CAN'T TAKE
MY EYES
OFF OF YOU

FIRST DATE

Shelby had no idea what "going Dutch" meant, but she was reasonably sure it had something to do with her buying her share of the beer. She'd already paid for the shoe rental, and chipped in toward the alley. Now beer? She'd have to work two or more hours to make that much money.

And then she smiled. Yes. She'd have to work to spend money. Not just ask Somerton. Not just tap her charge card. Not just spend and spend, without a thought to how much she was spending.

How wonderful!

"Sure," she said, getting into the swing of being just one of the guys. "I'd be happy to pay my share. But aren't you any good at all?"

"Oh, I'm good, Shelley," Quinn told her, picking up her right hand and placing it palm to palm with his own, measuring the length of her fingers. "I'm good at a lot of things."

Shelby's fingers tingled all the way up to her elbow. Her stomach turned to mush. Her knees all but buckled. She was being hit on. Oh, yes. By a tall, dark, and gorgeous man. A man who didn't know she was worth thirty million dollars. A man who just might be hitting on her because he thought she was . . . nice.

Or not so nice.

That wasn't so bad, either.

CAN'T TAKE MY EYES OFF OF YOU

Kasey Michaels

Zebra Books
Kensington Publishing Corp.
http://www.zebrabooks.com

ZEBRA BOOKS are published by

Kensington Publishing Corp.
850 Third Avenue
New York, NY 10022

ISBN: 0-7394-0838-0

Printed in the United States of America

For John Scognamiglio,
one of the good guys.

"If everybody minded their own business," said the Duchess in a hoarse growl, "the world would go round a deal faster than it does."

—Lewis Carroll
Alice's Adventures in Wonderland

Chapter One

There aren't a lot of pity parties for beautiful young women with eight-figure trust funds. Then again, there aren't a lot of people who have lived the life of a young woman with an eight-figure trust fund, not a lot of people qualified to know what life could be like inside a well-cushioned bubble.

Which is probably why Shelby Taite really didn't give a good damn what anybody else thought. She was miserable, it was her own misery, and everybody else could just shut up about it and let her get on with her own life.

Sure, like that was going to happen.

Case in point. Shelby stood in the large drawing room of the Philadelphia Main Line Taite mansion at the moment, being read a lecture by her dear, and only, brother, on the duties and responsibilities of being a Taite. It was June, it was hot, and she was dressed in a cotton, Peter Pan–collared shirtwaist and sensible, if expensive, white pumps.

She owned a dozen pairs of shorts, but they were all

tennis shorts, to be worn only on the courts. A halter top, cutoff jean shorts, and a pair of strap sandals were, in her social strata, completely beneath her. But not beyond her imagination.

Every naturally blond hair on her head was in place, sleekly falling to just above her shoulders. The style was classic Grace Kelly, as were her features, as was her lineage. Pedigreed, that was what Shelby Taite was. Thoroughbred, all the way down to her slim ankles.

But her wardrobe, her appearance, were just a part of what it meant to be a Taite. There was more. So much more.

Taites didn't go to war; they went to school. They didn't protest against wars while they were in school. Taites did not set trends, or follow them. No Taite ever spent so much as an hour in jail. Or at a rock concert. Or walking the streets. Or, God forbid, in politics. They had television sets, but the station was always tuned to PBS.

Taites were well mannered, well behaved. Well educated, well groomed. Their wedding pictures were reproduced in the best magazines. Their children attended private schools. Their friends were found among their peers, of which there weren't a whacking great lot.

The men followed their fathers into the family business, the daughters married well, and the mothers planned charity balls and croquet tournaments.

Not a lot of giggles, being a Taite.

"Are you listening to me, Shelby? I hesitate pointing this out, and don't wish to be cruel, but I don't think you're listening to me."

Shelby turned away from the window overlooking the boring, well-groomed gardens outside the Taite mansion and smiled at her brother. "Of course I'm listening, Somerton," she told him as she ran a hand through her hair, recklessly daring to shove a heavy lock of it behind her right ear. "The limousine will be here at seven, and for just once in my life you'd appreciate it if I would please be downstairs on time so that everyone else isn't kept waiting. After all, who on earth could ever want to miss so much as a moment of the evening?"

Somerton Taite cleared his throat nervously, not quite looking at his sister. "Don't be like that, Shelby. Is it really too much to ask that you be prompt? To hope that you'd make the least effort to enjoy yourself?"

Shelby sighed, shook her head. "No, Somerton, it's not. I'm sorry. It's just so *asinine,* that's all." Taites were allowed to be vulgar, but only articulately vulgar. Something could be asinine, for instance. It could not be a pile of bull—. Well, whatever.

Shelby took a discreet breath, then continued. "How many charity balls can one be expected to attend, Somerton? Is there a quota somewhere? When have we saved enough whales, or trees—or is it homeless Dalmatians this week? And wouldn't it be more cost-effective to cancel the orchestra and florist and caterer, and simply send a check?"

Somerton didn't have an answer to her questions. And why should he? They were Taites. They were fourth-generation Main Line Philadelphia. They attended charity balls. Why? Because they always had, they always would, into infinity.

Older than Shelby by four years, and shorter by three inches, Somerton Taite was slight, blond, aesthetically handsome, and rather fragile-looking, with his wet-combed blond hair and rather weak blue eyes. He was the sort of man who wore suits, never sport coats, and even his tennis whites dared never to wrinkle. He did not, Shelby believed, sweat. When one was a Taite, perspiration was simply not allowed.

And now Somerton was pouting. He did pouting quite

well as he pursed his lips, twisted them about a bit, then sat on one of the Sheraton sofas with his legs primly crossed at the knee, his arms folded and just sort of plopped in his lap, his dimpled chin rather high, nearly wobbling.

He'd broken one Taite rule himself, Somerton had, an unspoken one, but a rule nonetheless. And, especially considering how timid Somerton believed himself to be, it had been a doozy of a transgression. The sort that would have had whole generations of Taites spinning in their marble mausoleum if they hadn't already been so stiff and rigid before death that spinning couldn't possibly be an option now.

He and Jeremy, his "very good companion," were fortunate that being gay was "in" this Season. And Somerton could overlook Shelby's small rebellions because Shelby had accepted Jeremy without a blink. He did not pursue the why of her acceptance, whether it stemmed from some hidden liberal, Democratic failing or if she just didn't care one way or the other what her brother did. The latter thought depressed him, so he neatly shoved it out of his mind.

Shelby sensed her brother's nervousness and smiled at him, hoping he'd believe his eyes and not look too deeply into hers.

"Oh, Somerton, I'm sorry," she said, sitting down beside him, putting her arm around him. "I forgot the Taite motto, didn't I? 'Ours is not to question why, ours is but to wine and dine.' " She kissed his cheek, then stood up once more. "I'll be on time tonight, Somerton, I promise."

He looked up at her, arms still folded, lips still in a pout. "No, you won't. You'll keep us all waiting for at least a quarter hour. Uncle Alfred will amuse himself by drinking half the brandy in the house, Jeremy will fret and change his tie a half dozen times, and Parker will phone from the club, sure you've been kidnapped. I think you could treat your fiancé with more consideration, Shelby.''

"I know, I know," Shelby said, ready to agree to anything Somerton had to say, just so she could leave the room. Not that she had anywhere to go except for upstairs, to her own apartments, to the bath her maid would draw for her and to the gown laid out for her on the bed. There were whole days when she believed she did nothing but dress and undress and get dressed once more.

"But don't worry about Parker, Somerton. I'd like to think he worries because he can't stand to be without me, even for a moment, but we both know that isn't true. The Taite-Westbrook marriage will be just another in a long line of matrimonial mergers.''

Somerton sighed, stood, and placed his arm comfortingly around his sister. He loved her; he really did. He simply didn't understand her anymore. "You know that's not true, Shelby. Parker has assured me that he's madly in love with you, and I believe him. He's a good, upstanding man from an impeccable family, and his wife will be a fortunate woman.''

Shelby slid out from beneath her brother's arm, surprised at her own vehemence. "Fine. You like him so much, *you* marry him.''

Somerton's grin bordered on devilish. "Jeremy wouldn't like that," he said, then looked around the room nervously. He'd finally moved Jeremy into the house six months earlier, openly acknowledging their relationship. But that didn't mean he'd quite gotten past the notion that his late father would show up at any moment and pummel him to death with a yachting trophy. "Perhaps we can get Uncle Alfred to marry Parker? He could use the income.''

Shelby put her arms around her brother and hugged him. "Oh, I do love you, Somerton.''

"And you'll admit you're being silly? You'll admit that

you and Parker will have a lovely wedding in September, and a lovely life after that? After all, you're the one who said yes, who agreed to the marriage. Nobody is forcing you to marry the man."

Shelby sighed. "No, of course not. I don't know what's wrong with me, Somerton. Chalk it up to prewedding jitters, okay? I guess I just thought there should be more romance in the thing, and less china patterns."

She gave Somerton another kiss, then went upstairs, determined to be dressed and ready to go to the charity ball before the limousine arrived. If it killed her.

Chapter Two

Quinn Delaney leaned his tall frame against the side of the limousine, pushed back the cuff of his tuxedo, and glared at his watch. Seven-twenty.

He'd had twenty minutes to devise suitable tortures for Grady Sullivan, his partner in D & S Security. Because it was Grady's fault that Quinn was here, playing bodyguard to the Rich and Repulsive.

This wasn't part of their deal, damn it. Grady handled the R&Rs, and loved it, and he handled the corporate security. Quinn acted as bodyguard for businessmen, captains of industry, or at least he had until he'd completely taken over the business end of their partnership, leaving fieldwork behind him in exchange for computer printouts. Of all the things he did do, he did *not* dress up in his tuxedo and spend the night watching a bunch of society morons eat, drink, and make asses of themselves.

So how in hell had Grady conned him into this gig?

Quinn frowned, his gray eyes stormy as he remembered

the magazine page Grady had waved in front of his face a few hours earlier. "Look at her, Quinn, old boy. Just look at her. Miss October, Quinn. Likes poodles and raspberry ice cream, hates hypocrisy, wants to be a marine biologist while working for world peace, and her favorite color is warm flesh on black satin. Not to mention having legs that go up to her neck. And she's *mine*, all mine, until her plane takes off in the morning. You can't ask me to give this up, can you? And the Taites insist on having one of the partners. That's you. I'll owe you, buddy. I'll owe you big-time."

Quinn looked at his watch again, then at the mansion beyond the circular drive, and thought about the Phillies game he was missing. He crossed his long legs and more slouched than leaned against the side of the limousine. "Yeah. Big-time."

The sun still shone on this early June evening, but the chandeliers inside the house were already blazing, the wide windows giving him a clear view of what looked to be a living room the size of the flight deck on an aircraft carrier.

He could see three men through the windows, each of them dressed in monkey suits much like his but undoubtedly with better labels sewn in the jackets. Each of them held a glass of something stronger than the Coke that had been all he'd allowed himself earlier, as he was working tonight. If anyone could call this working.

Okay, so maybe the idle rich needed protection. Maybe they got robbed once in a while. Once in a very long while. The rich didn't really hire D & S for security. They hired them for the prestige, so that they could say things like, "Do you mind terribly if my personal security hides behind the flowers while we're dancing?"

And, if Grady could be believed, to help carry them home after they got themselves thoroughly sloshed at their society parties.

Quinn frowned again, stabbing his fingers through his too-long black hair. Give him a suicidal Libyan terrorist any day.

He pushed himself away from the back door of the limousine and nodded to the driver as the three men seemed to turn as one and head out of sight. "Heads up, Jim. I think the exodus has begun."

A few moments later the huge front door opened and an older gentleman carefully navigated his way down the few stairs to the drive. Uncle Alfred Taite, Quinn decided, mentally running down the list Grady had given him. Tall, sixtyish, silver-haired, and still with some claim to handsomeness. The obligatory black sheep, the hanger-on, the poor relation kept on an allowance and a stout leash as long as he was willing to be the extra, unattached gentleman so necessary to society parties. A lovable wastrel right out of Central Casting. Smiling, jolly, and always half in the bag.

Quinn nodded to the man as he watched him approach, held the door open for him. He'd already recognized Uncle Alfred's too-careful, poker-up-his-ass walk, and decided that, if part of his job description was to keep the guy from drowning in the punch bowl, it was going to be a long night.

Next to make his appearance was a tall, painfully thin man with a head full of black hair that looked as if it had been cut with hedge clippers then blown-dry in a wind tunnel. He wore his tuxedo like a cadaver in a rented suit laid out for viewing. His shirt collar stood away from his skinny neck; his fat, flowing bow tie and cummerbund were both powder blue. The fellow didn't walk. He pranced.

"Do hurry, Somerton," the man Quinn was sure could only be Jeremy Rifkin whined as he minced along. "You know how Mrs. Peterson *grimaces* at latecomers. Ghastly! And are you sure, quite sure, this tie is right? I agonized, you know, but was assured color is all the rage this season."

Still looking behind him, the man bumped into Quinn, giggled an apology, made a small *O* of his mouth as he patted Quinn's muscled shoulder, and then climbed into the back of the limousine.

Quinn made a mental note to make Grady very, very sorry.

"My apologies—Mr. Delaney, isn't it?" the man who, through the process of elimination, could only be Somerton Taite said, holding out his hand to Quinn. Had to be a relative; same poker-up-the-ass walk. Maybe it wasn't booze; maybe it was genetic. "I made her promise, but that never means anything. Not to my sister, not when she's forced to do what she doesn't want to do when she doesn't want to do it. Being tardy is her little rebellion, you understand. Oh, I'm Somerton Taite. Mr. Sullivan informed me that you'd be taking his place this evening. You shouldn't have much to do. I'd forgo a bodyguard if it were up to me, but with the jewels my sister will be wearing—well, the insurance company rather insisted."

"Yes, sir," Quinn answered shortly. "My partner explained everything to me. Will Miss Taite be much longer, sir?"

The slam of the front door served as his answer, and Quinn turned around to see Miss Shelby Taite walking down the stairs, still threading a length of sapphire silk through her elbows. A shawl? Were they still calling them shawls? Sounded too old–fashioned to Quinn, too matronly, especially on her.

She was a vision of money and breeding: a sweep of sleek blond hair drawn back into a severe twist, a long, narrow-hipped body wrapped breasts-to-toes in white silk. She had a choker of diamonds around her slim throat, a matching bracelet on her left wrist, a pair of sapphires the size of robin's eggs and wrapped in diamonds in her ears.

There was a diamond on her third finger, left hand, that could have choked an elephant.

She was beautiful. Stunning. Skin like warmed cream. Facial bone structure any supermodel would envy. A body that went on and on and on.

And brown eyes as lovely, and as vacant, as an empty church. But then, everyone had to have a flaw, didn't they?

"I'm here, Somerton," she announced wearily as her brother stood back to allow her to enter the limousine ahead of him. Her voice was rather low, faintly husky, and Quinn began to rethink his coming revenge on his partner. Looking after Miss Taite for the next five hours suddenly didn't seem like such a chore.

"And only twenty minutes late," her brother said, smiling at her. "My compliments, Shelby. Allow me to introduce Mr. Delaney, who will be taking Mr. Sullivan's place this evening."

Shelby didn't really care. She merely glanced in Quinn's general direction, then returned her attention to her slipping wrap, not really having registered him in her mind as being more than tall, dark, and in her way. "Drew the short straw, did you? How unfortunate for you, Mr., um, Mr. Clancy," she said coolly in that whiskey-over-velvet voice, then ducked her head and entered the limousine, giving him a fleeting view of a jaw-dropping, silk-clad derriere.

"That's Delaney," Quinn corrected before Somerton Taite followed his sister and he could close the door on the whole motley crew. Who did this Taite dame think she was? People *liked* him, damn it. They looked into his face when they spoke to him. They remembered his name. "Whoever said it was right, Jim," he grumbled as he took his place in the front seat beside the driver, the glass divider between employee and employer firmly in the up position. "The rich damn well *are* different."

Chapter Three

Shelby stood on the balcony, looking out over the gardens, looking out over the night. She and Parker had been there for over ten minutes, standing under a romantic full moon, and all Parker had talked about was the stock market and the rumor that Merilee Throgmorton had just had her second nose job.

When Parker finally paused in his monologue, she spoke up, hoping to change the subject. "It's beautiful out here, in a stodgy, uptight sort of way, isn't it, Parker? Everything so neat, so orderly. *Too* neat and orderly. Don't you just wish there were a dandelion or two?"

"Hardly, darling." Parker Westbrook III leaned a hip against the wrought-iron railing, folded his hands across his chest. Tall, thin, but sleekly muscular, Shelby's fiancé had blue eyes to her brown, his hair an even lighter, sun-bleached blond. Dressed in his custom-tailored tuxedo, he could have been posing for a liquor ad, one of those with the hidden phallic symbol somewhere in the background.

Sleek, handsome, subtly sexy. Shelby used to be impressed. Lately she wasn't quite so sure, and actually wished Parker could sprout a dandelion or two himself, just to make him look more human.

"Do you really think we should be out here, darling?" he said at last, barely able to keep the boredom out of his voice. "I mean, those diamonds are shining like beacons. Insured or not, they're around your neck, and I don't like feeling as if I am now in charge of protecting both."

Shelby ran a finger along the heavy choker. "What, these old things?" she teased, referring to her grandmother's diamonds. "You really think someone would go to the trouble of climbing through all of this considerable security for the chance of stealing these few pieces, when it would be so much easier to break into our house and scoop up the entire Taite collection? I know the combination to the safe, Parker," she told him, leaning close, wishing the man would relax, be spontaneous, just this once. "Do you want to know it? Twenty-three right, sixteen left—"

"Oh, for God's sake, Shelby," Parker interrupted, looking around as if he expected to see half a dozen masked thieves standing there, pens and scratch pads at the ready. "Is that why you insisted on coming out here? To be ridiculous?"

Shelby could have cheerfully strangled this man she was marrying. Not that she'd say so, because that would cause a scene, and Taites never caused scenes. Except for Uncle Alfred, but that was rather expected of the man.

Still, she decided maybe it was time to be at least a little bit daring.

"Actually, no," she told Parker, twining her arms around his shoulders, "I came out here so we could neck. Don't you want to neck, Parker? I want to neck."

"Now, Shelby. The night has eyes, remember?" Parker smiled, and Shelby thought, not for the first time, that when he smiled he was really quite handsome, in a sterile sort of way. She liked that he was tall, at least four inches taller than her own five feet, nine inches. His hair was getting just a little bit thin on top, but he used one of those hair-restoring formulas now, and she knew better than to try to run her fingers through his hair, mussing up the careful arrangement meant to cover the more sparsely populated areas. He played enough squash to keep himself trim, and he was quite intelligent, having taken over his father's investment firm three years earlier when the old man had died.

In short, he was perfect. Perfect Parker.

Shelby grimaced, still hearing the echo of that "the night has eyes" ridiculousness.

Perfect Parker picked a peck of picayune platitudes.

But he *was* perfect, at least as far as prospective mates went. Good family, solid financially, handsome enough to sire handsome children. Socially accepted. He was her perfect match, as Somerton had pointed out to her, as Parker had pointed out to her the night he had proposed.

It hadn't exactly been a whirlwind courtship, as they'd known each other for years. In fact, Parker had paid very little attention to her over those years, until a few months ago, when he seemed to have "discovered" her much in the way Columbus discovered America. Everything was suddenly "Hello, Shelby, how are you, Shelby, I would be honored to have this dance, Shelby."

Somerton had thought all of this wonderful. Somewhere in the back of her brain, Shelby thought all this new attention had a bit of a smell to it, but Parker was handsome. She'd always give him that. He showered her with flowers and poems and treated her as if she were made of glass.

When he proposed their "merger," she tried to see that proposal wrapped up in pink ribbons. She'd been trying hard to keep seeing it that way, and their marriage as well.

Then he went and came out with "the night has eyes."

This trying to be wrapped up in the romance of the thing was getting more difficult to pull off every day.

"Come on, Parker, be a little naughty," she pursued now doggedly, rubbing up against him, hoping to feel some sort of spark, see some flash of fire in his eyes. She had to know, needed to know—was something wrong with Parker, or with her? Was he a passionless stick, or was she still the Ice Maiden?

She touched his cheek with her hand, stroked its smoothness. "We're engaged to be married, remember? Forget where we are. Forget everything. Kiss me. Don't you want to kiss me, *need* to kiss me? Don't you ever think you'll just *die* if you can't kiss me, hold me? Don't you want to go a little mad—right here, right now?"

Parker reached up and disengaged her arms from his neck, placed kisses on the back of each hand as he lowered them to her sides. "How much have you had to drink, Shelby?" he asked, smiling indulgently.

"Not enough, apparently," she shot back at him, pushing past him as she all but ran down the length of the balcony, intent on returning to the ballroom—and bumped into a tall wall of well-tailored muscle.

" 'Evenin', ma'am. I was just coming out to check up on you, doing the bodyguard thing and all of that."

"Yes, yes. Whatever." She kept her head down, refusing to look at him, concentrating instead on the shine on the tops of his shoes. How dare the man have been here to witness her embarrassment! Didn't the fool know the meaning of the word *discretion?* She sailed past him, mortified, hating to hear the man's soft chuckle as she stepped inside the ballroom once more, then immediately forgot him.

Chapter Four

In vino veritas. "In wine is truth." And, for once in her life, Shelby had drunk enough to see all the truth wine held.

She'd come to a few conclusions.

The movies lied. The books lied. There was no such thing as romance. Happy endings were a crock. Maybe she was crocked, or cracked, or whatever the word was.

These were Shelby's profound if wine-fogged conclusions as she stood at her window, staring out at the darkness.

She was always at a window, always looking out. Even when she was outside, she was looking out. Looking, never doing. Seeing, never being a part of anything.

But well dressed. Well groomed. Well protected.

Cushioned.

Cocooned.

Trapped.

She was twenty-five and still as close to a virgin as some-

body could be after having a single one-night disappointment her second year of college. She'd been in love; she
swore it. Until the next day. Until she found out that her
"lover" was bragging about "bagging the Ice Maiden" to
anyone who would listen.

And Parker? The man treated her as if she were made
of imported crystal. He said he respected her and, respect-
ing her, he would wait for their wedding night. What a
prince . . .

Private schools. Private life.

Cosseted.

Smothered.

*Do the right thing, Shelby. Stand here. Smile. Remember that
you're a Taite. Guard your privacy, guard your honor, never
betray your family name.*

Marry well.

Marry now.

Marry? Why?

"Miss Taite? Will there be anything else?"

Shelby sighed, turned to face her young maid. "No,
thank you, Susie. And you really didn't have to wait up for
me."

"Yes, miss. Well, then, if there's nothing else?"

"Go, go," Shelby said, turning back to the window, to
the view of nothing. She stood there for at least five minutes
more, watching as a cloud passed over the full moon then
drifted on, leaving the gardens washed in silver.

Below her a door opened, and a shaft of yellow light
spilled onto the kitchen patio. She watched as Susie, now
dressed in shorts and a knit top, crossed the patio and ran
down the steps to the lawn.

Shelby pushed the drape back further and rolled open
the large casement window in time to hear a man's voice
call out to Susie. The young girl broke into a run as a
shape separated from the shadow of the trees. Within

moments Susie was in the man's arms, being swung around in a circle, being held, being kissed.

She could hear their laughter, feel their joy.

What would it feel like to have Parker wait in the moonlight for her? Pick her up, kiss her madly, carry her off into the trees, lay her down on the ground, make mad, passionate love to her?

Sure, like that was going to happen . . .

Chapter Five

D & S Security took up the entire sixteenth floor of a large, modern office building on Market Street in the center of the city. Grady had wanted the twentieth—and top—floor, but Quinn had put his foot down, reminding his rather flamboyant friend and partner that the rents rose with each floor the elevator traveled. D & S was successful, but that didn't mean Quinn wanted to throw money around just so he could share a roof with some Philadelphia pigeons.

But Grady had been born to money—earning it the old-fashioned way: he'd inherited it. If it had been left to him, not only would D & S occupy the penthouse offices, but those offices would be furnished in antique carpets, real leather, and with original paintings on the walls. As it was, Grady's office looked like something out of a private men's club—with Quinn always expecting to walk in and see some white-haired old geezer snoring in one of the burgundy leather wing chairs.

Quinn had grown up in the typical middle-class family, if it could be considered typical to move from state to state every few years, following his father's job. He'd been college age when they'd moved to Ardmore, outside Philadelphia, and when they moved on to Florida, Quinn had stayed behind, still in his sophomore year at the University of Pennsylvania.

His sister had done much the same thing four years earlier, and still lived in Chicago, while his parents had now retired to Arizona. They all called each other weekly, visited on holidays, stuff like that, but for the most part Quinn considered himself to be pretty much on his own. At thirty-two, that suited him just fine.

He'd allowed himself the privilege of arriving late at the offices the morning after the Taite assignment, figuring he'd earned a few hours of combat pay for having put up with the Rich and Repulsive. Not that it had been all that bad. Somerton and his little wifey had behaved themselves quite well, and Uncle Alfred had gotten himself quietly tanked and spent most of the evening propping up a pillar in the ballroom, leering down the necklines of all the passing ladies.

Only Shelby Taite had bothered him, and Quinn was still smarting at her deliberate refusal to acknowledge him, to, for crying out loud, at least take the trouble to *look* at him, remember his name.

And then there was that arrogant, brain-dead jerk she was engaged to marry. Quinn tried to imagine the two of them in bed together.

Talk about your sterile procedures.

Although Shelby Taite seemed to have some hint of fire behind all that ice. She'd pretty much thrown herself at old Parker, trying to get a rise out of him, pressing that long, sinfully lush body against him, asking him if he ever felt he'd die if he couldn't be kissing her.

She'd probably have had more luck if she'd whispered stock quotes into the jerk's ear.

Quinn really, really disliked the rich, Grady being one of the few exceptions. They had everything dumped right into their laps, and none of them seemed all that damn happy about it. Most of them had shrinks on retainer, divorced with the change of seasons, and spent their time saying they were helping the economy by buying three-million-dollar yachts because that kept the laborers in the shipyard employed. Scary. That was what the rich were.

What the rich needed was a good kick in the ass. What Shelby Taite needed, in the crudeness of an expression from Quinn's misspent youth, was to have her clock cleaned. She needed some hot, sweaty, steaming sex. Someone to rip the pins out of her too-perfect hair, strip her of her designer virgin robes, and make mad, passionate love to her until those damned dead eyes rolled back in her head.

Not that Quinn was volunteering for the job.

He rocked on his heels as the elevator climbed to the sixteenth floor, then stepped out onto the black and white marble floor Grady had called a necessary expense, as first impressions can be made only once.

Maisie sat at her large, semicircular desk in the reception area, the white marble wall behind her displaying the words *D & S Securities, Inc.* in large brass letters. Very impressive, for those who felt the need to be impressed. Many of their clients did.

Maisie had a portable telephone headset clamped over her riot of artificially red, artificially curled hair. The receptionist was short, a bit pudgy, and with a round, round face that might have been drawn by Charles Schulz. She was murmuring, "Uh-huh. Uh-huh," into the mouthpiece as she filed her French-manicured nails.

When she saw Quinn she smiled at him, pointed to the

headset, then pulled a face that made her look like a cherub with dyspepsia. She leaned forward, hit the mute button, and said, "Morning, honey. You're late, but the crazies were all up bright and early this morning. A question for you. Does D and S want to ride shotgun on a couple dozen elephants while the circus is in town? Nah, didn't think so. I'll get rid of this bozo. Bozo—get it? Oh, and wait until you see Grady!"

Quinn waited for her to explain, but she grimaced suddenly and hit the mute button once more, reopening the line. "No, honey, free peanuts won't make us reconsider. Uh-huh, yeah, I can assure you that D and S are animal lovers from way back. But that's just the point, honey— they want to be *way back* from them. But thank you for calling. Have a nice circus."

Maisie was their first line of defense, and she had exactly the right attitude for her job: Quick, sharp, with a very necessary sense of humor for the wackos, and definitely ballsy enough to handle their most demanding clients.

Quinn laughed, shook his head, and headed through the glass doors into the large, square, windowless room that functioned as the nerve center of D & S Securities. Five secretaries serving the two dozen bodyguards who made up the staff sat at their desks, all of them busy enough to warm the cockles of Quinn's heart—and pocketbook.

Hallways to the left and right led to five offices each, shared by the associates when they weren't in the field. On another morning, Quinn would have visited each office, checked on his employees' cases, shot a little bull, lingered over some bad coffee. But not today, not when he still wanted to make Grady pay for badgering him into a night with the R&Rs.

Smiling his hellos to the secretaries—executive assistants all, at least in their politically correct job descriptions— he made his way to the opposite end of the room and the large hallway that ended at the double doors to the conference room, with his and Grady's private offices flanking it on either side. All three rooms had window walls, glass from floor to ceiling, and a great view of the evolving skyline of Philadelphia—at least at sixteenth-floor level.

His secretary, Selma, was out on maternity leave, and had been for nearly two weeks, so Quinn gave himself a moment to grimace at the stacks of paperwork sitting on her desk, knowing he'd have to wade through them sooner or later. Preferably later. Definitely later.

Right now all he wanted to do was check his phone messages, then go choke Grady until his tongue turned purple. It wasn't much, but he believed it would satisfy him.

Quinn's own office was modern and more functional than fashionable, all chrome and glass and white paint and rugs with gray and navy accents and outfitted with two, count 'em, two state-of-the-art computers. A locked cabinet held his fairly extensive arsenal of shoulder holsters and nightscope rifles, as well as a flak jacket his mother had given to him for his thirtieth birthday. You could grow up, you could move away, but you could never really cut through that cast-iron umbilical. You could even tell yourself that you'd retired from fieldwork because it was time, and not because Mommy worried.

He checked the phone messages written in Maisie's large, looping scrawl, decided none of them were earth-shatteringly important, then took off his suit jacket and slung it over his gray leather swivel chair. It was Grady time.

"Good morn—*afternoon*, Quinn," Ruth, Grady's secretary, said a few moments later when he entered her office. Ruth had been with them from the beginning, a matronly woman of more than fifty who considered herself to be right-hand man and surrogate mother to both of them.

She chuckled as she looked at him. "What's the matter, sweetie? Rough night on the baby-sitting squad? Did Uncle Alfred jump in the pool again? Grady says he swears he'll let the old lush drown next time. He's ruined three tuxedos in the last year, jumping in after him. Not that replacements don't go right on the old expense account. Oh, and wait until you see your partner. He won't tell me what happened, but I've got some really great ideas, all of them having to do with Miss October. And maybe a trapeze or something."

Quinn's eyebrows rose on his forehead. "Trapeze? What are you trying to do, Ruth? Corrupt me?"

"Any way I can, sweetie," she told him with a wink, then pointed to the door leading to Grady's office. "Make him suffer, Quinn. I'm pretty sure he's been a bad, bad boy."

Quinn entered Grady's inner sanctum, stepping onto a plush Oriental carpet, instinctively halting just inside the dim room until his eyes adjusted to the relative absence of light, reflexively checking behind him as he closed the door. Maybe he was mostly a desk jockey now, but habits were habits, and good habits could someday keep a guy alive to crunch numbers another day.

Grady wasn't behind his oversize cherry desk with its protective glass top, having chosen instead to recline on the burgundy leather sofa that had enough deep tucks in it to look as though it had been sucking three dozen lemons.

His rangy frame filled the couch from end to end, his shaggy, sandy head propped up on a tapestry pillow, his laughing green eyes shining bright in his tanned, aristocratically handsome face. He wore a stark white dress shirt open at the neck and rolled at the cuffs, a pair of midnight blue pleated slacks, handmade loafers, and a color-coordinated blue sling on his left arm.

"What happened? She forgot to mention that she was ticklish, *and* a black belt?" Quinn offered as he walked over and sat down on the edge of the cherry wood coffee table in front of the couch.

Grady carefully jackknifed to a sitting position, glaring at his friend and partner. "Very funny—*not*. But then, you didn't have much time to rehearse, did you? Do you want to go out, think up a better line, then come back in to torture me?"

"No, not really," Quinn answered, grinning. "But I'll give you a quarter if you tell me what happened. A dollar if you've got photos. Videotape, and price is no object."

Grady reached into his back pocket and pulled out a folded square of snow white linen bearing his initials in navy thread. "Here," he said, extending his arm, "drool on this."

"No, seriously, Grady, what happened? Is it broken or just sprained?"

"Separated shoulder," he told him, grimacing as he got up, walked over to his desk, and threw two pills into his mouth, washing them down with a sip of water. "It was the damnedest thing, Quinn. One minute we're rolling quite happily on the bed, and the next I'm stuck between the bed and the nightstand, my shoulder on fire. Miss October fainted, which wasn't much of a help, and I had to get my own self up after pushing her off me—stop laughing, damn it!—then call the hotel doctor. Ever try pulling on your pants with one hand, Quinn? I don't recommend it. And let me tell you, it wasn't easy boosting Miss O back up onto the bed and getting her lovely little fanny under the covers before the doctor showed up."

By the time Grady was finished Quinn was doing a little rolling of his own, rocking on the edge of the coffee table, laughing until tears rolled down his cheeks. Then, with a suddenness that nearly had *him* falling on the floor, he sobered, glared at his partner. "How long will you be out of commission? Two weeks? Four? And before you answer that, *no,* I'm not going to take over any more of your R and R gigs. Got that?"

"No sweat, old son," Grady promised. "There's nothing pressing on either of our schedules for weeks and weeks. In fact, maybe you should think about picking up some sort of hobby, just to fill the time."

"Yeah, right, Grady, *old son.* That would be between running this place, doing the end-of-year reports, and spoon-feeding my invalid partner his gruel so that he doesn't slop all over his designer suits. I'll be in my office," Quinn ended, and headed out the door.

Behind him, he could hear Grady chuckling.

Chapter Six

After charity balls, Shelby rated garden parties second on her list of her least-favorite things to do. Yet here she was, the afternoon after the ball—and with only a slight headache to remind her of the previous evening—sitting in the back of the limousine in her uniform of the day, her full skirts carefully arranged on the seat, a huge straw picture hat jammed onto her head. Wouldn't be a proper garden party without that damn picture hat.

"Jim?"

"Yes, Miss Taite?"

Shelby scooted over onto the jump seat and leaned forward, closer to the opened divider that separated her from the Taite chauffeur. "Are you and Susie happy here?"

"Happy, miss?" Jim Helfrich took a quick look into the rearview mirror, then redirected his attention to the highway. "We're both happy enough with the work. You and Mr. Taite are very kind."

Shelby took off her hated hat, tossed it onto the back

bench seat. "That's good, but that's not really what I meant. Are you happy *here*, Jim, in Philadelphia? Where are you from, originally?"

"Where are we from?" Jim had an annoying habit of repeating everything that was said to him. He was also probably nervous, as Shelby had never asked him a personal question before today, even though he and his daughter had been in the Taites' employ for nearly a month. "East Wapaneken, miss. That's about sixty-five miles from here, up near Allentown. We're sort of stuck between Hokendauqua and Catasauqua, just a little bit of a place." He chanced another look in the rearview mirror. "Um . . . why do you ask, miss?"

"No real reason, Jim," Shelby said carefully, leaning her forearms on the back of the bench seat. More. She wanted to hear more. "It's a small town, then, East Wapaneken?"

"Is it small? So small there's no *West* Wapaneken, miss," Jim said with a chuckle. "I hated to leave, to tell you the truth, but with Susie's mom gone and the steel plant closing down, I needed to find work where I could watch over my Susie. She's been accepted at Temple, you know, right downtown. Did her first two years at our local community college, and now she's ready for the big time."

"I didn't know that," Shelby admitted, feeling more than a little ashamed. Granted, Susie had only been in her employ for a relatively short time, and only as temporary summer help, but she should have known *something* about her by now, shouldn't she? Or was she merely floating through life now, not acting, not even reacting? Just existing. Not to mention feeling sorry for herself. "So you liked living in a small town?"

"It's the only place to live, to my mind, miss. Good friends, deep roots. Oh, everybody knows your business, that's for sure, but everybody cares about you, too. Good people, good friends. That's important. It's . . . it's *real* in

East Wapaneken, miss. Yeah, that's it. It's the real world. Once Susie's got her degree, we're heading straight back there, no question."

"Thanks . . . um . . . thank you, Jim," Shelby said, sitting back against the jump seat, biting at her bottom lip as she thought about all he'd said.

Real. The real world.

Shelby smiled, her first *real* smile in a long, long time.

Chapter Seven

Shelby looked up from the book she'd been pretending to read ever since dinner, watching as her uncle made his way to the mahogany table holding an assortment of his favorite liquid refreshments.

She loved her uncle, loved him very much. He was happy, silly, sometimes profane, and totally outrageous. Such a handsome man, with his thick shock of silver hair and neatly trimmed beard, his boozy-red cheeks and nose, his twinkling blue eyes. His devilish smile, his lust for life. Sort of like a trim, dapper Santa Claus on speed. "Uncle Alfred?"

"Umm? Yes, my pet?"

She almost lost her courage, then asked her question anyway. "Have you ever wondered what life would be like if we were . . . normal?"

Alfred Taite leaned an elbow against the mantel, balanced his brandy snifter in his free hand, and stared at his niece. "Define normal, my darling."

Shelby stood up, began to pace. "You know—*normal*."
She spread her arms to indicate the magnificently furnished Taite drawing room, the entire Tudor mansion,
their entire world. "As opposed to this, which is about as
abnormal as it gets."

"Oh," Alfred said, taking a sip of brandy. "You mean
poor, don't you? I try not to think about that, actually. I
wouldn't either, Shelby, if I were you. You don't want to
see how the other half lives, and nobody certainly wants
to *live* as the other half lives. Just the thought is giving me
shivers. It would only deject you. Trust me on this."

Shelby drew her hands into fists, trying to find the words
to say what she meant. "I don't mean poor, exactly, Uncle
Alfred. I mean . . . I mean *real*. Yes, that's what Jim called
it. Real. I want to feel *real*. I want to experience life as a
real person. A *normal* person."

"No, you don't, darling. I have it on good authority that
the *real* people don't think real life is all it's cracked up
to be. And you said Jim? Who, pray tell, is Jim?"

"Our chauffeur, Uncle Alfred. Surely you know his
name."

He blinked at her, pushed himself away from the mantel,
truly not comprehending. "Why? Is there a reason I
should? It's enough that he knows me, knows he's supposed to pick me up, take me places, not lose me."

"You're insufferably arrogant, do you know that?"
Shelby asked, smiling at her uncle.

"A large part of my charm, my darling," he said, saluting
her with the snifter. "Now, if you'll excuse me, I believe
the esteemed Jim is waiting for me outside. Wouldn't it
make Somerton happier if we were to call the man James?
Well, never mind about that. Do you remember who I'm
squiring this evening, my pet, and, for God's sake, why?"

Shelby grinned, shook her head. "Mrs. Oberon, Uncle

Alfred. To a special summer presentation of the opera, which explains your tails.''

"Oh, yes, yes, the penguin suit," Alfred said, trying to turn about to look at his own backside. "Well, I'll be on my way then. Unless you want to discuss more of this real-life business?''

Shelby shook her head again. "No, Uncle Alfred. That's all right. I think this is something I'll just have to work out for myself.''

He patted her cheek. "Splendid idea, darling. Just don't say *work*, all right? You're a Taite, remember? Work. What a horrible four-letter word. Why, next thing we know, you'll be abusing my sensitive ears with words like *industry* and *discipline* and—ye gods!—*social conscience.*''

Shelby bit her lip. "Uncle Alfred? Aren't all those words somewhere on the Taite family crest?''

"What a depressing reminder. Somerton wears the damn thing on those ridiculous blazers he wears at the yacht club, which is horribly embarrassing." Alfred looked at her owlishly. "How you've pained me, to remind me of those nagging Taite responsibilities. *Responsibility*—another horrible word. You're so unlike me at times. In fact sometimes, Shelby, I wonder if I had anything to do with your birth.''

"You didn't, Uncle Alfred.''

"Oh, that's right. Pity. My brother was so like Somerton, right down to that horrible cleft in his chin—which is why I wear this beard, you know, to camouflage mine own. You'd have more spirit if I'd cuckolded your father, damn me if you wouldn't. But then, I never could abide your mother, God rest both their starchy souls.''

Shelby's smile faded. Not because of his comments about her parents, who'd both died a dozen years ago after living lives quite separate from those of their two obligatory offspring. It was her uncle's comments about her lack of spirit that upset her. "I don't have any spirit, Uncle Alfred? Do you really believe that?"

Alfred laid down the top hat and cape he'd picked up and walked over to his niece. "Did I say that? Oh, I'm sorry, darling. But you have been moping a bit of late, haven't you? Chin—blessedly not cleft—dragging on the carpets and all of that? You've been unhappy. Probably because you're so very proper and upright otherwise."

"Unlike you," she said sadly.

"Ah, yes. I remember my own youth, long gone and sorely lamented. Was asked to leave two prep schools and three colleges—a Taite record, and one of which I remain inordinately proud. But I lived, darling, I experienced! I toured Europe, traveled across America, rubbed elbows with the little people, learned all about this real life you've been hinting at so longingly tonight."

Shelby's heart began to beat faster, excitement at her uncle's adventures warming her blood, speeding her pulse. "You did? I never knew, never guessed. You broke out, Uncle Alfred? You broke away from all this, went your own way—experienced life?"

"Oh, I most certainly did, my child." He sighed, bent down, and picked up his snifter once more. "And then I . . . settled. Being cut off from one's allowance while sitting in a broken-down Thunderbird in the middle of an Arizona desert tends to bring one sharply to his senses. Now I drink, and I squire old ladies wearing too much old family money and definitely too much scent, and I drink some more. But I do have my memories. Those I do have."

"Memories," Shelby repeated, chewing on her bottom lip. Perhaps, she thought, being settled wouldn't be so bad, not if she had memories. Her smile began to grow again, the fairly crazy idea that had knocked on her mind earlier now finding an open door and a welcome mat.

She put her arms around her uncle and kissed him

soundly on his flushed cheek. "Oh, thank you, Uncle Alfred. Thank you so much!"

He stepped back, holding on to her arms, looking deeply into her eyes. "Thank me? For what?"

"Why, for helping to create me, of course," she said, kissing him yet again. "I've got some of your spirit somewhere inside of me. I must. And it's about time I did something with it, before I *settle.*"

Chapter Eight

If Shelby had taken the time to plan her every move, she probably wouldn't have done it. She'd have thought of a dozen reasons, two dozen reasons, why she should just forget any thoughts of—the word she sought, then found, was *freedom*—and simply go on existing, not living.

Go on being Somerton's sister, Parker's fiancée, the Ice Maiden. Spend the summer attending prewedding parties, unwrapping silver salad tongs, picking invitations, having fittings of her gown. Organizing the Taite–Westbrook merger—er, wedding—so that it would be the sensation of the year.

Strangled by ivory peau de soie, trapped in a web of Alencon lace. Grandly wedded, politely bedded, and then spending the remainder of her life attending parties, hosting parties, volunteering in the hospital gift shop three hours a week, turning a blind eye to Parker's little sexual peccadilloes with a string of disposable females, drinking just a tad too much wine after dinner . . . and quietly going insane.

So Shelby didn't think. She didn't plan. Well, not much anyway.

Mostly she acted.

Five days after the charity ball, she pulled Susie into the bedroom, flung open the doors to her walk-in closet—the one with the rotating hanging rods, the one that held enough clothes, shoes, hats, and purses to stock a large, upscale consignment shop—and told Susie to pick out some "normal" clothes for her.

Susie Helfrich dutifully took two steps into the closet, then stopped, screwed up her pug nose, and looked at her employer. "Huh? Um, that is, pardon me?"

"Normal, Susie," Shelby repeated, waving her arms a time or two, then pointing at her maid's denim skirt and pink summer sweater, her scuffed white Keds. "*Nor*mal. Like yours, Susie. The sort of thing people would wear in . . . well, what people would wear in a small town."

Susie looked at the clothing hanging on padded hangers and shook her head. "You don't own anything like that, Miss Taite. You shop in New York and Paris twice a year. Nor— Um—most people shop in malls and outlet stores. Your clothing is really beautiful, but you don't exactly have anything that I'd wear back home or anything like that."

Shelby's shoulders slumped, a princess who longed to be Cinderella before the fairy godmother showed up. "No, I haven't, have I? Very well, let's do the best we can with what we've got, all right?"

"I have a DKNY shirt I got at T.J.Maxx last year," Susie offered helpfully, pulling out a pale green Donna Karan suit and looking at it critically. "So I suppose it wouldn't be impossible that someone could have something like this. And Patty O'Boyle, my friend from back home in East

Wapaneken, she finds lots of designer clothes at the outlets in Reading.''

Shelby nodded her approval, even if Susie did seem to be speaking a foreign language. What on earth was a T.J.Maxx? "Well, then, that's fine. We'll start with the Donna Karan. I'll want skirts, a few Armani pantsuits, and matching tops. You pick everything. Enough for, oh, three weeks or so, Susie, plus shoes and other accessories. Do you think you could pack everything up for me? My luggage is in the closet in the hall.''

"You're going on a trip?'' Susie asked as she pushed the button that set the rolling rack into motion, eyeing the clothes assessingly as they passed by. "That's nice.''

Shelby was already rummaging through the built-in drawers that lined one wall of the closet, pulling out handfuls of silk underwear. "Yes, very nice, Susie. And our little secret, all right? I—I just feel a need to get away for a few weeks before the wedding preparations begin in earnest. My brother would try to talk me out of it if I told him, so I'm just going to pack and leave. You can give him my note when I'm gone.''

"Are you all right, Miss Taite?'' Susie asked as some of the underwear slipped from Shelby's hands, sliding to the floor. "I mean, it's none of my business, but you seem, well, upset. Did you and Mr. Westbrook have some sort of argument or something?''

"Ha! Parker? He'd never argue, Susie,'' Shelby told her, bending down to gather up her unmentionables. "Oh, he might frown and ask me if I'd slept well because I seemed a bit cranky. But argue with me? No, Susie, I can't see it.''

"Wow,'' the young girl said, shaking her head so that her tawny ponytail slapped against her shoulders. "My mom and dad used to have some real humdingers. But they always made up afterward, went out to dinner, then locked themselves in their bedroom until late the next morning. I remember being able to hear them giggling through the walls. Mom explained to me that husbands and wives do argue, that it's natural, and that it didn't mean that they didn't love each other.''

She leaned against the wall of the closet, blinking back sudden tears. "They loved each other very much, Miss Taite. Dad's only half a person without her.''

Shelby looked at the young woman for a long moment, unable to speak. Her parents had never argued. They'd had a few discussions, but those discussions had been more like low, hissing contests of wills, and usually ended with her father going to his club and her mother going to her lover of the month. Dying in the same plane crash was about the only thing they'd done together since Shelby had been conceived.

"I envy you your memories, Susie,'' she said at last, walking past her to dump the underwear on her bed. "I'll start sorting out my toiletries, all right? And remember, this is all our little secret.''

In the end, Shelby had added another full suitcase of clothing to that which Susie had packed, just to be certain she had enough. Traveling with less than five suitcases seemed impossible to Shelby, who at least congratulated herself that she'd forgone the elaborate, custom-made steamer trunk she usually used for trips lasting more than a few days.

She went down to dinner on time, nervously picking her way through three courses as Somerton and Jeremy got into a small spat over Somerton's preference for very rare steak.

"It's barbaric,'' Jeremy told them all, shuddering. "I expect you to come home at any time, Somerton, panting, your tail wagging, some limp-necked game hanging from your jaws. Vegetarianism, it's the only healthy way to live.''

"Nonsense, Jeremy,'' Somerton countered testily, his

nostrils flaring. "I am a carnivore. *You* are a carnivore. You just won't admit it. And I must say, Jeremy, that I resent your comparing me to an animal. I think you should apologize, frankly."

Jeremy's thin, aesthetic face flushed, and a tear came to his eye. "Apologize? Perhaps next week, Somerton, after you've dropped dead, your arteries clogged. Have you thought about that, Somerton?" He drew himself up and sniffled. "Have you thought about what would happen to *me* if anything should happen to you? I should think you'd have a little more consideration, Somerton. Really I do."

"You'd survive," Somerton snapped right back at him. "You certainly wouldn't starve. After all, all you'd have to do is go outside and *graze.*"

Jeremy gasped, lifted his linen napkin to his lips.

"Now, children," Uncle Alfred cut in, winking at Shelby. "Somerton, apologize, if you please. You're a naughty, naughty boy, upsetting the little woman, who only has your best interests at heart. Jeremy?" he then asked, leaning his elbows on the table as he held a glass of wine in both hands, "you're doing something new with your hair, aren't you, son? Adorable, really."

With Somerton still stiff-backed and silently sputtering, and with the easily diverted Jeremy now preening and posturing, Shelby was thankful to be left alone to push candied yams around on her plate and mentally word the note she'd write after dinner.

At nine the next morning, while the rest of the household either slept or breakfasted in their rooms, Jim Helfrich loaded Shelby's luggage into the back of the limousine and then drove her to the downtown bus station.

Nobody would ever think to look for her at a bus station.

And if anyone asked, and they probably would, Jim could only tell them about the bus station, not her destination.

Hers may have been an impromptu plan, but Shelby believed it had its moments of brilliance. She'd be arriving at the bus station in Allentown before noon, and well on her way to blissful oblivion in East Wapaneken.

She settled back against the plush leather seats of the Mercedes limousine, considering herself to be halfway to freedom.

Chapter Nine

What Shelby was two hours later was hot, dusty, and stranded outside the Allentown bus terminal. She'd enjoyed the ride, not having ever ridden on a bus before except for the summer she'd spent at horse camp. And the driver had been very nice to her, once she'd handed over a twenty-dollar tip as he glared at the pile of luggage he was expected to load into the compartment beneath the bus.

She'd struck up a conversation with a young woman also traveling to Allentown, heading home from a visit with her boyfriend. Brenda was a bubbly sort, talkative enough for both of them, and Shelby felt she'd handled her end of the conversation very well, including the fib that she was heading to Allentown to start a new job—managing a McDonald's. Shelby could think of a "normal" sort of employment, but she still thought at management level.

Brenda had been met by her parents, who then drove away, waving good-bye, and Shelby suddenly realized that she was now very much alone in a strange city, in a not-very-nice section of that city.

She walked to the sidewalk and looked up the street—all the way up the street—to the signpost marking the closest LANTA bus stop.

She could have taken a taxi, but taxis could be traced, as anyone who'd ever read a detective novel knew, and Shelby had read her share. A bus, on the other hand, was completely anonymous, and nobody would remember her.

They might, however, remember her luggage.

All the clothing she'd brought had seemed absolutely necessary at the time but, as she walked back to her luggage, slung bags over her shoulders, tucked another under her arm, and began dragging the other two, she had a sudden flash of insight. Nobody in East Wapaneken could possibly have, or need, such an extensive wardrobe.

Visions of a documentary she'd seen one night on PBS when she couldn't sleep came back to haunt her as she stepped, dragged, stepped again on her way to the sidewalk. The documentary had depicted a wagon train moving west, the camera panning over the pianos, trunks, and other luggage left behind on the trail as the road got longer, harder.

She was already mentally discarding the suitcase holding her shoes. She could always buy new shoes. She enjoyed buying shoes.

"Need some help, lady?"

"Pardon me?" Shelby, who had been concentrating on putting one foot in front of the other, looked up to see a skinny, T-shirted boy of about seventeen standing in front of her, blocking her way.

His brown hair was shaved except for a single two-inch-wide strip running down the center of his skull. His T-shirt fit like a second skin, so that she could actually count his ribs. Faded jeans hung somewhere below his waist, the crotch bagging to his knees, the hems as wide around as any of her ball gowns and dragging on the ground—making him look as if he were standing in a puddle of denim.

And he had a tattoo on his right forearm: the word *Killer,* incongruously surrounded by rosebuds.

Shelby opened her mouth to say thank you very much, but no, then looked toward Hamilton Street once more. Her arms were pulling loose from her shoulders and she still had half a block to go before she made it to the corner.

"Well, actually, I believe I could use some help, thank you," she told him, her smile rather tremulous as she let the luggage slide to the ground, then searched in her purse for another twenty-dollar bill. "I just need to transport all of this up to that bus stop at the corner. I'd really appreciate—"

The twenty disappeared from her hand. Five seconds later, she watched in horror as all five pieces of her luggage went bounding up the street in the boy's grasp as she chased after him, not liking the way he seemed to be running away more than he seemed to be transporting her belongings to the bus stop.

When he reached the bus stop and turned the corner, heading down a side street, Shelby broke into a run, unable to think of anything else to yell but "Stop! Thief!"

So trite. So embarrassingly melodramatic.

And yet, she thought thankfully, so very effective.

She rounded the corner in time to see the youth being held by the scruff of his neck, his feet so far off the ground that his jeans no longer dragged on the pavement, her luggage lying in a heap.

"These yours, ma'am?" the boy's captor was asking, and Shelby blinked, nodded her head a time or two, then stared at the mountain of a man who had rescued her luggage.

No taller than Shelby, he looked to be in his early to mid-thirties and was solid muscle from the neck down:

barrel chest, brawny arms, rock-solid thighs beneath tight, faded jeans. His hair was a brown buzz cut that did not flatter his beefy face or jug ears, but his smile was wide, his blue eyes kind. He wore thick work boots, and his T-shirt bore the words *Rainy Day Construction.*

The kid still squirming in the man's one-handed grasp had probably felt he'd run into a brick wall. Twice.

"Yes," Shelby said, catching her breath. "Yes, that's my luggage. Thank you so much, sir. Er, I think you might be able to put him down now."

"You sure? I could call a cop, you know, put this little bas—er, kid in the local lockup. Are you sure you don't want to press charges?"

"Killer," who had been squirming in the man's grip, now went rather slack, looking at Shelby with puppy-dog eyes, pleading with her not to send him to jail. He was "Only funnin' with you, lady," and would have turned around, brought the luggage back to her. "Honest to God, lady."

Now here was a dilemma. Shelby would like nothing more than helping this boy realize that actions had consequences. But if she did that, if she allowed her rescuer to bring the local police into it, her name would be on some police bladder or blotter or whatever, and Somerton would know where she was within the hour, perhaps less.

"I'd like my twenty dollars returned, if you please," she told the boy, "and then you may be on your way. In fact, give it to this nice man, who has more than earned it."

The twenty changed hands and Killer took off down the sidewalk, looking as though he had a good chance of breaking the four-minute mile—if he didn't fall over his pants legs and break his neck instead.

"Thank you again, sir," Shelby began as the man stepped closer, holding the twenty out in front of him.

"And really, please keep that. You've certainly earned it, and much more."

"Sorry, ma'am, but I can't do that," he told her, handing over the bill. "My mother would have my hide if I told her I took money for helping a lady. Now, where were you heading with all this luggage?"

Shelby sort of waved toward the bus stop behind her, then realized that, even if the man helped her to the bus stop, she would have no one to help her get the bags back off the bus once it reached East Wapaneken. "I . . . I'm not sure," she said at last, running a hand through her hair, which had fallen into her face as she chased after Killer.

She was overheated, rather hungry, and her legs had begun to feel like rubber. Much of the excitement she'd felt as she left Philadelphia had drained away, leaving her painfully aware of the fact that, in twenty-five years, she had never had to fend for herself, find her own transportation, make her own decisions. It was all very depressing.

"Name's Mack, ma'am, Gary Mack," the man said into the sudden silence, rubbing his hand on his pants leg, then extending it outward for Shelby to shake; rather like an overgrown puppy performing a trick. "I don't mean to be pushy or nothin', but how's about we get you a place to sit down for a while, and get you something in your stomach? You're looking sort of pale, you know."

"Why, thank you, Mr. Mack," Shelby said, retrieving her hand, which felt as if it had just been crushed in a vise. She had been stupid to trust Killer, but there was something about Gary Mack that told her it wouldn't be foolhardy to trust him. "That would be lovely, actually. Oh, and I'm Shel—um, *Shelley*. Shelley, um, Smith. I'm very pleased to meet you."

Shelby was doubly pleased, ten minutes later, to be introduced to Gary's fiancée, Brandy Wasilkowski. The two had planned to meet for an early lunch close to the employment office where Brandy worked, and Brandy accepted Shelby's presence with an indulgent smile that told her Gary had brought home strays before, and she was used to it.

Short and pleasantly rounded, Brandy Wasilkowski bounced herself down on the barely padded booth seat in the small restaurant, kissed Gary on the cheek, then beamed across the scarred Formica table at Shelby. Her blue eyes twinkled, her chestnut curls bounced, and her short, upturned nose displayed a dusting of freckles that were more large than cute. She had a rounded chin, wide smile, and an obvious liking for jewelry, as there were rings on every finger—and thumb—of both hands.

She seemed closer to Gary's age than Shelby's, but her youthful-looking ankle-length flowered dress and sandals told Shelby that, to Brandy, age had nothing to do with her choice of clothes.

"Hi, Shelley," she said, winking at Shelby. "Did Gary drag you and that mountain of designer luggage in here, or did you come along willingly?"

"Now, hon . . ." Gary began, but Brandy waved him off, still staring across the table at Shelby, her expression part amusement, part concern.

"Gary rescued me, and my luggage," Shelby told her, "and then invited me to lunch. I hope you don't mind."

Brandy reached across Gary, snagged one of the menus stuck between a bottle of ketchup and a large container of sugar. She deliberately didn't look at their luncheon companion, although she'd already seen and heard enough to know that something a little weird was going on. She'd find out what it was sooner or later, but right now she just wanted to eat. Brandy would rather eat than do pretty much anything else. "Nope. Don't mind at all. You guys already order?"

Gary removed the menu from her hands. "I ordered yours, too. You're getting the garden salad, hon, remember? That's what you told me to order for you, anyway. Although I still say there's nothing wrong with—"

"Isn't he sweet?" Brandy said quickly, cutting him off. "He says I'm not fat." She turned to him, kissed his cheek again. "Liar. I do love you. And if I'm going to fit into my wedding gown I've got to lose twenty pounds, minimum. A garden salad, huh? Why do you always pick the wrong times to do what I say? I think I could kill for a cheeseburger."

Shelby looked at Brandy's hands, sorted out from the other rings the small diamond on the third finger, left hand. She'd left her own diamond in the jewelry case at home, knowing its two-carat size would make her entirely too memorable if anyone were to begin asking questions about her. "When's the wedding, Brandy?" she asked as the waitress appeared with garden salads for both of them, and a huge, long roll stuffed with chipped steak and smothered in cheese for Gary.

He looked at Brandy for a moment, then ducked his head, began concentrating on burying a plate of French fries under a gallon of ketchup.

"Darn right you can't look at me, Gar. Pick a year between now and infinity, Shelley. I bought the gown when I was a size eight, if that gives you any hints as to how long we've been planning this thing," Brandy said, stabbing a cherry tomato and then popping it, whole, into her mouth.

"Now, hon, don't start—"

"Don't start? Yeah, Gar, Lord knows we don't want to *start* anything." Then she smiled, kissed his cheek a third time, seemed to regain her good humor as quickly as she'd lost it. "We've been engaged for twelve years now, right, Gary?" She leaned over the table and whispered loudly, "He's cute, but a bit of a slow starter, if you know what I mean. That," she ended, leaning back once more, "and the fact that his dearest mommy has yet to run out of excuses for postponing the date."

Gary flushed to the roots of his buzz cut. "Now, Brandy, that's not true. Mom—"

"Hates me," Brandy declared, another cherry tomato impaled on her fork. "Hates, loathes, and detests me. How dare I take her little baby away from her, leave her alone, a poor, sick old woman like her, yadda yadda."

She looked at Shelby, made a face. "Let's see. There's been the flooded basement, the new roof, the bad back— that was *twice,* Gar, remember—unexplained fainting spells, failing eyesight, and so much more. She once tried out agoraphobia—you know, that thing where you're afraid to leave your own house? That lasted about three weeks, until Tony ran one of his buses to Atlantic City." She snapped her fingers. "Presto! Agoraphobia all cured."

"Brandy, we've set the date for September, and we're by God going to go through with it this time," Gary protested, looking fairly embarrassed. "Besides, Mom has run out of good excuses."

"Shame she never tried dropping dead the day before the ceremony. I could live with that, and it would only work once," Brandy said, winking at Shelby. "Well, enough fun stuff. So, what brings you to Allentown, Shelley? From the look of things, I'd say you plan to be here for a while."

Shelby chewed on a small bite of salad, turning it into mush in her mouth as she tried to summon a convincing lie. Failing that, she swallowed hard and went with the first thing that came into her head.

"I was living in New York, Brandy, and simply got tired of the hustle and bustle of a big city. So much noise, so much traffic."

"And crime," Gary added helpfully.

"Yes!" Shelby leaned forward, pressing her forearms

against the edge of the table, grabbing at Gary's help with both hands. "I was *mugged*. It was horrible, Brandy. I was, um, jogging in Central Park. Suddenly there was this *man*. This huge man! In broad daylight. He took my purse—you know, one of those things that ties around your waist?—and was about to drag me off the path, into the bushes, when the police arrived."

She sat back, pleased with herself. "Well, let me tell you, I was shaken. I resigned my position—er, quit my job the next day, packed up everything I could, and took the first bus leaving the city. It just happened to be heading for Allentown."

"Wow," Brandy breathed, definitely impressed—impressed with how very bad a liar her new acquaintance was, not that Gary had seemed to notice. "That's so scary."

"Yeah, and what happens the second she gets off the bus?" Gary said to prove Brandy's point, his beefy hands balling into fists. "Bam! She gets mugged again. Talk about your rotten luck."

Shelby agreed happily, not knowing that her luck had undergone yet another change.

It had just gotten worse.

She'd handed her credit card to the waitress as the three of them were talking, and now the waitress was back, holding the platinum card in one hand, scissors in the other.

"This card isn't any good, hon. The girl at the company told me it's been canceled just this morning. They told me I'm supposed to cut this up right in front of you," the waitress said, sounding apologetic. "Sorry about this."

As Shelby watched, openmouthed, the waitress did just as she'd been told, and Shelby was left with her only access to cash beyond the four hundred dollars in her wallet lying in two uneven pieces on the table. She was without money. For the first time in her life she was without money. Real life had just hit with a vengeance.

"But . . . but . . ." she stammered, picking up the pieces, vainly, stupidly trying to stick them together again. And then, as Brandy slid onto the bench seat beside her and put her pudgy arms around her commiseratingly, she began to cry.

Chapter Ten

Because she rarely needed to do more than express a
wish for something before it was handed to her, Shelby
wasn't quite as overwhelmed by her good fortune as she
might have been. Still, she did know that she could have
done a lot worse than to be taken in by Brandy Wasilkowski.

What she considered to be the best of good luck was
finding out that Brandy lived in the Allentown suburb of
East Wapaneken, residing in a second-floor apartment in
an old, converted school building.

Within hours of her silly collapse into tears at the diner,
Shelby found herself firmly under Brandy's wing, and she
and her five suitcases were transferred to the spare bedroom in that same apartment.

She even found it possible to smile as Gary had put down
the luggage, as the two of them stepped first right, then
left, trying to make enough room for him to pass by her,
back into the hallway.

The bedroom was infinitesimally small, half the size of

Shelby's closet. It was stuffed with what had to be someone's mistaken impression of white French Provincial furniture, the narrow bed was covered in stuffed animals of varying vintage, and shelves on the walls were lined with cute little things called Beanie Babies that Brandy had already told her were someday going to be worth a small fortune.

Considering that Shelby had spent a lifetime around all-but-priceless pieces of art, she thought she'd done a fairly good job of looking as impressed as possible.

The walls of the room crowded in on her, painted a dark green and barely visible behind the shelves, pictures of Persian cats, and half a dozen very large posters of country music singers. Garth Brooks. Tim McGraw and Faith Hill. Reba McEntire. Shania Twain. And somebody else, her poster not favored with a signature, as if everyone should automatically know her—or recognize her by the size of her blond wig and the absolutely magnificent display of breasts beneath a jeweled gown and above a wasp-thin waist.

Well, Shelby thought, turning away from those unbelievable breasts, at least she wouldn't feel alone in here. A person couldn't possibly feel alone in this room.

She picked up one of the dozen photographs from the dresser, seeing a smiling Brandy as she made her way through the years—and the dress sizes—all while surrounded by dozens of other smiling faces that could only be other Wasikowskis, if she could tell something like that merely by counting freckles.

Shelby took a deep breath, let it out slowly, and then smiled. She was in a real bedroom in a real town, living with a real person, and she was about to have the adventure of her life. As she'd heard someone say on the bus, "It just doesn't get any better than this."

Then she remembered the two pieces of the credit card Somerton had canceled on her stuck in her purse, and felt her first real pangs of what it must be like for all these nice, normal people when money got tight, when there were too many days and too few dollars between now and their next paycheck.

Not that she even had a paycheck to look forward to. Damn Somerton for taking all the fun out of her adventure!

She felt sorry for herself for a moment, until a huge silver-shaded Persian with a neon pink collar flounced into the room, meowed at her briefly, hopped up on her bed, and began lazily cleaning herself. A cat. A pet. She'd never had a pet. What a simple, simply wonderful homey and fuzzy life Brandy lived. And now, if just for a little while, so did she.

Brandy and Gary were the good people Jim had talked about when he'd told her about East Wapaneken. They were the down-home, small-town folks who did more than host a charity ball for the less fortunate. They took them in, fed them, gave them a roof over their heads, *cared* for them. It was so wonderfully small town, just the way she'd imagined it.

It was real life, just as Shelby had wanted to see it, experience it. Even if, as she remembered Jim saying, everyone in a small town felt a right to know all your personal business.

As if to prove that fact, and over a dinner of home-delivered pizza (and while feeding pepperoni to Princess the Persian), Brandy promised not to ask any personal questions until her new friend was ready to answer them— and then asked at least two dozen of them.

Shelby pretty much held her own throughout Brandy's questions, or so she'd thought, making up lies as fast as she could. But later that night, as she shared her narrow bed with Princess and a big, red plush dog with one ratty ear, she could hear Brandy and Gary talking in the living room down the hall.

"Those were Gucci loafers, Gary. *Gucci.* And did you see her watch? Solid gold, with *diamonds.* Not chips, Gar— real diamonds. I'm telling you, Shelley isn't just a French Literature professor running away from New York, like she says she is. Professors don't make that kind of money."

"They do if they run up their credit cards until some waitress cuts them in half in front of you," Gary pointed out reasonably. "I like her, too, babe, but she could be on the lam or something. Running away from the police. Did you think of that before you invited her to move in with you?"

"She *cried,* Gary," Brandy pointed out. "Just broke down and sobbed. Criminals don't cry like that. She was shocked out of her gourd when the waitress cut up her card. And did you notice how she stumbled over her own name, like she wasn't used to saying it? Or answering to it, come to think of it. No, Shelley's in some kind of trouble. I'm sure of it. Maybe she's running away from a boyfriend, or even an abusive husband."

"It did look like she'd been wearing a ring on her left hand," Gary had put in, playing detective now himself. "You know, like her hand is a little bit tanned, but there's this one spot on her finger that isn't. You may be right, hon. Still, what are we going to do with her? She can't just stay here, can she?"

"And why not? She needs help; she needs a job. I'm an employment counselor, Gar, remember? She couldn't have it any better than to be here. I can get her a job, keep her here with me until she earns enough to afford her own apartment, gets back on her own two feet. What could be easier?"

Indeed. What could?

That was when Shelby had finally fallen asleep, smiling at the thought that she had somehow become a woman of mystery. A very lucky woman of mystery who was about to embark on what could only be a wonderful adventure out in the "real" world.

Chapter Eleven

The real world arrived at five-thirty the next morning as Brandy's three different-sounding alarm clocks went off on the other side of the thin bedroom wall.

Shelby sat up all at once as Princess deserted her, clapping her hands over her ears, listening to Brandy grumble and complain as her bedsprings creaked as she got out of bed and turned off the alarms one after the other.

Not that the silence lasted for more than a few moments before Brandy knocked on Shelby's door, then stuck her head in to say good morning, to be followed by her short, slightly chubby body, which was currently wrapped in a red-and-black-flowered faux-silk kimono. "Sorry about the racket. Should have warned you, I guess," she said, wrinkling her freckled nose. "Gary says it's like waking the dead, trying to get me up in the morning. You want the shower first, Shelley, while I put some coffee on?"

"Um . . . well . . . sure, sure," Shelby said, pushing her fingers through her hair, trying to remember who she was, where she was, *why* she was. "That . . . that would be just fine. Oh, and Brandy? Is my clock right? Is it really five-thirty?"

"Yeah. Scary, ain't it? But I've got to be at work by eight, and I usually stop at Tony's for breakfast before I catch my bus. You'll go with me, of course."

Shelby's head was still struggling with the idea of being up before the dawn. "To work? I'm going to work with you?"

"No, silly, to Tony's. You do want to eat, don't you? I mean, you don't really think I *use* the kitchen, do you? Now come on. Chop, chop."

Once Brandy was gone, padding off down the hallway toward the kitchen, Shelby collapsed against the pillows once more, thinking she'd had enough of real life for one morning and planning to sleep until at least ten. She turned onto her side, tucked one hand beneath the pillows, and snuggled beneath the blankets.

Her eyes flew open once more as the apartment filled with the sound of a twangy male voice happily complaining that "nobody gets off in this town." Brandy joined in seconds later with an off-key accompaniment that told the story of a town so small the trains didn't stop there, there was only one stop light, one dog, and if the bus stopped there people got on but nobody got off.

"Like that?" Brandy asked, sticking her head inside the door once more. "That's Garth Brooks, king of the world. You know, if anyone had told me I'd like country and western a year ago I would have laughed myself silly. Now I'm taking line-dancing lessons at the bowling alley on Friday nights, not that Gary will go with me, the jerk. Hey, you want to come along next time? It's fun, honest. Oh," she said, opening the door fully and walking into the room, "here's your coffee. As I remember it, you take it black. I'll hit the shower first, okay, keep the bathroom warm for you. But I'm warning you, unless you get into the shower before Mrs. Leopold in One B starts filling her tub, you'll be showering in cold water.''

Shelby opened and closed her mouth a few times, unable to think of a single thing to say, finally settling on a weak "Thank you" as Brandy passed over the coffee mug with the drawing of some hairy, widemouthed cartoon monster on it.

Forty-five minutes later, with the punch line of a bad joke told on the radio by someone named Howard Sterm, or Stern, or something like that echoing in her ears, Shelby was following Brandy down the stairs and out into the already bright sunshine. A two-block walk ended at Tony's Family Restaurant, located on a corner and, according to her new friend, converted from a gas station just five years earlier and now the favorite eating spot for most of East Wapaneken.

"Charming," Shelby said as she followed Brandy across the parking lot to the dull pink stucco building, watching as two men in plaid shirts, a pair of ladies wearing hats and carrying prayer books, and a uniformed policeman— with pistol—entered the restaurant ahead of them. She'd had no idea so many people got up this early in the morning.

Brandy was immediately greeted by a young waitress dressed in a black T-shirt and matching leggings, her arms full of dishes she quickly deposited in front of four patrons sitting closest to the door. "The usual, Brandy?" the girl asked. "Who's your friend?"

"Shelley, this here is Tabby. Shelley's staying with me for a little while, Tabby. Oh, and she takes her coffee black."

"Black, gotcha," the waitress answered, never stopping in what seemed to be a well-orchestrated perpetual motion that had her now picking up empty plates, dropping a check on the table, and joking with the patrons, calling all of them by their first names.

It was all too much. Tabby, and three more women very much like her, were all equally busy, as nearly every chair, every booth, was occupied by talking people, laughing people, people reading morning newspapers, people nursing hot coffee or just staring into space, still trying to wake up.

Barely controlled chaos, that was what it was, and Shelby shook her head as she sat down, and looked across the table at Brandy. "How do you stand it?" she asked. "All this noise so early in the morning."

"Oh, it's always like this at Tony's," Brandy explained as Tabby upended the brown ceramic mugs already on the table and poured coffee into them. "Isn't it, Tabby? Shelley, do you need to see a menu?"

"Hmmm?" Shelby asked, realizing that Brandy was talking to her. She'd been watching a man built more for sitting than moving pouring maple syrup over a stack of three pancakes that were already smothered in blueberries. "Oh. Oh, no, I suppose not." She smiled up at the waitress. "I'll have the fresh melon, thank you. Perhaps a small slice of prosciutto."

Brandy and Tabby laughed at the same time. "Melon?" Tabby repeated as she pulled out her order pad. "Honey, the closest thing we've got to fruit is orange juice. You want some of that? And some bacon and eggs, of course. You like your home fries light or dark?"

"I—I . . ." Shelby gave up, watching Tabby scribble on the pad. "That will be, um, just fine. Thank you, Tabby."

Brandy watched Shelby across the table, smiling at the other woman's confusion. "You're not used to this, are you, Shelley? Didn't you ever eat out in New York?"

"In New— Oh! Oh, yes, of course I did. This is . . . this is very nice. Really."

"Yeah, right," Brandy said, putting her elbows—and her cards—on the table. She'd tried half the night to think up subtle ways to worm the truth out of Shelley, then decided she didn't know subtle from Saturn. "Look, Shelley—if that's really your name—don't you think it's time you told me the truth?"

Shelby took refuge in sipping her coffee, which was amazingly good. The entire restaurant smelled quite good. Her stomach must have agreed, because it grumbled at her as she decided that a scrambled egg might not be such a bad idea. Unless her rumbling stomach was trying to warn her that she'd run out of lies and she was about to be found out for the fake she was. There was that.

"The truth, Brandy? I did tell you the truth last night."

"Sure you did, kiddo, even though I was sort of holding out on you. I forgot to mention that I'm the queen of England." She reached a hand across the table, squeezed Shelby's fingers. "You've run away, haven't you? What happened? Did you cause some scandal at the country club? Did Daddy cut off your allowance? Are you pregnant?"

"Pregnant? Good God, no!" Shelby withdrew her hand. "I'm sorry, Brandy. I'll pack and leave immediately."

"Oh, don't be a jerk," Brandy said easily, then sat back as Tabby arrived with two heaping plates of bacon, toast, scrambled eggs, and home fries. "Let's eat, okay, and then you can tell me whatever you want to tell me. And if you don't want to tell me anything, then that's okay, too. I just want to help, that's all."

"Thank you, Brandy," Shelby said sincerely, then looked down at the plate in front of her, her eyes going wide in her head. "Good Lord, am I really supposed to *eat* all of this?"

"Beats the hell out of Slim-Fast, doesn't it?" Brandy said, laughing. "I don't know why I think I'll ever get back in a size eight. Not when Tony's doing the cooking. Now eat up, Shelley. It'll do you a world of good."

"I highly doubt that," Shelby said, gingerly picking up her fork and stabbing it into a fluffy mound of scrambled eggs. She remembered Jeremy's views on cholesterol, believing the man would fall into a swoon if he could see her plate now. Who was she kidding? Jeremy would fall into a swoon if he even *heard* of East Wapaneken. "Um . . . the wait staff—do they all know CPR?"

"What, you want to live forever?" Brandy asked, her mouth full of delicious, greasy home-fried potatoes. Then she went for the whole thing, because she wasn't subtle, and the suspense was killing her. "But if you're not going to eat you're going to have to talk to me. Which is it, Shelley?"

Shelby put down her fork and dabbed at her mouth with the thin paper napkin. "What gave me away?"

Brandy held up a finger as she chewed and swallowed. "What *didn't* give you away? Your clothes, your shoes, that watch on your arm. Eating pizza with a knife and fork, for crying out loud. You're about as out of place as . . . as, well, as you look sitting here in Tony's right now. Admit it, Shelley; you're rich. And on the lam from something. Or some*one.*"

Shelby looked at the eggs, looked at Brandy, and gave up. "I suppose I should tell you the truth. I thought I'd *blend* better than I have, but I can see now that it was only wishful thinking on my part. All right, here goes. My name is Shelby Taite, Brandy, and I've run away from home, my fiancé, and a rich and pampered life that is slowly driving me insane. I had this crazy idea: I wanted to taste real life, with real people, and I wanted to disappear for a while as I did that."

Brandy looked at Shelby, her fork stopped halfway to

her mouth. "Running *away* from the good life. Now there's a switch."

"And you think I'm being ridiculous, don't you? But it would have worked, really, except my brother canceled my credit card, probably thinking that would have me running home before dark. I've got four hundred twenty-three dollars and fifty-three cents in my wallet, and I'll absolutely have to kill myself if I have to call Somerton and beg him to come get me. And, even though you didn't ask, no, I've never been in a place like this before this morning. I didn't even know anything like this existed. I mean, I once saw a PBS documentary on diners and the changing culinary scene in America, but . . . Well, I think I've been talking long enough."

She sat back against the wobbly wooden chair and folded her arms across her chest as she blinked back annoying tears. Less than twenty-four hours on her own, and she had already failed. It was more than depressing. "There. Is that honest enough?"

Brandy's jaw had dropped halfway through Shelby's confession and she popped some eggs into her mouth, then used her fork to push her chin back up before saying, "Wow. Oh, wow. This is like that movie. You know. Clark Gable and that girl—don't remember her name. *It Happened One Night,* that's it. Old movie, dead old. This rich girl swan dives off Daddy's yacht and runs away—takes a bus, too, if I'm remembering right—to see how the other half lives, or something like that. You're really rich, Shell— Shelby?"

"Filthy," Shelby admitted with a weak grin. "I'm sorry."

"Sorry?" Brandy shook her head. "What are you sorry about? I think it's cool. And you're engaged? What's the matter? Don't you love him?"

Confession must be good for the soul, because Shelby was beginning to feel better. Much better. Good enough to say exactly what she thought. "I don't know." She looked at Brandy, shrugged her shoulders. "I really don't know for certain. But I don't think he loves me. We're just sort of merging two old families."

"Ah, honey, that stinks."

Shelby reached into her pocket for her handkerchief, Brandy's sympathy starting up the waterworks yet again. But, somehow, these were cleansing tears. "It does, doesn't it? But I could be wrong," she added hopefully. "I mean, Parker *could* love me. He just doesn't seem to know how to show it very well. And Somerton says everything will be fine, that it's a splendid match. And . . . and we've already picked the china pattern."

"Screw the china," Brandy told her bracingly. "And eat your breakfast. God knows you could use a little meat on your bones. That's a good girl—take a big bite. Now, let's talk about what we're going to do, okay? Because if it's a few weeks out on your own that you want, to see if this Parker guy comes after you, worried sick and telling you he can't live without you, then we're going to have to get you a job or something until he does the white-knight bit, right?"

"A job? Brandy, you can't get me a job. My degree is in French Literature. Besides, I've never worked a day in my life."

"Never? Jeez. And you're what—twenty-four, twenty-five? I should be so lucky. I've been working at least part-time since I was sixteen. Okay, we'll work on it. You wouldn't believe some of the jerks I've gotten jobs for. You must have some skills, Shelby."

"Shelley," Shelby interrupted. "I think, if Somerton is going to be looking for me, that I really should continue being Shelley Smith. Don't you?"

Brandy shrugged, already concentrating on the project at hand. "Whatever works for you, I suppose, *Shelley*. Now, tell me what sort of skills you have, and I'll check out the files when I get to work. You do have a Social Security card, don't you? I mean, rich people still need those, don't they?''

Shelby smiled, liking her new friend very much. "Yes, we still need them. You know, Jim was right. There's nothing better than a small town.''

"Jim?''

"Our chauffeur,'' Shelby told her. "He used to live here, right in East Wapaneken, and told me about how happy he and his daughter were here, how they can't wait to come back once Susie is finished with college.''

"Oh, Jim Helfrich,'' Brandy said, nodding her head. ''That was real sad when his wife died. We knew he moved to Philly to be near Susie. Your chauffeur, huh? Well, it sure is a small world. A chauffeur. Man, you weren't kidding, were you? You're really rolling in it, aren't you?''

"Rolling in— Oh. Oh, yes. I suppose you could say that. But not right now, Brandy, which is why I'd like to hear more about how you think you'll be able to find me employment. Nothing permanent, you understand, as even Uncle Alfred won't be able to convince Somerton that I should be out on my own for more than a few weeks. Because I do have to go home again, Brandy. Sooner or later I have to go home.''

"Somerton? That's your brother? Never mind, of course he is. And Uncle Alfred. And Parker. Sound like names out of a book, not real names. I don't know, Shelley, but it also sounds to me like you've got a lot of people who are probably real worried about you right now.''

Shelby's jaw stiffened. "They're so worried about me that Somerton had my credit card cut up,'' she reminded her new friend. "Now it means twice as much to me to prove that I can survive on my own, live the way ninety-nine percent of the world lives, working every day, paying their own way. I can't go home with my tail between my legs, Brandy, I just can't. Not until I experience real life, make some memories."

"Uh-huh, uh-huh, memories. Got it," Brandy agreed, her head turned as Tony pushed open the door leading from the kitchen and walked into the restaurant. "And here, I'm thinking, comes the answer to your first problem, Shelley. I don't know why I didn't think of it before now, considering I've had to listen to Tony griping about Thelma all the time these past two weeks. I mean, how dare she have the nerve to go see her first grandchild, right? Now tell me quick—you go to parties, don't you? You *give* parties. You'd have to. Rich people are probably giving parties left and right, acting as hostess, greeting guests, that sort of stuff?"

"Well, yes, I've hosted a few parties. And I organized the ball for Saint Christopher's Hospital for Children last year. Why?"

"You'll see. Tony! Hey, Tony—can you c'mere a minute?"

Shelby watched as a tall, thin man about forty years old and wearing plaid Bermuda shorts, a green Philadelphia Eagles shirt, and a greasy white apron over all of it, shambled across the room, heading in their direction.

The man stood at least six feet, five inches tall, or he would if he didn't walk with his knees bent slightly, his nearly nonexistent shoulders hunched as if he spent most of his time working over a table too low for his comfort. He had a shock of sandy red hair, a long, angular face, and looked as if he was wearing most of the food he'd been cooking, and never eating any of it.

"What's up, Brandy?" he asked as he rolled to a stop at their table, totally ignoring Shelby. "I gotta get back there before Julio goes after Tabby with a knife. I'm telling you, if I had a single waitress who knew how to write down an order without screwing it up . . .''

"Just another day in paradise, huh, Tony?" Brandy interrupted, grinning. "I'd like you to meet someone. A new friend of mine, Shelley Smith. She's a hostess."

"Brandy, I—" Shelby sighed, held out her hand. After all, she had wanted an adventure, hadn't she? And this would really be something to tell her grandchildren, a memory to make her smile as she sat at some string quartet recital pretending she wasn't bored clear to her toes. At least it would be, if Brandy was about to do what Shelby thought she was about to do. "How do you do, Mr., um . . ."

"Just Tony," the man told her shortly, ignoring her outstretched hand. "Where'd you hostess?"

"Where?" Shelby repeated, then felt Brandy's kick under the table. "Philadelphia," she said quickly. "I hostessed—er, was a hostess in Philadelphia."

"Philly, huh? Fat lot they probably know about running a place busy as this. But okay. I only need someone for a coupla weeks, until Thelma decides to get her butt back from Oklahoma. Hours are noon to nine six days a week, with Tuesdays off. You can start today."

"I can . . . *today?* But . . . but you don't even know me."

"Brandy vouched for you. That's good enough for me." Then he turned away and made a shuffling beeline for Tabby, already telling her that Texas French toast and regular French toast were two different things and when in hell was she going to figure that out, damn it.

"Um . . . charming man," Shelby said, swallowing hard on a very large lump of nervousness.

"He's all bluster," Brandy told her, grabbing the check Tabby had thrown onto the table as she ran by, muttering under her breath about how she didn't need to be insulted, she had better things to do with her life than be insulted. "They all love him, really. And so do the customers. To tell you the truth, I think it's all an act. Otherwise they'd run all over him. He paid Thelma's way to Oklahoma, you know, not that he wants anyone to know that. Just stand up to him, don't take any guff, don't take anything he says to heart, and you'll be fine. Just fine."

"Just fine? Brandy, I don't have the faintest idea what a hostess *does* in a place like this. Do you?"

Brandy led the way out of the restaurant. "Nope, not really. But you'll manage. Of course, you probably should have asked him how much he's going to pay you, but then you'll probably be fired by tonight anyway. Ah, there's my bus, right on time—only ten minutes late. Here's the key to the apartment. I'll be home before six. In fact, Gary and I will come by for dinner, let you seat us, hand us our menus."

"That's all I have to do? Seat people?" Shelby walked to the bus with Brandy. "That doesn't sound too difficult."

"Made in the shade, babe," Brandy told her, patting her arm. "Have fun, you grand adventuress, you!"

Shelby stood at the corner until the bus was out of sight, then slowly walked back to the apartment. She'd been on her own for only a day and she had friends, a place to live, and now a job.

Now she was going to discover what it was like to be a normal person living in a normal world. She was having an adventure, being a *real* person. She could do this. She *would* do this.

"Made in the shade," she repeated to herself as she kicked at a stone with the toe of her Gucci loafer, not having the faintest idea what that meant.

Chapter Twelve

"I said no. *N*, as in not hardly, and *O*, as in it's out of the damn question."

Grady sat back in his desk chair, deliberately wincing as his shoulder made contact with the plush leather, and looked up at his hovering, glowering partner. "It wasn't an either/or question, Quinn," he pointed out calmly. "It was more of a 'So when can you start' question."

"And the answer is never," Quinn told him. "And you can stop playing the wounded warrior, because I don't give a damn. The Rich and Repulsives are yours, remember? Besides, we're nearing the end of the fiscal year, and I'm up to my ass in paperwork. I've already fired two temps, and if Selma doesn't come back soon we're all in trouble."

"True enough. But I can't do this one, and you know it. For one, I'm injured, not in the line of duty, granted, but injured just the same. Two, she knows me. I've been squiring the Taites around town for three years, while you've already told me you're willing to bet she wouldn't recognize you again if she tripped over you. By the way, that really pulled your chain, didn't it—that she didn't even notice the great Quinn Delaney—or was that Clancy? Anyway, we can't take the chance of spooking her, sending her running again before we can get her home. Oh, yeah, and three, the Taites always insist on a partner in the firm, remember?''

"Fine," Quinn spit. "Promote Maisie; she's all but running the place anyway. Because I'm not doing it, Grady. I'm not playing Chase the Heiress. As far as I'm concerned, the woman wanted to get lost. Let's all do her a favor and let her *be* lost. Besides, she's probably on the French Riviera with some gigolo and having the time of her life.''

Grady shifted in his chair. "Are you sure? The note could have been written under duress, you know. Maybe she was actually kidnapped.''

Quinn stopped pacing, considered this for a moment, then retrieved the faxed note from Grady's desktop. The fax had arrived an hour earlier, more than twenty-four hours after the Taites had discovered Shelby's disappearance. It was short, and more than a little obscure:

Don't worry about me, Somerton. I just felt a need to be by myself for a few weeks. Uncle Alfred understands and will explain. Please, Somerton, let me do this. I need to do this.

"Call it a wild hunch, Grady, but I'd say she wasn't kidnapped. She's just gone AWOL. Did anyone talk to Uncle Lush?" he said, replacing the note. Not that he cared, not that he was interested. So the Taite heiress did a flit. So what. Maybe she'd get lucky, come back with a little bit of life sparking in those empty brown eyes. Those lovely, perhaps sad brown eyes. *Damn.* He'd always been such a sucker for sad eyes.

Grady told his secretary to enter when she knocked,

then sat forward, saying, "Yeah, Somerton told me he talked to the uncle. He said something about Shelby wanting to find out how the other half lives, be normal, and make herself a few memories. You know, all that stuff that sounds so good in theory, then hits the fan in a big way when someone like our pampered runaway hits the real world and it hits back, hard. So yes, I agree, Quinn. She's run away from home, and now she's a target for any nut out there. Or do you really think this woman knows the first thing about survival outside of her expensive glass bubble? She's a babe in the woods, Quinn, a rich, pampered, spoiled, probably clueless and most definitely exploitable babe in a big, dangerous woods. If we both know nothing else, we know that the rich need keepers like us. What is it, Ruth?"

"The Taites are here, boys," she told them, then pulled a face. "And a Mr. Parker Something-or-other the *Thurd*. That one's really got his shorts in a twist, let me tell you. You want I should show them in? Oh, and it might be a good idea to keep your discussion a little under the shouting match you've been at for the past ten minutes. These walls are thick, but they aren't soundproof."

"Quinn?" Grady asked, looking up at his partner, noting the thundercloud expression in his friend's eyes. Smiling as he saw that his last words had hit home. Quinn had two dogs, mostly because he couldn't say no to a pair of sad eyes. And if Grady knew nothing else, he knew the sad look he'd seen in Shelby Taite's brown eyes the last few times he'd guarded her.

Quinn could ignore physical beauty. He could ignore wealth and position, and usually did so, with a vengeance. But he never could pass on a pair of soulful brown eyes. In fact, if Shelby Taite had four legs and a tail, Quinn would have been on the job an hour ago. "So, partner? What do we do? Send them away, lose a cushy account and probably a dozen more once Somerton tells his friends how unhelpful we've been? Let that poor, helpless little rich girl fend for herself out there in the big, bad world?''

"Oh, shut up," Quinn gritted out, then waved in Ruth's general direction, so that she retreated to the waiting area to gather up the Taites and the fiancé.

The Taite menagerie didn't just walk into a room; they made an entrance, sailing into Grady's office like a small fleet of very expensive sailboats with the wind at their backs.

Somerton Taite entered first, his rather prissy walk still filled with determination, although his pinched features showed obvious signs of distress and probably a sleepless night. He was followed hard by a shuffling Jeremy Rifkin, whose eyes were suspiciously red as he held a large white handkerchief to his mouth, stifling a sob. Somerton immediately led his friend to a chair, patted his shoulder.

Quinn waited for him to say, "Sit; stay," but it didn't happen.

Uncle Alfred seemed to have lost his rudder, as his progress into the office was far less direct, although his meandering steps did eventually lead him to the small table in the corner—the one with the cut-crystal whiskey decanters on it. He immediately lifted the lid of the ice bucket, smiling when he discovered that it was full.

And then there was Parker J. Westbrook III. He arrived last, still stuffing papers into a briefcase, and barking out orders to Ruth that had a lot to do with getting him some coffee—black, two sugars—and perhaps a stenographer.

Just as Quinn thought the gang was all there, another man slipped into the room, staying very close to the open door and looking as if he'd really rather be somewhere else. Anywhere else.

"Hello, Jim," Quinn said, bypassing the Taites and the "Thurd" to shake hands with the nervous chauffeur. "Why are you here? No, let me guess and see if I'm right. You drove the getaway car, didn't you?"

Jim Helfrich nodded miserably and wiped at his perspiration-dotted forehead with a big red and white handkerchief he'd pulled from his pocket. "I didn't know," he said plaintively. "I honest to God didn't know."

"Wrong. You didn't *think*," Parker bit out peevishly, settling himself on the couch and opening his briefcase once more, pulling out papers and photographs and carefully arranging them on the coffee table. "A bus station. Christ! If you were mine you'd be history."

"Yours, Westbrook?" Quinn asked, stepping in front of Jim. "Into owning people, are you?"

Parker's handsome face darkened. "You know what I mean, Delaney. The man's incompetent, and we've already wasted enough time," he said, slapping down a last pile of typewritten pages. "Now shall we get on with it? I have a meeting down the street in twenty minutes."

Quinn took another step in the man's direction. "Real worried about your fiancé, aren't you? Tell me, which chart is she in? Have you run a cost analysis as to how much time you're willing to expend finding her, compared it to how much money you'll lose every minute you aren't out wheeling and dealing? You have, haven't you? God, you really are a pr—"

"Quinn!" Grady interrupted, knowing his partner was about to insult the paying customers. Then he remembered that Westbrook wasn't the customer. "Sorry, old man. Didn't mean to interrupt. You were saying?"

"Never mind, it's not worth my trouble," Quinn said, rubbing at the back of his neck as he wondered, not for the first time, what Shelby Taite saw in this stiff-backed horse's ass. Not that he cared, of course.

Somerton Taite delicately cleared his throat from his seat beside Jeremy Rifkin, who was still weeping softly into his handkerchief as he moaned something that sounded very much like, "Our poor little girl." It was a nice touch, lent a certain softness to the moment, having someone cry over the missing socialite.

"As I informed you when I telephoned earlier, Mr. Sullivan," Somerton began carefully, "my sister has gone missing as of yesterday morning. We, of course, do not wish the police involved, or the press, as the last thing we want is for Shelby to be out there somewhere with the whole world looking for her as if she were the prize in some contest. Which is why we first thought to conduct our own investigation. However, we soon realized we were not equipped for what we finally decided must be done."

"That was so wonderfully succinct of you, dear Somerton," Jeremy complimented from his chair, beaming at the assembled company. "Wasn't that wonderfully succinct of him?"

"Thank you, Jeremy. Now, as you can see by the fax I sent you after our phone conversation, Mr. Sullivan, my sister's farewell note was not especially helpful to us, nor was my uncle Alfred, who seems to believe Shelby is simply off having the adventure of her life, as he calls it, and we should all just . . . just . . ."

"Butt out, Somerton. I told you all just to butt out, let the girl have her head for a while, not that you've ever listened to me," Uncle Alfred supplied from the corner, lifting his glass to Quinn in a mock salute before circling it beneath his nose. "Ah, pure ambrosia. Don't you just love the smell of good whiskey in the morning?"

"The bus," Jeremy whimpered from his chair, shuddering in very real horror. "She traveled on the *bus*."

Quinn's head pushed forward on his neck as he looked at Jeremy, then turned to the chauffeur. "He's kidding, right? You really took her to the bus station, Jim?" he felt forced to ask, knowing he was upsetting the man. "How did she explain that one to you?"

Jim ducked his head. "How did she explain it? She didn't, sir. She just had me load the luggage, and then told me where she wanted to go. I figured she knew where she wanted to go."

"Of course, of course," Quinn said, patting Jim's shoulder. "Don't worry about it."

"The dirt, and the *smells,* and the *humanity,*" Jeremy said on a groan. "All those people, shoved in together like cattle, cheek by jowl. Oh, I don't think I can bear thinking about it another second, Somerton, truly I don't."

"I told you to stay home," Somerton reminded him, gratefully taking a cup of coffee off the tray Ruth was now passing around and handing it to Jeremy. "You aren't going to be ill again, are you?"

Jeremy lifted his chin and gave his head a shake. "No, Somerton, I am not. I am going to sit here and support you in your time of trial. It is the very least I can do."

"And the most," Uncle Alfred commented, winking at Quinn. "Tell you what, Jeremy, how about we pour a splash of whiskey in that cup? Make a man of you, put some hair on your chest. You'd like that, wouldn't you, boy?"

"You're not helping, Uncle Alfred," Somerton said sternly as Jeremy sank back against the cushions, folding in on himself, hugging his misery to him.

Quinn shot a look at Grady, who smiled at him and purposefully patted his sling. "Yeah, right," Quinn said at last, knowing he'd have to handle this one without any help from his friend—his friend who was enjoying himself way too much. "She hasn't been gone all that long, gentlemen, although it would have been better if you'd contacted us yesterday. Still, if you'll just answer a few questions for me, I think I can guarantee I'll have her home safe and dry by tonight, tomorrow night at the latest. Figuring con-

servatively, as I don't think Miss Taite has read any books
on how to disappear without a trace."

"Oh, no!" Somerton said quickly, shaking his head.
"Oh, no, no, no. We don't want her *back.*"

"Pardon me?" Quinn said, but Parker interrupted
before Somerton could elaborate.

"Somerton, we discussed this and I thought it was settled," Parker said, still shuffling papers. "You and your
uncle may think it a laudatory lesson if Shelby is left to
her own devices for a while, that this is something Shelby
seems to want, but I cannot disagree more strenuously."

Quinn hated saying it, but heard himself agreeing with
Westbrook. "I also think she should be brought home as
soon as I locate her, Mr. Taite. You'll pardon me, but I
don't think your sister was built to be out there somewhere,
roughing it. I mean, if you'll recall, she left town on a *bus.*
It isn't as if she's flown to Aruba for the sun. She's probably
already seen enough of life outside the Main Line to have
her welcoming you like a shipwrecked sailor when I tell
you where to find her."

"But that's precisely what she needs to do," Somerton
explained as Jeremy resorted to his damp handkerchief
yet again. "See more of life, that is. From everything I've
learned from my uncle, and from Jim, even from Shelby's
maid, Susie, it's also precisely what Shelby wants. She asked
Susie what *normal* people wear, then had her pack *normal*
clothing for her."

"Versace," Uncle Alfred said, lifting his glass in a toast.
"What the well-dressed Everywoman is wearing this year,
don't you know."

Quinn mentally ruled out his earlier thought that Shelby
might have waved Jim good-bye at the bus station, then
called a hired car to transport her to the airport, then out
of the country. She was still in America, and still close by,
if he was figuring the thing correctly. But close could still

be pretty damn far away, if she was out there alone, a woman with less street-sense than a two-year-old. Immediate rescue wasn't an option if he was right, if Somerton was right. It was a necessity.

Parker tried to speak, but Quinn glared down at him, warning him to silence as Somerton pressed on with his explanation.

"She asked Jim here if he liked living in a small town, what it was like—that sort of thing. And, no thanks to my uncle, who filled her head with fanciful notions, I really do believe my sister is off to have herself an adventure before she settles down and marries Parker here."

"In short, Mr. Taite," Quinn said, still glaring at Westbrook, "your sister has gone slumming, right? She's gone slumming, and you want to let her have at it. Well, bully for her, and bully for you, and where does that leave us? What do you want from D and S?"

"We want you to find her," Somerton said.

"We need you to protect her," Jeremy added.

"We want to give my niece her head but make sure she's fully protected while she's out there exploring real life or whatever it is she thinks she's doing," Uncle Alfred concluded. "Consider yourself her guardian angel, if you like, Delaney. Anything that keeps these two happy and upsets Parker is just fine with me."

Quinn held out his hands, pushing away their words as unacceptable. "Oh, no. No, no, no, gentlemen. I thought you wanted me to find her so that you could come carry her home. Now you're saying you want me to *baby-sit* her until she's had her fling and come home on her own, and I'm not going to do it. There isn't enough money in the world to make me do that."

"Well, finally a man of some sense!" Parker said with satisfaction, gathering up some of his papers and replacing them in the briefcase, then standing up, ready to rush off to his meeting.

Parker didn't know it, but his words had finally convinced Quinn that maybe being a baby-sitter for a few weeks wasn't all that bad an idea. After all, anything Parker Westbrook wanted definitely had to be the opposite of what Quinn wanted. Westbrook did that to a person, made him want to do anything he could to, as Ruth had said, put the man's shorts in a twist.

"There is also the fact that Miss Taite is a grown woman, gentlemen, which means I could find her, you could go to her, and she still wouldn't agree to come home. It would be rather difficult to make her come home if she didn't want to. So how long?" he asked as Westbrook tapped his foot impatiently and pushed back his cuff to check his watch. "How long do you want her out there? Is there any time limit before I call you in, let you convince her to come home?"

"Ha, I should say there's already a limit, if we're going to persist with this foolishness, and I can see that we are," Parker said, showing off the results of some pretty damned expensive orthodonture. "The first thing we did was to cut off her credit card. American Express, you understand, with no monthly limit. She could have gone on indefinitely with that sort of resource. That said, I imagine we'll be getting a call within a few days, begging for Somerton here to send the car for her, wherever she is. Shelby is many things, but she has no notion of economy. She'll have spent all her money on a new pair of shoes, then belatedly realize she has no money for food. It was a perfect solution, and so I told Somerton."

"You goddamn jackass!" Quinn longed to rearrange Parker's handsome face. "One phone call and I could have traced her through credit card receipts. Now not only is she out there somewhere on her own, she's out there somewhere without money."

"Oh, dear," Somerton said, standing up quickly. "We hadn't thought of that. I'll make another call at once."

"Poor Shelby. Alone *and* destitute!" Jeremy shuddered delicately. "Indeed, yes, Somerton. You must do something at once!"

Grady, who had been content to act as silent audience these past minutes, spoke up. "Won't work, Mr. Taite. Canceled is canceled. If your sister has already tried to use the card, she's already found that out and won't try again. We'll call the credit card company, of course, but I think there's little hope we'll learn anything very productive. Quinn, looks like this one is going to have to be solved with good old shoe leather."

"In that case, I think these will be helpful." Parker smiled rather smugly as he handed over a dozen copies of a blown-up photo of him and Shelby at a charity dinner the previous winter, as well as a three-page listing of names of friends, telephone numbers, and his thoughts on where Shelby might have gone. "Personally I think your services aren't even necessary. We were right to cancel her credit card. Shelby will come to her senses the moment her purse is empty. And for God's sake, man, if you are going to call anyone, be discreet. We can't have word of Shelby's disappearance making the papers, now, can we? And now, if you'll excuse me?"

"What a horse's patoot," Uncle Alfred said to no one in particular when the door closed behind Parker. "I wonder how much Shelby is running off for an adventure and how much she's just plain running away from *him*. Sucks the air right out of a room, doesn't he?"

Jeremy staggered to his feet, laid both hands on Quinn's sleeve. "You will find her, won't you? Watch over her, protect her? She's such a dear, dear child. Not just anyone would have accepted me so calmly, you understand.''

"Yeah, right,'' Quinn said, more than a little impressed by Rifkin's genuine concern. "Now, Mr. Taite, if we can get down to business? Fifteen hundred dollars a day, plus expenses. I report to you, and only to you, and I pull the plug at any time if I think she's in any sort of trouble. Other than that, you want me to find her, watch her, and otherwise pretty much leave her alone until she decides to come home, if I'm understanding you correctly?''

"Yes, yes, that's precisely what I want,'' Somerton agreed. "And I'm so sorry about the credit card mistake. I promise you, there will be no more interference from any of us. Just find her, Mr. Delaney. Find her and watch over her, *guard* her. In the meantime, we'll just have a mention in the Society pages that my sister is sailing somewhere in the Greek isles.''

"That was my idea, wasn't it, Somerton?'' Jeremy said, preening. "Everyone should go sailing in the Greek isles sometime, don't you think, Mr. Delaney?''

"Anything you say, Mr. Rifkin. And yes, Mr. Taite, that's the plan,'' Quinn said, ushering everyone out of the office, then asking them to please wait there while he spoke with Jim in his own office.

Five minutes later Grady was in the room, holding out a slip of paper. "I called American Express, Quinn, pulled a few strings, and Shelby did try to use the card yesterday. A small diner in Allentown. I looked it up, and it's only two blocks from the bus station. Of course, where she went from there is anyone's guess.''

"Allentown,'' Quinn repeated, looking at Jim. "How far is that from East Wapaneken?''

"East Wapa-what?'' Grady interrupted, aware that Quinn had gotten as far with Jim as he had done with the phone call.

"How far? About seven miles," Jim said, shifting in his chair. "Do you really think that's where she's gone?"

"Yes, Jim, I do. Using deductive reasoning, listening very carefully to your recollections of your conversation with Miss Taite, and calling on all my years of experience— and because Miss Taite appears to be more in the Secret Squirrel rather than the Mata Hari school of intrigue— I'd also say I'm probably going to be heading out to the wilds of East Wapaneken in a couple of hours."

Jim nodded and sighed. "Well, I gotta tell you I'm feeling a whole lot better now, sirs, because Miss Taite could do a whole lot worse than to end up in East Wapaneken. Oh, and Mr. Delaney? If you're going to be heading up there, stop in at Tony's for a meal. You'll love it."

Chapter Thirteen

The drive to East Wapaneken took little more than ninety minutes, and that was with highway construction sending Quinn on three separate detours and missing his exit from Route 22.

Seventy miles from Philadelphia.

It was as if he'd turned his watch back fifty years.

East Wapaneken boasted one real stoplight, one blinking red light that only really operated when the Berry Street Fire Station got a call and the hook and ladder pulled out onto the main street—which, in true small-town tradition, was called just that, Main Street.

As he'd come over the bridge that led into the town backward, from the neighboring Catasauqua, the two boroughs divided by the Lehigh River, the first thought that struck him was that the place had been caught in some kind of time warp.

He passed Elm Street and saw the town's main attraction, a really impressive baseball park with three separate diamonds, bleachers, even lights for night games. Took their baseball seriously, he decided. But then, what the hell else was there to do in a town so small it didn't even have a movie theater, let alone a gas station?

Following Jim's directions, Quinn continued down Main Street until he saw the large white sign for Tony's Family Restaurant. It wasn't as if he was hungry; he'd eaten at home before he left and taken the dogs to Grady's house for the duration. But if Jim said Tony's was the nerve center of East Wapaneken, then that was where he'd start his search.

If Shelby Taite had made it to East Wapaneken. If that even had been her planned destination. If she hadn't already decided she'd seen enough of real life and wasn't already back in her sprawling Tudor mansion, downing bonbons and making an appointment for a pedicure.

He pulled his Porsche into the lot, parking between a Ford pickup and a '67 Caddy that still had all its own chrome. He climbed out and spent a few moments admiring the Caddy before two little old ladies of the blue-haired, stooped-posture variety came out, leaning heavily on their canes. The taller one might have reached five feet.

They smiled at him, said, "Hello, dearie," and then the shorter one climbed behind the wheel of the Caddy. Looking through the steering wheel rather than over it, she backed the car up as Quinn made a quick jump to his right.

He was still smiling as he entered the restaurant, passing by the pair of poker machines that had to be as illegal as they were profitable. There was a cop in a tan uniform, pistol strapped to his waist, playing the one closest to the door.

Quinn decided he was going to like this town.

But his smile faded, and faded fast, when he walked through the small inner foyer, half wall to his left, cash register to his right, and came face-to-face with Miss Shelby Taite.

"Good afternoon," she said brightly, her arms full of menus. "Welcome to Tony's Family Restaurant. Smoking or non, sir?"

It took a good five seconds until Quinn could find his tongue, another two before he remembered how to use it. "Um . . . smoking's fine, thank you."

"Fine. If you'll just follow me?"

He followed her. He really didn't have much choice. It was either follow her or turn on his heels and make a run for it—which seemed fairly unnecessary, considering the fact that she looked happy to see him but not within a million miles of recognizing him.

He threaded his way through the tables, taking in her designer suit of softest gray silk, her slim bare legs, her thin high-heeled pumps. Her blond hair was swept up in a French twist, and she had about ten thousand dollars' worth of fine gold jewelry around her throat and wrists and stuck in her ears. She smelled like two-hundred-dollar-an-ounce perfume.

And she was working as a hostess in a greasy spoon?

Shelby had been at Tony's for only two days, so she didn't know if this new customer was one of the "regulars," although he certainly didn't seem to be. As a matter of fact, he looked as if he'd never seen a restaurant before today. Much the same way she had felt yesterday.

She felt an immediate kinship with the man. Besides, he was of the tall, dark, and handsome variety, and if Shelby was going to learn more about the real world, well, this man certainly could make for a good start on that particular project.

Shame, shame on me, she thought, then had to suppress

a giggle. Maybe she'd overdosed on home fries that morning, or had been listening too closely to Brandy's stories, but she certainly was having a good time. A fine time. The time of her life, actually.

She quickly pulled out his chair for him, one of the four mismatched chairs arranged around a small square table with an oilcloth tablecloth and dotted with four paper place mats and four sets of utensils. "There you are, sir. Our luncheon specials are chipped prime rib—on a toasted kaiser roll and a cup of either bean and barley or Italian Wedding soup, or a tuna hoagie and pierogies. I highly recommend the prime rib. John will be with you shortly to take your drink order. Enjoy your meal."

Quinn only nodded. It was either that or open his mouth to say something intelligent like, "Ah-hum, ah-hummina-hummina." Which really wouldn't have a been a good thing, hardly professional, and probably would have had her saying something else to him so that he would be left at a loss as to how to answer her yet again.

So he let John take his drink order, and told a gum-popping waitress with purple fingernails that the prime rib sandwich and bean soup would be just fine. He looked around the restaurant, wondering if he was the only one who could see that Shelby Taite looked as out of place here as a peacock in a henhouse.

Then he mentally slapped himself to attention and remembered that he was a professional, here to do a job. Whatever that was, for the Taite woman certainly looked as if she'd landed on her feet.

He mentally began preparing his first fax to Somerton Taite, grinning around a mouthful of what was actually some pretty decent bean and bacon soup. Definitely home-made.

Let's see, how would that report go? Mr. Taite: Have located the subject and she is well. My only question so far is whether or not she accepts tips.

Quinn felt himself recovering from his initial shock, which really wasn't anything close to the one he'd felt the day he'd suddenly found himself disarming his then-client's former mistress before she could skewer the guy with a steak knife.

That was what he had to do. He used to be The Man. A guy who could keep a cool head in a crisis. He had to get some perspective here, find his feet, locate his head, and get on with the job.

Which wasn't going to be easy. Not when Shelby Taite was blowing his every preconceived notion about the Rich and Repulsive straight to hell as she helped an old man with a walker and an oxygen tank into the no-smoking section, a separate area in the back of the restaurant.

He searched in his pocket for the small notebook he always carried and pulled a pen out of his shirt pocket. He began to take note of his surroundings.

Greasy spoon. Occupancy, according to the Fire Department sign on the wall, eighty-five. Average age of customers, according to his quick appraisal, eighty-five. If the owner gave a senior citizen discount, he'd be out of business in a week.

The decor was early rummage sale. Square tables with chrome center posts . . . and not quite level, he noted when the table rocked as he wrote. Three red imitation leather booths lining the half wall beside the entryway, a larger wraparound booth occupying the corner. Pink walls, blue vases on the tables, fake pink flowers in the vases. Ketchup bottles on the table, glass sugar containers as well. A sort of "You want it, here it is" sort of service, and "If you don't see it we don't have it."

The service bar, or whatever it could be called, sat right out in the open, piles of dirty dishes stacked in plastic bins, the coffeepots jammed in alongside piles of plastic glasses and stacks of stuff Quinn didn't feel necessary to add to his inventory.

Definitely not top-drawer. Probably not even bottom-drawer. The whole place was sort of a stand-alone hatrack, straining under a load of mismatched coats.

He began sketching the interior of the restaurant, the better to remember it, the better to pick what he'd already decided would be his table—the one in the far corner, where he'd have an unobstructed view of Miss Taite at all times. He might only be playing baby-sitter, but he was going to do the job right.

The door next to the service bar flew open and his waitress approached with his sandwich, plopped it down in front of him as he quickly rescued his notebook, and told him to enjoy his meal.

Quinn looked down at his plate and spared a moment to wonder where they'd put the other half of the cow. He turned the plate and looked at the sandwich from another angle, trying to decide how to attack it, then looked at the table next to him, at the four men dressed in jeans and T-shirts chowing down on their own meals.

He'd seen steak sandwiches before, but he didn't remember any that were piled so high that the roll didn't have a chance of closing around it.

Then he noticed something else as the lunch crowd began to thin out. Nearly everyone heading toward the cash register was carrying a Styrofoam box. Okay, that was good. He wasn't actually expected to eat the whole damn thing. Hell, Godzilla after a ten-day fast couldn't eat the whole damn thing.

He cut the sandwich in half, then did his best impression of eating the smaller piece. As he ate, he watched Shelby Taite.

Someone handed her their check and a pile of bills and

she thanked him very much, then looked frantically toward one of the waitresses, who quickly relieved her of the check and rang the sale on the cash register while Shelby watched, her hands behind her back, her blond head nodding a time or two as she tried to learn the mysteries of the simple machine.

"Next time, you're on your own, hon," the waitress said, slamming the drawer and walking away. "And don't worry, Shelley, you can do it."

Shelley? Oh, this was good. She'd taken an alias. Quinn mentally bet himself a quarter that her last name was now Smith. Or Jones. Shelley Smith. Secret Squirrel. It fit. Pitiful.

He lingered over his sandwich, had a second glass of soda, and pretended to be scribbling in his notebook, just as if he had the entire afternoon to sit here doing pretty much next to nothing. Which was just about right, although he'd spend a long night with his laptop and modem, catching up on company business, working on the end-of-fiscal-year reports.

He bit his lip, trying not to smile as he watched Shelby struggle with the cash register, then cursed under his breath as she smiled brightly, having at last mastered this business of taking money and making change. Did she have to look so damn pleased with herself? So damn happy? Anyone would think she'd just figured out that pesky formula for cold fusion, for crying out loud.

When he couldn't justify spending another minute in the place, Quinn asked for a take-out box, dropped a three-dollar tip on the table, and headed for the cash register himself.

"Did you enjoy your meal?" Shelby asked, taking the check and the ten-dollar bill he'd handed her. The bill had only been six dollars and twenty-six cents, and he'd toyed with giving her the ten and a penny, just to watch as she tried to figure out that she'd then owe him an even three dollars and seventy-five cents' change. But then he decided that would just be plain mean.

"The meal was fine, thank you," he told her as she turned to the cash register, sighed, and began punching in numbers with her beautifully manicured fingertip. "This is a nice place. Have you worked here long?"

"Hmmm?" she asked, still concentrating on what she was doing, then grinning as the drawer opened and she could count out his change. Okay, so he wasn't one of the locals, or he wouldn't have asked that question. He was just a very handsome man, passing through. How nice for him, and why did he have to be so nosy? "Have I worked here . . . ? Oh. Oh, yes, *yes,* I have. East Wapaneken born and bred, as they say."

Liar, liar, pants on fire. Quinn raised one eyebrow as he looked at her, called her on her fib. "Must be a new cash register then," he remarked, motioning toward the battered piece of machinery. "I mean, I couldn't help noticing that you've been treating the thing as if it might bite you if you press the wrong button."

"You've been watching me? Why?"

Well, that was better, Quinn decided. *Never explain, Miss Taite, that's the ticket. Just go on the attack, ask a question of your own. Keep this up, lady, and you might last out here in the big bad world for, oh, another twenty minutes or so.*

"Sorry, force of habit, I guess," he said, quickly falling back on his prepared story. "I'm a writer, you see. I guess watching people is just something I do. The human condition, all of that."

Man, but she smelled good.

"A writer? Would that be for a newspaper? A magazine?"

He sensed her panic at coming face-to-face with the fear of discovery. He could tell her he wrote for the Philadelphia *Inquirer,* then watch as those lovely brown eyes filled with panic. But that wouldn't do him any good.

"I was," he said instead. "I wrote for a magazine, that is, a travel magazine you probably never heard of. But now I write travel books, going around the country on road trips, writing about the people, the sights, the little out-of-the-way places like East Wapaneken. I'm my own boss, and it does pay the bills. I'm really glad I discovered this place, you know. Full of local color, that down-home, small-town ambiance everybody loves to read about even if they wouldn't set foot outside their penthouses even to look in this direction. I guess you could call me the Charles Kuralt of the coffee-table book set. Oh, and please let me introduce myself. The name's Delaney. Quinn Delaney."

"How very nice to meet you, Mr. Delaney. Your change?"

Quinn stopped smiling, feeling as if he'd just described a great set of encyclopedias to the little lady of the house who was now going to slam the door in his face. Not only had he made *no* first impression on her, he was making a pretty damn lousy *second* first impression on her.

He really didn't like this woman. Not even a little bit. Worse, he wasn't even feeling sorry for the poor little rich girl anymore. Not now that she seemed to have landed on her feet. Yeah, landed on her feet, and taken a good job away from some poor schmuck who really needed it. No, he really didn't like Shelby Taite.

"Sir? Your change?"

"Oh, right," he said, taking the money; then he decided to push at her one more time. "Thanks. Say, you wouldn't know of a good place to stay around here, would you? I'm figuring I'd like to make East Wapaneken sort of my home base as I tour the area, drink up the local flavor. I mean, you did say you've lived here all your life, right?"

He watched as Shelby almost visibly squirmed inside her designer suit that screamed "Made anywhere but East

Wapaneken.'' *Gotcha, sweetcakes! That'll teach you to have me stuck in this one-stoplight burg until you're ready to cry uncle and rush back to your cushy life and your dipstick fiancé.*

"Two blocks up, just past the Pouting Petals flower shop. It's the old East Wapaneken schoolhouse. You might try there. It . . . it has high ceilings.'' She was staring at him. She knew she was staring at him. *Why* was she staring at him? "You know, ceilings,'' she said to fill the sudden, tense silence, raising one hand above her head. "High ones. And big windows. Now, if you'll excuse me? I understand I'm to—that is, I have to refill the sugar canisters before customers start showing up for the early-bird special.''

"The early-bird special? Pure small-town gold for this scribbler. What's that?''

"Pork and sauerkraut. All you can eat if you get here before five o'clock,'' Shelby told him, mentally beating herself back under control. Goodness, you'd think she'd never seen a man with gray eyes before. And she could read the word *adventure* in both of them. Did they put something in the water here in East Wapaneken that she was now suddenly sensing a second, quite interesting definition for the word *adventure?*

Quinn patted his stomach, held up the Styrofoam container. "Nice bit of folklore for the book, but I think I'll pass on the actual thing. But, hey, thanks for the information. And I'll see you again, I hope. If I can get a room, I'll probably be eating most of my meals here.''

"I would imagine so. Most of East Wapaneken does,'' Shelby told him, then turned and walked away. It was either that or throw her silly self into this handsome stranger's arms and say something dreadfully clichéd like, "Take me. Take me *now!*''

Oblivious to Shelby's designs on his body, Quinn left with nothing else to say. More than a little mad—at her, at himself—Quinn returned to his Porsche and headed up the street until he passed the flower shop, then spied the large, square, redbrick building that still had the words *East Wapaneken School* visible in gray granite over the front door.

There was also a sign nailed to the front door: *Aparts to let. Rooms, fernished and unfernished. Bye the week, bye the month.* Inventive speller, his prospective landlord. No wonder they'd closed down the old school.

He pulled to the curb, got out, gave a passing thought to the brand-new motel he'd seen as he'd gotten off the highway, then climbed the cement stairs two at a time and walked inside. Because if Shelby Taite knew about this place, it was dollars to doughnuts she was living in this place. That was what all good detectives would call real logic, not that Quinn considered himself a real detective, but it was better than calling himself a baby-sitter. Damn better.

There were three rows of mailboxes built into the vestibule, one for each floor of the building, he imagined, and there were only names on six of the twelve mailboxes. None of them were Shelley Smith or Jones, which wasn't surprising. He doubted if she was going to advertise the fact if she did live here.

Quinn pressed the doorbell on top of the mailbox labeled *Manager,* and waited less than a minute before a large, low-to-the-ground woman in a flowered muumuu that could have served as a dustcover for a 1956 Buick rolled out of the first door to the left beyond the vestibule.

"Afternoon, son," she said, smiling around a smear of cherry red lipstick and a filtered Marlboro. "Need some help?"

God. East Wapaneken was so small-town cliché he almost didn't believe any of this was actually happening.

"Yes, ma'am," he said in what he hoped was a nonthreatening, not-so-big-city tone. "I was just down at Tony's, and the hostess there told me I might be able to rent a furnished room here for a couple of weeks if you've got one."

"The hostess? But Thelma's out of— Oh, yeah, the new girl. She's staying with Brandy a couple of weeks. No more, mind you, or I'll have to up the rent. Told Brandy that. Now, you want a room, right? I've got five, so you can have your pick. What is it you're doing here in East Wappy?"

Brandy, huh? Now, that name he *had* seen on one of the mailboxes. The lies were coming easier now, as Quinn was more than halfway comfortable with his cover story, and really pretty damned pleased to have been proven right. Miss Shelby Taite did live here, ludicrous as that seemed. "I'm a writer, ma'am, and I'm just here for a few weeks to take in some of the local color, maybe pound out a few chapters of my next book."

"A writer, huh? Right." Suddenly the woman was all business. "I don't know nothin' about any couple of weeks, though. Rent's by the month for writers and musicians and such, in advance. You have references?"

Quinn grinned, at last feeling himself totally in familiar territory. "No, but I've got five hundred dollars in my pocket ready to hand over to you, if that counts?" He probably could have gotten a room for half that, but all his expenses were being paid, and he decided Somerton Taite would be getting off cheap at twice the price.

The manager motioned with her head for Quinn to follow her into her apartment, talking around the cigarette once more as she took a key off a rack hanging inside the door. "No pets, no loud parties, no putting your beer bottles on any of my tables without using a coaster, 'cause that's what they're there for. Just act like your mama's gonna be stopping in and checking up on you, because since she isn't, I am. I dust, run the vacuum cleaner, and scrub the sink and bathroom once a week. If you make that too hard for me, you're gone. Didn't put up with it from my kids, ain't putting up with it from anyone else. Got that?''

"Yes, ma'am," Quinn answered, unconsciously straightening his spine. He took a quick look around the living room, a classroom-size area jammed with overstuffed velour furniture, a snowstorm of white lace doilies, and dominated by a big-screen TV currently showing a half-naked pair of lovers making out on a sandy beach that had never seen the outside of a Hollywood soundstage. He could smell ham and cabbage cooking on the stove in the unseen kitchen, and was only mildly surprised to see the long-neck beer sitting on a coaster and resting on a table in front of the couch.

"Got it," Quinn added, stepping farther into the East Wapaneken twilight zone. "Anything else?"

"Nope. Just the five hundred." He handed over the bills and they disappeared down the front of the muumuu, probably to be lost there forever. "And my name's Mrs. Brichta."

"I'm Quinn Delaney," he offered in return. "You may call me Quinn."

"And you can call me Mrs. Brichta. Only thing the man gave me that's worth hanging on to. You're in Two B, up the steps and to your left. I clean that room on Friday mornings, so's you'd better be up and out by seven on Fridays unless you want me seeing you in your skivvies. Now let me get back to my soaps."

"Maybe I *should* write a book about this place," Quinn said to himself as he unloaded soft-sided luggage from the trunk of the Porsche, then laughed and shook his head. "Nah, who'd believe it?"

Chapter Fourteen

There were too many of them. And they just kept coming.

Shelby had been regretting the choice of four-inch heels since about two o'clock, and had begun cursing those heels in earnest by five as that old saying "run off her feet" hit home with a vengeance.

How many people lived in East Wapaneken anyway, and why did they all want to have dinner at Tony's? Didn't they have homes? Didn't they have kitchens?

Didn't Tony know the meaning of the word *reservations*?

She had no clean tables, three parties unconscionably lingering over dessert, and twelve people standing in line next to the cash register, making it nearly impossible for her to open the drawer.

A party of twelve was in the small no-smoking room in the back. East Wapaneken had probably never heard of the Surgeon General's warnings or, if they had, didn't believe them. The party was to celebrate somebody's seventy-fifth birthday, and they'd damn well better hurry up and eat because another party, sixteen in this one, was due in the door in less than an hour for another party for an eighty-seven-year-old—Tony had given the eighty-seven-year-old permission to smoke in the back room.

And it was only five o'clock!

The first day had been fun, a lark. She'd played hostess and everyone had smiled and everyone had helped her.

Now, well into her second day, she suddenly seemed to have been thrown to the sharks, everyone thinking she knew what she was doing, everyone ignoring her pleas for help.

"You'll get the hang of it, hon."

"Don't seat them until we get the setup down, babe."

"Where in Philadelphia did you say you did this?"

That last one had come from Tony just ten minutes ago, when he had stepped out of the kitchen to see her trying a loaves-and-fishes sort of division between tables as she ran out of menus.

She'd lifted her chin at him and told him she most certainly had time to chat if he had time to be away from the kitchen. He'd turned on his heel and shambled off, looking back at her over his shoulder in what might be called an expression of amazement. Maybe even of respect.

If there was one thing Shelby could do, it was handle the serving staff, although she doubted Tony would like to be slotted into that particular category.

But it had been her only victory.

She knew she was doing everything wrong, but she didn't know how to do it correctly.

Tabby had told her that yesterday had been the exception, not the rule, and the only reason they hadn't been crowded was because the high school baseball play-offs were being held up the street.

Shelby hadn't believed her, because she'd returned to

Brandy's apartment a little after nine o'clock, too tired to shower before she fell facedown into bed, one arm around the stuffed dog, her mind and body numb with fatigue.

She hadn't even hung up her clothes. She'd never hung up her own clothes, but this was different, because if she didn't hang them up when she took them off then she'd have to hang them up later, and probably press them first. She thought about Susie, about all the maids she'd had over the years, about how she had always left a trail of discarded clothing for them to pick up, never even thinking about it once, let alone twice. But before she could feel too bad, she fell asleep, her nose all but buried in the pillow, and woke to find Princess sleeping on her Armani suit, which was now covered in white fur.

But she had made it through her first day, and had barely even flinched when Brandy's alarms started going off.

Now she knew that yesterday had been a walk in the park when stacked up against the mayhem going on right now.

Well, there were two things she could do about it, weren't there? She could either throw down the single menu she had left, stamp her feet, and shout "I quit!" or she could suck it in, or up, or whatever, and stop allowing events to dictate to her instead of the other way around.

There must have been a Taite in the army at some time, probably the Revolutionary War or something else dramatic, because somewhere deep down inside Shelby suddenly arose the belief that, yes, she had been born to command.

"Tabby," she said as the waitress all but ran past her on the way to the kitchen, "I need you to clear table six so that we can seat some of these people."

"Are you freaking nuts?" Tabby countered, giving a quick nod of her head in the direction of the service bar.

Tabby had six kids and worked double shifts five days a week to keep food on the table. She was known for her efficiency, but not her gracious manner. "Tell Bobby to get the stick out of his ass and do it. All he's doing is serving drinks because you haven't told him what else to do."

"He's supposed to clear off the tables? But why isn't he doing it?"

"Honey, you have to tell Bobby to inhale, and I'm not talkin' weed here. He's supposed to be busing tables, and I'm supposed to be serving food. You, hon, are supposed to be making sure we're all busting our humps."

"I . . . I'm the *manager?*" Shelby asked, and suddenly her feet didn't hurt quite so badly. She'd spent the day filling sugar, salt, and pepper containers. Surely managers didn't do that, did they?

Tabby tried to walk past Shelby, but she stuck out a hand and grabbed her arm. "About those sugar containers . . ."

Tabby snorted. "Yeah, we were all wondering when you'd figure that one out. The guys do that stuff, Bobby, Tom, Pedro. Good joke, huh?"

"Hilarious," Shelby said, and now her feet didn't hurt at all.

She let go of Tabby's arm, turned around slowly, with great purpose, and drew a bead on Bobby, who was leaning a hip against the service bar, sipping a glass of soda.

"Robert, clear—er, bus and set up table six, please. Then tables twelve and fourteen. *Now.*"

The teenager dropped his chin onto his chest. "Busted. Knew it was too good to last," he muttered, then picked up a plastic bin and headed for table six.

Shelby then made a quick circuit of the room, stopping at every table, smiling widely, asking if the patrons were enjoying their meals, asking the lingerers if they'd received their checks and if everything had been satisfactory.

It was the old heave-ho, and it was done by the master, a woman who had emptied more rooms after charity balls than young Bobby had probably had fast-food burgers. Clearing Tony's didn't hold a match to moving a herd of tipsy revelers out of the local country club before the committee was assessed an extra fee for the use of the ballroom.

She punched numbers into the cash register, took names and how many were in each party from those milling about in the vestibule, complimented Bobby on his efficiency, and personally helped the birthday boy maneuver his walker through the crowd to the exit.

Order. That was what was needed at Tony's. Just some semblance of order. Someone in charge.

She could do *that*. She hadn't filled a single sugar container without making a mess all over the table, but she could do that.

And if Tony knew what was good for him, he'd stay in his kitchen and let her get on with it.

At six-thirty the doors opened and Brandy and Gary walked in, followed closely by a familiar face, one she'd seen that afternoon, playfully casting him in the role of Excellent Adventure.

"Hi, babe," Brandy said, winking at Shelby surreptitiously. "Look what we found wandering the halls; our new neighbor. Two B to our Two C. And, being really nice small-town types, me and Gar invited him along to dinner. Quinn Delaney's his name. He says you told him about the apartment, right?" Then she leaned closer and whispered, "Black Irish, I'm betting, and handsome as sin. Nice work if you can get it and hubba-hubba and all that."

"Subtle, Brandy, very subtle," Shelby hissed back at her through her professional, welcoming smile. "Mr. Delaney, how nice to see you again. I'm afraid you're too late for the early-bird special."

"My loss, I'm sure," Quinn said, watching as a very becoming pink flush crept into Shelby's cheeks. He suddenly had the feeling he hadn't been "lucky" enough to bump into Brandy and Gary so much as he'd been singled out by them for some project they had in mind. Just as he had singled them out for his own reasons. Now, what could they have in mind for him?

Cleaning Shelby's clock was the first answer that popped into his mind, and he deliberately quashed it.

Then he smiled. What the hell, every job should have fringe benefits.

"Yes, well, um," Shelby said, the man's smile doing something very strange to her insides, "if you'll all just come this way?"

Chapter Fifteen

"I think I know him from somewhere, Brandy," Shelby said as they walked toward the ladies' room. The restaurant had quieted down after the busy dinner hour, and Shelby had been sitting at Brandy's table for the past fifteen minutes, most of that time staring at Quinn Delaney without letting it appear that she was staring at him.

"I do, too," Brandy said, poking Shelby in the ribs. "I think he was the subject of Brandy's erotic dreams, episodes five through eight, the dark and dangerous years. My God, Shelley, did you see those sexy gray eyes? Bedroom eyes, that's what my Aunt Betty used to call them, and she should know, considering she's been married three times. Did I tell you that? Yeah, it's true. Three times. Can you imagine? And I can't get Gar to the altar *once*. No wonder I had two desserts."

Shelby washed her hands as she examined her appearance in the mirror above the sink. "I suppose you're right. He does look like a *GQ* advertisement, doesn't he? Black slacks, black shirt, black hair, gray eyes. Definitely *GQ*. But does he have to keep *looking* at me that way?"

"What way would that be?" Brandy asked, sliding her own hands beneath the lukewarm water. "Like he could eat you with a spoon? Because that's what I'm seeing, Shel, and Gary must think the same, because he's been kicking me under the table for the last hour. I think I'm supposed to invite you guys along when we go bowling tomorrow night. You game?"

Shelby was somewhat diverted by this question. "Bowling? I don't know; I've never been."

Brandy ripped off two pieces of paper toweling and handed one to Shelby. "You've never been *bowling?* Oh, my dear, my dear, you have led a sheltered life, haven't you? Well, that settles it. Now come on, let's get back to the table before Gary says something dumb that gives you away. He's a doll, but he sure can talk too much."

"I would have thought he'd be lucky to get a word in edgewise," Shelby whispered under her breath, shaking her head as she smiled, followed after her new friend.

She'd taken no more than three steps into the restaurant proper when Tony's gruff voice reached out and touched her right between the ears. "Hey, Philadelphia!"

Her shoulders slumped for a moment; then she stood up very straight and walked over to him. He wasn't going to fire her. She might have messed up earlier, but for the past few hours she'd been right on top of things and she knew it. "What can I do for you, Tony?" she asked him, chin up, even if her stomach was doing small flips.

Tony looked around, then glared at Tabby until she threw up her hands and backed away from the two of them. Whatever he was about to say, he was making sure no one else heard him say it. "Good job," he said, almost in a whisper, then turned on his heel and headed back into the kitchen.

"Well, I'll be damned," Shelby said, watching him go. The man *was* a marshmallow, just as Brandy had said.

And she was a success.

"Bobby, bus that table, please, and then take those dishes in to be washed. It doesn't add to the ambience, seeing them piled there. Thank you." She turned to Tabby, who was adding up a check. "Good work tonight, Tabby," she said brightly, almost laughing out loud when the waitress's head snapped up in surprise. "Thank you."

"You're . . . you're welcome."

"But Tabby?" Shelby continued, feeling rather drunk with her own new power. "In the future, I would really appreciate it, and it would be so much nicer, if you greeted the customers with a simple 'Hello,' or 'Good evening.' "

"Yeah. That's what I do," Tabby countered, looking confused.

"No, Tabby, you don't," Shelby persisted. "And I really do believe that 'How's it hanging' is *not* a proper greeting in a family restaurant, don't you?"

"Jeez," Tabby said, shaking her head as she stabbed a pencil into her ponytail and stomped into the kitchen. "Like this place's got *class* or something . . ."

"It will when I'm through with it," Shelby vowed quietly, then headed back across the restaurant and sat down in the chair directly across from Quinn Delaney.

"You're looking pretty smug," Quinn said, as he seemed to think he could say anything that might be on his mind, anything that might pop into his mouth. The man had no reticence, no respect for the fact that they were strangers, or at least near-strangers, having only met that afternoon. "What happened, you get a raise?"

"That would be personal," Shelby told him primly, then couldn't contain her smile any longer. She leaned her elbows on the table and looked at Brandy and Gary. "He likes me. Tony *likes* me."

Brandy looked at Quinn. "Translated, that means he didn't bite her head off. Good going, Shelley. I told you you'd be fine."

"Yes, you did, didn't you?" She sat back and sighed. "I don't believe how *good* I feel. I've never felt like this before, never—"

"So why did Tony call you Philadelphia?" Quinn broke in quickly. He could foresee Shelby rhapsodizing herself right into giving away her true identity, so he stopped her. He didn't take the time to figure out why he stopped her, why he didn't let the charade end now so that they could both go home to civilization. He just acted. "I thought you said you were East Wapaneken born and bred."

"She is," Gary said quickly.

"I am."

"Hey," Brandy interrupted, "anybody want to go bowling tomorrow night?"

Quinn looked from Gary, to Shelby, to Brandy, and said, "Bowling? You're kidding, right?" He tried to imagine Shelby Taite in rented bowling shoes, trying to navigate the alley. It just wasn't happening. Talk about your piece of fine china in a bull shop. "I don't know, Brandy. . . ."

But, being so grateful for Brandy's timely interruption, and not knowing Quinn was actually trying to save her, Shelby quickly said that bowling sounded just fine, and why couldn't they go tonight instead of tomorrow? After all, it was almost nine, and she was wide-awake, and . . . and . . .

And twenty minutes later she was gingerly holding on to a pair of red and green bowling shoes that still smelled of the disinfectant the young boy had sprayed in them and wondering when she was going to be smart enough to keep her big mouth *shut*.

The bowling alley smelled of disinfectant, cigarettes, and spilled beer, all nicely underlain with the odor of hot dogs that came from a nearby snack bar. It sounded like thunder on a rainy night, and looked like something out of a surreal painting, all overhead lights and wood and people in funny shirts and electronic signs showing the scores of those already on the alleys.

"Come on, I'll help you pick out a ball," Quinn told her, taking hold of her elbow and steering her toward racks and racks of bowling balls.

Shelby looked over her shoulder, hoping to locate Brandy, but couldn't find her. "A ball?" she said weakly. "Do I really need one?"

"If you want to bowl, you do," Quinn told her, doing his best not to laugh in her face. That lovely face that was no longer marred by dead brown eyes. Now she had Bambi's wide eyes, and they'd just been caught in head-lights. "Let me see your right hand."

"My right . . . Oh, this is ridiculous. I'm repeating every-thing you say, aren't I? I'm sorry. But I think I ought to tell you, Quinn. I've never bowled before in my life."

"You haven't?" Quinn questioned, raising his eyebrows as he grinned at her. "Who'da thunk it?"

"Now you're making fun of me," she answered, bristling. "That's not nice."

"No, not telling me you've never bowled before until after Gary and Brandy put me on your team wasn't nice. We're going to get creamed."

"And that bothers you? Losing a simple bowling . . . session?"

"Match," he corrected. "And no, it doesn't bother me. Except that I've got a feeling Brandy and Gary have high league averages to go with their matching bowling shirts and custom shoes and balls, so we'll probably be buying all the beer frames. We'll go Dutch, all right? You bring your wallet?"

Shelby had no idea what "going Dutch" meant, but she

was reasonably sure it had something to do with her buying her share of the beer. She'd already paid for the shoe rental and chipped in toward the alley. Now beer? She'd have to work two or more hours to make that much money.

And then she smiled. Yes. She'd have to work to spend money. Not just ask Somerton. Not just tap her charge card. Not just spend and spend, without a thought to how much she was spending.

How wonderful!

"Sure," she said, suppressing a desire to wipe a hand under her nose, as she'd seen Tabby do when she was talking, getting in to the swing of being just one of the guys. "I'd be happy to pay my share. But aren't you any good at all?"

"Oh, I'm good, Shelley," Quinn told her, picking up her right hand and placing it palm to palm with his own, measuring the length of her fingers. "I'm good at a lot of things."

Shelby's fingers tingled all the way up to her elbow. Her stomach turned to mush. Her knees all but buckled. She was being hit on. Oh, yes. She'd heard the term only that afternoon, listening to two teenage girls complaining to each other about their dates of the previous evening, but that was what was happening. She was being hit on. By a tall, dark, and gorgeous man. A man who didn't know she was worth thirty million dollars. A man who just might be hitting on her because he thought she was . . . nice.

Or not so nice.

That wasn't so bad, either.

"How . . . how do we find a ball for me?" she asked as Quinn let go of her hand and bent over the ball rack to hide a satisfied smile. Forget his name, would she? Not remember him? *Oh, baby. You're going to pay for that one.*

He fitted his fingers into a ball, found the fit tight, and picked it up and handed it to Shelby. "Here, try this one."

She looked at it for a moment, then placed her fingers in it the way he had done. Quinn let go and the ball hit the floor, missing his foot by no more than an inch. "Hey! You're supposed to hold on to it."

"With what? My *fingers?* That heavy thing? Oh, don't be ridiculous. Nobody could do that."

"Lighter ball," Quinn muttered, replacing the black one Shelby had dropped. In the end, he finally fitted her with a child's ball, one with large red and blue triangles painted on it, not that Shelby knew the difference. She just told him that at least this one was "pretty."

Ah, the rich. Let them loose in the real world and they wouldn't last five minutes. He didn't stop to consider that he hadn't added the usual "and repulsive" to that last thought.

Quinn was having a good time. A really good time. A ball. Watching Shelby slide out of her Prada shoes and into rentals was worth the trip to East Wapaneken all by itself. But when Gary got up onto the lane, bent down low over the ball, went into his approach, then sent his green and white ball singing down the lane two boards from the edge only to veer into the pocket and send all ten pins reeling—well, that was when Quinn really did have to laugh out loud.

"I'm supposed to do *that?*" she asked him, clutching his forearm with both hands. "I can't do that. Can *you* do that?"

"We'll soon see," Quinn said, disengaging her fingers from his arm and going up onto the approach to pick up his own rented ball. A few moments later Brandy was writing down his strike and Gary was high-fiving him as he returned to his seat.

"Hey, he's the enemy, remember?" Brandy admonished

Gary, who only winked and grinned. "Okay, Shelley, your turn. I've got to take off these rings anyway."

Shelley had been watching, doing her best to learn enough not to look like a complete idiot when she took her turn. But Gary had nearly bent himself in half over the ball, and Quinn had stood nearly upright. Which was right? Could she do either?

Quinn waggled his eyebrows at her—the louse—and bowed to her, throwing one arm out in a flourish, indicating the approach lane.

"I see it, I see it," she muttered as she passed by, wiping her suddenly sweaty hands on her skirt.

She picked out her ball, spun it in the rack until the finger holes appeared, speared it, picked it up, and turned back to walk to the very end of the approach lane.

Quinn was standing there, waiting for her. "It's simple enough, Shelley. Just do as I say, okay?"

"Okay," she said, then lifted the ball in both hands, cupping the bottom with her left hand, holding her right hand directly below her nose. "Now what?"

"You're a quick study. Your hands are right for a novice, as I don't think you're ready to throw a hook. But bend your knees a little. I said a little, Shelley; you're not curtsying to the queen. Okay, that's good. Now, look at the pins. Stare at them, Shelley. Glare at them. They're the enemy. They're everybody who ever slipped into a parking space ahead of you. They're your third-grade teacher, the one who stood in front of your desk while she talked, and sprayed you with spit."

Shelby turned around and looked at him. "My third-grade teacher was a doll. She'd never do that."

Quinn turned her back to face the pins, his hands cupping her elbows, his sweet breath close to her ear. "Work with me, Shelley, work with me. Now relax your shoulders.

What you're going to do is simple. Right, left, right, slide. Can you remember that?''

"Right, left, right, slide. Okay. But what happens to the ball?''

Quinn sighed. This wasn't easy. Especially when he was close enough to smell her perfume, feel the sweet warmth of her blond hair against his cheek. ''Push out the ball, straight in front of you, on *right*. Bring it down to your side on *left*. Bring it behind you on *right*, throw it on *slide*. And Shelley? Don't let go until you're on slide, okay? Not on the backstroke, okay? I'm not as fast on my feet as I used to be. Do you want to practice a few times without the ball?''

She shook her head, not wanting to speak. *Right, push. Left, drop. Right, back, don't let go. Slide, let go.* She had enough to do, to remember, without having Quinn hover over her while she practiced. With him being so close she could feel the heat of him, feel his thigh against the back of her leg. Close her eyes and imagine turning around, going into his arms, beginning a mad adventure that she'd only dreamed of before tonight.

"Okay, then. Let her rip," Quinn said as he let her go; then he walked back to stand beside Brandy as she sat at the scoring desk. "Be ready to duck, guys," he told his friends, and Shelby, hearing him, stiffened her shoulders once more. Kiss Quinn Delaney? *Ha!* She didn't even *like* him.

And she'd show him. It was only a ball, after all. Only a few pins. Only a few pins about five miles away from the ball that was still in her hand. Stuck to her hand.

She relaxed her fingers slightly, before they went into a cramp, took a deep, steadying breath, and set off.

Right, push. Left, drop. Right, swing back. Slide, push front, let go.

Let go!

She finally released the ball and it went nearly straight up into the air, then traveled about ten feet down the lane before finally dropping onto the boards with a dull thud. And then it began to roll.

Quinn walked up onto the approach and stood beside her as the ball rolled toward the pins.

And rolled. And rolled. *Ba-bump, ba-bump, ba-bump.*

"Want to catch a bite to eat before it hits?" he asked, his breath tickling her ear.

"What happens if it stops before it gets there?" Shelby asked, feeling as if every eye in the bowling alley were on her, or on the ball now making its painfully slow *ba-bump, ba-bump* progress down the lane.

"I'm not sure," Quinn said, biting his bottom lip. "You get to meet the manager?"

"Oh, God," Shelby breathed, pressing her hands to her mouth. And then, finally, the ball made contact with the pins. Nearly bounced off the pins, actually.

"Three," Quinn said as the pins tipped over in slow motion, as the ball finally rolled off the alley and into the gutter. "Not bad. Not bad at all."

Shelby dropped her hands from her mouth and turned to look at him, her smile wide, her eyes shining. "No, it's not bad, is it? In fact, it's very good for my first bowl."

"Well, I'm glad you like it, Shelley," Quinn said, retrieving her ball from the return rack, "because now you get to do it again."

"Again? Really? But you and Gary had only one turn. I don't want any special favors, Quinn. I want to be treated just like everyone else."

After Quinn sketchily explained the rules of bowling, Shelby colored slightly. "Oh. I get two turns because I didn't hit them all down. I suppose that's only fair."

"Gonna be a long night, guys," Quinn said as he left

Shelby on the approach and returned to his seat. He felt good. Felt like he was her date. Her boyfriend. Her mentor.

Her mentor?

Damn, what a thought. But an interesting one. She wanted real life? He could give her real life. In spades.

"Did you see? Did you see?" Shelby called out excitedly as she ran back to him. "I got four more! Isn't that wonderful?"

Quinn looked up at her smiling face, the delight in her eyes. Miss Main Line Philadelphia, ecstatic because she knocked down a few bowling pins.

"Wonderful, Shelley," he said, standing up and holding out his arms. "That deserves a hug."

"Yes. Yes, it does, doesn't it?" she answered, and stepped forward into his arms.

Behind them, Brandy and Gary exchanged high-fives.

Chapter Sixteen

Quinn was up early the next morning, wincing only slightly as he rolled out of bed, his "bowling muscles" aching in protest.

What a night! They'd bowled three games, with Shelby low scorer, but more than happy with her final game of eighty-seven. It didn't take a lot to satisfy the woman. She was just so damn thrilled with everything, like a child set loose in Santa's workshop or something.

It was strange. Here was a woman who traveled to Rome on a whim, who could buy and sell half of the people in Philadelphia. She was used to the best of everything, having the world placed into her hands whenever she wanted it there. And there she was last night, glowing after Tony's small compliment, jumping up and down, clapping her hands when she finally made a spare, and downing her strawberry Italian ice after the match with all the enjoyment others would show for the finest caviar.

Simple pleasures. She was awash in simple pleasures after a lifetime of indulging in the most major of them.

He'd have to watch himself, remember that this was all a game to Shelby Taite, that she knew she could do an E.T. and phone home at any time, go back to her well-cushioned life. How badly did she worry about her lack of money, her job, when she knew that?

And how long would she be amused by these simple pleasures? How long before she missed the country club and breakfast in bed and dancing until dawn with the rich, handsome fiancé she had left behind?

Who was the real Shelby Taite? The rich socialite, or the eager, happy, actually giggling girl who had thrown herself into his arms last night, hugging him because she'd knocked down a few bowling pins?

And how well could he guard his heart when she had fit into his arms so well, so naturally?

He didn't know. But he was damn well going to find out.

Quinn showered quickly, while there was still enough hot water—he'd learned his lesson on that one the previous evening while everyone else in the building must have been using water at the same time—and dressed in his usual black over black.

He brewed coffee in the small, automatic coffeemaker that came with his furnished apartment, knowing it couldn't hold a candle to Tony's special blend. But Tony's wasn't on the menu this morning.

Philadelphia was on the menu. Philadelphia and Somerton Taite. He'd promised a personal report today, and figured to get it out of the way before he faced Shelby again, looked into her trusting brown eyes, and remembered what a bastard he was.

*   *   *

Ninety minutes later he was ushered into the drawing room of the Taite mansion. Somerton stood near the mantel. Jeremy Rifkin, clad in a striped bathrobe, sat with his legs crossed at the knee, sipping tea, his pinkie raised toward the chandelier. And Uncle Alfred, looking very dapper in red-and-green-plaid slacks and a white pullover, stood behind the decanters on the drinks table, frowning into the empty ice bucket.

"Delaney," Somerton said, stepping forward, his right hand out. "You made good time. We didn't really expect you for another half hour. Parker, I'm afraid, has been detained."

"Now there's a disappointment," Quinn said, and smiled as he heard Uncle Alfred's short, sharp bark of laughter.

"I like this boy, Somerton," Uncle Alfred said, having contented himself with slipping a little vodka into his glass of orange juice. "Pity he's working for us. Shelby could do with a little fun."

Quinn's head shot around sharply as he looked into Uncle Alfred's merry eyes. What did the man mean by that? What did he see? How did he know?

Fortunately nobody really listened to Uncle Alfred, especially Jeremy, who took this opportunity to tug at Somerton's sleeve, asking him to be a dear and ring for more coffee, as they had guests.

Quinn had time to recover as the butler brought a fresh coffeepot into the room, assuming his stance in front of the fireplace now that Somerton was sitting beside Jeremy, spreading a linen napkin across the man's knees.

"I've come to report on your sister, of course," he began

quickly, taking out his notebook but not bothering to open it. "The subject, Shelby Taite—"

"We know who she is, boy," Uncle Alfred interrupted. "So why don't you just do this one in English, without all that 'subject' and other ridiculousness?"

"Yes, sir," Quinn said, wanting to get this interview over as quickly as possible. "Mr. Taite, your sister has secured an apartment with one Brandy Wasilkowski. A credit check and other background information assure me Ms. Wasilkowski is just what she appears, a young woman of moderate means and with a true concern for those she considers less fortunate than herself. In this case, that would be Miss Taite."

"Less fortunate than herself? My sister? I don't understand."

"No, sir, I didn't think you would," Quinn told him, pressing on. "That is, however, how I see the situation. Your sister has been taken in, as it were, by a good Samaritan and is in no danger. She has also procured employment as a hostess in a local restaurant, and is actually doing quite well. I might even say you could be proud of her resourcefulness."

"She has a *job?*" Somerton's watery blue eyes all but popped out of his head before he could control his reaction. "How . . . how enterprising of her, surely. A hostess, you say? This would be an upscale restaurant, I'm sure? Top of the line?"

"Best restaurant in all of East Wapaneken," Quinn declared, tongue very firmly in his cheek, as Tony's was also the only restaurant in East Wapaneken. "So, all in all, sirs, I'd say Miss Taite is doing very well out in the big bad world on her own. Which is why," he said, taking a deep breath, "I am here to tender my resignation as Miss Taite's bodyguard as of this morning. My office will contact you about the final billing."

"Somerton, I feel faint," Jeremy said, clutching the man's forearm.

"Not now, Jeremy," Somerton admonished him, rising and walking over to stand in front of Quinn, his wet-combed blond hair nearly shivering in his agitation. "Mr. Delaney, I don't understand. You can't possibly mean to leave my sister . . . *out there* by herself, can you? You've seen her. She has no conception of what she's doing, what she's opening herself up to, a woman alone in a hostile world."

"A babe in the woods," Jeremy added helpfully. "Little Eliza on the ice floe . . ."

"Yes, Jeremy dear. Thank you, we understand. Now, Mr. Delaney. Surely you can stay with her a while longer, until she has this . . . this *adventure* out of her system and comes home to us?"

Uncle Alfred, who moved quite sprightly when the spirit moved him, stepped between his nephew and Quinn. "Oh, be quiet, Somerton, and let the boy talk," he said, looking up at Quinn. "There is more, isn't there, son?"

Quinn had already known that the old man was sharp. "Yes, sir," he said, grinning. "There is more. I have no intention of allowing Miss Taite to sink or swim on her own while she's out having the time of her life, living what she calls 'real life,' if we're all still operating on that assumption. I just can't ethically accept money for my services."

Uncle Alfred clapped him on the back, nearly sending him reeling. "Attaboy, son! And let's hear it for my little Shelby. Quite the woman, isn't she? Bowled you over, hasn't she?"

"Bowled me over? Almost, sir," Quinn told him, once more hiding his tongue in his cheek, watching as Somerton's expression went from confused, to totally blank, to dawning comprehension.

"You intend to . . . to *romance* my sister?" he said at last, stepping back a pace. "You do know that she's engaged to be married, don't you?"

Quinn's jaw tightened. "I know she's in East Wapaneken and Parker Westbrook is here—or, in actual fact, *not* here—more concerned with his business affairs than the whereabouts of his fiancée."

"Somerton, Somerton! Isn't this the most delicious news?" Jeremy clapped his hands and hopped to his feet. "It's like . . . like Cinderella." He pulled a face. "Only backward, I think."

Somerton was back to frowning. "But . . . but what do I tell Parker?"

"Tell him I'm on the job, because I am," Quinn told him as he looked at Somerton levelly. "But if you love your sister at all, don't tell him where she is. I promise you, she'll come to no harm, but I think it's time you all let the girl grow up, make a few of her own decisions."

"Somerton?" Jeremy said, patting the man's shoulder. "Didn't I tell you? Didn't I say there was something *haunted* in Shelby's eyes these past months? I did, didn't I? And now she's off on her own and about to have an adventure. Surely you can't begrudge her a small adventure?" He shivered delicately. "Although I must say I can't be happy hearing she has a—horror of horrors—*job.*"

Somerton rounded on his companion. "Adventure? Is that how you see it? When this . . . this *man* has the nerve, the unmitigated *gall,* to stand here and all but announce he's about to *seduce* my sister?"

"I'll drink to that," Uncle Alfred said, lifting the orange juice to his mouth as he winked at Quinn. "Best thing that could happen to her, in my opinion."

"I didn't *ask* for your opinion, Uncle Alfred," Somerton spit at him. He pressed a hand to his head and began to pace. "I have to think."

"You do that, Mr. Taite," Quinn told him, replacing his

coffee cup on the silver tray. "But while you're thinking, think about your sister and what she wants, why she left."

"She . . . she doesn't love him?" Jeremy, always the romantic, questioned, collapsing onto the couch. "That's it, of course. What have we done, blithely going on and on about the wedding, when she doesn't love him? Oh, Somerton, our poor, dear girl. How *dreadful!*"

"Bingo, my pretty little man, bingo!" Uncle Alfred congratulated Jeremy. "And damn well about time, too. Or did you two think she's really run off just to see how the other half lives? She wouldn't *care* how the other half lives, Somerton, if she was happy with her own life, now, would she? If I can see that drunk, you certainly should be able to see it sober."

Somerton stumbled to the couch and sat down beside Jeremy. "I've been a fool, such a blind fool! I just thought she was having an adventure, *playing* at life because Uncle Alfred put some silliness in her head. I didn't think, didn't see— Parker! You've arrived, I see."

Quinn looked at the man as he strode purposefully into the drawing room, his briefcase clutched in his right hand. He couldn't leave the damn thing in his car? What the hell was in there that was so damn important? What could— *should*—be more important to him than Shelby?

"Forgive my tardiness, Somerton, everyone," he said briskly, helping himself to a cup of coffee. "But now that I'm here, shall we begin?"

"We're already finished," Uncle Alfred said, leering at his nephew. "Aren't we, Somerton?"

Somerton stopped himself, as he'd been biting his nails, something he hadn't done since childhood. "What? Oh. Oh, yes. We're done, Parker. Shelby is fine and Mr. Delaney will continue watching her. Isn't that right, Mr. Delaney?"

"Yes, sir, it is. I'll be watching her very closely, and promise that she will come to no harm."

"I'll hold you to that, son," Uncle Alfred said, passing by him on the way back to the drinks table for another small splash of vodka. It really wasn't done, anyway, to drink anything with color in it until at least five o'clock.

Quinn inclined his head to Parker, who was opening and closing his mouth like a fish. "Mr. Westbrook? Good to see you again, sir. Now, if you'll excuse me, I have a job to do."

"A job? Oh, naughty, naughty!" Jeremy said from his seat, the one he was nearly dancing in at the moment. "Somerton, I believe we're being decadent. Isn't it wonderful?"

Parker looked at each man in turn. "What in hell is going on here? That's it, Delaney? That's your idea of a report? She's fine? Is this what Somerton is paying you for? Because, let me tell you, it isn't enough. Not by a damn lot it isn't enough! I want particulars. I *demand* particulars."

"You don't pay me, Westbrook," Quinn all but growled, really wishing he could pop the guy one, just on general principles.

"No, he doesn't," Jeremy piped up, giggling. "And neither does— Whoops!"

Luckily, Parker Westbrook rarely listened to anything Jeremy, or almost anyone else, ever said, and only went on: "Very well, gentlemen. I see I'll simply have to hire my own investigators."

"I wouldn't do that if I were you," Quinn slid in quietly just as Parker stood, clearly intent on making a grand exit. "Miss Taite is having a small vacation from reality—or *in* reality; I'm really not quite sure which it is yet. I'm already one new face on the scene in a very small town. So far I've been accepted. But if you were to interfere, if some clumsy investigator were to let it slip that you were watching her, monitoring her? Well, I don't think you'll be hearing wedding bells ringing if that happens. And that is what you want, isn't it, Westbrook? Miss Taite home, and your wedding going off as planned?''

Parker seemed to chew on his tongue for a moment, then nodded shortly. "All right, Delaney. I guess I have no other option than to allow you to continue as Miss Taite's bodyguard. But I still want her home within the month, sooner if possible, and see no reason for her to stay away any longer. After all, the bloom has to go off the rose quickly when one is living hand-to-mouth, as she most certainly must be doing."

"She is eating well," Quinn couldn't help saying. "I'll report in person again in a week, gentlemen. Until then I suggest you content yourself with the information that Miss Taite is healthy, well, and seems to have landed on her feet."

"For now," Uncle Alfred whispered as Quinn walked by. "And good for you, son. About time one of us Taites had herself a little adventure."

"Yes, sir," Quinn said, not wanting to get into a long conversation concerning Alfred Taite's idea of what his niece needed.

His next stop was the offices of D & S. Maisie greeted him with her usual big smile, even as the reception area was crowded with at least a dozen suits in various stages of meltdown.

"What's going on?" he asked, leaning over the desk.

"The board of directors of Swindale Memorial Library," Maisie told him, still successfully avoiding all the many eyes trained on her in what appeared to be increasing fury. "They want us to guard their art exhibition but can't seem to get it through their heads that we aren't a nonprofit organization. They want us for nothing. Zilch. *Nada.* Grady has decided to take a profit. They're back this morning to take another shot at him, and he's keeping them waiting.

How're you, honey? You're looking good enough to eat, as usual.''

"I'm doing fine, thanks," Quinn said, keeping his own back turned to the angry board of directors. If they knew he was a partner in D & S they'd be on him like white on rice. "So he's in? Really?''

"Really," Maisie told him, sitting back in her chair, ready to punch at the telephone, which had begun to ring. "But you didn't hear it here, okay?''

He found Grady in the conference room, stretched out on a massage table, stripped to his waist, with a gorgeous young thing bending over him, working his back muscles.

"Are you supposed to do that with a separated shoulder?'' he asked as he slammed the door behind him, making Grady jump.

"Damn it, Quinn, don't you know how to knock? I was just beginning to relax.''

"Yeah, well, this happens," he told him, signaling for the massage therapist to leave the room for a few moments. "We've got a problem. Or we did. We don't now. I resigned from the Taite case this morning.''

"You did what? *Ow!*'' Grady grabbed at his shoulder as he pivoted to a sitting position. "I know she's a stick, Quinn, one of the Rich and Repulsives, but is she really that bad?''

"She's not a stick." The moment Quinn uttered the words he knew he'd made a mistake. His friend was much too quick on the uptake.

Grady cupped a hand to his ear. "What? What did you say? No , I couldn't have heard that right. You're defending the little heiress? Now, why, I've got to ask myself, would my good friend Quinn be defending the lady—*and* handing in his resignation from the easiest job he'll ever find? Could it be? Is it possible? Ah, be still my heart.''

"Put a sock in it, Grady," Quinn gritted out, flinging

himself into a nearby chair. "I'm off the case, not off the job, if you must know. But it's getting personal, and I can't ethically take money now that it's personal."

"Personal? Oh, more, more. I want details, Quinn. *How* personal is it?"

"Personal enough that I can't reconcile myself to being paid for chaperoning her, or whatever you want to call it."

"I can think of many things I want to call it, old sport. What do *you* call it?"

Quinn scratched the side of his head. "I don't know. But I'm interested. She's interested."

"Interested? All right, we'll go with that one. You're both interested. Which means, naturally, that you've not only found Miss Taite but you've been in personal contact with her. How personal? Never mind, we've already been there, right? That's what these pain pills will do to you. So you're going back to East Wapa-whoositz to see what happens?"

"She's looking for a fling, Grady, pretty determined to have one, I think," Quinn told him, not really happy that he believed what he was saying. "At least with me she'll be reasonably safe."

"What a man. So sacrificing, so very *giving*. You know, that might have worked, except I've *seen* her, remember? You're not making any great big sacrifices here. And then what? You let her have her mad, passionate fling with you, then walk away as she gets tired of the game, goes back to her cushy mansion—and her fiancé, remember?"

Quinn's jaw muscles tightened. He stood up and pushed back his chair. "I always walk away, Grady, remember? It's what I do."

"And what if she falls in love with you? What then, Quinn? What if you fall in love with her?"

"That isn't going to happen. You just keep holding down the fort and consider me on vacation, okay?"

"You're not by chance staying somewhere called Heart-break Hotel, are you, Quinn?" Grady asked as he slowly lay back down on the massage table. "Because if you're not, you might want to think about it. Now call Ginny back in here if you please, so that I can lie here and decide if you've resigned from the case so that you won't feel like a rat, or if this leaves you free to be a rat."

Quinn left the door open when he brushed past the massage therapist and headed for the door. Grady's soft laughter followed after him. He didn't really care. He just wanted to be back in East Wapaneken in time for lunch.

Chapter Seventeen

Shelby had never considered shopping an adventure. But that was before she'd gone shopping with Brandy.

With Brandy, shopping was more of a "search and destroy" mission, as Shelby had learned as she followed behind her friend and a metal shopping cart as, together, they took on T.J.Maxx.

Brandy could wheel between crowded aisles, her eyes boring like lasers into the racks, picking and discarding with the precision of a berry picker sorting out rejects. "Yup. Nope. Wrong color. Oh, this is good. Come on, let's check out the clearance racks."

Shelby followed along, remembering well-appointed showrooms, complimentary glasses of champagne, clothing being brought to her rather than the other way around.

And clerks. Shelby remembered clerks. Helpful clerks.

"Where are the clerks?" she asked as Brandy played a quick game of chicken with a woman who'd dared to push a cart toward her as she was already halfway down an aisle.

"Salespersons," Brandy corrected. "I'm in employment, remember? We don't call them clerks anymore. It's demeaning."

"Sorry. So, where are the salespersons? I mean, what if I want to try something on and it's the wrong size?"

"Then I schlepp out of the dressing room and get you the right size, silly. The only salespersons you'll see in this place are cashiers. How do you think they keep the prices so low?"

"I hadn't thought about it, actually," Shelby admitted. "Although they probably are saving quite a bit of money in not carpeting the floor. Or cleaning it very often."

Brandy pulled out a black summer sweater that was more of a crop-top, held it up to Shelby, nodded, then tossed it into the cart. "You're not getting this, are you? Shopping, that is."

"Am I buying that?" Shelby asked, eyeing the sweater. "And no, I don't think I am. Getting this, that is. It's just so . . . so *alien,* somehow."

"Ah, poor baby," Brandy teased, patting her cheek. "All this not being waited on hand and foot must be a real pain. Can I get you a cookie?"

Shelby pulled a face. "Very funny. And let me see that sweater." She reached into the cart, realizing that she was worried about a price tag for the first time in her life. Trying to read the tag was like deciphering Greek. "I don't understand. There're stickers all over it."

Brandy took hold of the tag and began pointing. "This is the price it should sell for, and this is the price you pay. Or the price you would have paid, except it's on clearance, so you pay what's on the top red sticker. *Comprende?*"

Shelby looked at the tag again, then grabbed the sweater, checking the brand name in the neckline. "But . . . but this is . . . my God, Brandy, what are designer labels doing in a place like this?"

"What do you care? You've just saved sixty bucks. Right?"

"Right," Shelby said quietly, then smiled. "I can get shorts, too, can't I?"

"Shorts, tops, anything your little heart desires. Even shoes."

"Shoes?" That was it. Shelby was in love. She stood on tiptoe, actually sniffed the air like a hunting dog going on point. "Where?"

An hour later, Shelby was the proud owner of the black sweater, three more midriff-hugging cotton tops, two pairs of denim shorts, and two pairs of sneakers, one red, one white. And she still had enough money in her pocket to buy some socks.

Ah, capitalism. She had a whole new understanding of the concept.

The hour she and Brandy had spent in the discount store had flown by, and Shelby panicked when she looked at her watch, realizing that she had to be at Tony's in a half hour. "Today's going to be really busy, Tabby told me. Actually, she said Saturdays are the pits, but I think I've translated correctly."

"You did. We'll hit McDonald's drive-through," Brandy told her reassuringly as they pulled out of the parking lot. "You have eaten at McDonald's, haven't you, Shelley?"

"Will you hate me if I say I haven't? But I have heard of it. That counts, doesn't it?"

"God, girl, you're *so* deprived. Nothing but artichoke hearts and caviar. Poor baby. Next time I'm wishing I was rich and famous I'm going to remember that I'd probably never get any more Mickey D French fries. That'll cure me. So," Brandy said, dropping Quinn into the conversation without bothering with subtlety, "did he kiss you? We left you alone out there in the hall so he'd kiss you, you know."

Shelby busied herself rearranging the seat belt strap, as Brandy's way of driving one way while looking another was a little unnerving. "We just went bowling, Brandy. It wasn't even a date. Not really. Was it?"

"If he didn't kiss you, then I guess not. Bummer."

Shelby sat back against the seat, remembering how Quinn had looked at her for a long time as they stood outside the door to her apartment. How he had actually put out his hand, begun to reach for her, then stepped back, said he'd hoped she'd enjoyed the evening. As if she were poison or something. "Yeah," she said as Brandy pulled into McDonald's parking lot. "Bummer."

Her disappointment faded soon enough as she munched on French fries that did things for her palate pheasant had never been able to do. "These are delicious," she said, her mouth full, her hand reaching into the bag for more. "I can't understand how I've lived this long without them."

Brandy reached over and patted her on the shoulder. "Ah, grasshopper," she said, her voice heavily accented, "the tings I will show you, the tings you will learn."

What Brandy showed Shelby next was how to weave in and out of three lanes of traffic while holding a soda cup in one hand and eating a hamburger with the other. But they arrived at Tony's in time for her shift, which had to mean something. Not much, Shelby decided, having believed they were going to die at least three separate times, but something.

As she was climbing out of the car, Brandy leaned over and said, "Oh, did I tell you? We're going miniature golfing tonight. The four of us. Gary arranged it all with Quinn last night, although he didn't bother to tell me until you'd gone to bed. And please don't tell me you've never played miniature golf. That's putting only, in case you didn't know."

Shelby thought about her bowling scores. Thought about the 238 Quinn had rolled—the showoff. Thought

about the silver cups and plates she'd won at the country
club. The big silver punch bowl had been for last year's
contest on the putting green, she remembered proudly.
And then she smiled. *Putting, huh?*

"Oh, yes, Brandy. I've played golf, not that we have to
mention that to Gary and Quinn. Well, this is going to be
interesting. What do you say we make it you and me against
the men?"

Brandy looked at her assessingly. "You're that good?"

"Good, Brandy? Oh, I'm better than that," Shelby said
confidently, grinning as she pushed the car door closed
and headed off to work. At her job. Her very real job. In
the very real world. Where she was having herself a very
real adventure.

And, tonight, damn it, she was going to have a very real
date or know the reason why!

Chapter Eighteen

Tabby slid two plates in front of Quinn and whisked off to take someone else's order. He looked down at a steak sandwich large enough to fill an entire plate, then at the mound of French fries on the other. And he figured it out. If he continued to eat three meals a day at Tony's for the next month, he'd weigh three hundred and fifty pounds. Conservatively. Which was why he had restarted his old habit of taking an early morning run before his morning trip to Philadelphia, purely out of self-defense.

Mrs. Brobst and Mrs. Fink entered the restaurant and called out cheery hellos to everyone before seating themselves at their usual table. They looked like wrinkled toddlers in orthopedic shoes, but the twinkles in their bright eyes were those of teenagers out on a spree. They both wore flowered straw hats on their gray heads and carried pocketbooks you could have packed for a long weekend.

"Afternoon, sonny," Mrs. Brobst said to Quinn, who returned the greeting.

"How's the car running today?" he asked, thinking about that really cherry '67 Caddy that, in Mrs. Brobst's hands, was more of an assault weapon with whitewalls.

"Fine, just fine. Hit a squirrel yesterday as we were leaving, didn't we, Bettyann? That's one little gray monster who won't be eating any more of my birdseed. Doesn't pay to play chicken with me, young man, and so I told Bettyann. You remember that next time you're out running in your undies and you see us coming as you cross the street. Now eat up before it gets cold; don't bother about us."

"That's true enough," Mrs. Bettyann Fink agreed happily. "You're much too *old* for either of us anyway. And those aren't undies the boy wears, Amelia, they're running shorts. Told you that. Honestly, if you don't get that hearing aid checked, I'm going to go hoarse, screaming at you."

Quinn hid a grin behind his napkin, adoring the two old ladies and their love of life even as they both headed toward their nineties.

Yes, he was getting to know the other customers in just these first few days, by sight if not all of them by name. Of course, he did know more names than Shelby did, because this was a woman who was beautiful, intelligent, remarkably hardworking—but a woman he had decided couldn't remember more than two names at any given time.

She called all the older ladies "ma'am," the children "sweetheart," and the regulars, a gang of crusty, middle-aged men who seemed to live in the corner booth, "the regulars." And the old ladies smiled, the children giggled, and the regulars blushed and dipped their heads to her.

Because, if she couldn't remember their names, she could remember what they ate and what they drank, and the denizens of East Wapaneken were nothing if not creatures of habit. She could already float from table to table, a pot of regular coffee in one hand, a pot of decaffeinated in the other, and pour refills correctly for everyone in the restaurant. And all with a smile and a personal comment, and an air of efficiency that still had the power to unnerve Quinn.

He sat in his corner and ate. And scribbled useless notes in his notebook. And drank gallons of coffee. And ate. Breakfast, lunch, and dinner.

And he watched Shelby.

She breezed in just before noon that Saturday, her cheeks flushed, her hair loose and flying, and with a smile in her eyes that bordered on wicked. She saw him as soon as she entered, as if her eyes had been drawn to him, and gave a quick wave before setting straight in on her job.

Her job. Quinn still couldn't quite get over that one. The heiress, if not slinging hash, was coming pretty damn close to it. And seeming to love every minute of her work-day. One by one, she was blowing his every conception of the Rich and Repulsive straight to hell and back. He didn't know whether he liked that or not. He only knew he was still fascinated, watching her.

She wasn't giving up. She wasn't crying "uncle," or "brother," or anything like that. She'd just rolled up her designer sleeves and dived in to Tony's, a very alien world, and was already in the process of bringing the whole place to its knees, or around her thumb, or whatever the hell you wanted to call it.

"Hello, sweetheart," she said now as she snagged two glass coffeepots and brushed past a little blond cherub who was lunching with her harassed-looking grandmother. "Don't you look pretty today? And even prettier, too, if you were to sit up straight and tuck your napkin onto your lap."

The little cherub, who had just been giving her grand-

mother fits with her fidgeting and whining, sat up straight
and reached for her napkin. The grandmother beamed.
And Shelby moved on. Quinn half expected her to leave
shiny fairy dust in her wake.

Tabby breezed by her, muttering under her breath.

"Good afternoon, Tabby," Shelby said. "How are you
today?"

"Compared to what?" the waitress answered automatically, and headed for the kitchen, her head leading her
body by a good two feet, to put in another order.

Shelby shook her head and smiled at Tabby's back.

"Ladies," she said to Mrs. Brobst and Mrs. Fink. "Aren't
you looking well. I must say, I simply *adore* your hats. So
wonderfully flattering. It's such a shame more people don't
wear them, as they're the very finest sign of a real lady.
Decaffeinated, am I correct?"

"Such a dear," Mrs. Brobst bellowed as Shelby walked
away, earning her a frantic bit of hand gesturing from Mrs.
Fink as the latter told her to "for God's sake, Amelia, turn
up your hearing aid so you can hear yourself bellow!"

Shelby glided between tables until she came to the corner booth. Six men sat there, a collection of frizzled, gray-
ing hair, leather jackets with skulls on them, beer bellies,
and hands and fingernails that could never be entirely
clean again. Family men, every one of them; two of them
already grandfathers. They'd all worked every day until the
local steel plant in Bethlehem closed down, and were living
on unemployment, Tony's coffee, and their memories.
They were, in Quinn's opinion, as harmless as kittens,
although most strangers wouldn't get close enough to discover that for themselves.

Shelby seemed oblivious to their appearance, the grinning skulls, the tattoos. "Ah, my regulars. How are you
fine gentlemen today?" she asked as they all held out their
coffee cups to her for refills.

"Hot. Too damn hot for June," one of them said conversationally.

"Yeah. Takes me back to Da Nang. Too damn hot," a second man—Quinn knew his name was George—agreed.

"Gentlemen, gentlemen," Shelby scolded, shaking her head. "Please, your language. I thought we had this discussion yesterday. There are children and ladies present, remember? Now, what do you say to me?"

Quinn watched, openmouthed, as the two huge, still heavily muscled men ducked their heads and murmured garbled apologies.

Shelby moved on, blissfully unaware that she had just admonished two of six ex-Green Berets who had, Quinn had learned from Gary, about three dozen medals for bravery among them. Not the sort of men who watched their language. Definitely the sort of men, middle-age paunches aside, who probably still knew how to kill people twelve different ways without breaking a sweat.

They laughed and joked with the waitresses. Never missed an opportunity to pat the gum-chewing Tabby's backside when she walked by. Roared loudly at their own jokes and more than once in the past days had fallen into rather loud arguments among themselves. But they were pussycats when Shelby walked in, smiled at them.

Twilight zone. Quinn felt that his move to East Wapaneken had definitely moved him a step or two into the twilight zone.

He watched as Shelby finished her circuit of the room, then brought the two coffeepots with her as she stopped at his table, politely waiting for him to stand up and pull out a chair for her. She didn't say anything. She just had that *way* of making men want to risk life and limb in order to open a car door for her, pull a chair out for her, throw their body on a grenade for her.

"How are you?" she asked, refilling his coffee cup, then

sitting back in her chair, smiling at him. "I had a very nice time last night. Thank you again."

So prim, so proper, even sitting in the middle of Tony's. A lady of white gloves and bread-and-butter notes written on the finest monogrammed linen stock. "No need for thanks, Shelley. I had a good time, too. Did Brandy tell you about our plans for tonight? If you're not too tired, that is. Miniature golf. Have you ever played?"

Shelby smiled, for he had framed his question in such a way that she didn't have to lie to him. "No. I've never played miniature golf. Is that a problem? I know I wasn't much help to you last night, bowling. As a matter of fact, I've already told Brandy that it would be the men against the ladies tonight, as you'd been such a good sport about losing so badly last night."

Quinn smelled a rat, but he only returned Shelby's smile. "Okay. If you don't mind?"

"I don't mind at all, honestly," she said, then lost her smile, looked to her left, toward the corner booth, and leaned forward, speaking quietly. "I don't know if I should say anything, but . . ."

Her voice trailed off and he leaned forward, too, waiting for her to go on.

She drew in a breath, let it out in a rush. She had thought about telling Brandy, but since Brandy couldn't do anything about it, that had seemed pointless. She didn't know why she thought Quinn could help her. She just did. He just seemed to be the sort of person who could handle, well, nearly everything. If nothing else, he could tell her to stop worrying. "I'm probably wrong, and nobody ever hears correctly when they only hear *part* of something, but . . ."

"Shelley," he said. "Out with it."

She went to look over at the corner booth again, then stopped herself, quickly ducked her head, pretended an interest in the salt shaker. "All right, but just remember it's probably nothing. Nothing at all. They're very sweet, if you just take the time to notice. Probably completely harmless. You know—like Tony? And you can't say anything to anyone. It's just too silly."

"Cross my heart," he promised, drawing a hand over his chest. "Now, spill it."

"I heard them talking. Yesterday afternoon, when they were all here for coffee and that marvelous chocolate cake that sweet little girl bakes at home and delivers here three times a week. I mean, I've tasted some of the best chocolate desserts in the—well, lots of chocolate desserts, and that has to be the best. . . . I'm rambling, aren't I?"

"You've left the road a time or two, but you're back on it now," Quinn said, smiling. "Let me help, okay? You overheard George and the others yesterday, right?"

Her forehead crinkled. "George? Who's George?"

"Never mind. Go on. Please."

"Well, it's the regulars. I guess you've already figured that out. I overheard them yesterday, talking about"—she leaned even closer, so that he could smell her perfume—*"killing* the mayor."

Shelby sat back, took another deep breath, and waited for Quinn to speak. She felt much better having told him, as now it wasn't only her problem but his as well. It was the least she could do for him, seeing that he'd actually allowed her to go Dutch last night.

Quinn sat for a moment, considering Shelby's words, then crooked a finger in her direction, motioning for her to come closer once more. "Kill the mayor? Shelley, Amelia Brobst is the mayor."

Her smooth forehead crinkled again. "Who?"

He sighed, trying very hard not to laugh. "Amelia Brobst. Eighty-five if she's a day, and admitted murderer of local squirrels."

"No."

"Yes. Do it slowly, not to draw attention to yourself, but turn around. She's the five-foot, eighty-pound Genghis Khan in the straw hat covered in pink roses."

Shelby counted to three under her breath, then dropped a napkin onto the floor, bent to retrieve it, and looked behind her.

"No," she said, looking at Quinn, her lovely brown eyes wide as saucers.

"Yes, Shelley," Quinn promised, remembering yet again that he'd already metaphorically shelved Shelby's cloak-and-dagger expertise next to his Secret Squirrel videos. "Mrs. Brobst has been mayor of East Wapaneken for six years, ever since her husband died. He was the mayor for thirty-seven years, by the way."

"How do you know that?"

Quinn smiled, pleased with himself and his ready-made lie. "I'm here to write about the local color, remember? All it took was one quick visit to the library. So tell me, why are the regulars going to snuff her? What did she do— drive that tank of hers over their motorcycles?"

Shelby sneaked another look at Amelia Brobst, who was having some real difficulty getting her heavy brown coffee mug to her lips without spilling its contents. She'd meant to have a talk with Tony about that. The mugs were all well and good for the gentlemen, but the ladies really should have regular cups, with saucers. Thin china ones, perhaps with flowers on them. It was just a little thing, but the little things added up, especially when one was trying to run a successful restaurant.

Obviously Shelby still hadn't seen Tony's account books. . . .

She shook herself back to attention. Smiled at the old ladies, turned back to Quinn. "They're going to kill *her?"* She all but hissed her next words: "That's ridiculous!"

"Hey," Quinn said, raising his hands. "Don't look at me. It was you who said it."

Her shoulders slumped. "Oh, yes. It was, wasn't it?" She sat up once more. "It has something to do with a war memorial, and how the mayor refuses to put one up in the town park. I believe, if I heard correctly—I was really, *really* trying *not* to hear—that the mayor believes the memorial that's there is enough to cover every war. The regulars don't think so."

Quinn nodded. "Okay. Now you're making sense. Sort of. The regulars, as you call them, are all Vietnam vets. They probably do want a special memorial. But that doesn't mean they're going to kill little Amelia. They're just talking, that's all. Men do that. They talk."

"Do they all talk about cutting brake lines?" Shelby asked, raising one eyebrow, waiting for Quinn's response.

He was silent for a few moments, considering this. He'd been a cop. He'd been a bodyguard. Now he was a desk jockey, out of the field for over a year. Part of him wanted to laugh off Shelby's concerns, but another part of him wasn't so sure. "That is pretty definite for a daydream," he admitted.

"Then you *do* think they might try to hurt her?"

"Let me get back to you on that, all right? I'll do a little investigating of my own."

"You'll be careful, won't you?"

Quinn's grin split his face. "Why, Shelley, you *do* care, don't you? I'm touched, really I am. That you confided in me. That you're worried about me."

Shelby felt her cheeks reddening. "Now you're just being mean," she said, wishing his smile didn't do such unexpected things to her, make her think such unladylike thoughts—thoughts no engaged woman should be thinking.

She pushed back her chair, motioning for him to remain

seated. She needed to get away from him before she reached out and brushed his black hair back from his forehead. Before she betrayed herself in any way. "I'd better go write tonight's specials on the board before Tony does it himself. I keep trying to tell him, two *Ls* in *fillet* if it's fish, only one if it's filet mignon."

Quinn deliberately pushed away thoughts of pulling Shelby into his lap and kissing her senseless and, in turn, got a mental picture of the tall yet stooped, shuffling man in the always dirty apron. "I don't think he cares," he said.

Shelby picked up the coffeepots and stood very straight. "Well, he should," she said. "But you're right. He told me yesterday that as long as he knows how to cook it, his customers don't care if he can't spell it."

There was a bellow from the other side of the room. "Ah, the master's voice," she said, pretending to wince as the not-so-dulcet tones of her employer began a crescendo having a lot to do with Tabby and an incorrectly added-up check. "If you'll excuse me, I think I have to pull yet another thorn out of the king's paw."

"Certainly." Quinn half rose from his seat. Purely a reflex action, he told himself as she walked away. He watched her for a moment, then realized the regulars had gone silent. They also were watching Shelby's progress across the restaurant. Not leering, not poking each other with their elbows and making quiet comments. Just watching. One of them actually took his paper napkin out of its tucked-in place in the vee of his shirt, smoothed it, and placed it in his lap.

Shelby stopped beside the cherub, put down one coffee-pot, and fished in her pocket for two quarters for the video game located in the hallway leading to the rest rooms. The little girl took the coins, then said, "Thank you very much," before running off to play the game, leaving her grandmother some peace in which to sip her coffee.

"Thank you, Shelley," she said gratefully.

"My uncle always taught me that good behavior should be rewarded," Shelby told her with a wink. "And, as you've been very good, I thought I'd give you a little reward."

The grandmother laughed and thanked Shelby again.

The regulars went back to their lunches, napkins in their laps.

And Tony, who had just begun the refrain of his well-known "why I put up with you people I'll never know" song, saw Shelby approaching, shut his mouth, glared at Tabby impotently one last time, and retreated to his kitchen.

"What a hoot! Do you think he was once frightened by Miss Manners? Anyway, I owe you, babe," Tabby said, giving Shelby a friendly whack on the shoulder that all but sent her staggering.

Quinn looked at his plate and saw that somehow he'd eaten all of the steak sandwich. Picking up his coffee cup, he walked over to the corner booth, motioned that he'd like to sit down, said he'd like to talk about the "great cycles" he'd seen in the parking lot. It wasn't much of an opening, but it might do for starters.

The regulars told him to join them, the one named George even kicking out beneath the booth so that the empty chair on the other side of it was pushed away and made ready for Quinn to sit down. "Why, thank you, George."

Civilization comes to East Wapaneken.

Civilization, and *a possible murder plot?*

Amazing.

Chapter Nineteen

Shelby looked at the windmill. Watched its blades rotate. Watched the cutout hole at the bottom of the windmill appear, disappear, reappear again as the blades passed by.

She turned to look at Brandy, leaned close, whispered, "You're kidding, right?"

Brandy was confused. She grabbed Shelby by the elbow and pulled her away from the first hole of the miniature golf course. "Kidding? What do you mean, am I kidding? What's the problem? I thought you said you were good at this. I've bet Gary a half hour of foot rubbing that we'd beat their pants off. Now get some color back in those cheeks, sweetcakes, and hit the damn ball."

Shelby dug in her heels and refused to be moved. "I said I could putt. I said I could golf. This isn't golf. This is . . . this is . . ." She looked out over the course. At a grinning alligator, its mouth wide open to receive the putt. At a wooden granny in a small rocking chair, alternating between blocking and exposing another hole she was supposed to knock her ball through to reach the hole. Eighteen holes, littered with obstacles, hidey-holes, twists, and turns. Even two water holes. "This is *nuts.*"

"Wrong. It's miniature golf. God, you are deprived, aren't you? Okay, I'll go first, and you watch."

While Shelby and Brandy continued whispering to each other in low tones, Quinn took advantage of this short time in which to admire Shelby's legs yet again and grin a little at her silly red sneakers. Damn, but those legs were long. And straight. No knobby knees on this girl, none whatsoever. She had legs like Chita Rivera. Cyd Charisse. Ann-Margret. Legs that could fill a man's dreams.

And that black sweater? Well, he'd seen black sweaters before, even ones that somehow stopped four inches short of the waist of a pair of tight, faded denim shorts. But he'd never seen one on Shelby Taite, and seeing one on that cool blond beauty was enough to make him damn glad he'd handed in his resignation. Otherwise, Somerton Taite would have to have him killed for what he was thinking, what he was hoping.

He watched as the ponytail she'd fastened in her hair with a red fuzzy something-or-other bobbed up and down as she argued with Brandy. Hell, Somerton probably wouldn't even *recognize* his sister.

Gary removed the pack of cigarettes from its place in the rolled-up sleeve of his T-shirt, smacked one cigarette out, and lit it with a heavy metal lighter with an enameled hula girl on it. He looked up at Quinn, one eye squeezed shut to keep the blue smoke out of it. "So, what do you think? They're planning some kind of strategy?"

"I don't know," Quinn admitted honestly. He would have thought Shelby's outfit to be strategy enough, as he was going to have a hell of a time concentrating on hitting the ball when all he wanted to do was pick her up, toss her over his shoulder, and take her someplace Brandy and Gary and the rest of the world weren't.

"Maybe Brandy's trying to make her put down that purse," Gary said, pointing to the large mesh shoulder bag Shelby had slung over one shoulder. "Shelley should have left that feedbag in the car, you know."

"She won't putt, holding it," Quinn said, then wondered why he'd said it. Shelby would do whatever she wanted to do. He was beginning to learn that. Without fuss, without muss, she was the sort of velvet steamroller type who just politely went through life expecting everyone to simply understand that she simply had to do what she had to do.

Quinn watched as Brandy said something, Shelby nodded, and the two of them returned to the first tee, a rubber mat with a flat, built-in rubber tee.

"I'm going first," Brandy said, motioning for Gary to get out of the way.

"But Shelley's name is first on the scorecard," Gary answered, confused. "That'll screw me up, Brandy."

Brandy rested the head of her putter on the mat, turned, and looked dispassionately at her fiancé for a long moment. "You scare me sometimes, Gar, you know that?"

Quinn bit his bottom lip, trying not to laugh, and walked over to stand beside Shelby, who was watching the windmill blades with the sort of concentration one usually reserves for looking down the barrel of a loaded gun pointed in their direction.

"Looks like fun, doesn't it?" he said, daring to slip his arm around her waist. Her bare waist. For a moment he thought his arm might catch fire . . . but what a way to go.

"Uh-huh, yes. Sure," Shelby said as she watched Brandy address the ball, look toward the moving windmill blades. "She's holding the club all wrong," she said quietly, as if to herself, before stiffening, remembering she was supposed to not know what she was doing. Which, in truth, she didn't. Doglegs she understood. Greens that broke to the left. Windmills, she didn't understand.

"Ah, now I get it," Quinn said, removing his arm so that he could step in front of her as Brandy stroked the ball, blocking her view. "You thought you could do this, didn't you? That's why you offered to be Brandy's partner. Not to let me win, but to make sure I'd lose. Come on, Shelley, 'fess up. You're a ringer, aren't you?"

"Ringer?" Shelby asked, trying to peer around him and watch Brandy putt. "Damn, you're in the way, Quinn. What happened?"

He looked back over his shoulder. "She made it through. Now she's doing a small dance, and Gary is still frowning at the scorecard. You're next."

Shelby approached the tee with all the enthusiasm of a French aristocrat heading up the stairs to the guillotine. She set herself so that her feet were no farther apart than her shoulder blades, then gave a large swing of her hips so that the mesh bag skidded onto her back, hanging just at the base of her spine.

"I could hold that, you know," Quinn offered.

"Not in a million years," she said, still looking down at the ball. "I wouldn't ask you for any favors."

"No, you wouldn't, would you," he said, stepping back.

Shelby placed her left palm against the back of the club, flexed her fingers a few times, then closed her fingers around the grip. Added her right hand, using an interlocking grip with her right pinkie and left index finger. Looked toward the windmill. Watched the blades. Began to count. Counted again.

Looked at the ball, still counting, and stroked it.

Brandy ran past the windmill, watching to see where Shelby's ball landed on the other side, and screeched, "Hole in one! *Aw-right!* I can feel that foot rub now."

Shelby smiled at Quinn, stepped back, and motioned for him to take his turn.

"Ringer," he whispered in her ear as he walked past and bent to put his ball on the tee.

"But a ringer with a handicap," Shelby said, lifting her purse, feeling as if she could leap tall buildings in a single bound. "Your turn now, Quinn. First thing you do is address the ball. It's an old joke, but you can start by saying, 'Hello, ball.' "

"Ha. Ha," Quinn said, already squinting at the windmill.

Five seconds later, Brandy said, "Nuts, he's got a hole-in-one, too, Shelley. I can see we're in for quite a battle."

"No quarter, no prisoners," Quinn said as he rejoined Shelby, who came as close to uttering a snort as someone born and raised on Philadelphia's Main Line ever could.

They arrived at the seventeenth hole tied for lowest individual score, but with Gary and Quinn up by a single stroke. It had been cutthroat all the way, with Shelby walking off distances, checking out the obstacles, even going so far as to wink at Brandy, then pull some grass, throw it up, and pretend to check for wind.

Quinn was pretty close to grinding his teeth. It was bad enough she tied with him. Did she have to do it while wearing that stupid purse? "Would you just hit the damn ball?" he complained at last, following after her, as Shelby had walked down the cement path next to the hole to check on the second tier of the hole.

He had spent sixteen holes watching her bend over her putts. Watching her sling that damn purse onto her behind, then waggle that behind before she hit the ball. He wondered if she even knew she waggled her behind in those denim shorts, wondered, if she did know, if she also knew what she was doing to him each time, with each sexy, come-hither waggle. Wondered when he could get her alone, damn it.

Shelby could feel Quinn's eyes on her. She'd been feeling those eyes on her all night. She tried to tell herself it was just the outfit, maybe even the red sneakers, but she didn't think so. He had to be feeling the same strong magnetism she was feeling. How could he not feel it? Was he already figuring out a way to leave Brandy and Gary somewhere so that they could be alone? She certainly hoped so.

But for now she studiously ignored him, bending down to look at the three exit holes that came out from beneath the old lady and the rocking chair. Hit the right spot, and the ball would come out the center hole, heading straight for the cup. Hit it left or right, and the ball would go off into side areas, making it impossible to sink the putt on the second try.

She had to get a hole in one. Brandy had already explained that everyone got a hole in one on the last hole, because that was the way it worked. Hit it up the ramp, and the ball disappeared into a storage box. Oh, you could miss the first time, not get the ball up the ramp, let alone in the center hole that meant getting a free game, but Shelby didn't believe Quinn wouldn't be able to get the ball up the ramp.

It had to be now. Now or never. And she really, *really* wanted to win. She didn't know why; she just did.

"Okay, I've got it now," she said, standing up and turning around quickly. And hitting smack against Quinn's chest as he bent over behind her. And putting him off balance. And watching him spin his arms like two windmills. And watching him slowly go rump-down smack in the middle of the water hazard on the seventeenth hole.

She couldn't help it. Actually, she probably could, but she really didn't want to. So she looked down at him as he sat in three inches of water, shook her head commiseratingly, and said, "Sorry. But I believe landing in a water hazard is a two-stroke penalty. We win, Brandy. Gary, get those foot massage fingers limber.''

They did play out the last two holes, Quinn with his golf cardigan tied around his waist, covering his soggy behind, and Shelby did end up with the low score, and a free game.

Quinn was a good sport about his dunking. Sitting in that cool water, looking up at Shelby as her brown eyes danced, as she laughed until she had to sit down beside him on the cement, had been worth three dunkings, maybe four.

As they rode back to the apartment in the backseat of Gary's four-door pickup truck—Quinn sitting on some old newspapers Gary had lying on the floor—he was still feeling dazed and amazed.

Here was Shelby Taite, heiress, with a pedigree that probably stretched back to the *Mayflower*, and beyond. Here she was sitting in the backseat of a pickup truck, still giggling like a child who'd just seen her first circus, and not giving a single thought to her family name, her station in life. Her—as she allowed Quinn to take her hand in his, squeeze it in the dark—fiancé.

She was having herself a fling. An adventure. He had to remember that. He had to remember that he was only here, only handy, and that he'd promised her family he wouldn't allow her to be hurt.

But he hadn't thought about himself, about the fact that he might be more attracted than interested, more serious than serviceable. That he might end up hurt, especially if Shelby really did see him as a part of her great adventure, the one she would have before returning to her family, to that stick of a fiancé.

He squeezed her fingers again, then let go and held out his arm in silence, hoping she'd understand and lean against his shoulder.

She did. She moved across the seat, curled up against

him, and rested her hand on his chest. They didn't say a word, didn't look at each other. They just sat there together in the dark, listening to Brandy and Gary singing along with the country tunes on the radio.

Gary had a really good voice. Brandy didn't. But the songs were upbeat and the rhythms infectious, so Shelby soon began patting her hand against Quinn's chest in tune with the music. In tune with his rapidly beating heart. In tune with all the questions that knocked on his brain.

As the truck pulled into the parking lot behind the apartments, he asked one of them. "If you'll come with me while I get into some dry clothes, we can take a walk?" Then, since this sounded pretty lame, even to his own ears, he added, "I think Gary and Brandy might want to be alone."

Shelby had been thinking the same thing. Since she was now Brandy's roommate, and Gary still lived with his mother, the two had not really been alone in several days. And, considering the look Brandy got on her face when she talked about the foot massage, she had a feeling she might be as welcome in the apartment right now as an infestation of cockroaches. "That sounds good," she said, easing away from him as the pickup stopped. "It is a nice night for a walk."

The quartet, now two sets of two, walked up the stairs, Brandy and Gary heading to 2C, Quinn opening the door to 2B and waiting for Shelby to precede him into the small apartment. She did, first looking at him shyly—that was shyly, wasn't it? Not slyly?

He stepped inside, flipped on the light, and got ready to hear Shelby laugh. She didn't disappoint him.

"Quinn, there's ruffles *everywhere,*" she exclaimed, walking around the small living room-kitchen combination. "And lace doilies . . . and . . . and all the flowers on the couch. And what's this?" she asked, picking up a pink lace-

and-ruffled thing from the kitchen counter, exposing the utilitarian toaster beneath it.

"A toaster cozy," Quinn said. "Mrs. Brichta made it herself. Since she comes in to clean, I'm afraid to put it away, as it might hurt her. Or make her mad," he added reflectively, and probably more honestly. "There's another one in the bathroom, stuck over an extra roll of toilet tissue. It has a plastic duck glued to the top of it. Very charming."

Shelby sat down on the couch—purple flowers against a pink background—and laughed. "Oh, Quinn. However do you *work* in all of this?"

"It isn't easy. Now wait here, and I'll be back in a minute."

Shelby did as he said, amusing herself by walking around the room, touching doilies, doing her best to admire the prints of large-eyed children on the walls. And then she saw the table in front of the windows covered in frilly priscilla curtains. On it was a portable computer—and several manila files, all of them looking very official.

Quinn's notes for his book, she thought, looking toward the closed bedroom door, her bottom lip tucked between her teeth, then looking at the piles of folders again.

What harm could it do? It wasn't as if he were writing about state secrets or anything like that. Besides, she might learn something about East Wapaneken from his notes, as he seemed to be quite good at researching the small town.

She was just reaching for the top folder when Quinn opened the door to the bedroom.

Three seconds later she was in his arms, and he was kissing her. Kissing her, and moving her away from the table, closer to the couch.

Shelby was lost in the quickness of it, the shock of awareness that struck her, slammed straight through her, left her with knees too weak to stand and with no reason to, either. She allowed him to push her back on the couch, slid her arms around his waist, and kissed him back for all she was worth.

She kissed him hard, kissed him long, kissed him because she'd die, just die, if she couldn't kiss him, taste him, feel his mouth against hers, his body aligned with hers.

What had begun as the quickest diversion he could think of had immediately turned into a clear and present danger Quinn recognized but didn't quite know how to fight. She was in his arms, alive and eager and wanting, and he suddenly wanted her more than he had believed he could ever want anyone.

His mouth slanted against hers, his teasing tongue sought and gained entry, his body fit against hers as if they both had been formed for this single purpose. His hand found her breast and he thrilled as she arched against him, allowing him the liberty.

And then, like a dose of cold water, like a full-body dunking in the water hole, Quinn was hit with an unexpected flash of conscience. Damned inconvenient, that flash of conscience.

How could he do this? How could he kiss her, touch her? Make love to her . . .

She was living a lie. He was living a lie.

He would not, could not, be a part of her adventure.

He could not tell her the truth, even if she told all her truths to him.

This wouldn't work. Couldn't work. She'd only end up hating him. And he didn't want that. He'd seen her beautiful brown eyes blank, he'd seen them flash in quickly tamped-down anger, he'd seen them dancing in delight.

He didn't think he could survive seeing them fill with hurt, disillusionment, all the pain his truths would give her.

And so he slowly pulled away and looked into her ques-

tioning brown eyes gone soft with passion. Kissed her one
single, last time, and then helped her to her feet. "Sorry,"
he said as she smoothed her sweater, suddenly realized he
was withdrawing, and withdrew herself, looking down at
the floor, anywhere but at him. "I didn't mean to get
carried away."

"No," she said, nodding, still avoiding his eyes. "Neither
did I. Probably all that hot competition on the golf course,
huh? It was bound to explode somehow. Well . . ."

"I guess you don't want to take that walk now?"

She nodded again, wishing her eyes weren't filling with
silly, stupid tears. "No, I guess not. It is late, isn't it? And
. . . and I do have to work tomorrow. So I guess I'll be
going. . . ."

"Yeah, going," Quinn said, walking her to the door.
"Don't forget to knock first when you get next door."

Shelby smiled sadly. She blinked back her tears, then
looked up at him, looked deeply into his shadowy gray
eyes. "Yes, I'd better do that, hadn't I? Well, thank you,
Quinn. I had a really nice—"

"Oh, hell," he interrupted, pulling her against him for
one last kiss, holding her close for long moments until she
began to relax in his arms. "I'll see you tomorrow?" he
asked, speaking against her hair.

"Tomorrow. Yes. Yes, that would be nice," she told him,
then slipped out the open door, leaving him very much
alone with his guilty conscience.

He closed the door after watching to make sure she got
inside 2C safely, then walked across the room and picked
up the top file folder. *Taite, Shelby,* it read. *Classification:
Nontypical bodyguard detail.*

He loaded all the folder, all the folders, into his attaché
case, then locked it, shoved it under the couch.

That was close. That had been way too close.

He went to the kitchen, pulled a long-neck beer out of

the refrigerator, and, avoiding the couch, slouched in the huge, overstuffed brown chair that sported doilies on each arm and the headrest. He picked up the clicker, planning to watch television, then put it down again.

It was going to be just him and his conscience.

And it was going to be a long night. . . .

Chapter Twenty

Shelby followed Brandy into the living room after closing the door on Quinn, who had stood in the hall until her friend answered her knock.

"Brandy, I'm so sorry to be back so soon. I didn't mean to, but—" She stopped in the middle of the living room and looked around. "Where's Gary?"

"Who knows; who cares?" Brandy said, falling into a chair, folding her arms across her belly. She had worn a peasant dress of blue and white flowers that evening, and it blossomed around her now like a giant mushroom. "I never want to see him *again!*"

Shelby looked back toward the door, toward Quinn's apartment. She thought about her own problems, which were almost more confusing than daunting, and then looked at her friend. Brandy was keeping her chin up, but that chin was wobbling, and she was blinking away tears.

"Ah, Brandy, what happened?" she asked, kneeling in front of the chair.

"Nothing. *Everything*. It ... it's *Mama*," she all but snarled. "*Mama* told Gary tonight that she'd forgotten to tell him she's signed up for a cruise the weekend of our wedding. That she signed up and gave a nonrefundable deposit months ago, before we set this date. And that ... that great big, stupid, dumb *doofus* bought it. He actually bought that idiotic story a two-year-old could see through, for crying out loud." She all but flung her head against the back of the chair. "I can't believe it, Shelley. She keeps *doing* this, and Gary still can't see what she's doing."

Shelby was at a loss. What could anyone say to a woman who had been both engaged and left at the altar—at least figuratively—more than a half dozen times in the past twelve years? "I think I saw some wine coolers in the refrigerator," she said at last, standing up and heading for the kitchen.

She was back a few moments later, having decided that, tonight, glasses weren't exactly de rigueur. "Here you go, black cherry. Drink up, Brandy, and so will I. I think we both deserve it. To men—may they all go straight to hell."

Brandy lifted her head from the back of the chair, so that a second yet still adorable chin formed beneath her jaw. "You too? What? You two seemed to be getting along like gangbusters. Is there something in the air around here? What happened?"

"What happened?" Shelby said, sitting down on the carpet, leaning her back against the front of the couch. "I don't know, Brandy. I honest-to-God don't know. He came out of nowhere, kissed me—practically mugged me—then tossed me out. He *apologized*, Brandy, which is just about the worst insult I can think of, and then he kissed me again and said he'd see me tomorrow." She lifted the bottle and took a long drink. "I highly doubt *that*."

"Oh, brother ..." Brandy slipped to the floor and

leaned her back against the chair. She took another long drink. "He didn't . . . I mean . . . he didn't *that*, did he?"

Shelby lifted her bottle, eyed the level of wine cooler left, and decided that, no, she couldn't be drunk. "He didn't *what*, Brandy?"

"You know—*that*. You said he darn near mugged you, didn't you?"

"Oh. No, Brandy, we didn't make love, if that's what you're asking. More's the pity," she added almost under her breath, lifting the bottle to her mouth once more.

Brandy giggled. "Good kisser, huh?"

Shelby nodded. "My toes are still tingling."

"But he stopped. He was a gentleman."

"I'm not sure what he was. I just know that one moment we were kissing and the next I was getting the 'Here's your hat, what's your hurry' routine. What's wrong with me, Brandy? Parker doesn't want to go to bed with me. Quinn just about threw me out. Damn it, Brandy, I want another wine cooler."

"It's not you," Brandy called after her. "It's the men. It's *always* the men. Trust me on this; Gary has made me an expert. I'll take another black cherry. Oh, shit, the phone. You know who that is, don't you? That's Gar, trying to apologize while he's telling me at the same time that Mama didn't mean any harm." She struggled to her feet, almost tripping over her hem. "Well, I'm going to tell him—"

Shelby ran back into the living room and put her hand on the phone that sat on the coffee table, blocking Brandy's way. "No," she said, shaking her head. "Don't answer it, Brandy. Let the machine take it. Let him stew tonight. He deserves it."

"But—but it's *Gary*," Brandy said in confusion. "He always calls first after we have a fight. I always answer. And then, damn it, I forgive him, the dope. It . . . it's what we *do,* Shelley.''

"Not tonight it isn't," Shelby told her sternly. "It's about time you stop doing what's expected, and do the unexpected. Maybe that will shock him into understanding you're more important than his mother's cruise. Now, the machine's picking up. How do we turn up the volume so we can hear him?''

Brandy hit the volume control, then slumped against the chair once more, wrapping her arms around her knees as she stared at the machine.

". . . so please leave a message after the beep," her own voice was saying.

"Brandy?" Gary's voice came through loud and clear, so loud that Shelby turned down the volume a few notches. "Brandy, baby, I know you're there. Come on, baby, pick up." There was a pause while Gary waited, while Shelby kept her hand on the phone as she stared warningly at Brandy. "I know you're mad, babe, and I don't blame you. But she showed me the tickets. They're for the same weekend we planned on, honest. And she's part of a group from her church, so if she cancels they lose their rate . . . or something like that. She's sorry; she really is. She even cried. Honest, babe, she's just sick about—''

Brandy had leaned forward and turned off the volume. *"She's* sick? I think *I'm* going to be sick," she muttered, leaning back once more and closing her eyes. "It's the same old same old, Shelley. She's going to keep doing this until the day she croaks, and I'm going to go down the aisle behind my damn walker. But, man, am I ever going to dance on that old lady's grave!''

"At least you've got someone who wants to marry you, even if he's got the mother from hell," Shelby said, making healthy inroads on her second wine cooler.

"What do you mean? You've got Parker, right? He wants to marry you."

"Does he, Brandy? Does he really? How am I supposed to tell?"

"Well . . . I dunno. When you make love?"

Shelby choked on a mouthful of wine cooler. "Make . . . make *love*? Brandy, we haven't made love. I mean, I got closer to making love with Quinn tonight than I've gotten with Parker in two years."

Brandy looked down the neck of her bottle. "Well, that's depressing."

Shelby looked over at her friend and gave a weak laugh. "Yes. Yes, it is, isn't it? Would you like another wine cooler? I know I would. My ears are starting to buzz. I think I want to keep going until my teeth are numb."

"Sounds like a plan," Brandy agreed, stumbling to her feet. "And I'll get us some munchies. No sense getting drunk without some munchies, right? It's why I wear these damn fool dresses. They hide the fact that munchies and me go way back."

Together they gathered a four-pack of wine coolers, a bowl of pretzels and potato chips, and an unopened box of cheese crackers—economy size.

Returning to the living room, Brandy picked up the clicker and turned on the television, keeping the volume low as an old B–movie came onto the screen. "Bet it's something sappy and stupid," she said, pointing to the television screen. "Just what we need right now."

"As my uncle Alfred would say—and does on almost any occasion or with no provocation at all—I'll drink to that!"

"You're okay, you know that, Shelley?" Brandy said, looking at her new friend through slightly blurry eyes. "You could have been a real stick, but you're not. You're actually pretty cool. Uh-oh, there goes the phone again. This could go on all night.''

"Don't answer it," Shelby warned as Brandy made a move toward the phone.

"I won't," she promised. "I'm just going to turn up the volume. Ah, here goes. . . ."

"Brandy? Pick up, Brandy. Aw, come on, I know you're there."

"Hmmm," Brandy said, smiling. "He's sounding a little bit miffed this time, isn't he? Well, good. About time I stopped this knee-jerk reaction, huh? Let him stew."

"Brandy? If you don't pick up I won't call back. I mean it, babe. I won't. I can't keep having these fights, babe, you putting me in the middle between you and Mama. It's not easy for me, you know. Brandy? Damn it, Brandy, pick up! Aw, the hell with it . . ." *Click.*

"Oh, this is good," Brandy said, hunting in the bowl for a burned chip, as she liked those best. "Now he's mad at me for having the nerve to be mad at him because he's so stupid. Just like a man. I'm so glad you didn't let me answer the phone, Shelley. This is quite educational, isn't it? We're right—women, that is—but that doesn't mean it isn't our fault that we're right." She shook her head. "Does that make sense to you, too, or am I beginning to get very, very drunk?"

"Does it matter?" Shelby asked, still pretty much sunk in her own misery.

"Probably not. Well, I'm turning off the ringer, too. You're right, Shelley; he should just simmer in his own juices for a while. Maybe being without his foot rubs and his . . . well, maybe without me being so damn *available* all the time, he'll smarten up some. Besides, this is old news; we've been through it a million times. Right now I think maybe we should be concentrating on you. So spill it, Shelley. What else is bothering you, because I know it's more than the fact that Quinn kissed you until your toes went numb.''

"Bothering me? *Everything*, Brandy, that's what's bothering me. I went to the same schools my mother went to, got the same grades. I joined the same clubs, I work for the same charities. I didn't get a job after college because Taites don't get *jobs*. I just kept doing what I was told. Go here, sit there, write this check, get engaged to Parker because . . .''

"Because you love him?'' Brandy supplied helpfully.

Shelby shook her head. "No, I don't think that's it. I think I got engaged because it was time I was married. Mother was married by the time she was twenty-five. Somerton was born when she was twenty-six. She did what she was told. Married, dutifully gave birth to a male child and major heir. Four years later, in the middle of one of Mother and Daddy's famous genteelly drunken sprees, I was conceived. Born to grow up just like Mother, the way Somerton was programmed—yes, *programmed*—to grow up just like Daddy. Well, Somerton broke the mold, and maybe I should, too!''

"How did Somerton break the mold?'' Brandy asked, glad of the diversion, because she really was weakening, feeling herself ready to pick up the phone if Gary dared to call one last time.

But Shelby wasn't listening. "So damned obedient. Obedient little Shelby, that's me. Don't do this, don't do that. Listen to everyone, do what they want, what is expected of a Taite. Now I'm getting married because it's time for me to be married. God, Brandy, I'm *sickening*.''

"He broke the mold *how?*'' Brandy asked, trying again, because she thought it might be important. She heard the near-silent click of the answering machine, heard the tape begin to whirl. And she ignored it. *Talk yourself blue in the face, bucko,* she thought. *Maybe you'll finally figure it out.*

Shelby looked at the level of liquid in her third wine cooler, and deftly reduced it by another two inches. Uncle Alfred had a point—a mushy mind was a happy mind, at least until it sobered up in the morning, something Uncle Alfred hadn't let his mind do in several decades. "He could have found me by now, you know."

"Who? Your brother?"

"No, Brandy, not Somerton. *Parker.* He could have found me, if he wanted to find me, if he isn't just glad I'm gone and hoping he can break the engagement. Except he won't do that. Too much old money merging for him to do that. Because Parker's practical, that's what Parker is. Practical Parker." She actually belched, something she couldn't remember doing in her entire sheltered life. "The prick. Practical Prick Parker picked a peck of . . . of . . . *something* with a *P.* Alliteration. I've always liked alliter . . . alliter-ashun."

"Hoo—boy, somebody's drunkie-poo," Brandy said, pulling the now empty bottle out of Shelby's slack grip. "Now, before you pass out, tell me about Somerton, Shelley. How did he break the mold?"

"Somerton?" Shelby questioned, her mind having left the distasteful subject of Parker Westbrook III and gone back to that of Quinn Delaney and the fact that he'd kissed her, then pushed her out of his apartment. Just when she was about to say the hell with everything and go to bed with him. Did he know that? Had he sensed that? Did he kick her out because he didn't want her . . . or because he had wanted her too much?

She smiled, rather sloppily, deciding on the latter explanation because it made her happy. She deserved to be happy, damn it. Personal happiness might not have been written down anywhere on the Taite Schedule for Life, but she believed she deserved some anyway. *So there.* Because things all seemed much nicer now. Fuzzier. Like Princess, who had climbed onto her lap and was now purring contentedly. Princess knew. It was time for some happiness, damn it. "You love me, Princess, don't you, honey?"

"Yeah, Princess loves you. Now, about Somerton," Brandy repeated, trying to keep Shelby from fading before she had some answers. "I mean, this could be important. If he broke the mold somehow, then it might not be so bad if you do, too. So tell me. What did he do?"

Shelby allowed her head to loll back against the couch cushions as her legs slowly slid forward under the coffee table. "He moved Jeremy in, that's what he did. Thumbed his nose at everybody and moved Jeremy—shazam!—straight into the old family mansion. Daddy's probably still spinning out in the gardens. The family mausoleum, you unnerstand. Potted right there, with the posies. Proper Papa potted with the posies. Pitiful."

"Okay," Brandy said slowly, still confused, although not nearly as drunk as Shelby, who clearly didn't have a head for alcohol, or much experience with it either, if Brandy had to guess. "Now, who or what is a Jeremy?"

Shelby brought her head forward and blinked a few times, trying to focus her eyes, her mind. "Who is Jeremy? Why, he's the sweetest, most silly, wonderful little *dear.*"

"Oh. Then it's a dog. What did your stuffy ancestors have against dogs?" The answering machine clicked, and the tape began to whirl. Brandy didn't even hear it.

"Look at that, Brandy," Shelby said, momentarily diverted by the movie playing on the television screen. "She's got a gun, she's backed into a corner by the bad guy, and she's not shooting him. He's going to kill her, and she's not going to shoot him. Does that make any sense, Brandy? Why does everyone think women are so *dumb?* So *afraid* of everything, so afraid that they'll ruin their own lives rather than stand up for themselves. *Shoot the bastard!"* she yelled at the screen, then sagged against the couch once more as Princess leaped up and ran away.

"Good for you, sweetcakes. Kill the bastards. Kill them all. Now, back to Jeremy, okay? Try to keep your eye on the ball, or whatever it is you told me tonight at the golf course. Is Jeremy a dog?"

Shelby sat up and tried to concentrate. She really shouldn't drink. It wasn't good for her. And she'd probably have a headache in the morning, just like she did the night of the charity ball. Once drunk was a lark; twice drunk was just plain stupid. She silently vowed never to drink again.

"No, no, no. Jeremy isn't a *dog*. He's . . . he's Somerton's soul mate. His lifetime companion. His sig . . . his significant other. And he's so *sweet;* Somerton's so *happy.* I'm *so* proud of Somerton. That's why I thought he'd understand. Why I left him the note. *He* did it. Why shouldn't I be able to do it?"

"I think you mean why can't you have an adventure, right?" Brandy said, laughing. "But you're right, Shelley. Somerton probably understands very well. If you told him how unhappy you are, that is. Did you tell him?"

"I told him to marry Parker if he thinks he's so wonderful, but he said Jeremy might object," Shelby said, remembering the conversation. Then she giggled. "That's funny, isn't it? Somerton usually can't make jokes, it's just not in him. But that was funny, wasn't it?"

"Hilarious," Brandy agreed, biting her thumbnail. "You know something, Shelley? I think you're really good at telling other people what to do—like me and Gar, Tony, Tabby, and everyone at the restaurant, even that gal in the movie—but you're afraid to do what *you* want to do."

"No, I'm not," Shelby protested, as the arrow hit home. She slumped against the couch. "Yes, I am."

Brandy felt instantly protective. "Well, no, you're not, actually. I mean, at least you've made a start, haven't you?

You ran away; you came here. You've got a job, a place to live . . . a boyfriend. . . ."

Shelby smiled and hugged herself. "He really is a wonderful kisser," she said, sighing. Then she looked at Brandy, her eyes wide. "I can't really call him my boyfriend, can I? I mean, he sent me home."

"And said he'd see you tomorrow, right? So, yeah, I'd say he's your boyfriend. If you want him."

Shelby picked up a pretzel stick that had fallen on her lap, and stuck it in her mouth. "If I want him." She turned to Brandy. "I think I do. Want him, that is. He's so . . . so everything that Parker isn't. Do you know what would have happened if I'd tipped Parker into that water hazard? No, you don't, because Parker would never think to *go* miniature golfing in the first place. Well, let me tell you, he wouldn't have been happy. Not Perfect Parker. But Quinn . . . he just laughed and said it was all right. . . ."

"What a guy. A real prince of a fellow, and with those bedroom eyes, too," Brandy agreed, watching as Shelby's eyelids fluttered, beginning to lose their fight with the wine coolers.

"I know," Shelby said in satisfaction. "What a guy. It's like I've always known him, you know? I mean, that first day, at Tony's, he looked so *familiar* to me. Do you think that means he's the man of my dreams?"

"Could be," Brandy said, grabbing one of Shelby's arms and pulling her friend to her feet. "And, speaking of dreams, I think it's about time you got to bed and had some. All in all, it's been a long day."

"Yes, ma'am, whatever you say, ma'am. May Princess sleep with me again tonight? Here Princess, here Princess . . ." Shelby said, walking with her head bent awkwardly, so that it could rest against the shorter woman's chestnut curls. "Didn't we have just the best time tonight, Brandy?"

Older by nearly ten years, and maybe not wiser in all things but certainly more experienced in many of them, Brandy sighed, smiled sadly as she heard the answering machine kick in yet again, and said, "Yeah, sweetcakes, we had us a hell of a time tonight."

Chapter Twenty-one

Grady Sullivan bent over the putt, eyeing the empty coffee cup ten feet away on the Oriental carpet. It was the final hole of the PGA and he was tied for the lead. If he missed this putt he and Tiger Woods would go to a sudden-death play-off, but his tee shot had topped Tiger's by thirty yards, and his second shot had landed him on the green.

Tiger had already missed his thirty-foot lag putt, which showed his disdain for Grady, and how Woods didn't think he had a chance in hell of sinking his own forty-footer. That meant, if Grady could sink this, get himself a birdie, he'd be the winner. Top dog. King of the world.

The crowd went silent; even the birds in the trees stopped singing, leaning over their branches, watching. Watching.

High above them, in the aerial booth, the ESPN commentators were reminding the home viewers that Sullivan had choked last year at the Masters, on a putt much this same length, and they doubted he'd make this one, or even his second putt, especially as he was just back at the game after a separated shoulder received in a freak home accident. In fact, a television crew had already headed out onto the course for the sudden death that would begin at the sixteenth hole.

But Grady couldn't think about any of that now. He could only think about this putt. This one putt. And the prize money. And the endorsements he'd get. And all the women who'd want to help him celebrate his win. He wasn't the selfish sort. He only wanted it all.

If he remembered correctly, there was a slight bump in the carpet right about where that vermilion thread stuck up, needing to be snipped. That would mean the putt would break slightly to his right.

This was it. King of the world or schmuck of the year. Which would it be?

He drew back the putter, squinted toward the coffee cup one last time, and stroked the ball home.

"And the crowd went wild," Grady exclaimed, modestly taking bows to the empty room.

"I hate to interrupt the celebration," his secretary said from the doorway, "but your partner is on the horn. Which was it this time? The Open, or the Desert Classic? Lord knows it couldn't be the Masters. You always choke on that one. But don't worry, you don't look all that great in green anyway."

"That's our Ruthie," Grady said, propping the putter against his desk. "Always my biggest fan. Did you say Quinn is on the phone? Why's he checking in, anyway? I thought he told me he was on vacation. And how did he know he'd find us here, at the office? It's Sunday."

"It's nearly the end of the fiscal year," Ruth reminded him, pointing toward the half dozen towers of paper haphazardly piled on Grady's desk as she walked across the room and confiscated the putter. "And until you're through at least two of those stacks, there will be no more playtime for Grady, got that?''

"Yes, ma'am," Grady said, walking around to sit down behind his desk, then pulling a face at Ruth's back as she sashayed out of the room, holding the putter as if it might turn into a snake at any moment.

He hit the button on the speakerphone and sat back in his chair, resting his feet on the desk. "Grady's Bar and Grill," he said, glaring at the towering paperwork. "How may we help you?"

Quinn's voice came through the speaker. "For starters, you can get me the hell off the speaker. You know I hate that."

Grady sighed, dropped his feet to the floor, and picked up the receiver. "There. Happy now?"

"Tell me I'm not a louse."

Grady took the receiver away from his head, then stared at it for a moment before putting it to his ear once more. "Come again?"

"I said, tell me I'm not a louse. That's why I'm calling you, damn it, so you can tell me I'm not a louse. So tell me."

Grady shrugged. "You're not a louse."

There was a short silence at the other end of the phone, then: "You can't say it with any real meaning, can you?" Quinn asked. "And you know why, Grady? It's because I *am* a louse. A board-certified, card-carrying louse."

"Don't be so hard on yourself, man. All right, so you left me in the lurch here, in paperwork up to my eyeballs. I can live with that. Dealing with auditors, hunting for forms I didn't even know existed. Trying to figure out your accounting system and those faxes you keep sending me. And all so you can go off and romance an heiress who also happens to be beautiful, with long legs, a killer figure—and

I'm not just talking about her bank balance. Hey, wait a minute. You *are* a louse."

"I kissed her last night."

Now, at last, Quinn had Grady's full attention, and he knew it. He sat back in his chair, automatically unfolded the bent doily on the arm, and waited.

"And . . . ?" Grady responded at last. "I mean, that can't be it. You kissed her? That's all? Hell, Quinn, that story wouldn't even have me turning back after the first commercial. Can't you give me more than that?"

"The word *ethics* never really meant a hell of a lot to you, did it, Grady?"

"What has ethics to do with anything? You gave them back their money, didn't you? This is purely on your own, with no connection to D and S. Of course, if you haven't yet told her that you were originally hired to baby-sit her while she played at real life . . ." Grady frowned at the desk calendar. "You *have* told her, right?"

"No, Grady, I haven't told her. She was in my apartment last night, snooping around the living room while I got out of my wet clothes—"

Grady interrupted, as his internal radar had gone on red alert. "Wet clothes? How did your clothes get wet? We're in the middle of a drought here, you know, and the weather isn't any different in East What-the-hell-you-call-it. You're skipping parts, aren't you? That isn't fair."

"Just try to stay with me, okay?" Quinn asked, getting up, beginning to pace the flowered carpet. "I came out of the bedroom and there she was, just about to pick up the file on her. Stupid! How could I have been so stupid as to leave that lying around?"

"Been out of the field for over a year, bucko. Sounds like you're losing your edge. I, however, haven't. So let me hazard a guess here. You saw her, saw the file. Grabbed her, kissed her, took her mind off the file. That's what I would have done. So, how am I doing so far?''

Quinn pushed his fingers through his hair. ''Not as well as I was doing, until I realized what a louse I was. How in hell am I going to tell her now, Grady?''

Grady pushed the speaker button and hung up the phone as he stood, began to pace in Philadelphia just as Quinn was pacing in East Wapaneken. ''You're serious, aren't you?''

''Grady, get me the hell off the speaker.''

''I can't. I have to pace. You know I have to pace. Besides, if you're worried that Ruth has her ear at my office door, I wouldn't worry about it. She's probably just sitting in her office, feet on her desk, eating chocolates, and recording all of this somehow, so she can hand out copies to everyone in the office tomorrow morning. You know she's the only one who really understands how to work these phones.''

There was a slight click, and the line became clearer.

''Oh, God,'' Quinn said, plopping into the chair once more. ''Just what I needed. You know she's going to call me later, ream me out, and then tell me what I should do.''

Grady grinned. ''Which would mean you don't need me. Isn't it great how all this is working out? But if you could explain the really rather nice bump in our second-quarter earnings, I'd really—''

''Good-bye, Grady.''

''Good—'' Grady looked at the speakerphone, listening to the dial tone. ''He hung up on me. Son of a gun. Damn if he didn't hang up on me.'' He headed for Ruth's office, poking his head out the door to get his secretary's opinion. ''So?''

''He's in love,'' Ruth pronounced flatly, then grinned. ''And he's in a hell of a mess. This ought to be fun.''

''Yeah, that's what I thought,'' Grady said, withdrawing

his head, then poking it front once more. "Can I have my putter back now?"

"Only if you want it somewhere you really wouldn't want it," Ruth warned, laughing.

"Forget I mentioned it," Grady said, wincing, and headed back to those leering, leaning stacks of paper as, in East Wapaneken, Quinn frowned as his doorbell rang with all the melody of an electronic pig stuck in a fence.

He walked into the hallway and looked down the stairs, to see Gary Mack standing there, looking more than a little lost. "What's up, Gary?"

Gary looked up at him and motioned for him to hit the buzzer that opened the inner door. A few moments later, having climbed the stairs two at a time, he was heading for 2C. "She wouldn't let me up," he told Quinn shortly. "We had a fight last night. A big one. Now she won't answer the phone, won't answer the buzzer." He raised his fist, ready to beat on the door, when Quinn grabbed him, turned him around, pushed him through the open door of 2B.

"Hey, what are you doing?" Gary asked as Quinn closed the door and locked it.

"Saving your life, it sounds like," Quinn said, motioning Gary to the chair he'd just vacated. "Never run after a woman, Gary, especially when she doesn't want to be run after. It's in the code."

Gary, who had spent a nearly sleepless night and had actually snapped at his mother when she commented that he hadn't eaten all his breakfast, looked at Quinn questioningly. "The code?" He shook his head. "Never heard of it."

Quinn sat himself down on the couch and smiled at his confused friend. Lots of muscle on the boy, with a fairly good proportion of it lodged between his ears at the moment. "It's simple, Gary. Never go after a woman who doesn't want you going after her. And, in section two, part A, never go after a woman who *wants* you to go after her. Either way you're going to lose. Now, which do you think applies to Brandy this morning?''

Gary hung his head. "She doesn't want to talk to me?" He looked up at Quinn. "I mean, she threw me out last night. Threw me out! She wouldn't answer the phone, won't answer the buzzer. So, yeah. She doesn't want to talk to me." His homely face rearranged itself in an attitude of what, for Gary, had to be deep thought. "Unless she really wants me to come crawling back, like I just tried to do. She could be doing that, too, couldn't she?"

"Ah, and there's your dilemma, Gary," Quinn told him. "Which is what she wants? Why don't you tell me what happened, and we'll see if we can sort this out, okay?"

Quinn didn't know why he was doing this, but it did keep his mind off Shelby. Off how she had felt in his arms. How her mouth had tasted. Of how much he wanted her, probably needed her. How much she'd hate him when she found out the truth.

Gary bit his bottom lip, then nodded. Gary was good at nodding. Explanations, however, were not his forte, as Quinn learned in the next few minutes.

"Okay, we were in the apartment, doing just great," he began, his brow creased. "I was rubbing her feet. Brandy loves when I rub her feet. And I was telling her about this great idea my buddy at work had. We were working on a renovation project out on the parkway. Big house, big addition. Two bedrooms, a sitting room, three bathrooms, if you can believe that."

"Gary? All of that is very interesting, but is this getting us anywhere?"

"Well, yeah," Gary said, a little insulted. "Because that's when Jim—he's my plumber buddy on the job site, you understand. Subcontract that stuff out, we do, because it's cheaper that way, and there's city codes and all, so you have to use a real plumber. Well, that's when Jim told us how the lady of the house was really piss—Um, that is, she was really *upset* about these low-flow toilets we were putting in the bathrooms. They are a pain, you know, but it's federal regulations. All new toilets have to be these low-flow kind, and they're a real pain, like I said. Like Jim says, what's the sense of using less water if you have to flush twice, maybe three times? But that's the federal government for you, Jim says, and I—"

Quinn jabbed his fingers through his hair. "Focus, Gary. Focus."

"Oh, right." Gary cleared his throat and began again. "So I tell him that Canada doesn't have these regulations about toilets. They're still making the same damn ones. Damn good ones. One flush and you're done. So Jim says to me, he says, 'You know, Gar, there's a fortune to be had, if we work it right,' and I say, 'What are you talking about, Jim?' and he says we could go up to Canada in my truck, buy us a couple dozen toilets, bring them back here, and sell them for about a thousand bucks apiece to people like this lady who's really piss— Er, really upset about these low-flow pieces of junk."

Quinn rubbed his forehead, thinking about illegal toilets and border guards and jail terms and, in general, Brandy's reaction to this piece of brilliance. "Brandy didn't like the idea?" he said, hazarding what he thought was a pretty good guess as to Brandy's reaction.

Gary began picking at the lace doily on the arm of the chair. "She said she wants to go to Niagara Falls on our honeymoon and that the only water she wants to see flowing is that on the Canadian side of the falls." He found a loose thread in the doily and began tugging at it, and Quinn quickly rescued the thing before Mrs. Brichta could see it and then probably murder him.

"And that's when we had the fight," Gary ended, sighing theatrically, or at least as theatrically as a man built like a brick house could muster.

Quinn nodded knowingly. "About the contraband toilets."

Gary looked up, clearly puzzled. "No," he corrected. "About the wedding. Weren't you listening?"

"Obviously not," Quinn said, deciding it was time for a couple of cold ones from the fridge. "But keep talking, Gary. I'm listening now."

It took another ten minutes, but at last Quinn understood the whole of it. "You're screwed," he said at last, draining his beer as he looked at Gary. "I mean, you are royally screwed."

"Yeah. I know," Gary said, putting his empty bottle on the table, so that Quinn found himself getting up yet again, this time to locate a coaster and slip it under the bottle. Mrs. Brichta sure did have him trained, he thought, then returned to the couch and stared at Gary, who stared back at him.

"What am I going to do?" Gary asked at last.

Quinn didn't have the faintest idea. "What do you want to do, Gar?"

"I want my mama and Brandy to be friends," he said at last, "but that's not going to happen. Oh, I don't blame Brandy; I really don't. Mama can be a little difficult, I guess, but then she's a widow, and lonely, and I'm her only child. She needs me, you know? But Brandy can't see that."

Quinn, who was also having a lot of trouble seeing that, carried the empty beer bottles to the kitchen in order to give himself time to think. What he thought first was that, considering his own predicament, he was probably the last person in the world who should be trying to hand out advice to the lovelorn.

Still, looking at Gary's problem was easier than spending any more time examining his own. He returned to the living room and sat down. "Tell you what, Gary. Give Brandy a couple of days to cool down; then ask her if maybe she wants the two of you to get tickets for this same cruise, then get married at sea. That would work, wouldn't it?"

Gary seemed to choke on his own spit. "Have Mama and Brandy together on the same boat? Are you *nuts*? They'd be screaming 'Man overboard' every ten minutes. Jeez, Quinn, I thought you said you could help me, but if that's the best you can do . . ."

Quinn looked at his watch. "It's eleven o'clock. The Phillies are playing at home. What do you say the two of us drive down to the Vet and catch the game?"

"Go to the ball game? But Brandy and I always go food shopping on Sunday's. I take Mama in the morning, and Brandy in the afternoon. We've been doing it that way ever since I can remember."

"But Brandy isn't answering the phone, Gary; she isn't answering the buzzer. Maybe if you left her alone today to get her own grocery shopping done, she'll be more willing to talk to you next time you call. Or are you planning to hang around her front door like some whipped puppy until she forgives you?"

"Well, yeah. That's how we usually work it," Gary said blankly, then straightened his shoulders. "You're right, Quinn. You have to know if they want you to come around or if they don't want you to come around. And I always come around, and Brandy knows it." His resolve seemed to weaken for a moment. "Of course, she always let me *in* before today."

Quinn walked over and patted Gary's shoulder. "She's pretty angry this time, Gar, I'll bet on it. I know how much she was looking forward to the wedding. Don't you think it's best that you leave her alone awhile, to cool down? Come on, Gar, the game starts at one. Interleague play, with the Yankees. I happen to know someone who has season tickets in one of the super boxes. We'll stop at his place, I'll run up and get the tickets, and we're all set.''

"Cool down? You think she'll cool down?" Gary said, standing up, hitching up his pants. "Yeah, that's what she'll do. She always does. Yankees, you say? A super box? And we could drive down in your Porsche? Damn, Quinn, what are we doing here? Let's go.''

Quinn hefted his key ring, looked at his apartment key, the one he'd use to get his tickets to the super box, and headed after Gary.

It was easier than having lunch at Tony's. Easier than seeing Shelby again just yet.

The phone began to ring just as he was locking the door to the apartment. It was Ruthie. Had to be Ruthie. She was calling to rake him over the coals, tell him he had to tell Shelby his true identity, and let the chips fall where they may. She sure wasn't calling to tell him to wait, to see what might happen between them, see if this was love— good God, *love!*—or if Shelby was interested in him only in the way of an adventure and he was only attracted to her because . . . because . . . well, damn, he didn't know why he was attracted to her.

But he was going to find out. And he couldn't find out if he told her the truth right now. Ruthie wouldn't understand that, but he did.

So he locked the door behind him and let the phone ring.

It was cowardly. He was a louse.

But he'd think about all of that later, when he met Shelby after work. . . .

Chapter Twenty-two

Keeping Brandy from becoming totally unglued had kept Shelby more than a little busy all of Sunday. Between waiting on patrons at Tony's, keeping Brandy supplied with tissues as she sat at the table closest to the kitchen watering the silk floral centerpiece with her tears, and trying to come back to life after her second—and definitely last!—bout of trying to find happiness in the bottom of a wine bottle, Shelby was almost too exhausted even to notice that Quinn was nowhere to be found.

Quinn *and* Gary were nowhere to be found. *The rats.*

Although Shelby believed Gary's absence was probably a good thing, because Brandy was ready to cave in, forgive him, and start up that same circle of ridiculousness that had kept her from the altar for twelve long years. Shelby didn't know why, but she felt it was sort of her mission in life to keep Brandy from making that mistake.

Which meant she'd been babysitting her friend at Tony's for most of the day, redoubling her efforts when Brandy had actually broken down and called Gary's house and ended up talking to Mama. "Why, dear, I don't know where he is," Mama Mack had told her sweetly. "He did mention something about going somewhere with someone for the day. Perhaps he has a date? But how are you keeping, dear? Still gaining weight? That's so sad."

Yes, Shelby had had her hands full, all right. And Brandy had had her mouth full. Turkey and all the fixings. Two slices of lemon meringue pie. An éclair for dinner. By the time the restaurant closed, Shelby's only thought had been how she was going to boost Brandy from her chair and maneuver her up the street to the apartment.

She had at least half expected Quinn to be sitting on the apartment steps, waiting for her. After all, he did say he would see her today, didn't he? But the Porsche was still missing, and his apartment was dark.

So Shelby and Brandy had climbed the stairs wearily, checked the answering machine to see that there were no messages, and crawled off to bed.

Men. That was what Brandy had said a time or two that long, long day. Just "men."

And that said it all. . . .

By Monday morning Brandy had rallied. She'd taken the phone off the hook the previous evening, and left it off until she headed out the door for her bus, having skipped breakfast at Tony's because she was starting a new diet. Her fifth of the year, one that had something to do with eating nothing but protein until she could turn a special testing strip blue with her urine. Shelby hadn't really listened to more, not after that test-strip business.

She had walked to the door with Brandy, gave her a kiss on the cheek before watching her go down the steps, then glared at the closed door to Quinn's furnished apartment for a full minute before going back inside, putting the phone on the hook, and taking a long, long shower.

She stepped out of the bathroom half an hour later, a towel turban around her head, a long bath sheet wrapped around her body, her feet bare. "Hello, Princess, darling," she said to the shaded silver Persian who had just come out of her bedroom.

And then she saw it.

It. An itty-bitty, great, gargantuan *it.*

The mouse. The mouse clamped tightly in Princess's jaws—and Princess was heading straight for her, as if ready to give her the still slightly squirming rodent as a present.

Shelby gave out a fairly ladylike "Eeek!" and raced for the telephone. She believed her feet must have touched the ground as she ran down the hallway and into the living room, but she wouldn't bet on it, especially as she vaulted over the couch and grabbed the phone, pushing the speed-dial for Brandy's office.

"Brandy!" she shouted a few years later, after having to deal with a lengthy "If you want form eleven A, press one; if you want to set up an appointment, press two," that nearly reduced her to tears. By the time Brandy finally came on the line ("If you wish to speak to one of our counselors, please stay on the line and someone will be with you shortly."), she had curled herself into a small ball on the back of the couch, daring to look down the hall every few seconds, just to make sure Princess still had the mouse in her mouth. Having the mouse in her mouth was bad, Shelby knew. But *not* having the mouse in her mouth meant it was somewhere else, and that, Shelby had decided, was worse.

"BrandyPrincesshasamouseinhermouth," Shelby said breathlessly.

"What?"

Shelby rolled her eyes, then winced as she saw Princess heading toward her. "I said, Princess has a mouse in her mouth. In her *mouth,* Brandy. And it's *wiggling.* No, wait.

Now it's not wiggling. I think it's dead, poor thing. Probably died of heart failure; I know I would have. What do I do? Brandy? Brandy, stop laughing. This isn't funny.''

Brandy stopped laughing long enough to say, "Oh, honey, yes it is," before going off into another round of giggles. "God, I needed this this morning."

Shelby took the receiver away from her head, glared at it, then pressed it against her ear once more. "Well, I didn't! What am I going to do? She won't . . . she won't *eat* it, will she?''

"I don't think so," Brandy said, still trying to control herself. "Look, just walk up to her, give the mouse's tail a little pull, and maybe she'll let go.''

Shelby suddenly thought of the Tudor mansion on the Main Line. Of all the permanent staff who could be relied on to keep even the *thought* of a dead mouse at bay. "You want *me* to touch that mouse? You've got to be kidding.''

"You could call Quinn. He's probably home, right?''

Shelby closed her eyes and did her best to straighten her backbone. "Do you have rubber gloves, Brandy?''

"That's my girl. Under the sink. Big yellow ones. Put one on, go over to Princess, grab the tail—that's the mouse, sweetcakes, not the cat—and then tell Princess to let go. I'll hang on.''

"Okay." Shelby put down the phone, dangled her bare legs over the back of the couch, and measured the distance between the couch and the kitchen sink. She could do this. She had to do this. It was either that or let Princess eat the mouse. *Ugh!* Or call Quinn and ask for his help after he said he'd see her yesterday and then didn't see her yesterday. *Double ugh!*

She found the glove, put it on, and approached Princess carefully, digging her bare toes into the carpet with each step. "Nice Princess. Pretty Princess. Give Shelby the mousie, Princess. That's a good— Damn it!''

Brandy was laughing hysterically as Shelby picked up the receiver once more. "Let me guess; it didn't work?"

"She *growled* at me, Brandy. I didn't know cats *could* growl. Now what do I do?"

Brandy gave the problem another moment's thought. "Water. Go to the sink, fill a glass, and pour it over the cat's head. She'll have to let go then, and you can quickly pick up the mouse."

"Brandy," Shelby said as calmly as she could. "I can do a lot of things quickly. I'm sure I can. But I cannot pick up a mouse *quickly.*"

"Shelley, you gotta stop. I'm dyin' here," Brandy told her, laughing. "Okay, change of plan. Pour the water over her head, then pick up *Princess* quickly, and throw her in the bedroom and close the door. Then you can pick up the mouse *slowly.*"

Doing as she was told, even if she wasn't happy about it, Shelby filled a glass and poured its entire contents over Princess's head. The cat let go of the mouse. Shelby reached down—quickly—and picked up the cat. "Damn it!"

"Now what?" Brandy asked, having put Shelby on the speakerphone so that all her coworkers could listen in. "Shut up, guys, and quit laughing. I can't hear her. Go ahead, Shelley. What happened?"

"She let go of the mouse, but when I picked her up she was so wet and slippery that she just fell out of my arms and picked up the mouse again. Growled at me again. Brandy, what am I going to do?"

A male voice came on the phone. "Shelley? This is Stan, one of Brandy's friends. Listen, what you've got to do is just ignore the cat. Sit down on the couch, twiddle your thumbs, look up at the ceiling—you know, ignore her. Then, when she drops the mouse, you sort of stand up slowly, go over to her, still looking at the ceiling, maybe even whistling, and quickly swoop up the mouse. It'll work, I promise.''

"Sounds like a plan, Shelley. Call me back,'' Brandy said, and broke the connection, but not soon enough that Shelby didn't hear an entire chorus of laughter and the words, "Whistle? Stan, you're a *scream!*''

Shelby looked at Princess, who was just standing there, sopping wet, still growling every once in a while. Still holding the mouse between her jaws. Shelby put down the phone. Smiled at the cat. Sat back on the couch.

"Nonchalant,'' she told herself. "Just sit here and be nonchalant.'' She smiled at Princess again, then picked up a magazine and pretended to read it. She began to hum. Humming was calming, wasn't it?

Two minutes later, Princess opened her mouth and dropped the mouse.

Shelby waited until she counted to ten, then slowly put down the magazine. Slowly uncrossed her legs. Stood up. Kept her head high and began walking toward the kitchen. Nonchalant.

She got within two feet of the mouse before Princess picked it up once more, growled, gave a flick of her bushy tail, and walked over to stand in front of the television.

"Damn, damn, *damn!*'' Shelby swore. "I'm going to be late for work if this keeps up. And now what?'' she asked herself as there was a knock at the door.

With her luck it would be Mrs. Brichta, come to check up on them—that would seem a motherly thing to do, except that Mrs. Brichta was a lot of things, but motherly wasn't one of them.

"Just a minute,'' Shelby said, putting a hand to the towel turban, adjusting the bath sheet where she had knotted it over her breasts.

She opened the door a crack to see Quinn standing

there, smiling at her. "Hi. Brandy called and said you needed a knight in shining armor. I'm here to volunteer."

Shelby's first instinct was to slam the door in his face. That reaction lasted about two seconds, because she really did need him, and she knew it. She stood back and opened the door. "It's Princess. She's got a mouse and won't let it go."

"I know," Quinn said, trying to look at the cat, but succeeding only in looking at Shelby. Under one towel she had her beautiful blond hair. Under the other she had . . . a whole bunch of things he'd better not think about right now. "Where does Brandy keep the cat food?"

"I don't—under the sink, I think. Why?"

"Because Princess is a well-fed cat. Well-fed cats don't eat mice. They play with them. That's what Princess is doing. Playing with the mouse."

"That's disgusting," Shelby said, shivering, and suddenly remembering that she was naked beneath the bath sheet that only covered her from the top of her breasts to just above her knees. "I . . . I'll get the cat food."

Two minutes later Princess was digging into some turkey and giblets, the mouse was running loose in the field behind the apartment building, and Quinn was standing in the hallway, knocking on the door to Brandy's apartment once more, wondering what the reward for mouse disposal ran these days.

"I thought I'd come back and tell you. Mighty Mouse wasn't dead, just playing possum. He'll live to find his way back in here another day."

Shelby felt a smile curving her lips. "Not dead? Oh, that's so good to hear. I mean, I don't want mice in the apartment, but I didn't want him to be dead, either. Thank you, Quinn. Thank you very much. Well, I've got to get dressed now, so . . .''

She went to close the door, but he'd already put his hand against it, holding it open. "I wanted to apologize for not seeing you yesterday after I said I would."

Shelby searched her brain for something to say, and settled on something Tabby had once said: "It's no big deal, Quinn. Don't worry, um, sweat it. Now, I really—"

"It was Gary. He was a mess yesterday," Quinn pressed on, still keeping his hand on the door. "I suppose you know he and Brandy had an argument? Anyway, I took him to the Phillies game, just to keep him from making things worse."

Shelby stepped back a pace and looked at Quinn through narrowed eyelids. *"You* took him away? I had to deal with Brandy and her eat-everything-in-sight depression all day yesterday because *you* decided Gary shouldn't see her or talk to her? You shouldn't have involved yourself, Quinn."

"Right," he answered, walking past her into the living room. "And you didn't involve yourself, Shelley? Gary told me he always calls Brandy after a fight and they always spend the night on the phone, talking through their problems, making up. Except she wouldn't answer the phone Saturday night. Now why do you suppose she wouldn't answer the phone Saturday night, when that's the way they play this game they've played for the past twelve years?"

"I have no idea," Shelby said, avoiding his eyes. "Oh, all right, so I meddled. So did you. But *somebody* had to step in and stop this silliness. They love each other, Quinn; they really love each other. But if each of them keeps reacting the same old way to the same old stimuli, keeps pressing the same buttons on the other, getting the same reaction, well, they'll be engaged until they're both eighty-six years old."

Quinn rolled his eyes. "Stimuli. Buttons. Reactions. Do I hear the echo of some Psych one-oh-one professor in here?"

Shelby yanked the bath sheet up higher around her breasts. "So what if you do? I'm right, and you know it. That old woman is running their lives, but at the same time Brandy is allowing it, and Gary is allowing it."

"And you're going to change all of that, right?"

She shrugged, averting her eyes. "Maybe. And what are *you* going to do, other than take Gary to a baseball game?"

He moved closer to her and smiled. "Nothing," he said, shaking his head. "I'm going to do nothing at all. I only took Gary away yesterday so he'd have some time to think about what he was doing, maybe even look at the problem from some other angle. Right now he's thinking a dozen roses. In other words, he's still got a long way to go, but he's trying. And I suggest you butt out as well, Shelley. People don't like other people interfering with their lives, even with the best intentions."

Shelby felt hot color run into her cheeks as his comment reminded her that she had just run away from all the people whose good intentions had been ruling her life for so long. "You're right, I suppose."

He stepped even closer, put a finger under her chin, and lifted her face to his. "Besides, I think we've got enough going on between us, don't you?"

"I . . . I don't know what you mean," she lied, realizing that her legs had begun to tremble.

"Yes, you do, Shelley," he told her, his voice low, intimate. "Because there's something going on between us, something neither of us wants to ignore. The only questions right now are why we feel this way, and what we are going to do about it. Right now I think I want to kiss you."

She moistened her suddenly dry lips with the tip of her tongue, a move that might have been nervousness on her part but that had an entirely different impact on him, making him feel bolder, more eager for the taste of her mouth.

"Shelley? May I kiss you? Please."

That did it. Her knees melted. She nearly fell against him as he put his hands on her bare shoulders and lowered his head to hers. All she could see was the black of his hair, the intense gray of his eyes, the slight smile on his full lips. And then her eyes fluttered closed and she gave herself up to sensations that had nothing to do with sight.

The kiss began tentatively, nothing like his first kiss on Saturday night. He kissed her as if he were in no hurry at all, as if he had all day to kiss her, taste her, draw her sweetness from her, drive her wild with desire.

His fingers held on to her shoulders, kneading the soft flesh she'd smoothed with body lotion, and he felt her arms go around him, reaching up to hold on to his shoulders, drawing him closer. Closer.

She was his for the taking, his for the giving. She was delicate and pliant, yet she burned with an inner fire that seared him chest to thigh as he pressed against her softness, as her mouth opened beneath his, allowed him entry.

Quinn lifted his head, looked down at her, at her closed eyes, her moist mouth, and he kissed her again. He wanted to go on kissing her until the last star died and the skies went forever dark.

He wanted to hold her, to love her, to have her. He stepped back slightly, his hand going to the knot in the bath sheet, beginning to fumble with it, his movements less sure than he could ever remember them being. But then he couldn't remember anything else he'd done in his life that was this important.

And the phone rang.

He broke the kiss, pulled her close against him, and

spoke against her hair. "Don't answer it. Pretend it isn't ringing."

She remained locked against him, allowing him to nibble at the side of her throat, but by the sixth ring she had pushed him away, mumbled a soft "Sorry, Brandy turned off the answering machine," and headed for the phone.

"Hello. Brandy? What?" She turned and looked at Quinn, who was doing his best to regain his normal breathing pattern. "Oh. Oh, yes. Quinn came over and the mouse is gone. I . . . I'm sorry I didn't call you back, but Quinn's still here and . . . Yes, you could say that. No, it's all right, really. I don't mind that you called, honestly. What? When? How many roses?" she asked, looking at Quinn, holding up her hand as if to say, "I'm sorry, but she just keeps on talking."

"It's all right, Shelley, I have things to do anyway," Quinn said, already heading for the door. He had to leave, or he had to have her. There was only that either/or; nothing else would do. Even if he still hadn't told her the truth, even if the moment he told her the truth she'd slap his face and tell him to go to hell.

Maybe later. Maybe tonight. Maybe he could tell her tonight, and then let the chips fall where they might. Tonight, before he got in too deep, before they both got in too deep. If they already weren't.

"Yes, Brandy, it is. It's wonderful of him. So you've forgiven him? Good-bye, Quinn," she then said, her hand over the receiver. "Um . . . later?"

"Later. That's a promise," he said, bending to pick up the mail the postman had slid through the slot, as all the mailboxes downstairs were rusted shut. "I'll just put this on the table," he said, and wandered out. He thought about taking a cold shower. Maybe two cold showers.

* * *

Shelby watched him go, wondering why she was letting him go when all she wanted was for him to pick her up, carry her to her bed surrounded by country and western singers and Beanie Babies, and make mad, passionate love to her.

As Brandy rambled on about how wonderful Gary was, Shelby picked up the mail and began idly looking through it, even though it was nothing but bills for Brandy or junk mail.

Then she saw an envelope with her new name on it, the address spelled out in block letters, and with no return address. Still with the receiver between her ear and shoulder, she slit open the envelope and pulled out the single sheet of paper, also written in block letters and all in capitals. There was only one line, in the center of the page:

LEAVE TOWN NOW. THERE ARE SAFER PLACES.

"Um, Brandy? I have to hang up now," she said as calmly as possible. "Yes, my hair is wet and still wrapped in a towel and I'm probably going to have to wash it again if I want it to look even halfway decent before I go to work. Yes, okay," she said, already bending down, the phone at her ear, heading it toward the receiver. "Um-hmm, later, bye."

Then Shelby sat down on the couch, her fingers trembling, her whole body shaking with shock, and read the few words again.

Chapter Twenty-three

Quinn had been sitting at the corner table in Tony's for the past hour, pretending to eat his lunch. So had the guy in the ripped jeans, faded T-shirt, and handmade leather loafers.

It was the loafers that gave him away. That and the fact that he kept watching Shelby. Not that everyone didn't watch Shelby. She was, in her designer clothes, her sleek blond hair, her perfect posture, her wide and genuine smile, and all that other stuff Quinn dreamed of at night, eminently watchable.

But this guy was different. For one, nobody knew him, even though he'd made a great business out of saying hello to everyone just as if he'd lived in East Wapaneken all his life. And, as the people of East Wapaneken were a friendly sort, they said hello right back at him. Then, Quinn saw, they looked at their table companions and whispered something like, "Who's that? Do we know him?"

Quinn had patted himself on the back, believing he had

slipped into town, and into the life of the town, without making much of a splash.

The guy in the handmade loafers was about as subtle as a Mack truck driving through Tony's front window. At least he was to Quinn.

Ten minutes ago he'd taken a walk outside, checked out the cars in the lot. Mayor Brobst's '67 Caddy took up two spaces right out front. Three motorcycles, as the regulars were three short until half the guys got back from the unemployment office. Three other cars he recognized from seeing them in the lot before, but he could place only two of them with Tony's everyday customers.

The third, a brand-new BMW, had to belong to Hand-made Shoes. Except that Quinn hadn't seen him inside the restaurant before today. He rubbed the back of his neck, dredging through his memories of his days at Tony's, pretending to write in his notebook while watching Shelby, and suddenly it came to him.

There had been another guy, late last week. Tall, thin, thirtyish, unremarkable. One of those invisible sorts witnesses later described as being "average height, average build, wearing khakis—no, maybe it was jeans. And a shirt. Yeah, he was wearing a shirt; I'm sure of that—was I any help?"

The guy had just come in, ordered coffee and cake, spoke with Tabby for a while, then left again. Spoke with Tabby? Hell, that was better, and more productive, than watching CNN for twenty-four hours straight.

Quinn pushed back his sleeve, checked his watch, then, with one last look at Handmade Shoes, paid his bill, waving good-bye to Shelby as she sorted menus. She nodded, then went back to counting out the small "Specials" cards that had to be paper-clipped to the menus. She did smile at him, but she looked preoccupied, and as if counting out cards were a job almost beyond her powers.

Now that he thought about it, she also had been rather pale, somewhat quiet, even while talking to Amelia Brobst, who couldn't hear much of anything below a bellow. He should have noticed that earlier, damn it, but he'd been too busy watching her move, admiring her long legs, remembering the taste of her kiss, anticipating tonight, when they'd be together again.

Now both his cop and bodyguard antennae began to quiver and he was no longer Quinn Delaney, hopeful lover, but Quinn Delaney, protector of the innocent.

He had his cell phone out of his pocket before he hit the door. "Somerton Taite, please," he told—not asked—the person who answered the phone at the Taite mansion. "Never mind who's calling, damn it, get the man on the phone. *Now.*"

Somerton was on the line moments later. "Delaney, is that you? I can't think of anyone else who'd be so rude to a member of my staff. Is something wrong?"

"You could say that," Quinn said, fishing in his pocket for the keys to the Porsche. "Have Westbrook in your living room in an hour. We have to talk." Then he broke the connection before Somerton could ask any questions.

Quinn headed for the parking lot behind the apartment building, then hesitated at the last moment and climbed the front stairs, thinking to get his jacket because it looked like rain would fall in another hour.

He got as far as the hallway outside his furnished rooms before he decided he really should have told Shelby he was going to be away for most of the day. After the way he had just disappeared on Sunday, she might not be too happy if he did it again today. He'd write her a note and slip it under her door.

And then the antennae wiggled again. He didn't know why. He never knew why. But he had also learned to follow his instincts.

Taking a moment to peer down the stairs, just in case Mrs. Brichta was out and about on one of her snooping rounds, he pulled a credit card from his wallet and approached 2C. The locks in this place, he already knew, were very much Mickey Mouse, and with a few good pushes and a bit of handle wriggling, he was inside Brandy's apartment, the door closed at his back.

Now if he only knew what he was doing here.

He didn't spend much time in the living room, as he'd already seen it, and he didn't expect to find anything of Shelby's there anyway. There wouldn't have been room. Brandy had every tabletop covered in knickknacks ranging from the tacky to the not so tacky. Still, the place was warm and inviting, and Shelby could have done a lot worse than to have met Brandy and been taken in by the bighearted woman.

Something touched his leg, and he looked down to see Princess rubbing against him. "No more mice?" he asked, bending to rub under the cat's chin, setting off a round of purring that sounded like the Persian's motor needed a tune-up. "Be good, and maybe I'll import one for you, if you promise to show it to Shelby when she's home alone, dressed only in a towel," he said to the uncomprehending animal, then set off down the hallway, toward the bedrooms.

Simple deduction told him the queen-size bed belonged to Brandy, the small single bed to Shelby.

He stepped into the room, shaking his head at the decorations, trying without success to picture Shelby sleeping in the middle of it, sleeping with the big plush dog that lay on the neatly made bed.

But there was a silver brush and comb set on the bureau, a bottle of her favorite perfume standing next to it. A pair of navy blue pumps pushed into a corner. A mountain of suitcases shoved into another corner. A pink lace bra draped over the cold metal radiator under the window, probably put there to dry after Shelby had washed it in the bathroom sink.

Funny, he'd never felt like an intruder before, never separated the person from the job, gave that person a human face. He'd carried out more than a few searches while on the job, and he'd known why he was doing what he did, the reasons behind it, even what the district attorney who'd ordered the warrant hoped to find.

But this was different. He wasn't a cop anymore; he wasn't, technically, even on the job anymore. This was breaking and entering, pure and simple. Or very complicated, as he didn't know why he'd thought looking through Shelby's personal belongings could be important, didn't know what he hoped to gain. He just knew she'd looked different at Tony's. Maybe even scared.

Quinn shook his head, turned, and left the room, knocking over the purse that had been sitting on the edge of the bureau. He'd already noticed that Shelby never brought her purse with her to the restaurant, preferring just to carry her key in her pocket. "Damn," he said, bending to pick up the scattered contents, wondering if it had purely been an accident, or if he'd subconsciously hoped something like this would happen so that he had a "reason" for going through Shelby's purse.

Still, no matter how lousy he felt, he had also felt the tingle, and he wasn't about to forget that. He wasn't about to forget that Shelby Taite was an heiress at least a few million times over, and that she was a possible kidnap victim every moment she was out in the wide, wide world, having her "adventure."

After all, what if she was planning to leave town again, take another flit? What if, right now, there were bus tickets stuck in this purse? What then? How would he handle that? And what if she'd been writing to someone? Someone who might not be blind to the profit to be made in selling Shelby's story to the tabloids?

There were so many reasons for Quinn to check the contents of Shelby's purse. So many reasons, and no good reasons at all, except that he cared for her. He really, really *cared* for her.

He picked up lipstick, a compact, a gold pen, a pair of Paloma Picasso sunglasses in a red case, a finely woven linen hankie with an *S* embroidered on one corner in dusky rose thread. He looked at her wallet for a long time, hefted it in his hand, then told himself that he'd been overreacting, and nosy. He put the wallet, unopened, back into the purse.

At the last moment, just when he was congratulating himself on his ethics, he felt the stiffness of paper behind the zippered compartment on one side of the purse.

And he gave in to temptation.

One hour and one speeding ticket on the Pennsylvania Turnpike later, he stepped through the Taite door before the butler had opened it all the way, and headed for the living room, smoke still coming from his ears.

"Where is he?" he asked without preamble, seeing only the two Taite men and Jeremy Rifkin scattered about the room like so many statues warily waiting for the pigeons to come flying in to roost.

"You would mean Parker?" Somerton asked politely.

"Yeah," Quinn said, realizing his hands were drawn up into fists. "That's who I would mean, all right. Parker Westbrook the freaking third. Where is he?"

"Oh, dear, the native has gone restless," Uncle Alfred said, pouring Quinn a tumbler of scotch and bringing it over to him. "Here, boy, I think you need this."

Quinn shook his head. "No, thanks."

"Very well, *I* need this," Uncle Alfred said, and wandered off again, sipping at the scotch.

"Somerton, I believe Mr. Delaney is upset about something," Jeremy put in, as if he was the only one in the room to have figured out that Quinn was ready to explode. "Oh, please don't let anything have happened to our dear Shelby."

Quinn looked at Somerton, gauging the man's expression, and saw only concern for his sister. He had thought about Somerton, thought he might be the one, wanted to keep an open mind before he popped Westbrook in the chops. "Shelby's fine," he told the man, and watched as Somerton visibly relaxed. "But she is in trouble."

"Oh, my good Lord!" Jeremy exclaimed, fanning himself with both hands. "I knew it; I just knew it. Somerton, didn't I tell you? She's in trouble." He stopped fanning himself and looked at Quinn. *"How* is she in trouble, Mr. Delaney? We thought she was working in a fine establishment."

"Is it money?" Somerton asked. "I know you said we couldn't fix that mess we made with her credit card, but if it's money, if she's desperate . . ."

"It's not money," Quinn said shortly. "As a matter of fact, you can be damn proud of your sister. She's working every day, earning a wage, and not spending like the drunken sailor Westbrook seemed to think her. But somebody's"—he hesitated, framed his words carefully—"somebody else is in town, watching her. Now tell me, have you sent another bodyguard after her? A private investigator, by any chance?"

"Ah, that would be me, Delaney," Parker Westbrook III said, walking into the room, making his dramatic entrance, as he seemed prone to do on any occasion. He was dressed in blue pinstripes, his suit custom made, his shirt a pristine white beneath his old school tie. He was tanned and smiling, and Quinn wanted nothing more than to pop him one in the chops.

"Parker," Somerton said, walking over to greet the man. "You sent a private investigator to watch Shelby? But we agreed—"

"No," Westbrook interrupted, "*you* agreed. *I* did not. It was an asinine capitulation to this . . . this *hireling* of yours, and I made my mind up to have nothing to do with it. Good God, Somerton, I'm her fiancé, and you wouldn't even tell me where she'd run off to. So, yes, I hired my own investigators. Top-notch, came highly recommended. They traced Shelby to a dreadful little place called East Wapaneken where, contrary to *your* man's report, she is working at some greasy spoon, putting in long hours for what is probably minimum wage."

"Minimum wage," Uncle Alfred repeated, shuddering, then took another deep drink of scotch.

Somerton looked to Quinn. "I thought you said—"

Quinn waved his arms, erasing Westbrook's words. Damn the man for putting him on the defensive. "It's a fine place, Mr. Taite. Well run, only two blocks from the apartment Miss Taite is sharing with Ms. Wasilkowski. And I've become a regular patron at the restaurant, besides taking the apartment across the hall from Ms. Wasilkowski's, so that I have Miss Taite under my surveillance and protection twenty-four-seven."

"Twenty-four-seven," Uncle Alfred repeated, heading for the drinks table. "Ten-four, over and out. Love that sort of thing, don't you? Macho, Jeremy, don't you think?"

"Yes, Uncle Alfred," Jeremy said, rolling his eyes at Somerton. "Quite macho. I'm all atingle."

Quinn listened to this short interchange, gathering his own thoughts. Mostly those thoughts had to do with drop-kicking Westbrook through one of the floor-to-ceiling windows of the Taite mansion, but he fought and gained control over his baser instincts, more was the pity.

"I want them called off, Westbrook," he said, narrowing his attention to the man and trying to ignore Uncle Alfred, who was holding the brandy decanter next to his ear and saying, "That's a copy. A five-twelve in progress at Fourth and Main. Ten-four, over and out."

"No," Westbrook replied, crossing his arms over his chest. And smirking. Quinn knew a smirk when he saw one.

"Look, Westbrook, I spotted your man this morning. Took me all of ten seconds. The guy blends into the background like a zebra against a red canvas. How long do you think it will take for Ms. Taite to figure out someone's set a keeper on her trail?"

He didn't mention the note, would not mention the note. Not for a lot of reasons. One, Somerton would go straight to East Wapaneken and personally escort Shelby home, which was the last thing Shelby wanted, the last thing Quinn wanted, if he wanted to be honest with himself. Two, there was something fishy about that note, something too cute, too pat, and he wanted to find out who was at the bottom of it. Three, he hoped it was Parker Westbrook III. Man, did he hope it was Westbrook.

He sure as hell didn't want it to be the regulars, who were his only other suspects, considering the fact that they were bound to know that Shelby had overheard them talking about offing the mayor. Shelby was a lot of things, nine-tenths of them wonderful, but she had a face a person could read by moonlight. The regulars had to know, from the way she smiled at them, from the way she watched them, that she knew what they were planning. Or dreaming. Quinn didn't put much credit in the idea that they were doing anything more than dreaming. After all—Amelia Brobst? It was ludicrous.

"Parker, I believe I must insist," Somerton said, standing stiffly in front of the man, both his chin and his voice wobbling a little. "I have every faith in Mr. Delaney, and everything has been working out quite well so far. Bringing in your own bodyguards, or private investigators, or whatever it is you've so clumsily done, can only provoke Shelby once she discovers what you've done and prolong her . . . her adventure. None of us wants that, now, do we?"

Behind him on the couch, Jeremy applauded happily. "Oh, Somerton, that was *so* perspicacious of you. Wasn't that perspicacious of him, everybody? I've been studying the dictionary, hoping to improve my vocabulary, and that's one of my very best new words. Perspicacious: having keen mental perception. Truly a wonderful word. And, Parker? You're being *un*perspicacious. Oh, dear. Is that a proper form of the word? I really should—"

Quinn watched, keeping his own counsel, as Westbrook's handsome face turned the color of an overripe persimmon. He leaned past Somerton and spit, "Shut up, you damned fairy!"

What happened next would be pressed between the pages of the picture book of Quinn's memory for many a year.

Because Somerton, known for his backhand but not for much of anything else physical, balled up his fist, brought back his arm . . . and punched Parker Westbrook III flat in the mouth.

Uncle Alfred roared his approval as Somerton then danced around the room, holding his punching hand to his mouth, sucking on his knuckles and whimpering.

Jeremy all but swooned on the couch, keeping one eye open to see if that was it or if there'd be a round two.

Which left Quinn to pick up Westbrook, dust him off, and send him on his way.

If he'd been a nice man, that is. Since, in this instance,

he decided he was *not* a nice man, he just stood there and watched as Westbrook climbed to his feet, brushed off his own clothing, then took out a handkerchief when he realized he had a bloody lip.

"Out of . . . out of the knowledge that I am soon to be a member of this family," he said, dabbing at his bottom lip, "I am going to forget this happened, Somerton."

Somerton bobbed his head up and down several times and swaggered a bit. "Yes, you do that, Parker. And fire those damn investigators. I mean it."

"Better listen to the lad," Uncle Alfred said, handing Somerton a linen napkin he'd filled with ice, to put on his knuckles. "We're bad to the bone, us Taites. Couldn't guarantee your safety if you were to insult the little woman again, because he's *our* little woman."

Then Uncle Alfred turned to Quinn. "You go back there and guard our Shelby, Delaney. Oh, and make sure she has a good time," he added, winking. "If you take my meaning?"

"Yes, sir," Quinn said, then left the mansion, eager to get back to Shelby in time to eat with her during her dinner break.

Still, all in all, Quinn had enjoyed his little trip to the Main Line very much.

Chapter Twenty-four

"You haven't told me if you've learned anything from the regulars," Shelby said as she and Quinn walked back to the apartment after she'd completed her shift. "Not that I think there's anything to it. I mean, the regulars? And the mayor? No, it's just too silly."

The June night was full of stars, with a full moon hanging over East Wapaneken, lighting their way home, lighting Shelby's upturned face.

And Shelby looked worried.

Quinn slipped an arm around her waist and pulled her close against his side as they walked along the cracked pavements that bore silent—and twice litigious, so far— witness to Amelia's late husband's last and worst idea, the planting of shade trees along the town's streets. The trees had grown, the shade was lovely, but the roots had pushed up pavements from one end of East Wapaneken to the other. Still, the unseen sidewalk was the perfect excuse for holding hands, for slipping a protective arm around a young woman's waist.

"I think they like to talk a lot," he told her comfortingly, or maybe not so comfortingly. After all, when one was getting threatening letters, it was at least some small comfort to believe one knew who was sending them. "But I guess you never know," he added in the belief that the small "hedge" might make her feel better.

She nodded, watching where she was stepping. "I've been giving it a lot of thought today," she told him. She wouldn't tell him how much thought she'd been giving a lot of things all day today, or how nervous she'd been and still was. "Their problem, you understand. And I'm willing to bet that if they raised the money for a memorial, then Mayor Brobst will allow it to be built in the park."

"Really?" Quinn said, trying not to smile. Why hadn't he already considered this? Put someone like Shelby Taite down in front of a problem, and the first solution that would most naturally come to her mind was to have a fund-raiser. Maybe even a ball.

He tried to picture the regulars at a ball. Balding or with long, flowing locks. Beer-bellied. Tattoos all around. More than a couple of missing teeth as they requested that the orchestra play some Willie Nelson. Nope. Couldn't picture it.

He offered another solution. "I guess they could have a bake sale, something like that. But Shelley, it would take a lot of cakes and cookies to raise enough money for a monument."

"A wall," Shelby corrected. "I spoke with the regulars this afternoon, and they want a wall, divided into two areas. One for those who served, the second section for those who died. Did you know that, for a town of only about four or five thousand people, East Wapaneken lost six men to that war? And thirty-seven more served. I find that rather amazing, and sad.''

"Sad, yes, but not surprising," Quinn told her. "The draft took kids who didn't go on to college, kids who worked in the local mills and factories. I'm willing to bet that back then there were more sons who followed in their father's footsteps—straight into the factories—than there were those who could get themselves a college deferment. You're right, Shelley, and so are the regulars. They should have a monument.''

Unless someone in that group sent you that cryptic message, he added to himself.

"I'm so glad you agree. Then you'll buy a ticket to our dinner?''

"Your *what?* I've been gone for only one afternoon. Have I missed something?''

They had reached the apartment building, and Shelby looked up the stairs to the doorway, then at Quinn. "Oh, I forgot. Gary, having been duly forgiven, is visiting tonight, and I've been told not to come home before ten. Do you want to talk out here?'' she asked, pointing to the steps.

"We could," he said, smiling. "But I've got some cold beers in the fridge upstairs.''

She returned his smile. "All right," she said slowly, and he knew she had answered quite another question. A question that had hung between them almost from the first, a question that had been partially answered this morning.

She settled herself on the couch up in his apartment, slipping out of her pumps and curling her long legs up beneath her, resting her arms on the back of the couch and watching as he pulled two beers from the fridge, then belatedly grabbed a single tall glass from the cabinet. The glass was decorated with bluebirds, in typical Mrs. Brichta fashion.

She wasn't sure what she was doing, why she was about

to do it. She only knew it felt right to be here, with Quinn, talking easily, feeling caught between that comforting feeling of not having to be on her best behavior and wanting to be on her very worst behavior—at least as it pertained to engaged ladies.

Was Quinn her adventure? Was this why she had left Philadelphia? Had she been in search of real life, or just of a real person? In other words, the opposite of Parker Westbrook III. A man of desires he wasn't afraid to show, a man who seemed capable of protecting her and enjoying her company, a man totally unimpressed by her birth or wealth, and a man willing and able to make love to her until she couldn't see straight.

A man she was stupidly falling in love with, knowing that the moment she told him the truth he'd either run as far and as fast as he could, or smile a hungry smile while she watched dollar signs flash in his gray eyes.

Could she chance either reaction? Could there be a third, a reaction she had not considered? Could he actually be falling in love with her? Or did he travel the country, writing his books and having his own adventures in every town?

Shelby swiveled back on the couch as Quinn walked around it and sat down beside her. He poured some beer in her glass and handed it to her. "So tell me about this dinner you're planning."

She frowned for a second, trying to remember what they'd been talking about. Which wasn't easy, now that he was sitting close beside her in the near-dark, his aftershave tickling her nose, the warmth of his long, lean body invading her every pore.

"Oh," she said after a moment, "the dinner." She took a sip of the cold beer, winced as she tasted it, and remembered how much she really had never cared for beer. She placed the glass on the small coffee table—on a coaster.

"Well, I've been thinking about it for a few days—nothing serious, you understand. But then today, as Tony seemed to be in a fairly good mood, I asked him."

"To host a fund-raising dinner at the restaurant? And he said yes? That's hard to believe."

"Not really," Shelby told him in all seriousness. "Brandy said he was solid marshmallow inside, and she's right. Beneath that lanky, slow-moving, crusty exterior, Tony's really a wonderful, generous man. He said yes immediately. Well, he said yes after I explained the usual percentage of the profit that would be his."

"The usual percentage?" Quinn asked, studying Shelby's face. Was this the opening he hoped for? Should he press her as to how she'd know that? And should he do it now, before he made love to her? Before he held her in his arms and knew, for sure and forever, that this was the one woman in the world he could never walk away from, could never leave?

She bowed her head, plucking at a wrinkle in her skirt. "I read about it in a magazine I found in that pile Brandy keeps stacked in the living room," she said, still avoiding his eyes.

"Oh," Quinn said, thinking that at least Shelby knew she was a terrible liar, then feeling pretty good about the fact that she couldn't look at him and lie at the same time. Did that mean anything, or was he so desperate he was clutching at any straw that came his way?

"Yes, and we'll have three sittings, so if we get the full eighty-five each sitting, well, we'll make a tidy profit, both the regulars and Tony. The restaurant is always crowded on Friday nights anyway, and the town's so small that we don't have to worry about advertising too much. We're pretty much relying on a sign out front, and Tabby, of course. Although there are a few sticking points still to be worked out."

"You certainly have had a busy day while I was out researching. But you said there are a few sticking points still to settle? Such as?" Quinn asked, truly amazed at Shelby's mind, how it worked, how she just stepped in, took over, and did it in such a way that even a crusty curmudgeon like Tony became putty in her hands.

"Well, for one, I told Tony that he really should consider renting real table linens for the event. You know, table-cloths and, most especially, cloth napkins. I told him cloth napkins make a *statement*. I told him that paper napkins also made a statement, but then—"

"But then who'd listen to anything they said?" Quinn finished for her, laughing.

"Yes! How did you know?"

Quinn coughed into his hand. "Just call it a lucky guess," he said, wanting to hold her, kiss her, love her. She was so innocent, for all her Main Line sophistication. "So did Tony cave?"

"If you mean are we having real linens, then yes, he did," Shelby said smugly. "Although I'll admit to less success with the regulars. I had thought black tie would be nice. . . ."

"Black tie? The regulars?" All his earlier thoughts about the regulars came rushing back. "You're kidding, right?"

Shelby could feel her cheeks flushing. She had been so nice to the regulars, and they had been so nice to her. Hardly the sort of men who would send an anonymous note to her, trying to frighten her into leaving East Wapaneken. But if not them, who? That thought had rattled Shelby badly, so that she had dived into the planning of the charity dinner headfirst, putting the memory of the note into a drawer in her mind, then locking it.

"They did show me the error of my thinking," she said at last, beginning to see the humor in the situation as she remembered the horrified looks on the faces of the regulars when she had first broached her ideas on formal dress. "They said they couldn't possibly afford to rent formal wear *and* buy tickets to the dinner. And, as Tony doesn't have a liquor license but patrons are allowed to bring liquor in with them, they said they really thought it would be better if, instead of black tie, the dinners be two keg affairs. They've very simple tastes, the regulars."

"That's a pity, actually," Quinn told her, finishing his beer and putting it down on a coaster. "I think I would have paid double to see George in a starched stand-up collar. So when's the party?"

She was back to avoiding his eyes, playing with the wrinkle in her skirt. "Because we're always busy then, we scheduled it for this Friday night," she told him, knowing that the party would also mark her last night in East Wapaneken.

She had to go home.

Somerton had been wonderful, not calling out the National Guard or whatever to find her, but Thelma was coming back after seeing her new grandchild, she'd have no job, and it really was time she went home. She'd wanted three weeks, maybe four. She'd have less than two. She'd only have a few more days in East Wapanekan, a few more days with Quinn.

She was going home.

Right after she found a way to settle Brandy and Gary once and for all.

Right after the fund-raiser, which she would then supplement with an anonymous monetary gift once she had access to her money once more.

Right after she made love with Quinn Delaney for the first and last time, told Quinn Delaney the truth, and then returned to Philadelphia to tell Parker that she could never marry him before locking herself in her rooms and crying for a month.

Unless she told Quinn now, tonight? She glanced at him out of the corner of her eye, considering this idea.

What could she tell him? That she was a fairly consider-able heiress out on a spree and she had decided that going to bed with him would just be the icing on the cake of her adventure?

Hardly.

Could she tell him about the note? Tell him that she had been worried that the regulars had sent it, but that she'd soon seen the ridiculousness of that assumption?

Could she tell him that, instead of the regulars, she had a feeling there was someone in East Wapaneken who somehow knew who she was, and that the first letter would be followed by another, probably demanding an outra-geous sum of money to keep silent?

Could she tell him that she thought she was falling in love with him, really in love with him, and that she couldn't *make* love to him until she told him the truth?

And chance him telling her to get out, never darken his door again . . . and never know what it was like to be held in his arms?

"Shelley? Earth to Shelley; come in, Shelley."

"Um, what? Oh, I'm sorry. I was woolgathering, wasn't I? Did you say something?"

"I just asked if there was something wrong, something you might want to tell me?" And that, Quinn knew, was true enough, as she might have been debating with herself as to whether she wanted to tell him about the note. But the moment the words were out of his mouth, he knew he'd made a mistake, as she stiffened beside him, her hands twisting together in her lap.

He reached over with both hands, taking hers in his, lifting them, one after the other, to his mouth. "We proba-bly shouldn't be talking, should we?" he asked, looking deeply into her expressive brown eyes. Those eyes that would haunt him to his grave, those eyes he never wanted to see looking vacant and expressionless again.

"Probably . . . probably not," she said quietly, her breathing suddenly uneven. Scarlett O'Hara had the right idea. She'd think about everything else tomorrow. But tonight . . . tonight the last thing she wanted to do was think.

He took her into his arms, moving slowly so as not to frighten her, for he instinctively knew that this was a woman who might have been taken to bed before now, but who had never really been made love to the way she deserved.

"Are you sure?" he whispered, his mouth inches from hers, her eyes already fluttering closed. Which was stupid, because if she said no now he'd have to go somewhere and kill himself for asking such a potentially dangerous question.

In answer, Shelby lifted a hand to his face, cupped his cheek, allowed her lips to curve upward in a small smile. A welcoming touch. A tremulous, welcoming smile.

He felt like a louse, making love to a woman who had no idea who he was, what he was. Ethics and fair play and his guilty conscience and all that sort of thing rose up in his mind, protesting. He told them all to go to hell.

There was a small explosion as their lips met, as their bodies melded together, as he slid his arms beneath her and picked her up and carried her into the bedroom on legs that were not quite steady.

Somehow the pins were out of her hair, so that its sleek blond beauty fanned out around her head on the flowered quilt. He would have undressed, except that he couldn't leave her, couldn't chance leaving her. So he followed her down onto the mattress, keeping his arms around her, kissing her again and again and again.

He had never tasted a mouth so sweet, felt a body so soft and pliant as hers. So yielding. So giving. And yet demanding everything of him. Everything and more . . .

Somehow their clothing disappeared, piece by tantalizing piece, until they lay there naked, pressed together from chest to knee, still kissing each other even as their bodies learned each other, as their hands traveled, explored. Found.

"You're so beautiful," he whispered against her ear as he tried to control his breathing, give her yet another chance to tell him they had gone far enough and she didn't want to go further.

"Love me," was all she answered, rather inexpertly but very provocatively pushing her hips against his. "Please."

Shelby kept her eyes closed as she heard herself plead with Quinn, as part of her became mortified as it stood back, watched her, told her that impulsive actions always had their punishment. But there was another part of her, newly discovered and already heady with desire, that was much more powerful in its arguments: *Take what you want now, while you can. Take it all. You deserve this. You* need *this.*

She felt his lips against her throat, on her breast. Taking her nipple into his mouth, laving it with his tongue.

Sensations she couldn't describe, had never felt before, exploded in small bursts from her skin, trailing all the way to her belly and beyond, creating a warmth, a softness, a burning need that could not be ignored.

She held him close against her, ran her hands through his night dark hair, learned the muscles of his back with her fingertips. Taking, taking, while she gave and gave, while his hands in turn found her center, brought her to the brink of something wonderful, some strange mystery she had to know or die in the trying.

Quinn knew she was ready for him, more than ready. Her soft, throaty moans had nearly driven him over the brink minutes ago, and it was only his firm promise to himself that she would know the fullness of completion that had kept him from driving himself into her, finding a release that he knew would be more than he had ever experienced, ever dreamed.

With one hand he somehow prepared himself, protected her, even as she moaned again, her eyes still closed, blindly trying to pull him down to her. Then he inserted a knee between her thighs, leaned down to kiss her as he levered himself completely on top of her and settled himself between her legs.

The small explosion on the couch faded into memory as the entire world exploded, imploded, burst into flame, shattered into a million pieces, raced through the universe at twice the speed of light. Everything. Loving Shelby was everything, all, the entirety of experience.

He plunged deep, and she answered him with a movement of her own. He slid his tongue into her mouth, and she began a duel with her own tongue, mimicking the thrust and withdrawal of their bodies. A lump of raw emotion formed in his throat, a sensation so alien, so fraught with thoughts of protecting, and loving, and forever, that he knew he was a goner, that he could never, ever walk away from this woman.

"Love me, please," Shelby sighed into his mouth.

And he did. Oh, God help him; God help them both. He did. . . .

Chapter Twenty-five

Shelby wandered into the apartment a little before midnight, still rather dreamy-eyed, having been loved by Quinn not once but twice, their second union so slow and languid, so explosive at its ending . . .

"So tell me something," Brandy said from her curled-up position on the couch. "If Snapple got into really big money trouble, as I think they were a while ago, could you buy them? I mean, you like their iced tea a lot. Are you *that* rich?"

"Gosh, I don't know," Shelby answered, then headed for the kitchen and a bottle of iced tea, since Brandy had reminded her that she was thirsty. And hungry. She picked up a pack of Tastykake chocolate cupcakes, too, on her way back into the living room. "How much money would it take? Because you're right; I really do like this stuff. But it would be a toss-up, if Tastykake was ever in trouble, because I don't think I could live without their chocolate cupcakes." She collapsed onto the couch. "And I thought

I knew so much. Brandy, how did I ever exist for twenty-five years without Snapple and Tastykakes?''

"I can't survive without them for ten minutes, and have the body to prove it," Brandy said, drinking from her own bottle as she eyed her friend. "Gonna buy stock?"

Shelby lowered her head, blushing. "I should take control of my own money, shouldn't I? I never really gave it much thought before, as there's always been somebody to do it for me. But, yes, definitely, and if just for self-protection, I promise to buy stock in both companies. Happy now?"

"Getting there," Brandy said, grinning. "So now that I have you all relaxed and off guard and everything—am I guessing right that you've just come from Quinn's apartment, where you have been well and truly made love to for, oh, two or three hours?"

"Brandy!"

Brandy readjusted her legs under her, pulling down the pink-and-yellow-flowered nightie to cover her dimpled knees. "What? Are we friends or aren't we? You know darn well what I was doing tonight, right? Now, fair's fair. How was it?"

Shelby let her head drop against the couch pillows and closed her eyes. "It was . . . it was *wonderful.* More than I'd ever hoped, more than I'd ever imagined possible." She lifted her head and turned to look at a grinning Brandy. "I think I love him, Brandy. Isn't that wonderful?" She blinked back sudden tears. "And terrible."

Scratching at her temple, Brandy winced a little as she considered Shelby's dilemma. "Because you haven't told him the truth, right?"

Shelby sighed and nodded. "Being rich is such a *trial.*"

"Yeah," Brandy agreed sarcastically. "I can't imagine how terrible it must be never to have to go to work, never to have to worry. Traveling, eating the best foods, shopping without looking at price tags. A real killer.''

''You'd get tired of it, Brandy,'' Shelby said, rolling her head to the side as she lay against the back of the couch, pulling a fringed silk pillow with the words *Love is Better in Atlantic City* crocheted on one side.

''I suppose so, sweetcakes—in about, oh, fifty or eighty years. But I definitely could hack it that long. I could even buy Mama a palace in Spain, or Katmandu, or maybe even Hawaii. Yeah, Hawaii. I've never really wanted to go to Hawaii. Spain or Katmandu hold some appeal.''

''You're crazy,'' Shelby said on a giggle, squeezing the pillow to her, still able to feel Quinn's arms around her, the warmth of his last, lingering kiss as he'd walked her across the hall, said his good nights.

''And you've really got a problem, don't you?'' Brandy said, looking at Shelby carefully. ''Do you love him? I mean, if you don't love him, then there's not much of a problem. But I can't see you climbing into the sack with anyone you didn't love. Not because you're rich, but because you're such a . . . such a *lady*. Hmmm, guess I answered my own question. You love him.''

''I love him,'' Shelby agreed quietly. ''Brandy, do you suppose there really *are* happy endings?''

''Ha! Look who you're talking to, sweetcakes. I've been engaged to Gary and his mama for twelve years now. I'm lucky to get a happy *middle*, yet alone a happy ending.''

Brandy's only half-joking remark lingered in Shelby's brain overnight, and she was almost glad when Quinn didn't show up at Tony's for the breakfast she'd shared with her friend before Brandy caught her bus and Shelby walked back to the apartment alone.

She was crossing the alleyway between the two long

blocks separating Tony's and the apartment building when, seemingly out of nowhere, a car screeched to a stop beside her.

There were two men inside, both strangers to Shelby, and the passenger jumped out, then approached her at a run. He took hold of her arm and tried to pull her over to the open back door of the sedan.

"Fire!" Shelby screamed, quickly figuring that would get more attention than simply screaming. Still, she followed that shout with a scream anyway, the one she'd learned during that weekend retreat of her college sorority, the one where they had been taught some simple self-defense.

Somehow the lessons came back to her. *Tell the aggressor that you will* not *be a victim. Tell him, and yourself, by shouting "no" as loudly, as forcefully as you can.*

"No!" she cried out, as loud as possible. *"NO!"* She grabbed at the fingers holding tight to her forearm and began pulling back the man's thumb, trying to break his hold, trying to hurt him enough that he would let go of her.

"Hey!" the man yelped, letting go, only to grab at her with his other hand. "That hurt."

"Good!" Shelby declared, following up her thumb bending with a quick, sharp kick to the man's shins, making him yelp once again.

She'd never know, and didn't care to know, if she would have been able to keep fighting until the man gave up, because just then Quinn came running down the street, his wash basket flung onto someone's lawn, his face a mask of blackest fury.

"Get in! Get in! He's coming!" the driver called out, and Shelby's attacker looked up the pavement, then said something strange: "About damn time." He threw himself into the car and it sped off just as Quinn reached her.

"Pennsylvania plate, partial reading, Adam, thirty-eight-something. Tan Toyota sedan, 1999. Probably a rental," Quinn said quickly as he skidded to a halt, mostly to himself, and almost, to Shelby's mind, as if he was accustomed to quickly committing such information to memory.

Then she was in Quinn's arms, and he was asking her if she was all right, was she hurt, had she recognized the man who'd tried to kidnap her.

"Kid—*kidnap* me?" Shelby pushed herself out of his arms, looking up into his face in delayed shock. "Is that what happened? Someone was trying to kidnap me? Why?"

Quinn knew one possible answer to that question.

Shelby knew the same possible, probable answer to that question.

That answer had a *lot* of zeros behind it.

But neither of them said so out loud.

"I don't know, Shelley," he lied quickly. "But I'm going to call this in to the police. Maybe there's even been a rash of attempted abductions in the area. I haven't seen anything in the paper, but sometimes the cops keep stuff like this hushed up so as not to scare the bejesus out of everyone. I got a partial on the license plate, though, and that could help."

"I . . . I suppose so," Shelby said, and then she noticed that she'd begun to shake, to shiver. Her teeth were actually rattling. She'd almost been kidnapped, Parker's worst fear! She had fought, just as she'd always told herself she would fight, never give in, never just say "please, don't," and let something terrible happen to her.

But she had touched him. Felt his hot, sour breath next to her head. Bent his thumb. Kicked him. *God!* Had she really done all of that? And what would have happened if Quinn hadn't shown up when he did? "I think . . . I think I'd like to sit down now."

Quinn put his arm around her waist, turning her toward the apartment, but she resisted.

"No, I'd like to sit down *now*," she said, and collapsed on the curb running along the corner of the alley. She felt Quinn put his hand on the back of her neck, push her head between her knees.

"Slow, deep breaths, sweetheart," he told her. "In through the nose, out through the mouth. And don't close your eyes or you'll get dizzier."

"Too . . . too late for that advice, I'm afraid. Sorry," she heard herself mumble as the lights behind her eyelids exploded a time or two in rather dazzling fireworks, right before her entire world went dark.

She resurfaced a while later, to find herself lying on the couch in Brandy's apartment and wondering what happened, how she had gotten there. Looking up, wincing as her stomach tried to revolt, she saw Quinn standing over her, the apartment key in his hand. She touched a hand to her skirt pocket, realized that he was holding her own key, and then wondered why she wasn't quite as thrilled to see Quinn as she'd been as she fought off her abductor.

And then she remembered.

"Get in! Get in! He's coming!"

"About damn time."

The men had *known* Quinn? Recognized him? And what did that mean: *"About damn time?"* It was almost as if they'd been expecting him, and he'd been late. But late for what? To help them kidnap her, or to pretend to save her?

"I—I think I'd like a glass of water, please," she said, averting her eyes from his concerned face. If that *was* a truly concerned face. How could she know, how could she tell? Could she say he was honest and true because he had taken her to bed? Lord, that was what all the silly, inane victims said. . . .

"Here you go," Quinn said, returning from the kitchen with half a glass of water, then lifting her head so that she could sip it. "You went in and out a couple of times, you know, not that I objected to carrying you home. Although I'd better go back and pick up my laundry, I suppose."

"Your . . . ? Oh. Oh, yes, I remember now. You were at the Laundromat, weren't you? You weren't at breakfast." She sat up against the pillows. "Why don't you go get your laundry, then, before somebody else does?"

"I already phoned the police, Shelley," he told her, "and since I saw everything you saw, he said it was all right if I just came down to the station later to give him a report. Unless you want to talk to him? Recognized either of them or could describe them?"

She shook her head, then regretted it, as now she had one killer of a headache. "I've never fainted before," she said, looking up at him, wishing she knew him, really *knew* him. "That's what I did, isn't it? Fainted?"

Quinn smiled at her. "You went out like the proverbial light, honey," he told her. "But you were very ladylike about it, even apologizing before you suddenly sort of slid into my arms. I rather like that part," he said, bending down to kiss the tip of her nose. "Me and my Hanes will be right back, okay?"

"Okay," she told him, smiling weakly. She watched him go to the door, and saw the stack of mail he must have put on the table. Once he was gone, she stood up— slowly—and walked across the room to gather up the mail. Two magazines, the telephone bill, a credit card bill, three pieces of obvious junk mail.

No letter addressed to her in block letters. She didn't know if that was good or bad. If one letter had been the first warning; if the near abduction this morning had been the second . . . ?

What on earth would be the third?

How she longed to tell Quinn. But what would she tell him? Could she tell him that the man seemed to recognize him, seemed to have been waiting for him to make an appearance? Because, now that she thought about it, really thought about it, she realized that she probably wasn't quite the master of self-defense she initially thought herself to be. That man could have had her into the car if he'd really wanted to.

Had he really wanted to kidnap her? Or had he been told just to frighten her?

And why?

She carefully put the mail back down the way Quinn had placed it, and returned to the couch. And thought . . .

Quinn had certainly shown up in East Wapaneken very opportunely, hadn't he? Had it just been coincidence that they both had come to town within a day of each other? Or had it somehow gotten out that Shelby Taite, the heiress, was on the run, out in the world, unprotected?

Somerton, now that she thought about it, had been rather quiet for someone who would rather see his sister locked in the velvet cage of marriage to Parker than out on her own, trying her wings. He'd shown that by cutting off her access to money, hadn't he?

But what else would he have done? If she, in his place, had learned that he had run off to find himself or have an adventure or whatever, what would she do?

"I wouldn't cut off his money," she grumbled to herself. "That was mean."

She took a sip of water and thought some more. She would not go to the police. She knew that. After all, Somerton was of age, wasn't he? He could go where he wanted, when he wanted. Certainly it wasn't a matter for the police.

But would she have left it at that? Just wished him well and hoped that he had a marvelous time and came home happy?

No. No, she wouldn't. Not Somerton, whom she loved dearly but believed to be about as capable of living in the real world as Princess would be able to survive in a real jungle. She closed her eyes and sighed. So she would have done *something*. Definitely. She would have phoned D & S Security and asked them to find him, that was what she would have done. Not to haul him home like some truant, but just to find him, tell her he was all right.

And then possibly watch him until he got whatever he wanted out of his system and come home.

That was what she would have done.

And then, like a quarter dropping into one of those bubble gum machines that sent the colored gum ball round and round down a clear spiral chute to land at the bottom, a proverbial gum ball dropped inside Shelby's brain and she balled her hands into fists and beat them against her knees.

She remembered the slightly mocking smile, the lift of a dark eyebrow. Her embarrassment as she had brushed past him, without really looking at him, without allowing herself to recognize him. He'd been a one-night replacement for Grady Sullivan, not worth more than a glance as she spent yet another evening in misery, wishing herself home and in bed. Anywhere but where she was.

Grady Sullivan. Quinn Delaney. D & S. Somerton always demanded one of the partners. It was all so obvious now.

"Delaney!" she gritted out from between clenched teeth. "D and S. It wasn't a coincidence," she said, her bottom lip beginning to tremble. "And you're not the man of my dreams. That's not why you seemed familiar to me. Damn you, Somerton, and damn you, Quinn Delaney. And damn me for a fool for not recognizing you, not paying attention to names, faces. You're my bodyguard. Damn you to hell, Quinn, you're my *bodyguard.*"

Tears running down her cheeks, she jumped up and went to turn the dead bolt so that Quinn couldn't just march back into the apartment as though he belonged there or something. She heard the bolt click into place just as Quinn turned the door handle.

"Shelley? Are you all right in there?"

She had to stay cool, calm, not give herself away. Not until she knew what she was going to do next. "I—I'm fine, fine. I just thought I should lock the dead bolt," she called through the closed door. "We're . . . we're just not as security conscious as we should be in East Wapaneken, don't you think? Many days Brandy doesn't lock the door at all. Isn't that silly?"

She bit her lips together between her teeth as she realized she was babbling. So she took a deep breath, closed her eyes, and said, "Thank you, Quinn, if I haven't already said it. Thank you so much. But I really want to be alone for a while, if you don't mind. Take a long bath, get the feel of that man's hands off me."

"Okay," he said after a moment, his tone more inquiring than agreeable. "Do you want me to go tell Tony you won't be in today? I'm sure he'd under—"

"No!" Shelby winced. "I mean, no, thank you. I really think I'd feel better if I were working, rather than just sitting here thinking. I'll see you later?"

There was another pause, during which time Shelby wondered wildly if he was contemplating breaking down the door, before Quinn said, "I'll see you for lunch, as always. And you have a free day tomorrow, remember? Maybe we can go on a picnic or something?"

"Or something," she said, then closed her eyes and leaned against the door, waiting to hear the sound of his door closing on the other side of the hallway.

"Damn, damn, damn," she muttered as she raced through the living room, stripping off her clothes as she went. Everything was falling into place, even as it all fell apart. Everything was suddenly making sense.

Quinn had been sent to find her, then stay and protect her.

While she had her little "fling."

"Does he get a bonus for being a *part* of that fling?" she asked herself as she turned on the taps and poured bath salts into the tub. "How would he write that up on his expense sheet? How much would he charge, for crying out loud!"

But you had to hand it to the guy. He really knew how to go that extra mile for his client.

He'd gotten himself an apartment right across the hall. *The better to watch you, my dear.*

She'd so wanted to be out on her own for a while, just living her life like other people, *normal* people. But she'd never been alone, not really. Never been on her own, not since that first day. Without knowing it, she'd had a safety net all along, someone close by, watching, waiting for her to stumble, ready to pick her up if she did.

Bodyguard. Babysitter.

Same thing.

He'd made up a story about being a writer—a writer, ha!—so that he had a reason to be free all day, free to sit at Tony's and watch her. Always watching her.

He was so damn good at his job that he'd fooled Brandy and Gary into having him tag along for dinner. They'd even set him up with her, on a sort of blind date.

Well, Shelby now knew who the blind one had been in that scenario, didn't she?

And the threatening letter. And that clumsy, failed abduction. The police didn't need to talk to her? No wonder, as Quinn most probably hadn't *told* them about it.

It was all so clear to her now. So horribly transparent. Quinn had sent the letter. Quinn had arranged the sloppy kidnap attempt, and all to scare her into packing up and going home, going back to being sweet, obedient, stifled Shelby.

"What's the matter, Quinn, are you that bored here in East Wapaneken? Are you that bored with *me?* Were my kisses that repugnant? Was I that much of a disappointment to you in bed?"

She pressed a hand to her mouth, holding back the sob that had risen in her throat, tamping down the hysteria that threatened to overcome her.

"You took me to bed," she said, rubbing at the tears that wouldn't stop falling. "How could you have done that, Quinn? How could you have *done* that?"

Chapter Twenty-six

IF YOU WILL NOT LISTEN YOU CAN BE SHOWN.
LEAVE NOW.

Quinn read the note he'd lifted from Shelby's pile of mail and stuffed into his pocket before putting the rest on the table, before Shelby could discover it, be frightened by it. Then he crumpled the single page and threw it in the general direction of his makeshift desk.

"Stupid, melodramatic crap!" He exploded as he collapsed onto the couch, grabbed his chin in his fist, and rubbed at the morning beard he hadn't gotten around to shaving yet today.

"Dangerous crap," he added, thinking out loud. He looked at the phone sitting in front of him, its cord dragging across the carpet from its anchor on the wall beside his desk. He'd been looking at the phone for nearly an hour, thinking, rethinking, knowing he needed help, reluctant to ask for it.

Grady would insist he take Shelby home now. Today. That was practical, logical. He would point out, as Quinn already knew, that his first responsibility to the client was to keep her safe, period. Letting Shelby walk around East Wapaneken after two threatening letters and one obviously halfhearted abduction? That was contrary to everything he knew to be right, knew to be ethical. Especially as he was there, on the spot, and could have her out of harm's way in an hour, back behind the sturdy iron gates of the Taite mansion.

That was the professional side of him.

The human side of him was thinking something else entirely.

The human side of him told him that he was falling in love with Shelby. Hell, he *was* in love with her.

How strange. She certainly wasn't the woman of his dreams, far from it. His single brush, in college, with what he imagined to be real love had ended in heartbreak when Barbara's daddy had offered him twenty-five thousand dollars to leave town.

That was what dealing with the superrich got you: a warm smile, a hearty handshake, and a warning that while he might be a real nice guy, he wasn't one of *them*. He wouldn't fit in, wouldn't be given the chance to try. So thank you very much for escorting our Barbara home from college, and good-bye.

Now, looking back on that time with older eyes, with more experience under his belt, Quinn knew that Barbara had never loved him. She couldn't have loved him; otherwise she would have disobeyed her father, eloped with Quinn to Maryland, and the devil with all that money.

Yeah, right. All he'd asked of her was to give up her family, her home, her cushy existence, her country club, her future, to take on a college sophomore with five hundred bucks in the bank and five thousand dollars' worth of student loans. Oh, and no job, only a vague idea that he might want to practice law. Or become a policeman.

That was what had really put Barb's father over the top. His son-in-law, a cop? Quinn hadn't even flinched when the man heard that, then upped the bribe to thirty thousand, even.

Still, although his love for Barbara had faded, to be replaced by a tough shell around his heart that had lasted for a long, long time, he had at last forgiven her. He'd asked her to give up too much, for too little return on her investment.

What rankled, what still got under his skin and itched like hell, was that the rich thought they could buy their way in or out of anything. Any problem, any trouble, any situation. He'd seen that during his years as a cop, too, when he'd been a lowly patrolman on the beat and was either offered money not to write a ticket or warned that the speeder knew the mayor of Philadelphia personally.

By the time he'd been promoted to Robbery and Homicide, his dislike of the rich had been firmly ingrained, with nothing he'd seen or heard changing his mind. Three years in Robbery and Homicide had been the clincher. The rich *were* different. They could buy a better brand of justice, and they could buy their way out of trouble that would have put a poor man's son behind bars.

It was one of the reasons he'd left the force when Grady had asked him to go into partnership with him, probably the driving reason. Sure, Grady was rich. Rolling in it. But Grady, Quinn believed, was the exception that proved the rule when it came to the Rich and Repulsive.

So what was he doing now, sitting here like some damn dumb jackass, hip-deep in love with one of them?

He picked up the phone, punched in the numbers, and waited for Maisie to go through her welcoming spiel.

"How are you doing, sweetheart?" he asked her. "Please tell me we aren't tending giraffes this week, or standing guard on the hospital book sale."

"Ah, honey, you know I wouldn't let you boys do that," the receptionist said, laughing. "But did you know that a giraffe's tongue is about a foot long? Gives you something to think about, doesn't it?"

"Not sober," Quinn answered, grinning into the phone. Leave it to Maisie to cheer him up, at least temporarily. "So what else is new?"

"Well, honey, let's see, shall we? Grady landed a new client, which means Burns and Arquette are off to Saudi Arabia this week."

Quinn raised his eyebrows. "Saudi Arabia? Not too shabby."

"If you like heat, oil, and sand, I suppose not, honey. Oh, and Selma quit. She says she can't possibly come back to work and leave her sweet little baby boy in day care."

"What? Selma? My secretary? Great. Now what am I going to do?"

"Well, honey, for one, I bought her a baby gift and signed your name to the card. You forgot that, you know. Probably because you don't have Selma around to do that stuff for you. And two, you can try not to laugh when you see Selma's pictures of little Zachary Semple. Honey, last time I saw ears like that, they were on a cocker spaniel. You want me to connect you with Grady?"

Shaking his head, caught between regret that Selma had left him and trying not to laugh at Maisie's description of the Semple heir, he told her that, yes, he did want to speak to Grady.

A moment later his partner was on the line. "Sullivan's Security and Dating Service," Grady said into the receiver after Maisie told him who was on the line. "Rent a security stud, and make your life a better place. How may we help you?"

"Swallowing your tongue works for me," Quinn shot back. "Listen, I've got a bit of a situation here, nothing I want to go into on the phone, but I need your help."

He could hear the front legs of Grady's chair hit the floor, and pictured his partner losing his smile as he picked up a pen and searched his desk for a piece of scrap paper. "Go ahead; I'm ready."

"I need you to track down a license plate for me and I've only got a partial. Pennsylvania license. I'm betting it's a rental, but we have to check it out, okay?"

After he told Grady the partial, and the make and model of the car, he sat back on the couch, waiting for his friend to start grilling him. Surprisingly, Grady just said, "Anything else?"

"Yeah," Quinn said, closing his eyes. "And this is going to be sticky, and pretty illegal, I suppose. I want you to do a full work-up on Parker Westbrook the Third."

"You're kidding, right?"

"Wrong. From the cradle until next month, and everything in between. I want full financial records, what he eats, who he sleeps with, who he talks to—in person and on the phone, including his cell phone. Rumors, innuendo, personal opinions, anything you can ferret out of anybody. Use all your hotshot connections at the country club for the gossip. A to Z, Grady, soup to nuts, whatever you want to call it, and all off the record, with no way to trace any of it to us. How long will it take?"

Grady, who had been scribbling on the scrap paper, quickly committed the partial license plate to memory, then fed the paper into the shredder he kept under his desk. "You couldn't have asked me to sneak into the Oval Office in Washington and plant a 'Kilroy Was Here' sign,

could you, or anything else that has to be easier than
breaking the thick green wall of silence that holds the
Main Line together? What's up? This sounds important.
Quinn Delaney doesn't ask for just this side—and maybe
the other side—of legal unless it's important. Is our gal
safe?"

"She's safe," Quinn assured him, looking across the
room at the door to the hallway. "Never out of my sight.
And I don't want to go into it any more than I already
have, Grady. I'm just scratching an itch, playing a hunch."

"Uh-oh," Grady said. "Last time you did that you ended
up on the wrong side of a thirty-eight and your mom made
you promise to get out of the field once and for all and
shuffle paper. Your leg still give you hell when it rains?"

Remembering all too well the day he'd had to disarm a
loyal follower of some obscure religion as he planned to
save the world by killing the rock star he'd been guarding,
he began absently rubbing at his left thigh, the site of his
wound. "No," he answered lightly, "but it throbs like hell
in warning every time you tell me I'm going to have a
simple assignment because you have a hot date and need
me to fill in."

"Yeah, like you're hating every minute of this," Grady
replied, laughing. Then he became serious again. "Give
me three days before you call again, and call me at home,
all right? That's for the easy stuff, like tracing a partial
license plate without first asking 'Mother may I.' The rest
is going to take longer, if you're looking for what I think
you're looking for. It's always harder to find buried stuff,
and these people really know how to burrow in deep."

Quinn heard Shelby's door open and close, looked at
his wristwatch, and swore. "Damn it, I've got to go. No
more than a week, Grady, okay?"

He pulled on his sneakers and managed to catch up
with Shelby by the time she'd reached the pavement, then

turned and headed toward Tony's. "How are you doing?" he asked, falling into step beside her.

"Did you go to the police station?" she asked, looking at him levelly with a lack of expression in her eyes that he'd hoped never to see again. "What did the officer say?"

He hadn't gone to the police. Going to the police would only muddy the waters. He knew that. Hell, Shelby knew that, considering she was trying to keep her identity a secret. Was that it? She was worried about the police? "Nothing much, just that he'd have the part-time officer make more drive-bys for the next couple of days. In the meantime he asked us not to say anything to anybody, that it was probably an isolated incident. I take it he doesn't want to alarm the populace."

He was such a good liar. So believable. She would have believed him without a doubt, if she didn't know what she knew. Shelby nodded and kept walking. That amazed her. That she could still put one foot in front of the other. Still move, still function. Even with her heart, and her trust, broken into small, jagged pieces.

"I won't tell anyone," she promised. "Not even Brandy. Especially Brandy, I suppose. She'd just be upset."

That, Shelby knew, was also true. Brandy would be upset, more than upset. She'd probably want her to call Somerton at once, have some armed guard come to escort her home. And that was the last thing Shelby wanted to do.

She was not going to run. Taites didn't run. They probably never *had* to run, but that was beside the point. Shelby Taite was going to stand her ground, right up until the moment she had decided to leave. Nobody, not threatening letter writers, not halfhearted abductors, not nosy bodyguards—not even her own unhappiness—was going to make her turn tail and run.

Not until she'd figured out a way to prove her supposi-

tions about Quinn. And make him hurt for them. Make
him hurt *real* bad.

With that in mind, and knowing now that he was a
professional, and probably not all that easy to fool, she
pinned a bright smile on her face and said, "Tell me more
about that picnic you spoke of earlier. It sounds like fun."

Quinn scratched at a sudden itch at the back of his neck.
Why were his antennae quivering? What in the hell was
going on? Shelby was acting as if the near-abduction was
nothing more than a very forgettable incident. She hadn't
cried on his shoulder or told him about the threatening
note. She hadn't asked for his help, or broken down and
confessed her true identity.

She'd done none of that, and yet now her mouth smiled
and her brown eyes remained blank, shuttered, like the
woman he'd first met the night of the charity ball. She
was looking at him, but she wasn't seeing him. Wasn't
connecting with him, not on any level.

Could she know? Could the incident this morning have
somehow jogged her memory, brought his face and name
together and let her come up with D & S?

No. That was impossible. If she hadn't recognized him
by now, she wouldn't have had some startling revelation
this morning because she'd been put into danger, had
automatically thought about how she usually didn't travel
anywhere out of her circle without someone from D & S
along, usually Grady.

And just that one time, him . . .

He stepped in front of Shelby and opened the door to
Tony's, motioned for her to precede him into the restaurant. "It's only eleven-thirty, half an hour until your shift
starts. You were planning an early lunch, weren't you?"

"Yes," she answered, glancing at the handwritten "Specials" board and frowning. *"Potatoe* soup? With an E? I
guess Tabby's running for president," she said with an

attempt at humor. "I talked Tony into adding two low-fat, low-calorie salads to the luncheon menu and I'd like to try one, as this is the first day. Do you care to join me?"

"For lunch, but not for the salad," Quinn replied honestly. "I think I'm forever hooked on fat, grease, starch, cholesterol, and those slightly burned onions Tony mixes in with his steak sandwiches. Are any of those part of the basic food groups?"

"Only if you harbor a death wish," Shelby told him, still outwardly happy, in control, still smiling. Still showing him those sad, empty eyes.

While she hunted for an eraser to fix the "Specials" board, Quinn walked around the dividing wall and over to the corner, taking up his position at his usual table, waving to four of the regulars on his way.

"Hey, Delaney. Good," George called to him. "C'mere a minute, would ya?"

Rising once more, he joined George and the others in their corner booth, sitting on the chair that always stood on the opposite side of the table, in case Tony wanted to sit down, have a chat. "What's up, guys?" he asked, motioning to the papers scattered all over the table along with four cups and two white thermal carafes. The regulars drank coffee by the gallon, so that Tony found it quicker and easier to charge them by the pot rather than the cup.

"You know about the dinner this Friday, right?" George asked, and Quinn nodded that, yes, he did. "Saw the signs out front? The ones the rest of the guys are putting up all over town?" Quinn nodded again. "Saw the banner Harry hung on the back of his hog?"

"Well, I wouldn't go that far," Quinn acceded, "but it sounds like a great idea. So is there a problem?"

"Yeah, there sure as hell is," George said, dropping his head nearer to his barrel chest, shaking it. "She wants me

to give a speech," he muttered, so that Quinn had to strain
to hear him.

"She? That would be Shelley, right? A speech?"

"Yeah, yeah, yeah, a speech. Didn't I say that?"

"Easy, George," Harry said, patting his friend's arm, the
one with the tattooed anchor and entwined snake on it,
as he looked across the table at Quinn. "I haven't seen
him this bad since his wedding. Passed out, right on the
altar. Took out a Gook sniper's nest without a blink, but
when it came to saying 'I do,' the guy goes down like a
tree. Who'd figure that?"

"Shuddup, Harry," George said, then looked straight
at Quinn. "She says somebody has to say something at
stuff like this. And not just once, neither, but for all three
settings, servings—whatever the hell she's calling them.
So, thinking that you're a writer and all . . ."

Now here was a dilemma. How did that go? Hoist by his
own petard? Maybe. But Quinn decided it was more like
he'd royally screwed himself. He couldn't write a speech.
Hell, he'd only gotten through English Composition in
college because he'd been dating the professor's daughter.
He was a numbers man. Facts, figures, reports. Not
speeches meant to empty somebody's pockets.

"Sure," he said brightly as George watched him through
narrowed eyelids. "Be happy to," he lied. "Are these your
notes?" he asked, picking up the many sheets of paper,
stacking them together.

"Yeah, those are them. Just some stuff about the boys,
you know. The ones who didn't come back. I want you to
do them proud, okay?"

Quinn looked down at the top sheet, which he noticed
thankfully was typed, probably by George's wife, who also
typed the daily menus for Tony. He read aloud, "Bender,
William, age nineteen. Gunner's mate. Missing in action,
in country, since 1971. Played second base for the East

Wapaneken Warriors. Altar boy, Saint Michael's Church.''
So stark, so simple. Yet those few lines said so much.

He looked at the regulars, at their double-chinned faces
with the faintly bulbous noses of men who spent a lot of
time outdoors and the rest of it drinking beer. Looked
into their eyes deeply for the first time, saw that they were
all one hundred years old in experience. Remembered
that, once, they had all been nineteen-year-old boys who
played baseball, maybe sang in church, probably made out
with their girlfriends in the backseat of a souped-up '57
Chevy, and went face-to-face with the horrors of war before
they were old enough to vote.

"I'll take care of it, George," he promised quietly, and
meant it.

"Hey! Come back here! Nobody leaves without paying."

Quinn whirled around, hearing Tabby yell as she
pointed to two boys of about thirteen or fourteen who
were laughing as they headed for the door.

Shelby, still working on the "Specials" board in the
entryway, and probably correcting more of Tabby's rather
inventive spelling, had flattened herself against the closed
door by the time Quinn skidded around the corner, her
arms out, blocking the exit. She looked like a sleek, upscale
version of one of those plush animals plastered spread-
eagle to the window of a car with suction cups, although
he didn't think he'd ever tell her that.

"Out of the way, lady," one of the boys told her, raising
a hand to her.

Big mistake.

Shelby abandoned her spread-arm pose at the door and
took two steps forward, putting her nose-to-nose with the
slight teenager, her chin thrust out, her eyes slitted and
glittering. "Boy, did you ever pick the wrong day to get
me angry," she told him.

And then, as Quinn took hold of the other teenager by

the scruff of his neck, Shelby put out one leg, did something rather strange, clumsy, but vaguely judolike as she
grabbed that upraised arm, and the threatening teenager
was looking up at her from the floor.

"Wow. Cool," the boy Quinn held said admiringly.

Quinn looked past Shelby, through the clear glass door
to the small vestibule, and saw the local police chief oblivi-
ously playing one of the video poker games. "You want
me to alert Barney Fife there, or will you let them go if
they pay for their food?"

"And apologize," Shelby added, still feeling rather
pleased with herself, even as she knew she was also very
much surprised at what she'd done. Twice in one day, for
goodness' sake. "In writing," she added when the boy on
the floor groaned. "An essay, as a matter of fact, on why
honesty is important."

"And safer," Quinn added, grinning.

With a little grumbling, and some halfhearted attempts
at swagger—hard to do in wide-legged jeans that dragged
two inches on the ground—the boys paid their bill and
promised to deliver their essays by Friday.

"And we know who you are," Quinn called after them,
just to remind them that he'd make sure the essays were in
on time. They stopped in their tracks and turned around,
shoulders hunched.

"We do?" Shelby asked, confused.

"Oh, yeah, Shelley, we do. Just listen." He lifted his
head, raised his voice, and called out over the partition,
"Anybody in here know those two kids?"

There came a definitive chorus of "I dos" that would
have done one of those large group weddings proud.

Quinn grinned as the boys' faces blanched. "See you
boys Friday," he said, and then laughed as the two turned
and ran. Quinn still didn't know where they lived, but that
didn't matter. Everyone knew everyone in East Wapa-

neken, and the boys' mothers would probably hear about their sons' little escapade before dinner was on the table tonight.

Once Shelby had closed the cash register her shoulders slumped and Quinn could hear her take a shuddering breath. He put his arms on her shoulders and turned her around to look at him. "Hey, you're a hero. Why are you crying?"

"I don't know," Shelby answered honestly. "But I think you were right. I can't work today. Those boys . . . I guess they were the icing on the cake or something. But I want to go back to the apartment."

Quinn fought the urge to gather her in his arms, knowing that her few tears could turn into a real gusher if he did so here in the restaurant. She was strong, damn strong, but she'd finally had enough, finally given in. "Done and done," he said bracingly instead, and went to tell Tabby she was in charge until Tony could get someone else to take over.

"Sure, you bet," Tabby said, balancing three platters on her left arm. "He'll probably get one of his church ladies to help," she added, referring to the older women who ate nearly every meal at the restaurant and often helped at private parties in the back room. "Better get Shelley home, though," she added, gesturing toward Shelby with a flip of her head. "She looks like she's about to lose her breakfast."

Shelby let him keep his arm around her waist all the way back to the apartment. Let her head rest against him as they walked along. Took his strength and his comfort because she needed them, wanted them, could think of no one else who made her feel so safe, so protected.

Even if she detested him for the lying sneak he was . . .

Chapter Twenty-seven

Shelby rested on the couch, her shoes kicked off and lying on the carpet, and watched as Quinn made her a cup of tea.

He looked so cute, being domestic. Cute, and a louse. Domestic, and a liar. Caring and loving and incredibly sweet. And a lying, no-good son of a—

"Two sugars, right?" Quinn asked, placing a small black plastic tray with *Loving is better in Maryland* painted on it in vibrant pink lettering on the coffee table. Brandy and Gary seemed to have tried loving in quite a few places. "And I have toast in the toaster. I figure you should eat, but nothing heavy, all right?"

And, crazily, Shelby found herself apologizing. Had she spent her entire life apologizing for not being perfect? Probably, but it was a hard habit to break. "Thank you; that's lovely. I'm so sorry to be such a bother."

Quinn handed her a steaming mug, took the second for himself, and sat down, cross-legged, in front of the couch.

"What in hell are you apologizing for? For nearly being mugged? For stopping two wanna-be punks who tried to stiff Tony? For crying, which is the same as saying for being human? I think you're pretty damn wonderful, if you really want to know."

Shelby felt her spine stiffening. "You're right. I shouldn't be apologizing, should I? All right, I retract that apology, and replace it with just saying thank you very much for being my rescuer today. Twice."

Quinn's smile showed in his eyes, made a physical impact in Shelby's heart. "Yeah, I'm wonderful, too, aren't I? In fact, we're a pair of heroes. And we deserve a reward."

Shelby continued to stare at him, astounded at how much she wanted to kiss him, be held by him, make wild, passionate love with him . . . and all while she knew he had deceived her, deceived her horribly. "A reward?"

He took the cup from her hands, then pulled her to her feet. "Yes, Shelley, a reward. Now, as I'm already sure you're going to tell me you feel honor-bound to work tomorrow, on your day off, to make up for today—"

"Of course," Shelby answered, this woman who never made a promise, or a bargain, without making sure she lived up to every last bit of it. But how did he know that about her? How did she know that he did things exactly the same way? Was that how he came to be in East Wapaneken in the first place? He had taken on the job of Taite bodyguard, and now was just finishing the job? And was it still just a job to him? Would a man actually make love to a "job?"

Many would. Quinn, she thought, probably would not. Definitely would not, now that she'd had some time to think sensibly, and not just with anger burning inside her.

That meant he liked her. She *wasn't* just a job, was much more than a job. She smiled, unaware that Quinn was watching her, as she suddenly felt very much better.

Still, he did lie to her. He was still lying to her. Just as she was still lying to him. How in the world would either of them ever get past that one horrible truth?

"Shelley? You look as if you're miles away," Quinn said, squeezing her hands. He'd kiss her, but his sixth sense told him that something in their relationship had changed since they'd made love. They were closer, naturally, but they were also farther apart.

He couldn't explain it, even if someone asked him to, but there was a new wariness in Shelby, even as she seemed more physically comfortable in his company. For a man who liked certainty, Quinn was having a real problem trying to figure out this woman he so unexpectedly loved.

"Hmmm?" she answered, still working out problems in her mind, deciding if it was such a terrible thing to make love to a man when both knew the other one was playing a game. If it was a game. What if their relationship had gone beyond games, and rules, and the silly restrictions of the world? And if love had somehow entered the equation . . .

Still, they were on even ground now, each knowing about the other, even if Quinn didn't know it yet. That, for the moment, seemed fair enough.

"I said, since you're going in to work tomorrow, how about we have that picnic on the parkway today? Just the two of us."

"We could do that," Shelby said, stepping forward, her mental addition adding up to a loving surrender, at least for the moment, entwining her arms around his neck. "Or we could just stay here," she added, nuzzling his neck.

Quinn closed his eyes, caught between a sharp, hot stab of desire and the niggling feeling that Shelby might be falling in love with who she thought he was, rather than who he really was. The thought hurt, the truth would hurt, and he should tell her the truth now and then wait for her to either slap or forgive him.

He felt her mouth moving against his bare skin, the tip of her tongue tracing small designs against his throat. Could he push her away, sit her down, tell her that her brother had hired him to watch her? Tell her he wasn't a writer, that he was pretty much a louse, but he loved her and would she forgive him, please? Take her so-far bad day and turn it truly lousy?

Or should he just go with the moment, hope Shelby really was falling in love with *him* and not the dream, the adventure? Would making love with her a second time be twice the crime, or help her know if what she felt was love, not just desire, or even some kind of physical release after her two recent scares?

"Oh, what the hell . . ." he said, the questions fading and his mind going mercifully blank as Shelby insinuated her thigh between his, gave a gentle pressure that slammed straight to the one part of him that immediately told him not to think at all, but just to react.

He lifted his arms, taking her fully into his embrace. Moved his head, seeking her mouth, finding it. The instant passion he had felt a moment earlier was replaced by this new sensation, so alien to him for all of his life until he'd made love to Shelby Taite.

He felt the passion, surely. The white-hot desire. But there was something else, some subtle, unidentifiable difference in his reaction to the stimuli of her mouth, her body, the sweet scent that was so uniquely Shelby's.

It was a feeling of protection, of completion, of wanting her pleasure more than his own. A feeling he could only describe as wanting to *cherish* her, make her understand that he would never hurt her, would always love her, could never possibly love her enough, even if they both lived another hundred years.

She still fit against him so well. Perfectly, as if they'd both been exclusively fashioned for each other.

His hands moved on her body, and Shelby moaned softly, welcoming his touch, knowing she had been only half-alive before Quinn had touched her, had loved her. If they couldn't have forever, if the truths they'd eventually have to tell would tarnish what they now had, was she to be condemned for taking what she could, for giving what she needed to give?

Tears flooded her eyes as, together, she and Quinn slid to their knees on the carpet, their bodies still close together from chest to knee, their hands busy, their mouths busier.

I want, I want, I want, Shelby chanted inside her head, eagerly, greedily devouring Quinn's mouth, even as he devoured hers.

For now, forever. For now . . . with the hope of forever . . . Quinn told himself as he finally lowered Shelby onto her back, looked deeply into her moist eyes, felt emotion begin to choke him, make him clumsy, as if this were the first time he had lain with a woman.

And in a way it was. Their first night had been magical, but this was different. Better. Sweeter. Hotter. More gentle. A memory in the making, one that would go on forever, even if there would be nothing else for them ever again.

Her skin was warm to the touch, the flesh over her ribs quivering slightly as he ran his hands down the sweet length of her, slid his hand beneath her panties, sought and found her with his fingers. Worshiped her.

She rose to meet him with no shame, no regrets, seizing the moment with both hands, taking all that he would give, giving all that she had and more.

They moved as one, touching, stroking, kissing, bothersome buttons and zippers yielding to reveal the hot, straining flesh beneath.

Together they sought release, completion. Together

they rode wave after wave of sweet passion, each wave growing higher, higher, their need more urgent.

Shelby dug her nails into Quinn's bare back and yielded her last defenses, allowing him to take her even higher and send them both racing, dancing toward the shore.

The only sounds in the room for some time were those of heavy breathing and the purrs of Princess as she nudged Quinn a time or two before hopping onto his back, then vaulting onto the couch, where she took up her favorite spot in front of the cushions.

Shelby, who had watched Princess's progress, giggled, then said, "Do you think we've corrupted her morals? Do cats *have* morals?"

"I don't know. They have claws; I can vouch for that. Have I told you that I love you? Because I do, you know," Quinn added, pressing a kiss against her forehead as he looked down at her, their bodies still joined, still one, never to be whole without the other again.

Shelby's smile faltered. Did he mean that? Could he mean that? Damn it, she shouldn't have made love with him again. She had been thinking so much more clearly before they'd made love again. Because he'd told her he loved her, but he hadn't told her the truth. He hadn't told her that he knew who she was, what she was. She'd wanted to fall in love with someone who she could *know* would love her only for herself, and not her inheritance.

"Shelley?" he prompted when she didn't respond.

He doesn't even call me by my right name, when he knows it; he has to know it. "I'd like to get up now," she said at last, rather ineffectually pushing against his bare shoulders.

Quinn knew when to push for answers, and when to wait for another time. He knew when he was being stonewalled, and when the person being asked the questions would do anything except give straight answers. Shelby probably wouldn't give him the right time of day right now, just because he'd asked for it. She certainly wasn't going to gush "I love you, too, Quinn," because he had stupidly, clumsily confessed his love for her.

Because, Quinn knew, felt deep in his gut, that she didn't trust him. He didn't know why, refused to believe that she might finally have seen through his cover story at this late date, and if he asked her why she'd suddenly turned so cool to him she'd only evade the question, or lie.

Although he might feel better with a lie than with the truth, if that truth was that he had been nothing more than a part of her adventure, if he had been part of something she had to "prove" to herself and, now that she had proven it, he was about to be given the old "Thanks, it's been fun, let's hope we can always be friends" brush–off. That was what happened to guys who didn't play by the rules, who ruined the fun of a fling by saying stupid things like "I love you."

He pulled on his slacks, avoiding looking at Shelby as she got dressed, knowing that she would feel his gaze now to be an invasion of her privacy. For a loving, giving woman of considerable passion, she was also modest, the sort of woman who believed people should make love in the dark, in a proper bed, and is now appalled at herself for being so wanton as to roll around a living room floor in the buff, without a thought for modesty.

She was his lover, and his lady. Always a lady, even as she turned wanton in his arms. God, but he loved this exasperating woman!

Quinn slipped on his shoes and got to his feet. So many thoughts. So many contradictions. Shelby Taite was a mass of contradictions. The cool blond heiress. The hostess at Tony's. The woman who'd panicked at the sight of a mouse yesterday, then taken on a possible kidnapper and two hopeful teenage felons single-handedly today. The woman who'd been fire in his arms a moment ago, now turning into the ice maiden who clearly wanted him out of her apartment, now.

She had her back to him as she lifted her hands to her French twist, taking out the few pins that still remained in her hair. "I really . . . um, that is, I think today would be a good time for me to catch up on . . . lots of . . . small chores, yes, chores I've been neglecting." She let her hair fall free, running her fingers through it, then turned to face Quinn. "Is that all right?"

Quinn wanted to tell her no, that *wasn't* all right. He wanted to take her by the arms and sit her down on the couch and confess everything, even going so far as to tell her she might be in some very real danger—even if he couldn't bring himself to quite believe that. No one ever killed the golden goose. No one but an idiot, that was.

But if he did tell her? Then what?

Well, first she'd probably slap his face. Which he'd deserve. Second, she'd probably run back to the Taite mansion as fast as she could, and marry Parker Westbrook III, refusing to see Quinn, talk to him, give him a few minutes to grovel at her feet, beg her to love him.

Time. He needed time. Time for Grady to complete his investigations. Time for Shelby to believe that Quinn really, truly loved her. Time to build up enough positives that the negatives would sting only for a little while, then be forgiven.

He pulled her close and kissed her cheek. "I'm sorry, Shelley. I shouldn't have said anything. I'm going too fast, aren't I? Will I see you tonight?"

She shook her head, avoiding his eyes. "I—I really need some time on my own, Quinn," she said, even as she raised her hand and stroked it down his cheek. "But I'll see you tomorrow, at Tony's?"

He took hold of her hand before she could lower it,

pressing a kiss into her palm. "At Tony's, on the moon. Where you are, Shelley, that's where I want to be."

"Oh, Quinn," she said, her voice breaking as she pushed out of his arms, already running out of the living room, toward the safety of her bedroom.

Quinn didn't need the instincts of a cop or a personal security expert to know that it was time he made his exit. He bent down, gave the purring Princess a quick rub behind the ears, and left the apartment, softly closing the door behind him.

When the knock and called-out greeting disturbed him hours later—Quinn blearily looked at his watch and saw that it was past eight o'clock—he stood up, swaying only slightly, and went to open the door a crack. Then he turned around, aimed himself at the couch once more, and collapsed onto the cushions as he said, "Come on in, Gary; make yourself at home. There's lots more beer where this came from," he ended, motioning to the empty brown bottles lined up on half a dozen crocheted coasters.

He was drunk, damn drunk, but that didn't mean he didn't still fear Mrs. Brichta if she were to find white water rings on her furniture. Drunk, yes. Entirely stupid, no.

"Wow," Gary said, heading toward the small kitchen area, "what truck hit you?"

"That bad, huh?" Quinn asked, stabbing his fingers through his hair and adjusting the golf shirt that had somehow come free of his slacks. Unless he'd never tucked it back into his trousers as he left Shelby—at her express request. "Maybe I should take a shower?"

Gary shrugged as he sat down on a chintz-covered chair and picked up the TV remote. "Suit yourself. I can watch the Phillies while I wait. The girls went to a movie, you know. One of those weepy female ones where somebody dies some slow, painful death at the end and they call that *uplifting*. I'll never understand that. Anyway, they won't be back until after ten, later if they stop for ice-cream sundaes, which I'm betting they will. Did you eat dinner? No, suppose not. I'll call for a pizza.''

Quinn stood, vaguely waving his hands in agreement, and left the room, already stripping out of his shirt. He needed company like he needed another beer, but the affable Gary seemed to think he was as welcome as the flowers of May, and Quinn didn't know how to tell him he wasn't.

Fifteen minutes later, his hair still damp after a lengthy, mostly cold shower, he returned to the living room to see Gary chugging down beer as he leaned forward in his chair, totally concentrating on the ball game. "A strike?" he exploded a moment later, talking to the television set. "You call that a strike? The strike zone ends at his knees, you jerk, not his ankles!"

Quinn raised both hands to his head, just to check that it was still there after Gary's impassioned outburst. If a guy wanted to drown his sorrows in solitude in this burg, he'd first have to find an old bomb shelter left over from the sixties, and lock himself in. "Um, Gar? You order the pizza yet?"

Brandy's fiancé of twelve years, going on thirteen, looked up as if he'd just remembered where he was. "Huh? Oh, sure, sure. Be here in another ten minutes or so. You look better. Not much, but better. What's the matter, you and Shelley have a fight?"

"A fight?" Quinn repeated, lowering himself onto the couch. "No, why do you ask?"

With one eye on the television screen, Gary said, "I dunno. Just that Brandy would barely let me in the apartment, pushing me out as I tried to talk to her, and then I saw Shelley for a moment and she looked kind of like she'd been crying. Oh, and you're drunk. That's the other reason I— *Well, awright!* Home run ties it up!" He punched a fist toward the ceiling. "Go, Phils!"

Quinn decided that twelve aspirin would probably be overkill, and headed for the kitchen to down three with a glass of water.

Either the aspirin or the first real food he'd eaten all day helped rid him of the worst of his headache by the time the Phillies had outlasted the Pirates in the bottom of the ninth, and Quinn suddenly realized the last thing he wanted was for Gary to leave, leaving him alone.

He had to talk to someone. Grady was out. Maisie was out. Brandy wasn't even an option. That left Gary.

He looked at the guy's simple, open face, that perpetual smile. Gary Mack was a great, big, muscle-bound teddy bear. He was also Brandy's fiancé, and Brandy had the sort of mouth Quinn's grandmother used to say "ran on wheels."

Brandy knew about Shelby. Quinn would bet on that. And if Brandy knew, odds were that Gary knew. And, pulling the thread of his thought all the way through, if Gary knew, then Gary might be able to help him. Or at least listen to him.

"Gar," he began, picking up the remote and clicking off the postgame show, "may I confide in you? I mean, I don't want to make you slit your palm and swear it on your blood or anything, but can I count on you to keep what I say just between the two of us?"

Gary looked blank for a moment, then shrugged. "Sure. Why not?"

"You won't tell Brandy?"

"Brandy? Naw. If I told her she'd just ask questions and then get mad at me because *I* didn't think to ask those questions, and then I'd ask her if she thought I was stupid and she'd say of course you're not stupid but you sure are *thick,* and we'd end up in a big fight. I don't tell Brandy lots of things, Quinn. It's easier that way. Besides, she talks enough for the both of us.''

So Quinn told him. He was still just drunk enough to tell him. He told Gary everything, then sat back and waited for the man to react.

That took a while, but it was worth it.

''A bodyguard, right?'' Gary said at last. ''Like with guns and armored cars and terrorists and stuff? Yeah, sure, it would have to be. Cool.''

Quinn shrugged and smiled. Obviously Gary still hadn't gotten the point. But he had faith in the man. He'd get around to it sooner or later.

So Quinn kept his silence and Gary thought some more. ''I don't know about ethical and all of that, but sleeping with the girl you're supposed to be protecting? That sounds downright dangerous to me, if she finds out. Except I guess you've already thought of that—a little late, but you've thought of it. Man, if Shelley's anything like Brandy, you're a dead man.''

''Thanks,'' Quinn said, and waited some more. Watching Gary Mack think was a real experience. He could almost see the thought processes moving along, slowly gathering themselves until there were enough to come to a conclusion. It was a slow process, rather like watching molasses make its way to the neck of the bottle, but fascinating.

Gary studied his fingers, touching one against the other, counting off facts, assembling them for distillation, distribution. ''How can she not believe he's been lying to her when he *has* been lying to her? How can she say she hasn't been lying to him, because she *has* been lying to him? And this Parker guy? What if he *is* the bad guy, not just a jerk who doesn't deserve her? What if he isn't?''

While Gary paused, chewing at his bottom lip, Quinn got up and got the man another beer.

"Can't say he loves her, because that could be a lie, too. Gotta protect her, watch her." He shook his head. "Shouldn't have made love to her. Shouldn't have said anything about love. And she's leaving, too, after the dinner for the memorial. Man, this is confusing. I don't—"

"Whoa, back up, would you, Gary?" Quinn said, sitting front on the edge of the couch. "Shelby's leaving after the dinner this Friday? Are you sure?"

Gary clapped a hand over his mouth for a moment and rolled his eyes desperately. "I don't think I was supposed to say that, was I? No, I'm sure I wasn't. But I promise, Quinn, I won't make the same mistake with Brandy. Promise."

"I believe you, Gary," Quinn said, not believing him at all. "And when you don't say anything to Brandy, make sure she understands that, if she believes I really love Shelby, want to marry her, and I do, she won't say anything to her. Okay?"

Gary's eyes slid back and forth as he repeated Quinn's words in his head. "You got it," he said at last. "And I sure do need this beer, because I understood that."

Chapter Twenty-eight

Quinn and his headache woke at nine-seventeen the next morning. He knew that because he looked at his bedside clock, then all but jumped out of bed, already knowing he was too late to take Shelby to breakfast at Tony's.

Holding one hand to his throbbing head, he searched for his pants, then remembered that he had to answer the continuing knocks at the door.

Shelby?

No, he doubted that.

Mrs. Brichta?

No, she'd use her key, the way she did the other day, to find him coming out of the shower with just a towel wrapped around him. She hadn't apologized, either, only told him she hadn't had such a great "cheap thrill" in years, then started dusting the living room furniture.

His mouth dry, and tasting as if he'd been chewing sweaty socks, Quinn stabbed his fingers through his hair as he blinked, shook himself like a wet puppy, and positioned himself in front of the closed door. "Who's there?"

"A friend. Now open the damn door and get me out of this hallway, *friend,* or I can safely assure you that we're both going to rue the day we were born into this mortal coil."

Quinn's eyes opened wide, letting in entirely too much light for a man suffering a hangover. He unlocked the door, pulled it open, and glared at the man standing there with a smile on his face and a suitcase in his hand. "Uncle Alfred?"

Alfred Taite swept past the stunned Quinn, deftly kicking the door shut with his foot. "One and the same, dear boy. Oh, my. You look like I usually do in the morning. Drink's the very devil, son. Stay away from it; that's my advice. Now, where do I put this?"

"Where do you put it?" Quinn shook his aching head. "Don't make me answer that; you wouldn't like it."

"Ah, not a happy drunk, I see."

"Not a drunk at all, damn it," Quinn protested, sinking onto the couch, one hand still pressed against his forehead. "I haven't had that much beer in one sitting since college. And I'm never going to drink that much again. I only wish I could believe I'm hallucinating, and you aren't really here. Other people get pink elephants, you know. Why do I have to see grinning Taites?"

"It's because of your good heart," Uncle Alfred said, looking around the small apartment. "I suppose this isn't the foyer, is it?"

Quinn chuckled in spite of himself. "Nope. This is it. Except for one small bedroom. Which doesn't matter, suit-case or not, because you aren't staying here. Not that you were thinking about that, right?"

Uncle Alfred walked over to the couch, bent down, and pushed on the cushions. "Ah, uncomfortable enough to be a pullout." He waved a hand at Quinn. "Stand up. That's a good boy." Then, as Quinn watched, the two floral cushions hit the floor and Uncle Alfred pointed to the pullout bed with some satisfaction. "I've slept on worse. You should do very well here, my boy."

"You're not—*I'm* not . . . Oh, hell," Quinn said, picking up the cushions and replacing them before he sprawled on the couch once more. "Okay, I've fought it long enough. Guess it's time for the sixty-four-thousand-dollar question. Why are you here?"

Uncle Alfred's grin was wicked behind his natty silver beard and mustache. "I thought you'd never ask." He motioned for Quinn to remove his feet from one cushion, then joined him on the couch, carefully pulling up his slacks so not to ruin the knife-sharp crease in the navy material. "I've been tossed out on my ear, actually. Somerton has threatened it often enough but, thanks to my dearest niece, he has at last turned threat to fact. Obstinate boy, Somerton, and nearly insufferably smug since he punched old Westbrook in the chops."

Quinn stared at the older man for a few moments, trying to make his brain work at least a little bit. "Coffee," he said at last. "I need coffee. About two gallons of it. Care to join me?"

"Charmed, I'm sure," Uncle Alfred said, standing up and trailing after Quinn as he made his way to the efficiency kitchen that was, in truth, still a part of the living room. He sat himself down at one of the two stools at a small serving bar, pulled a silver flask out of his pocket, and placed it in front of him. "I take mine black, dear boy, with a chaser. Although I don't suppose I could interest you in a . . . what do the lower orders call it? Oh, yes, of course. Would you care to join me in a *belt?*"

Quinn eyed the silver flask as he loaded the coffeemaker. "You probably put that stuff on your cornflakes." Then he walked around the bar and perched himself on the second stool. "Talk to me, Uncle Alfred. Talk slowly, and don't raise your voice. But talk to me."

"Tsk, tsk," Uncle Alfred said. "I hadn't known you had this flair for the melodramatic, son. Oh, very well, I suppose if I must, I must. It would seem that I'm, er, financially embarrassed. That's dead broke, to you, and more in debt than I care to think about this early in the morning. I am also between allowance checks, which is highly embarrassing, and dangerous, when one considers to whom I am in debt, if you catch my drift. Catch my drift. My, I'm doing very well with the vernacular, aren't I? Must have something to do with all that consorting I do with those nasty gambling types."

Enough coffee had dripped into the pot to send Quinn over to the counter, pulling the pot aside and replacing it with his cup, which he watched fill as he replayed Uncle Alfred's words in his head. After filling a cup for the older man, too, he replaced the pot and returned to the serving bar.

"You're broke, you're in debt to some gamblers, you're between allowances, and Somerton threw you out on your ear. That much I understand. What I don't understand is why this is Shelby's fault, and why the hell you're *here.*"

Uncle Alfred took a sip of coffee, then followed it with a sip from his flask. "Ah, that's better. I haven't had a nip since Jim drove me here in the limousine. Can't go off into oblivion, I say, unless you travel in style. Not us Taites, anyway. Now, where was I? Oh, yes. If your head weren't so clogged with drink, son, you'd have figured it out by now."

"No, I wouldn't have," Quinn said, drinking deeply of the coffee, cursing as he scalded his tongue. "I would never, not in a million years, be able to figure out why in hell, of all the places you could have gone, you've shown up here in East Wapaneken.''

Uncle Alfred took a last sip from the flask, then returned it to his pocket. ''Somerton believes that his sister is a heroine of sorts. A true Taite. Independent, fiercely so, and able to stand up on her own two feet, find herself— Lord help us—*employment,* and make her own way in the world. I, on the other hand, am an embarrassment to the Taites, pure and simple. So when I asked Somerton for an advance on my allowance, just a piddling twenty thousand, he said no. Absolutely, positively no. I was to do as Shelby has done: go out in the world, fend for myself, and come back with a paycheck made out to me in my own name. Then, and only then, will he take me back into the Taite fold. So, considering how fertile the—what do you call it, the job market?—is here in East Wapaneken, it seemed quite natural that I toddle off here. I have a relative here, I have a friend here—that's you, son—and my friend has an apartment here. It was the only logical step, truly.''

Quinn looked at the man through slitted eyelids. ''I'll tell you what's logical. Who's after you?''

Uncle Alfred reached for his flask, then thought better of it. ''Well, so much for dulled wits. That's very astute of you, son, surely. But not to worry. They couldn't have possibly followed me here. I mean, who'd come *here?*''

''You were driven here in the Taite limo, Alfred. I suppose it never occurred to you that whoever you owe this piddling twenty thousand to just might have had someone watching the estate?''

''Oh, dear,'' Uncle Alfred said, and this time he did take the flask out of his pocket. ''I hadn't thought of that. Do you really think I've been followed? I mean, what are the odds?''

''I don't gamble, Alfred,'' Quinn said, walking over to the counter and tossing the remainder of his coffee into the sink. "And I don't think you were unaware that you could have been followed. After all, you didn't go to Shelby, did you? No, you came to me, the Taite bodyguard. I'm supposed to keep you safe from the knee-breakers for the next ten days, aren't I?"

Uncle Alfred picked an invisible bit of lint from the sleeve of his brand-new golf shirt—just the sort of thing he believed would make him inconspicuous in East Wapaneken. "I do hope Somerton pays you enough, son. You're definitely worth every penny. Oh, and don't worry about Shelby. I'm sure to see her soon enough, and I will quickly take her aside and explain that I, on my own, figured out where she was after talking with Jim, and have come to support her in my way, and have an adventure of my own. She'll believe me. She's a good girl; she always believes me."

"Uh-huh," Quinn said, having his doubts, but keeping most of them to himself. "But how are you going to explain staying here, in my apartment? Which you're not going to be doing, by the way."

"You don't want me? Well, I'm crushed. However, I did speak with the most delightful woman downstairs, and she told me there's an apartment just like yours available on the third floor. Can you believe it, son—there's no elevator in this building. Shocking! Now, if you wouldn't mind advancing me a month's rent, I'm sure I could be out of your way in no time at all."

Quinn reached into his pocket and pulled out his wallet. "This is blackmail, you know, in some twisted way I don't want to examine right now."

"Now, now, no name-calling," Uncle Alfred said, pocketing several one-hundred-dollar bills. "Everything is going splendidly so far, and will continue to do so, I'm sure. But now that that's all settled, what do you say you find me a job? Nothing too involved, you understand. Just something where I can stand about and pretend to be busy. Jim said something about a company he called Wal-Mart, I believe. His uncle is a greeter there, as I understand it. I do believe I could do that, and I've brought my tuxedo.''

"A tuxedo for a Wal-Mart greeter? Damn, that tears it,'' Quinn said, laughing as he went off to take his shower. A cold shower. With the faucets turned on full. In the hope he might wake up and learn that he'd only been having a nightmare.

But he'd been wide-awake, which he already knew as he walked back into the living room to see Uncle Alfred trying on a pair of whiter-than-white sneakers with enough purple and blue trim to hurt the eyes. He finished tying the second one, wiggled his toes a bit, then stood up and walked across the carpet as he kept his head bent, inspecting his new footwear, until he all but bumped into Quinn.

"Ah, son, what do you think? I've never worn anything quite like these. Oh, tennis sneakers, of course, but nothing like this. Still, Jim said they're all the rage, and I do want to fit in. Even bought ten of these shirts,'' he added, patting his flat stomach. "One in every color of the rainbow, plus two white ones. And slacks. These are new, too. Can't go roughing it without the correct wardrobe; that's what I say.''

"I thought you were broke.''

"I am, I am, my boy. And that's the only thing one can do when one is financially embarrassed—buy something. It lifts the mood considerably, not to mention concentrating the mind.'' He sucked in a deep breath, then released it slowly. "So where are you taking me to procure me this employment Somerton believes I must have to lift my morals, or scruples, or some such nonsense?''

"That depends,'' Quinn said, walking over to the window and looking down at the street below. He knew every car that was usually parked there, and today there was a new one. Black coupe, but not a rental. Rentals didn't have illegal darkened glass on the driver's-side window.

"I think Tony needs a dishwasher," he said as he turned to Uncle Alfred, grinning from ear to ear. "I think you'll do nicely."

Uncle Alfred put his hands out in front of him, as if to ward off a blow. "Oh, no. Oh, no, no, no. I don't think you've quite grasped this, son. Taites don't *do* menial labor. Why, I just had a manicure . . . and I haven't the faintest idea what a kitchen looks like—not that I have any burning curiosity to find out—and . . . and . . . Why do you keep looking out the window?"

"Because I think we have company, that's why," Quinn said, walking over to Uncle Alfred and ruthlessly pulling the man's shirttails out of his two-hundred-dollar slacks. "Because if I'm going to watch you and Shelby, it'll be easier to have you both in the same place. Now ruffle your hair a little. Okay, that's good. And we'll scuff up those sneakers when we get outside—we're leaving by the back door, by the way. Do you smoke?"

"The occasional cigar. Havanas, of course. Why?" Uncle Alfred asked as he dutifully mussed his gorgeous mane of silver hair.

"You're a cigarette man now, Alfred, that's why. I've got a pack around here somewhere." He found the pack in the drawer. He opened it, shook out three cigarettes, slipped a matchbook between pack and cellophane, then rolled the pack up in the sleeve of Uncle Alfred's shirt. He stood back and inspected his creation. "No beard trimming from here on out, all right? Now, what shall we call you?"

"You can call me Al. I've always wanted to be called Al."

"I'd rather call you a cab," Quinn told him, "but Al it is. Al what?"

"Smith?" Uncle Alfred offered, then winced. "Al Smith. No, can't do that. Democrat, wasn't he? Yes, I'm sure of it. I'd have Taite ancestors for five generations rolling in their graves. How about O'Hara? I've always thought the Irish had such a good time, and nobody will mind my flask.''

"I'm Irish, *Al,* so don't make me knock you down,'' Quinn said as he reached into Uncle Alfred's pocket and pulled out the flask. "This, my friend, stays here. Got that?''

"You're not seeing this as the great adventure I'm seeing it as, are you, son?'' Uncle Alfred asked as he followed Quinn to the door; then he gulped as Quinn turned and glared at him.

"Look, old man. Shelby likes you. I like you, too, although I don't know why. If not, you'd be out on your ear right now, and whoever is in that car out there could practice their batting swings on you. But this is *not* a great adventure. Shelby is going to smell a rat, for one thing, and she's already got enough going on to make her cut and run.''

Uncle Alfred automatically reached for his slacks pocket, then drew himself up and said, "She's in some sort of trouble, isn't she? You mentioned that the other day, but didn't elaborate, so I thought you weren't serious. But you're looking far too fierce now for it to be anything else but real trouble. How can I be of assistance?''

Quinn looked at the old man with the full silver beard, sparkling eyes, and a nose as rosy as his cheeks. One of the Main Line's finest, if most unique, dressed "down'' to look like a dishwasher and still looking more like some visiting count or something. He took hold of Uncle Alfred's elbow and drew him back toward the couch. "Sit down. We have to talk. . . .''

A half hour and several dozen questions later, they were on their way out of the apartment once more, only to be met at the bottom of the stairs by Mrs. Brichta, who seemed to be wearing a newly ironed muumuu, and who definitely smelled as if she'd just taken a bath in perfume.

"Hello again, Alfred," she all but cooed, patting her tightly permed hair. "Have you decided to rent one of my furnished apartments? You said you might, after you visited with your friend." She looked at Quinn, her eyes hard, then looked back at Alfred, those same eyes melting and soft.

Uncle Alfred took her hand and lifted it to his lips, which set off a trill of girlish giggles that nearly floored Quinn, who had seen Mrs. Brichta in a lot of moods, but none of them had much to do with humor or any hint of girlishness. "My dearest Bertha, how could I not, after seeing Mr. Delaney's exquisite quarters? In fact, I have my deposit right here. . . ."

He let the words trail off as he slowly, so slowly moved a hand toward his trouser pocket.

"Oh, don't be silly, Alfred. I certainly don't need a *deposit*. Why, if I'm nothing else, I'm a fine judge of people. You can just pay me next week, or at the end of the month. Whenever, *however,*" she ended, tracing a finger down her chest, giving the neckline of the muumuu a slight downward tug.

"I am overwhelmed," Uncle Alfred said, kissing the giggling, blushing woman's hand once more, then allowing Quinn to lead the way down the hall toward the back door.

As he walked along, Quinn—definitely "overwhelmed"—wondered what good ol' Bertha would think if she knew Uncle Alfred was flat broke, and would probably leave without paying his bill. "Gimme," he said, turning in front of the door and holding out his hand, waiting for Uncle Alfred to cross his palm with the borrowed money.

"Now, son, you wouldn't—"

"Give. Now." He took the bills and counted them. "All

right, you can keep the two hundred still in your pocket. But that's it.''

"And to think that I liked you," Uncle Alfred said, shaking his head sadly. "I can see now why Bertha said she made you pay your rent before she'd let you in. You don't have a very trustworthy face, now that I consider it. Much too dark and brooding. No wonder Somerton demands Mr. Sullivan.''

Quinn bent down in the gravel parking lot and scooped up some dirt, which he smeared on the too-new, too-white sneakers. "Yeah, that Grady. What a prince. Okay," he said, standing up and brushing his hands together. "Let's go introduce you to Tony and get you settled before Shelby shows up for her shift. When, by the way, *I* will be nowhere to be found. I'll come in later, and we can meet for the first time. Are you up to this, Al?''

In answer, Uncle Alfred removed the cigarette pack from his sleeve, thumped out one cigarette, and lit it with the match held in his cupped hands. He took a deep drag, blew the smoke out his nose, then rubbed at his nose with the back of his hand. Snorted. Spit. "Yeah, man, I'm ready.''

"Sweet mother of God, we're all dead," Quinn breathed quietly, then headed off down the street, bad boy Al following behind.

Chapter Twenty-nine

Shelby had stood at the window in her bedroom, the one overlooking the parking lot, and waited until she saw Quinn get into his Porsche and drive off. Only then did she grab a light sweater and head off to Tony's for her shift.

He had come to the door, as usual, to escort her to the restaurant—or at least that was what she thought he'd say. But it wasn't. He'd only wanted to tell her he had to go "interview" somebody for his book, and wouldn't be back until closer to the dinner hour, and would she be all right in his absence.

The rat. Of course she told him she'd be all right. After all, she'd only almost been kidnapped. Not that he seemed to be all that worried about her safety today. Which he wouldn't be, if he was the one behind the kidnap attempt, the attempt to get her frightened enough to turn tail and run home so that he could get on to more exciting assignments. After all, he'd already bedded her. Already told at least a million lies. He had to be getting bored by now.

The rat.

She looked both ways before going down the steps from the apartment onto the pavement. She walked with her head up, her long legs striding purposely; alert, her key stuck between the fingers of her right hand, ready to use as a weapon. Every once in a while she remembered to breathe.

Quinn watched her from behind a bush he'd belatedly realized was full of inch-long thorns as one of the branches caught him on the face. He wiped blood from his cheek as he continued to watch Shelby, watch the way she walked, the way her hips swung, the way her sleek, shoulder-length blond hair bounced slightly, swayed with her every step.

"Oh, yeah, sweetheart. We bad, we bad," he said under his breath, chuckling at her aggressive gait. God, how he enjoyed her, how he loved her.

Only when the door swung closed behind her did he relax, retreat to the Porsche he'd parked on a side street, and return to his apartment. He was getting too old for this; he needed a nap.

Shelby said hello to the police chief as he stood at the poker machine, using quite a bit of body English on it as the cards flipped over on the screen, then entered the air-conditioned chill of the restaurant proper.

She automatically checked the "Specials" board, wincing at Tabby's inventive spelling, then grabbed one of the pile of inserts for the afternoon menu, which listed the entrees. Ostrich filet, she saw, shaking her head at Tony's flights of fancy in a town the size of East Wapaneken. And yet, the alligator *had* gone over fairly well.

Still concentrating on the menu as she walked toward the service bar, she murmured a quick "Excuse me" as she bumped into someone holding a heavy gray plastic tub filled to the brim with dirty dishes.

"Yeah, well, watch where you're goin', all right?"

Shelby kept her head down, although her eyes somehow had gone right, looking at nothing in particular as her brain engaged, zeroing in on the voice she'd just heard. Then she looked up. "Uncle Alfred?"

"Al, honey," Uncle Alfred said, a little more loudly than necessary. "Al O'Hara. And you must be that Shelley girl, whose always making the busboys nuts with all her 'do this, now do this' stuff. Wanna go out back and share a smoke? I'm up for a break."

Shelby opened her mouth to speak, but found that she couldn't get a single word past her lips. So she raised one hand and held up one finger at Uncle Alfred's already retreating back. He didn't even hold open the swinging door to the kitchen for her. Her mouth still open, her finger still raised, she stumbled after him, through the busy kitchen, and out the back door.

"How . . . why . . . *what* are you doing here?" she growled at him when she finally found her voice. She spread her arms wide, as if to encompass him in full busboy regalia, including a huge white apron that hung around his neck and fell nearly to his shins. "Like *that?*"

"Why, darling, the esteemed Tony has seen fit to allow me employment as a busperson. I said busboy, but it's really busperson, did you know that? Probably not. Pedro says he likes you well enough, but you can be a real pain in the butt. In fact, that's the general impression around here. Lovely girl, sweet, kind. But a pain in the butt. Sorry, darling, it is what he said."

Her head buzzing as if a family of bees had taken up residence between her ears, Shelby fought for control as she tried to listen to her uncle, to take in the fact that he was standing in front of her. "How? How did you find out where I was?"

Uncle Alfred unwrapped the pack of cigarettes from his sleeve and kept his eyes averted as he lit one. "Simple enough, darling. I asked Jim. If you'll remember, you did speak of our dear family chauffeur with me before you did your absolutely inspired little flit. Not that I told Somerton what I found out. Oh, no. Not me. Not when I wanted you to have this little adventure. By the way, aren't you going to kiss your uncle hello?"

"I, um, but—oh, come here, Uncle Alfred. I'm so glad to see you!" she said, opening her arms and walking toward him to give him a big hug. She felt tears stinging her eyes, surprised to realize just how much she had missed her uncle, still missed Somerton, and Jeremy. But not Parker. Strange. She really hadn't thought much about Parker at all. Well, maybe not so strange . . .

Finally she pushed him away and inspected him again. "I still don't believe it. You're *working* here?"

"Honest labor, darling. Money earned for services rendered. The American way, and all of that. Do you think I look dashing? I really think I look dashing. Almost roguish. Except for the apron, you understand."

"And you did this on your own? You decided to come to me, share my adventure?" She cocked her head to one side and looked at him closely. "I don't believe you, Uncle Alfred."

"Al, darling. Call me Al, if you please. And of course you don't believe me. Whoever knows me *would* believe me, in anything?" He sighed deeply. "I'm financially embarrassed, darling, and, because of your example, Somerton decided to toss me out into the great wide world to fend for myself. Said it would straighten my spine, if you can believe that. Jeremy lobbied for me, explained quite succinctly that your brother was being quite unreasonable—he actually told Somerton he was being recalcitrant, Jeremy's new word of the day—but all pleas, alas, fell on deaf ears. So here I am, and here I will be until I can show Somerton a paycheck."

"Which was it, Uncle Alfred?" Shelby asked, shaking her head. "Cards or the ponies?"

"A little of both, dearest, but most unfortunately with the same quite unlovely group of people. Terribly worried about their money, you understand. So I thought it might be best to, um, *disappear* until my next allowance is due. Your brother had no sympathy for me, no care for my old, frail physical form and what a few fists might do to it, so I asked Jim to bring me here, sure you must already be in town. How surprised, pleasantly, I'm sure, I was to hear that a Miss Shelley Smith worked as hostess. I knew in a moment that she must be you. Serendipity, that's what I call it."

"I don't think that's what I'd call it," Shelby said, positive that Quinn had told Uncle Alfred where she was, not Jim. Deeper and deeper. The more she thought about it, the deeper the hole she'd already put Quinn Delaney into got. Until it would take him a dozen shovels to find his way out of there.

"You working today?"

Shelby spun around to see Tony standing in the doorway, allowing the doorjamb to hold up his long frame. "Oh, Tony, forgive me. It turns out that Al here is an old friend. We were just catching up."

"Well, ain't that grand. Catch up on your own time," Tony said, then slowly pushed himself away from the doorjamb and shuffled back to the kitchen.

"He's a sweetheart, really," Shelby told her uncle as the two of them headed back inside the kitchen.

"A diamond in the rough," Uncle Alfred agreed amicably. "Now, if you'll excuse me, Pedro promised to teach me how to skin carrots. Or was that *peel* carrots? Never mind. I'm sure Pedro knows."

Shelby pushed open the swinging door to the restaurant and stopped just on the other side of it, trying to collect her thoughts, until Tabby slammed the door open, carrying out three platters of Tony's special hamburgers.

Shelby quickly turned to help balance the platters, apologizing as she remembered she'd been told never, *never* to stand in front of the single swinging door to the kitchens. "I'm so sorry, Tabby."

"No harm, no foul, babe," the waitress said, then leaned her head closer. "Did you see the new guy? Al? We're going out tonight. Hot, hot, hot babe!"

"How, um, charming," Shelby said, then winced as the customers yelled to Tabby that they didn't have all day to wait for her to serve them—to which Tabby replied, "Hold your water, boys; I'm coming."

"Yes," Shelby mumbled, withholding a grimace. "How very charming . . . all of it." She kept her smile tight as she watched the thin, wiry waitress with the rubber band–wrapped ponytail and the black high-top sneakers head for the nearest table. "So very, very charming," she repeated to herself dully, shaking her head.

She snapped to attention as she felt a sharp poke in her side, and turned to see that Mrs. Miller had entered the restaurant. Her day was just getting better and better.

"Hello, Mrs. Miller," she said as cheerfully as possible, looking down at the five-foot-nothing woman with the largest store-bought teeth in the history of the world. Scary, that was what Mrs. Miller was. And, as always, armed. "How are you today?"

Mrs. Miller slowly lowered the pointy umbrella she carried in good weather and bad, and which she employed to poke Shelby in the ribs every chance she got. "Hummph! As if *you* care. Bet you're the one making my lumbago act up. Lumbago was fine till you got here. Now step aside. I know how to find my own table. Don't need no idiot girl leading me around like a dog on a leash."

"Yes, ma'am," Shelby said gratefully, then watched the old woman all but skip across the room, her lumbago miraculously in remission all of a sudden.

Mrs. Miller was the one conquest Shelby had been unable to make. Everyone in East Wapaneken had been so nice, so welcoming. But not Mrs. Miller, who was, unfortunately, a twice-daily customer. Carol, one of the part-time waitresses, had finally told her that Mrs. Miller believed Shelby to be an alien. "And I don't mean you don't have your green card," Carol had said. "She's talking Mork from Ork alien. But don't worry. She also calls Bert down at the police station twice a week to say there's a man under her bed. She should be so lucky, the old bat. She hates everybody."

And that was when Shelby smiled. She shouldn't be smiling. Lord knew she had little to smile about, even less since Uncle Alfred had shown up, ready to play out his little farce. But still, Shelby smiled. She pushed open the door to the kitchen and found her uncle. "Al? I need you out front for a setup. The lady at table six. Get her a place setting and a cup of coffee. And be sure to ask her how she is today. Mrs. Miller is a positive doll. She just loves to chatter."

"That was mean," Tony said, sidling up to her in that slow, soundless way he had. "I thought you said Al was an old friend of yours."

"True enough, Tony. But I wouldn't want you to think I would play favorites, just because I know Al."

"Sounds more like you hate his guts," Tony remarked, scratching his head. "Women. I'll never understand them. Yeah, well, gotta get back to work. Ostrich filet tonight, you know. We're going to be crowded, which should make you happy, because ostrich is low in cholesterol, and tastes a whole lot better than cottage cheese."

And Tony had been proved right in his prediction. The restaurant was crowded, starting at four o'clock with the early birds, and not slacking off one bit. And Mrs. Miller, hogging a table for four, still showed no signs of budging. Not with "Al" hovering over her every other minute, kissing her hand, telling her little nonsense stories, calling her—Shelby couldn't believe it—"Althea, dear."

Uncle Alfred had hours ago—about the time Mrs. Miller arrived at Tony's—abandoned his "tough boy" pose for one of professional courtesy and his own innate elegance that had all the women swooning—and it wasn't all that easy to make the geriatric set swoon. How could she have forgotten that Uncle Alfred could charm the birds out of the trees? In fact, the only two things he couldn't seem to charm were cards and ponies. Not that he hadn't spent a lifetime trying.

The regulars had also spent the day, two of them coming in and three of them leaving for a time, then all six of them digging into ostrich filets after an afternoon of coffee and talk.

Two other customers had spent the entire afternoon at Quinn's usual corner table, and showed no signs of leaving anytime soon, before Quinn appeared, wanting his dinner.

Shelby didn't recognize the two men, which wasn't an uncommon occurrence for her, but these two she was sure she would never forget. They were both huge. Huge heads, huge arms, huge bellies, huge thighs. They both smoked incessantly, and had already ordered four plates of spaghetti between them. And that was just a snack, for now they were eating porterhouse steaks with all the fixings. They both wore open-throated, patterned polyester shirts and plaid polyester slacks that strained to hold together below their bellies.

And they didn't talk. Not a word beyond grunting out their orders to Tabby, who rolled her eyes as she wrote on her pad, then shuffled away. "Big bad boys," the waitress stage-whispered to Shelby at one point. "Very big bad boys, and I should know. Had their kind around more than a few times before my idiot husband took off, knocking on my door, scaring the kids. Stay away, honey; they'd eat you for a snack."

The strangers didn't seem to bother Uncle Alfred, who had been assigned to bus tables and serve drinks for the remainder of his shift. In fact, he had lingered at their table for quite a long time, refilling their coffee mugs and passing the time of day with the two mute, unsmiling men. But, again, that was Uncle Alfred. He could charm anyone. Even Mrs. Miller. Although he didn't seem to be having much luck with the two polyester men.

She wondered, thought about Tabby's assessment of the two men, and wondered some more. Could it be? Could these two men be here to watch Uncle Alfred? Hurt Uncle Alfred? No. That was silly. Just silly. She was seeing plots everywhere now, from the regulars, to Quinn, to the polyester men. And yet . . . ?

"Hi, am I too late for the ostrich filet? I saw it listed on the sign outside. And should filet be spelled with two *Ls*, or did you just give up?"

Shelby turned to see Quinn standing behind her, smiling. Her stomach dropped to her toes, then shot back up into her throat. God, but she loved this man she hated.

His eyes twinkled, so that she remembered how they clouded with passion. His smile hypnotized her, so that all she could think about was how he had felt, tasted, as his mouth had devoured hers.

She wouldn't even dare look lower than his neck, for there lay real trouble, especially as she tried to remember that he was the lowest of the low, a bodyguard. A hired baby-sitter who had taken his client's sister to bed. Lower than low . . .

"You really want the ostrich?" she asked at last, unable to think of anything else to say.

Quinn smiled, shook his head. "Not on your life," he told her, flicking at a wisp of blond hair that had somehow dared to be out of place. He wondered what would happen if he were to pick her up, throw her over his shoulder, take her back to the apartment, and make love to her until her bones melted. Would her eyes look more alive then? Would her smile be more real? Would she finally tell him she loved him . . . or at least tell him what in the hell was making her look so sad, seem so distant? Even if he was pretty sure he didn't want to know. Not, at least, until he had her in his arms, well loved, and then made his idiot confession.

"Some . . . er . . . your table is occupied, I'm afraid," she said finally, handing him a menu and indicating that he should follow her as she headed toward the worst table in the house, and the only one still unoccupied. She pulled out his chair, then stepped back. "Is this all right?"

"It will be, if I'm on time for your dinner break and you'll agree to eat with me."

He watched as her eyes went dull, as her shoulders slumped almost imperceptibly before she returned to her usual model-erect posture. "I'm afraid I've already eaten. Sorry."

"Then I'll see you later? Walk you back to the apartment?"

She shook her head. "Thank you, no. Brandy and I are going to the movies. We saw the coming attractions the other night, and decided we'd really like to see Julia Roberts's new romantic comedy. But really, thank you for asking. I'll . . . I'll see you tomorrow . . . the next day. I'm sure you have a lot of work to catch up on, considering you've been spending most of your days here. I thank you for your concern about those men, but I'm fine now, I promise. So you can just concentrate on your book."

"Sure," Quinn said, nodding as he lied, pretending not to realize he'd just been given the proverbial brush-off. "Thanks. I do need to do some catching up, maybe type up some of my interview notes. And I've got to write George's speech for him. . . ."

This was so awkward. Shelby could see that Quinn thought so, too. So damned awkward. Two people who'd been to bed together, for crying out loud, acting as if they were both trying to find some polite way of saying, "Thanks, but no thanks."

She dipped her head and looked at him again. "Look, Quinn, I . . . I just need some time, okay? You said . . . well, you know what you said." Everything but the truth, she reminded herself. "I'm afraid I need some time to think about that. About us."

"Sure, Shelley," Quinn agreed, wondering if it would be possible to kick himself all the way up the street. It was Tuesday. She was leaving Saturday, after the big dinner. And he was rapidly running out of time. "But how about Thursday night? A late dinner after work? Two days apart, Shelley, two days for thinking. Is that enough time?"

"Thursday night," she repeated, relaxing slightly, believing she'd have herself back under control by then. If she didn't think, didn't dream, didn't love him so much.

The rat. "Yes, that would be fine." And then she stepped back as Uncle Alfred approached the table, a glass of water in one hand, a glass coffeepot in the other.

"Good evening, sir," Uncle Alfred said smoothly, putting down the plastic glass. "Would you care for coffee this evening? I highly recommend the brew."

"Yes, I know," Quinn said, holding up his cup. Here we go, he thought, refusing to look at Shelby, to see her reaction. She had to believe they didn't know each other, that Uncle Alfred—Al—had really discovered her whereabouts on his own. Otherwise there could be only one other answer—and that answer was him. She'd already been looking at him strangely, been behaving strangely, so that he'd worried she might have finally remembered him. *Damn Uncle Alfred!* Damn everyone who was making a rotten situation even worse. And that would include the two muscle-bound thugs sitting at *his* table, damn them twice. "You're new here, aren't you?"

"Oh, indeed, indeed," Uncle Alfred said. "Such a lovely little hamlet, don't you think? I've already found myself the loveliest apartment just up the street, in a converted school building."

"Really," Quinn said. "I happen to live there as well, as does Miss Smith. Isn't that a coincidence?"

"Yes, isn't it?" Shelby said, her smile so bright it hurt her cheeks as she turned away from the table.

She might not have seen through Quinn's lies as he pretended not to know her uncle, but she'd spent her entire life around Uncle Alfred. Jim hadn't told him where she was. He hadn't questioned Jim and come to some happy conclusion that brought him to East Wapaneken when Somerton tossed him out to fend for himself.

Oh, no. Uncle Alfred knew where she was because Quinn Delaney told him. Told him, told Somerton, told Jeremy. Told Parker? And, she could now tell from Quinn's glittering eyes, he was about as happy to see Uncle Alfred here in East Wapaneken as he would be to find his bed filled with rats—which might not be a bad idea.

"Coincidence," Shelby muttered under her breath as she returned to her post. "Isn't it just?"

Chapter Thirty

Brandy sat with her legs wrapped around a stool in the ice-cream shop, licking whipped cream off a long spoon with such obvious enjoyment that the boy behind the counter walked right into the open freezer door.

"You know what, Shelley?" she said, oblivious to the teen's hopeful dreams. "It's getting so you can't tell the players without a scorecard. And, by the way, if I see one more movie this week, so that you aren't actually lying to Quinn—which you've been doing all along, I won't be so rotten as to point out—I think I'll qualify for some kind of discount. Now, run this all by me one more time, okay? You're telling me that Al is your *uncle?* Sweetcakes, do you think you may have overdosed on popcorn?"

After several hours to think about it while pretending to watch the movie that had entirely too happy an ending to suit her mood, Shelby was at last beginning to see the humor in this latest development. Sort of. "I'm not kidding, Brandy. Al is my Uncle Alfred, and vice versa."

"The guy who had his own adventures before he *settled,* right? The one who sort of put it into your mind that taking off, living a *normal* life among the little people for a while, would be a barrel of fun? The one who, um, *drinks* a bit? Is he that Uncle Alfred?"

"One and the same. And now I think I've figured out why he does it. Drinks, that is. Although my only two dives into a bottle didn't end all that well. Brandy, how do I face a life like Uncle Alfred's after this? How do I settle? Especially when, as you've already pointed out to me, I can't hold my liquor. Poor Uncle Alfred. I hope he's enjoying himself. With Tabby. They were going to go to some club Tabby likes. I can just imagine it. God." Shelby sighed, her elbows inelegantly propped on the bar as she used a long spoon to play with the hot fudge that was rapidly melting her ice cream.

Brandy was silent for a few moments; then she said in a small voice, "He pinched me. Tonight, as Gar and I were leaving Tony's. Honest to God, Shel, he *pinched* me. Right on the . . . well, you know where, right? He said Brandy was his favorite name of all time. Now I understand why. What a sweet old man."

Shelby turned her head and looked at her friend. "That's Uncle Alfred. When I was still a child, I used to watch him walk through a room during a party, and watch all the elegantly clad ladies giving these little jumps and *eeks* as he walked by pretending he was as innocent as a newborn lamb. I think it's Uncle Alfred's version of the wave, you know, that thing we saw the fans doing when we watched that Phillies game," she said, then dissolved into giggles as Brandy's face went cherry red, nearly blotting out her riot of freckles.

Brandy smiled, then shook her head. "So glad you've finally found something to laugh at, Shelley, even if it's mostly at *me.* But, you know, if anyone else had pinched me I would have turned around, hauled off, and swatted him a good one. But there's something about your Uncle Alfred . . . something so twinkling and full of fun, that the pinch felt more like a compliment."

"Thus the secret of Uncle Alfred's success," Shelby agreed, nodding. "He's such a gentleman, but with that little imp of mischief about him that has you laughing right along with him."

"Everyone but your brother, at least right now," Brandy pointed out, digging into the second level of her sundae, as that was how she ate them, starting with the cherry, then the whipped cream, and only then the caramel syrup and ice cream. "Do you really think he tossed him out on his ear?"

Shelby pushed the half-eaten sundae away from her. "Yes, I think he has, much as it surprises me. Quinn didn't look shocked to see him, but that could be because he met him earlier in the day. Plus the fact that the man lies like a rug, and without flinching. In other words, I can't be sure Quinn knew Uncle Alfred had come to East Wapaneken, but I'm betting he isn't thrilled. Which makes two of us, or four, if you want to count those two great, hulking men who camped out at Tony's until we closed tonight."

"Bone crushers," Brandy said, bobbing her head knowingly. "Will they hurt him?"

"I don't think so, at least not yet. From what I remember from another famous episode in Uncle Alfred's life, they won't really hurt him unless he looks like he's running away. Running to East Wapaneken, then appearing in plain sight, even *talking* to the men, isn't exactly hiding, is it? I think those men are still trying to get over the shock, figure out what he's doing. Besides, he gets his quarterly allowance in another few weeks. Uncle Alfred always pays his debts; he just doesn't always pay them on time."

"Which takes us back to Quinn. He confessed everything to Gary."

"What!" Shelby's eyes went wide and she sat up so quickly she nearly toppled off the high stool. "He *told* him? Oh, God, then it's true. It's all true."

Brandy waved her hands in front of her, saying, "Whoa, whoa. I thought you said you already *knew*. Knew he was hired to find you, probably told to then watch you until you came to your senses and went home. Right? You *knew*."

Shelby rubbed at her forehead, tried to hold back the tears threatening to fall. "No, Brandy," she admitted miserably. "I *thought* so. It seemed logical; then I was sure of it when I finally made the connection between Quinn and D and S, finally remembered seeing him the night of the charity ball. Except I still didn't *want* to believe it. Just in this small part of me, I *didn't* believe it, ridiculous as that sounds. God, what a fool I am, what a stupid, *stupid* fool."

Brandy looked at Shelby's melting sundae, sighed, and tried to lighten her friend's mood at least a little. "Man, do I ever wish I couldn't eat when I was upset. Instead I eat everything that's not nailed down, even stuff I don't like." She took another bite of her own sundae, giving Shelby time to collect herself, then said, "Okay, so he came here to watch you. You were a job, plain and simple. Then he met you, talked to you, got to know you. And he took you to bed. You can't tell me that was part of his job, Shelley, because I won't believe it. I've seen how he looks at you. He looks at you the way I look at sundaes."

Shelby lifted her bent head and looked at Brandy, her smile tremulous, but there. Real. "He does?"

Brandy rolled her eyes theatrically. "And contained within those two words or others much like them, madam, is the reason why men get away with murder, and always have. Yeah, Shel, he does. And you'll forgive him almost anything, just because *I* think he loves you. No wonder

I've been engaged for twelve years. That's us dumb, gullible women. Lord, I'm the poster child for forgiving a man for being impossible, just because he looks at me with love in his eyes. Right after he tells me Mama has the gout and we can't have the wedding because she refuses to walk down the aisle with a cane.''

"I have *not* forgiven him, Brandy," Shelby asserted, paying the check before Brandy could snatch it from her, then following her friend out into the warm June evening. "Or are you forgetting that clumsy kidnap attempt? 'About damn time.' That's what the man said when Quinn came running toward him. As if he was late for the show the guy was putting on, a show meant to scare me into going home. Unless you think the regulars hired those men because I overheard them threaten the mayor? And I didn't even tell you about the letter. I think he just got tired of being here, and wanted me to panic and—''

"Back up, Shelley. Letter? What letter?"

The next fifteen minutes were pretty much taken up by Brandy, who berated Shelby for not confiding in her, about the letter, about her suspicions about the regulars and Quinn—at least for not telling her right away. Shelby apologized about six times, as the bouncy Brandy seemed to cool down, then set off again, saying it stank pretty bad when she had to learn stuff from Gary, who knew nothing most of the time. How *dared* he know more than she did?

Before Brandy could work up a full head of steam that would undoubtedly culminate with a blistering phone call to the hapless Gary, Shelby stopped, hugged Brandy, and gave her a kiss on the cheek. "I adore you, you know."

"Well, of course you do, silly," Brandy said, wiping away quick tears. "That's what I am. Adorable. Now, when are you going to confront Quinn and tell him that the jig is up, that you know who he is and why he's here? Before or after you hit him, if you're so sure he's the one playing games with notes and stuff?''

"When? *Never.* I just can't.''

They'd reached the apartment, and Brandy pulled her down on the steps beside her, a full moon casting eerie shadows all around them, warring with the streetlight on the corner. "Never? You're kidding, right? You're just going to walk away? Say nothing? Go back to Philadelphia? *Marry* Parker?''

"He's the one who lied," Shelby declared mulishly. "So why should I be the one to say anything?''

"Meaning, of course, why should you tell him that *you* were lying to him, saying you were brought up here in East Wappy, and all the rest of it? Oh yeah, I can see your point. He lied, and you're as honest as Abe Lincoln. Jeez, Shelley, give me a break. You're *both* lying to each other, both of you. He's known it all along, and you've figured it out.''

"But *he* knew from the beginning. I didn't.''

"Oh. Oh, yeah. Okay, I see it now. We're talking *pride* here, aren't we? Tell me, how warm do you think pride keeps you on cold winter nights?''

Shelby felt herself becoming angry. "Just because you let Gary and his mother run roughshod over you is no reason for me to lie down and let Quinn turn me into a doormat.''

"So I don't have any pride?" Brandy began poking herself in the chest with one finger. "Me? I don't have any *pride?* Is that what you're saying? Well, *that* stinks. What am I supposed to do, Shelley? Throw away the only man I love, just to satisfy my *pride?* You know something, Miss Shelby Taite? I don't think you love Quinn. I don't think you have the faintest idea what love *is.*''

Shelby buried her face in her hands and shook her head miserably. "Oh, Brandy, I'm sorry. I didn't mean that. Really, I didn't.'' She dropped her hands and looked at her friend. "I'm just lashing out, hurting everyone, ruining everything. I guess I'm just not *real* enough for real life. I'm too scared to really *live* a real life. I—I'm a *mess!*"

Brandy gathered the weeping Shelby into her arms, rocking her as she would a child, and let her cry. Just let her cry.

A long time later, they walked up the stairs together, arm in arm, and Brandy fished in her purse for her key as Shelby blew her nose one last time.

"Is that our phone?" Brandy asked, taking a quick look at her watch. "It's nearly midnight, for crying out loud. No, wait—it's not our phone; it's Quinn's. I wonder who could be calling him this late at night."

Shelby looked toward Quinn's door, imagining him rousing from sleep, his dark hair tousled, his eyelids heavy, half-shut, the way they were when he looked down at her after loving her, a slow grin forming on his lips.

She hugged herself, stupidly remembering her maid Susie telling her that Jim was only "half a man" without his wife. That had seemed so sad to Shelby, but it wasn't until this very moment that she really understood. She was half a woman without Quinn, would probably spend the rest of her life as only half a woman.

Which was still more of a woman than she'd been before he appeared in Tony's restaurant.

Could she remain only half a woman? Did she really believe she couldn't walk across this hall, knock on Quinn's door, and confront him with what she knew? Could she spend the rest of this night alone, the rest of her life alone? *Before I leave,* she told herself bracingly, *I'll tell him before I leave. Oh, please, let him tell me first. If he truly loves me, let him tell me first. . . .*

"I can't imagine who it could be," she said at last, giving Quinn's closed door one last, longing look before following Brandy into their apartment even as she heard the rumble of Quinn's voice, low and gruff, as he answered the phone. "Not that he'll tell me. Not that he's ever told me anything . . ."

If Quinn could have heard Shelby's sad comment he would have flung down the phone and gone to her, told her everything, begged her forgiveness. But he didn't hear her, and he really couldn't tell her everything because he didn't know everything.

But maybe, with Grady on the other end of the phone, he was finally going to learn what *everything* was.

"What've you got?" Quinn asked as soon as Grady identified himself as Agent 006, one better than "Bond, James Bond."

"It's not what I've got, bucko," Grady then told him. "It's what you've got. And you've been holding out on me."

Quinn brushed a hand over his hair as he went into the kitchen area and hit the button on the coffeemaker, which was already filled and set up to go on in the morning. "It's midnight, Grady, and I haven't exactly had a great night, or a great day, either, come to think of it. What are you talking about?"

"Your crystal ball, of course, unless you read tea leaves or tarot cards, or something like that," Grady answered.

Quinn balanced the receiver against his shoulder as he pulled out the glass coffeepot and replaced it with his cup when the coffee began its slow drip. "I was right?" he said, already waking up, without the coffee.

"More than right," Grady told him. "But, dramatic sort that I am, first I want you to tell me why my poor good buddy has had such a lousy day. I thought you and Miss Taite were happy as hell in your fool's paradise. What's the matter, Quinn, the snake show up?"

Quinn replaced the coffeepot, made his way to the kitchen bar, and sat down on a stool. He gathered up pen and paper, the ones he'd left on the bar, and got ready to take down the information Grady had gathered. But first he'd give Grady his moment, let him build the suspense. "That depends. Would you call Alfred Taite a snake?"

"Uncle Lush?" Grady's voice broke on a sudden, delighted laugh. "God, Quinn, don't tell me Uncle Lush is there."

"He's here, he's real, and he's busing tables at the same restaurant where Shelby is working as a hostess. Stop laughing! He's blackmailed me into advancing him money for his rent, here in this same building—and then he charmed our landlady into letting him move in without putting down a deposit. Grady, damn it, I'm not going to tell you anything else if you don't stop laughing."

"I'm not laughing, Quinn; I'm *howling*. More, more. Tell me more. Is he washing dishes? I'd pay real cash money to see a Taite washing dishes."

Quinn took a sip of hot coffee, giving Grady a moment to collect himself. "What else is there? Oh, yeah. He wants everyone to call him Al." At this point, even Quinn was smiling, because—and he faced the fact—the whole thing *was* funny.

"You can call him Al? Didn't Paul Simon do a song like that a few years back? Hey, is he pinching the ladies? *Al* really enjoys pinching the ladies."

"Let's just say all the dear old ladies didn't need their heart-stimulating medication today, okay, and get on with it. I'm running out of time, Grady. Shelby is going home on Saturday, Sunday at the latest. Somehow, between now and then, I've got to tell her who I am, why I'm here, and hopefully tell her who's been writing her threatening letters, faking a damn kidnapping, if you can believe that."

"All of that, huh? And I guess I'm supposed to help?"

"Only if you've got information for me, which you said you do. Come on, spill it."

"All right, but afterward we're going to have a small talk about fake kidnappings, poison-pen letters, and why in the hell Shelby Taite isn't home in her mansion, writing out wedding invitations."

"You know why," Quinn said, picking up the pen. "You damn well know why. Besides, I think she's made me. I don't know for sure, and it certainly took long enough, but I think she has. Which just makes everything worse."

"Bucko, I don't think it could *get* worse. Not unless Somerton and Jeremy show up. I don't think East Wapa-thingamigig would ever fully recover from *that*. Somerton punching Westbrook—I still can't get over that one, old Stiff Ass nailing Westbrook, more power to him—and Jer-emy asking Shelby to make sure the kitchen help cuts the crust off his sandwiches."

"Right, whatever. Your information, Grady. If I'm going to hell, at least I first want to know that I'm right, and that no matter how Shelby will hate me, probably already hates me, she won't marry that jerk."

"You know," Grady said, dragging out his end of the conversation as long as he could, "it still could be those Vietnam vets who sent her the notes, tried to kidnap her. It doesn't have to be Westbrook, just like I told you yester-day when I called with the information on the license plate."

"It was a rental, picked up in Philadelphia. And it wasn't the regulars. Shelby's planning a huge fund-raising dinner for them this Friday. They worship her, for crying out loud. Which reminds me—I still haven't written George's speech. Damn."

There was a short, pregnant silence at the other end of the phone; then Grady remarked conversationally, "Quinn, old buddy, I can't tell you how much I've been enjoying these little late-night conversations of ours. You're better than summer reruns, a damn sight better. You're writing a speech? Quinn Delaney, who had to romance the prof's daughter to get a C in Lit? Why haven't I heard that one before now?"

"Because I knew you'd react just as you have, that's why," Quinn said, feeling the world rolling straight over him, flattening him beneath a mountain of problems, only some of them caused by his own actions. Well, okay, a *lot* of them caused by his own actions. "Now give me what you've got, or I'm coming down there to choke it out of you."

Chapter Thirty-one

Quinn was knee-deep in computer-generated reports, bits of information that still had to be brought together in something coherent enough for the auditors, and had been all morning, only taking time out to surreptitiously watch Shelby on her walk down the street to Tony's just before noon.

The reports had to be done, and it was better than thinking about Shelby, thinking about how he was going to approach her, what he was going to say.

It would be so much simpler if he could just kidnap her, take her to Vegas, and set her down in front of some justice of the peace.

"She knows," he said out loud as he went to refill his coffee mug. A few more cups of coffee and he could probably fly Shelby and himself to Vegas without a plane. "She has to know. But she doesn't know all of it, can't know all of it. Which makes you either her savior, Delaney, or some

smug son of a bitch who's going to be told to keep his
damn nose out of her business.''

Grady's information about Parker Westbrook III had
been even better—no, *worse*, he really should think *worse*—
than he had thought, and a lot easier to obtain than either
he or Grady had believed it would be.

Joining a few mutual acquaintances at their club at
lunch, then mentioning—just in passing—that Westbrook
sure seemed to have a lot of irons in the fire and he
wondered if he could keep all those irons hot, had been
all that was needed to get the men talking.

And talking. Once one said something, the rest seemed
more than eager to join in, add their bits to the evidence
that was fast going to bury Westbrook. Unless he had a
very large infusion of funds before all those irons fell out
of the fire and burned his hotshot ass.

Marriage to Shelby Taite, and her money, would be
Westbrook's salvation.

He needed her, needed her badly.

Badly enough to try to scare her into coming home?

"It's so far-fetched," Quinn told himself as he walked
across the room to answer a knock that showed no signs
of stopping. "Oh, it's good old Al. Yippee," he said sarcastically to Uncle Alfred as he turned away from the open
door. "What happened? Were you fired already?"

"Honest toil for an honest dollar," Uncle Alfred said,
making himself at home on the couch, "does not mean
working one's fingers to the nub. My presence is not
required at Anthony's establishment until two o'clock."

"And in the meantime, you've decided to come in here
and visit with me. Once more with feeling—yippee."

"Yes, thank you, I will have coffee."

"Did I offer any? You pour it all day at Tony's. I think
you can muddle through here and find your own cup."

"How the high have fallen. You know what, I've decided

something. The next time I think about living a *real* life—
which I doubt I will do, Somerton or no Somerton—I'm
going to bring at least one Taite employee with me. The
cook, I think, or one of the maids, as I don't think I have
whatever it takes to repair what I seem to do to bedding
in a single night. Thank heaven for Bertha. Good woman,
good woman, but unnervingly like the ladies I squire about
town in her own way. Now Tabitha. Ah, that's another
matter entirely, and part of the reason my sheets were in
such disarray.''

Uncle Alfred sighed, remembering his evening, then
retrieved a cup and filled it, leaving just enough room for
a dollop of the Irish whiskey he had in his flask. "I may
be wrong here, but I do believe you're unhappy about
something?''

Quinn gave a short laugh, saved his work on the laptop,
and shut it down. "What was your first clue?''

"I've been in love a time or three myself, son, and recognize the symptoms. That hearts-and-flowers business is just
so much claptrap. Suffering. That's what love is, which is
why I ran far and fast when I found myself sighing and
moping. But you're not running, are you, son? And neither
is Shelby. Interesting.''

"Yeah, a real nail-biter,'' Quinn said, then quickly caught
himself as he realized he was about to sigh. "I've got to
tell her, Al, tell her all of it. Soon. Even if I think she
already knows some of it, most of it.''

"Well, of course she knows,'' Uncle Alfred said, sipping
his spiked coffee, then sighing himself, but in satisfaction.
"She's my niece, isn't she? Do you think she's stupid? Now
ask yourself something else—why hasn't she confronted
you? Why hasn't she left town? And don't tell me it's just
because of this little charity soiree she's tossing, because
that's ridiculous. She may have planned it, but it's running
along quite splendidly on its own, according to Tabitha—

a dear girl, by the way, and quite talented. In any event, Shelby isn't needed anymore, not really. So—and this will be rhetorical, because you look as if you've swallowed your tongue—why is my niece still here? She's still here because she loves you. Now tell me what you're going to do about it before I begin to think she's lost her heart to an idiot.''

Quinn looked at the older man for a long time, measuring him, deciding what to tell him. ''Westbrook needs Shelby's money,'' he said at last.

''Well, of course he does, son. We all never have all the money we want, even if we have all that we need.'' Then he frowned. ''Oh. He *needs* her money? How do you know this?''

''Does it matter?'' Quinn asked, beginning to pace. ''I just don't know if I can tell Shelby.''

The flask came out once more. ''She could be grateful, I suppose. But I doubt that. She'd probably want to know what the devil you were doing, meddling in her affairs. I don't think I'd blame her. You know, pointing out that Westbrook isn't the perfect fiancé, all that sort of thing, as if she's about to make a terrible mistake—and you're going to save her. Why, I wouldn't be surprised if she hauled off and hit you.''

Quinn pushed his fingers through his hair. ''Yeah, that's about how I see it. Except if Westbrook is behind the letters, that pseudo kidnap attempt, I'll have to tell her, explain the reasons behind them. As it is, she thinks it might be the regulars. Or maybe me,'' he said, his voice trailing off as that thought hit him and seemed to make some sort of twisted sense.

Uncle Alfred slapped his knees and stood up. ''I'd say you're well and truly hung on the horns of a dilemma, son. Pity. Now, if you could turn your mind to another subject, I'd appreciate the return of the rest of the funds you so generously advanced to me. I've a game going, you understand, with that marvelous group Shelby calls the regulars. Oh, and Tabitha, of course, and Mutt and Jeff, too. Those two were more than happy to join us, especially as they seem to want to keep me in sight. We stayed after Anthony closed up last night, doing a few rounds of poker in the back room, and, sadly, I find myself financially embarrassed today."

Quinn pinched the bridge of his nose and winced. "Poker. At *Anthony's*. And Mutt and Jeff? Those would have to be the knee-smashers. Figures." He shook his head, reached into his pocket, and pulled out another three hundred dollars. "I don't know why, but it figures. You'll never learn, will you?" he asked as Uncle Alfred pocketed the bills.

"Hopefully not, son, hopefully not," he answered, grinning through his well-trimmed beard. "I'm old now, and this is one dog who isn't interested in new tricks. You, however, are young, you and Shelby both. You don't yet have a grasp on the fact that you're mortal, that life is short, and to be lived hopefully without regret. Life is to be grabbed at greedily, and with both hands. In other words, *talk* to the girl. Now, today."

Quinn stared at the door for a long time after Uncle Alfred left, thinking. He knew Uncle Alfred would watch Shelby today, Uncle Alfred, and Tony, and the regulars, even Mutt and Jeff—they'd all watch her. For many reasons, Shelby was immensely watchable. She'd be safe, and safely at work until nine o'clock.

Then he went back to work, forgetting to eat lunch, slapping two pieces of ham between some almost stale bread for dinner. But by eight o'clock that night, the reports were all done, both those he sent via E-mail attachments to the Philadelphia office and those he'd printed out and faxed to the auditors.

He was free and clear, with nothing standing between

him and Shelby but their mutual lies . . . and so he thought
as he walked into Tony's just before closing and leaned
against the wall beside the cash register.

Then, belatedly, Quinn realized something else. Something surprising, actually unnerving. Unsure. Nervous. Was
this Quinn Delaney? It sure wasn't any Quinn Delaney *he*
remembered. He knew himself to be calm, self-assured,
the kind of guy who could walk away from anything, anyone, with no regrets. Just move himself on to greener
pastures. And now here he was, looking for fences. Praying
for fences.

"I've come to escort you home," he told Shelby as she
made change for a customer. "If that's all right?"

Shelby silently congratulated herself for not literally
jumping out of her skin. She'd been missing him all day,
wondering where he was, worried about where he was,
what he might be thinking. Running conversations in her
head, trying to approach the subject of their mutual lies
from so many directions she had nearly become dizzy, not
to mention sticking her thumb into Mrs. Miller's bowl of
creamed cucumbers. Only Uncle Alfred could keep her
from complaining to Tony that Shelby was trying to poison
her.

"Thank you. That would be nice," Shelby answered,
shutting the drawer, but not looking up, not looking at
him. "Have you eaten? You haven't been in all day."

"Now that you mention it, I could eat something. We
could go back to my apartment, order a pizza?"

And talk, he ended silently.

"I'll just tell Tony I'm leaving," she said, wishing her
voice didn't sound so weak and quavering. "He's, um, he's
going to be here until at least midnight anyway."

"Playing poker," Quinn said, grinning. When she
looked at him, frowning, he added, "Let's just say there's

been a rumor to that effect. Is the police chief in on it yet? I'll bet he is, and I'm not a betting man.''

Shelby nodded, still frowning, and went to talk to Tony. She knew how Quinn knew about the game. Uncle Alfred had told him. There could be no other way, considering that he'd not been to the restaurant all day. How nice that the two men could "chat." About a whole lot more than poker, she'd bet, and *she* wasn't a betting woman.

"Let's go,'' she said as she came out of the kitchen, brushing past Quinn, pushing open the door.

He followed her like a puppy just graduated from obedience school, then took her hand and slowed her rapid gait. "Let's enjoy the night, all right?''

Shelby didn't want to "enjoy the night.'' She wanted to talk, damn it. Or maybe she didn't. Maybe she wanted him to talk.

Maybe she didn't want either one of them to talk.

They climbed the stairs together, Shelby waiting as Quinn unlocked the door to his apartment. "There's a pink scarf tied around Brandy's doorknob,'' he told her, and she looked across the hallway and grimaced.

"Great. Now what am I supposed to do?''

"Eat pizza,'' Quinn said, pulling her into the apartment, bringing her against his chest. "I'll call for it . . . in a moment.'' He lowered his head toward hers, aware that this might be the first of the last kisses he'd ever share with her. "In a minute . . .''

Shelby felt his lips brush against hers, lightly, teasingly. Once, twice, a third time. He wasn't holding her; he wasn't really kissing her. What he was, she felt sure, was waiting for an invitation.

She gave it to him. Slid her arms up and around his shoulders, stepped closer against him. Finally grabbed onto his head with both hands and ground her mouth against his, her need overwhelming everything else—including what she believed to be her better judgment.

She needed him. She wanted him. She loved him.

Nothing else mattered, not for this moment. Nothing else could.

She sighed into his mouth as he lifted her and carried her into his bedroom. Reached up for him blindly as he put her on the bed, then left her for a few moments, a lifetime, before joining her again. Before undressing her, slowly, his warm mouth following after his hands as he slid her clothes from her body, pressed his own nakedness against her.

His kisses were long, drugging, and she felt tears stinging her eyes as she held on to him, held on to him because she could not let go. To let go was to lose him, to face the truth, to ruin this glorious perfection.

Quinn found her breasts with his mouth and hands, devouring the taste of her, skimming his fingers over her, glorying in her soft moans, her automatic response to his touch that couldn't be faked, was never a lie.

I love you, I love you, he chanted inside his head, not daring to say the words. Not now. Not yet. He'd said them once, and frightened her. He had to tell her the truth, all of the truth, or else his words of love would be meaningless.

He lingered over her, committing each curve to memory, until Shelby reached down, clasped him in her hand, and whispered into his ear, "Please, please. Please, now."

Shelby's tears flowed freely as he eased onto her, slid between her welcoming thighs, sank deep inside her. She wrapped her legs around him, high on his back, and held him to her with hands that caressed, urged, imprisoned. She wanted all of him, even as she gave all, praying her body could tell him how much she loved, even as her mind hid how little she trusted.

Their mouths clung, so that neither could tell lies, neither could say the truth. For the lies had hurt, but the truth could destroy.

Afterward they showered together in the old-fashioned claw-footed tub with the brightly flowered shower curtain enclosing them beneath a round curtain rod. They laughed as they stood together on rubber cutout daisies pressed to the bottom of the tub, their laughter dying as Quinn soaped up his hands and began washing Shelby, who became suddenly modest, turning her head as she tried to still his hands.

But Quinn persisted, not going too fast, but only fast enough to keep her from bolting, to wait until she melted against him, her blond hair darkly wet as she threw back her head and gave herself over to his ministrations. Until her body became one throbbing center, until her muscles forgot how to work and she nearly slid from his arms.

He lifted her from the tub as the water turned cold, wrapped her in a huge bath sheet he'd brought from his Philadelphia apartment, and sat her down on the small bench in the bathroom. He used a smaller towel to dry her hair as she sat there, looking at him, occasionally leaning against him, sighing against his chest.

"Hungry?" he asked against her ear, and felt her head move in the negative, followed closely by a yawn. He smiled, kissed the tip of her nose, lifted her in his arms, and carried her to the bed. "We should talk," he said as she lay down on her side, curled into a fetal position.

"I know," she answered, her eyes closed as she snuggled deeper into the feather pillow.

Quinn turned off the light and crawled into the bed beside her. "Do you want to talk?"

"I don't think so," Shelby answered honestly, two days of near-sleepless nights catching up to her with a vengeance. "I just want to sleep. Here, with you. Can we do that, please?"

Quinn reached out a hand and brushed her damp hair behind her ear. "But you *know,* don't you?" he asked, watching her face carefully.

"Yes, I know. You're a rat," Shelby murmured after a moment, feeling as if she were within a dream, safe in a fantasy where she could have everything she wanted, say anything she wanted, always win and never lose. "I'm in love with a rat." Then she yawned, sighed, and fell asleep.

Quinn watched her for a long time, the bed a mass of dark and light gray stripes thanks to the full moon coming in through the blinds, before carefully sliding off the bed, pulling on a pair of shorts, and returning to the living room.

He turned off the television and the single light he'd left burning, and sat down on the couch. There was nothing else, he knew, that he could say to Shelby. No explanation, long or short, no graphs, no spreadsheets, no smooth or not-so-smooth massaging of the truth to make himself look better.

It was over. The worst was over, with neither of them saying much of anything, actually. The only thing left was to wait for the morning, and learn whether Shelby loved him enough to forgive him.

That was the question. The last question. Unless she'd already said everything she meant, all he needed to know.

I'm in love with a rat. Shelby's near-comatose confession had just about said it all.

Chapter Thirty-two

Shelby smiled as she walked to work Thursday morning, secure in the knowledge that Quinn was going to have a very stiff neck, if his position on his couch could be any indication.

Which served him right, she had thought as she'd tiptoed through the living room and closed the door behind her.

Because he'd tricked her. Kissed her. Made love to her. Held her, caressed her, took her to the brink and over so many times that she had all but passed out in his bed without a word spoken between them about his lies, her lies.

She stopped to listen to a robin high in one of the sidewalk shade trees, smiling as she remembered Quinn's conniving ways, his avoidance of discussion, his mouth hot and moist against hers. The way he treated her body like a fine musical instrument he had mastered, creating a symphony so seductive that there was nothing she could do but succumb to the magic.

"You're good," she said, looking up at the robin. "But he's better." Then she smiled and walked on, and decided that this morning was just about the best morning of her life. Quinn loved her. She loved him.

They'd talk about their mutual lies some other time. Maybe in fifty years. And they'd laugh about them.

Yes, fifty years. That would be a good time.

Time.

About damn time.

Those three damning words . . .

Shelby stopped, her smile disappearing as those three words echoed in her mind. Quinn loved her. She loved him. They wouldn't talk about that man, that threatening note, those three words. They couldn't. Not now, not in fifty years. Because, if it were true, it would mean he was definitely a rat, and if it were false, then she'd be shown as a person who could believe something so terrible about the man she loved.

That realization slid a single cloud over Shelby's lovely morning, but she didn't have time to feel sorry for herself once she opened the door to Tony's and went straight to dealing with the lingering morning crowd and the early lunch crowd—which many times were the same people.

It seemed as if many of the citizens of East Wapaneken had decided to make a day of it at Tony's, including at least a dozen who offered their help in preparing for the three-seatings fund-raiser the regulars had officially dubbed "The Official Fund-raiser for Our Sons, Fathers, Husbands, and Brothers." It wasn't exactly a catchy title, but it worked. At least for the most part. *And Cousins,* someone had scratched onto the end of the long banner that hung sort of at half-mast across the restaurant's front windows.

Thelma had come back from Texas a day early when she heard about the dinner, intent on taking up her duties as hostess. A tall, rangy-looking woman who had a lantern jaw and black raisin eyes, she'd introduced herself to Shelby at three, intent on letting this upstart young woman know who was in charge. At three-fifteen, she was folding cloth napkins in the shape of swans, just as Shelby had taught her, and telling anyone who would listen that she was going to wear her purple dress that night—the one with the bugle beads she'd bought for her daughter's wedding—and content herself with being a pampered customer for a change.

One after another, crises came up. One after another, Shelby shot them down. Although she did have some small trouble with Tony and the matter of presentation.

"Presentation is everything," she told the man who thought a garnish was a fat wad of iceberg lettuce with a chunk of orange perched on top of it.

"*Food* is everything," Tony countered, scowling down at her as he shoved another huge rib roast into the oven. "*Taste* is everything. You got your linens. You got the fancy cups for the ladies. And that's all you're getting, understand?"

Thoughts of exotic greens and perhaps a tomato slice in aspic were waved a reluctant farewell as Shelby returned to the dining room, put her hands on her hips, and took one last look around the room. They'd closed the restaurant at three to remove the oilcloths and replace them with the rented linens that gleamed a soft ivory, accented by the deep rose "swans" Thelma had made.

Silverware glinted on each table, the spoons, knives, and forks arranged correctly instead of simply rolled up inside a paper napkin. There were new silk flowers in the holders, the ketchup bottles had been removed, and tonight sugar would be served in paper packets rather than in huge silver-topped containers. Small folded papers marked each table with the name of the party that had reserved it for the first sitting.

Crepe-paper streamers of ivory and navy crisscrossed the ceiling and trailed in the corners. Shelby had personally washed the leaves of all the hanging plants and placed blue crepe-paper bows around each pot.

She looked around, smiling softly, and realized that each napkin, each tablecloth, each new silk flower, had been a victory. Her victory. Such a warm feeling of accomplishment swept over her, ten times stronger than it ever had when she'd been on committees for various charity balls. Because this was different. This was East Wapaneken. And she had done this herself, for a truly wonderful reason.

The satisfaction of a job well done.

She pressed a hand to her stomach. *And all the butterflies of a first-time hostess, praying nothing too disastrous will occur before the evening is over.*

"You're looking smug, my dear," Uncle Alfred said from behind Shelby, so that she nearly jumped out of her skin.

She turned to look at him, amazed to see him dressed in his tuxedo. "Where . . . ?"

"Darling, no one travels without being prepared for all possibilities, didn't you know that? Now help me with this tie, won't you? I can't seem to be able to do it by myself."

He lifted his head and Shelby expertly completed the job her uncle had started, then kissed him on the cheek before stepping back to admire him once more. "You really are a handsome devil, you know. The ladies will be swooning all night long."

"As long as they tip me first," Uncle Alfred said, winking at her. "This is nice, isn't it, my dear? I feel so *American,* if that's the word. Why, it's almost like a barn raising, or whatever it's called. One for all and all for one and . . . well, let's just say I'm enjoying myself and have done with it. Not that you're to tell Somerton any such thing. I want him to believe I am suffering unbearably, am learning a lesson about my profligate ways, and will be like a tame lamb once he allows me back under his roof."

"Looking for a raise in your quarterly allowance, aren't you?" Shelby said, shaking her head.

"It could happen," Uncle Alfred said, then turned on his heel to go open the door, as someone was knocking on it. "Ah," he called over his shoulder as he advanced toward the door. "Joseph and Francis are here, isn't that nice."

"Joseph and Francis?" Shelby asked, stepping around the divider to see the two hulking men she had actually believed were named Mutt and Jeff coming into the restaurant carrying . . . a small organ? "Unc—I mean, Al—what on *earth?*"

"Our dinnertime entertainment, my dear," Uncle Alfred said as Joseph—carrying a padded bench—and Francis—hefting a small electronic organ over his head as if it weighed no more than a feather—passed by, heading for a small cleared spot on the opposite side of the room.

"No," Shelby said, shaking her head. "You're kidding. You *are* kidding, aren't you?"

"On the contrary, my dear. It seems that Joseph is quite accomplished on that musical machine. He's had, oh, at least five lessons beyond what he has taught himself, and is very proud of himself. They broached the idea to Anthony last night, during our game, and he agreed." He stepped closer, bent down, and whispered in Shelby's ear, "They also promised to knock two grand off my bill if I told Anthony they were professional musicians."

Shelby watched as the organ was plugged in and set up on its metal legs, as the padded bench was positioned behind it. Joseph sat down as Francis placed a thick music book—*Beginners Broadway*—on the small stand, then stood back, his beefy hands folded at his belly, a grin as wide as a carved melon on his face.

Joseph opened the book. Selected a page. Frowned. Stood up.

Francis repositioned the bench.

Joseph sat down, flexed his fingers a few times. Touched the open book.

Frowned. Stood up.

Francis repositioned the bench.

"Oh, my God," Shelby groaned under her breath. "It's like watching a pair of hippos in pink tutus performing *Swan Lake.*"

"Nasty girl," Uncle Alfred scolded, chuckling. "Nasty, nasty. I prefer to see them as two rather, er, *large* devotees of musical theater."

Joseph sat down, flexed his fingers once more. Tested the organ by playing a few chords.

Frowned. Stood up.

Francis—well, it was obvious by now what Francis would do next.

"Do you think Joseph and his artistic backside will be ready before the last seating?" Shelby asked, beginning to see the humor in the thing.

"Darling, do you honestly care?" Uncle Alfred asked, then flipped a snow white towel over his left forearm as he walked off to answer yet another knock on the front door. "Ah, Quinn, my boy. Who have you here? Well, never mind. I've been commissioned to locate the nearest grocery establishment and purchase several dozen tomatoes. Anthony was good enough to lend me the keys to his truck, so I didn't wish to bother him with the mention that I haven't driven myself anywhere in twenty years. You may take over in my absence, all right?"

Shelby heard Quinn's name and immediately found herself checking her hair, making sure no wisps had come free from the French knot she'd placed it in earlier. She had begun to brush down the front of her softest lilac Armani suit before she realized what she was doing, and deliberately stopped before Quinn could poke his head around the divider and say, "You had visitors waiting outside, Miss Smith, totally stymied by the 'Closed' sign on the door. I thought I'd rescue them."

"Visitors?" A quick, panicked thought was that, since everyone knew where she was anyway, Somerton and Jeremy might have decided enough was enough and come to take her home. Or Parker. God, she hoped it wasn't Parker. . . .

"Miss Smith?" a young teenager Shelby didn't recognize said as she walked around the divider to see not just him but a second boy standing in the entranceway, scrubbed, well combed, and dressed in shirts and clip-on ties. The one who spoke was carrying a bouquet of flowers.

"Yes," she said slowly, then saw the folded papers clenched in the second boy's hands, and remembered. "Oh, yes. It is Friday, isn't it?"

"Yes, ma'am," the one who seemed to be the appointed spokesman agreed, running a hand beneath his collar, which was too tight, and then tugging at his sleeves, which were too short. Some rather major growing had gone on since the last time either of these boys had needed to wear a white shirt, that was for certain, but they both looked so adorably uncomfortable that Shelby wanted to hug them.

"Are those for me?" she asked, pointing to the flowers.

"Yes, ma'am, they are. Me and Jimmy here, well, our moms said ladies like flowers. And we've got the essay, too. We both wrote it, all by ourselves."

"Except my sister, Jen, she typed it up on her computer,"

Jimmy added, obviously having learned the lesson of honesty with a vengeance. "She says it's pretty good."

"I'll bet it is," Shelby said, taking the essay from him, tucking the flowers into the crook of her arm. "Your parents must be very proud of you both," she told them, her throat tight. "I know I am. I'm very, very proud of you both."

"Yes, ma'am," Jimmy said, ducking his head. "Like Richie here said last night, we sure have learned our lesson. Especially Richie. His dad was really piss—um, really angry. He can't go to the mall for a *month*. I'm just cutting grass. For my folks, for my aunt, and for one of our neighbors. But that's all right," he added hastily. "I mean, we did something wrong, ain't that right, Richie? And we learned our lesson."

"Boy, did we learn our lesson," Richie agreed heartily, then smiled a little when Quinn put out his hand and affectionately rubbed the boy's neatly combed head. "Yeah, well, we gotta go, right, Jimmy? Gotta get home before anyone sees us."

Jimmy grimaced and rolled his eyes. "Too late. Jen took a picture of me when I came out of the bathroom."

Quinn threw back his head and laughed, then watched as Shelby stepped forward and kissed both boys on the cheek before they ran out, grinning. "That was probably worth all of it," he said as Shelby kept her head down, pretending a great interest in the daisies in her arms. "You did good, Shelley. More kids ought to have lessons like that, and parents who care that much."

"Uh-huh," Shelby said, turning on her heel and heading for the service bar, grabbing a tall glass and putting the flowers into it. She still held the essay, all three pages of it, but knew she couldn't open it right now, read it right now.

How she loved this place, this life. It was everything Jim Helfrich had said. *Real.* And tomorrow it would be a memory.

Quinn stepped up behind her and placed a hand on her shoulder. "Hey, are you all right?"

She shook her head, the first tears spilling down her cheeks. "No. I don't think so."

He turned her in his arms and cupped a hand under her chin so that he could look into her eyes. Could this be the Main Line socialite? This wonderfully emotional woman who cried because two teenagers combed their hair and brought her flowers? This woman he knew he loved with an intensity that still stunned him. Loved her heart, loved her mind, loved her very human soul. "Ah, sweetheart," he said, then pulled her close against him, cradling her head against his shoulders. "It's all right. I promise, everything is going to be fine, just fine."

Shelby held on, held on tight, trying to regain control of her emotions. By tomorrow she would be gone. By tomorrow she would have told Quinn everything and he would have told her . . . whatever he decided to tell her. By tomorrow she would be back in her old life. By tomorrow she could be alone.

And then, wonder of wonders, the exacting Joseph seemed at last to have found a comfortable positioning of his padded bench, the proper placement of his music, the correct spot for the huge brandy snifter Francis had placed on the organ in case anyone wanted to pay to have a special song played.

And then—could there be room in the day for more wonders?—as Joseph hit the first chords, Francis cleared his throat and began belting out the first few bars of "Oklahoma."

Quinn's arms encircled Shelby more closely as her shoulders began to shake, until he realized that she wasn't crying anymore. She was laughing. It had started as a quiet giggle, but had rapidly grown into a full-throated laugh so full of genuine amusement that it was impossible not to laugh along with her.

Until Joseph couldn't find a chord, and Francis had to hold a note—"O-o-o-o-o-o-o-o-o-o-o-o-o-o-kla"—for a full ten seconds until the next notes were located, at which point their laughter began to border on the very nearly hysterical.

With Shelby's face still buried in Quinn's shoulder, he hustled the two of them into the kitchen, where they pressed themselves against the wall and laughed like loons.

Tony merely looked up from his worktable and said, "What? You're music critics now? Shame on you. I think they're good. Now get out of my kitchen." Then he lifted his cleaver and cut another cabbage neatly in half.

Brandy arrived ten minutes before the first sitting was to officially begin, and cornered Shelby in the small back room, the famous no-smoking room that was always the last to fill in a town like East Wapaneken. She was dressed in a green-and-pink-flowered dress that skimmed her ankles, her freckles standing out in relief against her white skin. "Pay me," she said, holding out her hand.

"Pay you? Brandy, you have this backward. You pay us for your dinner. Although," she added, grinning, "you might be eligible for a small rebate if, as I remember, your table is next to the musical entertainment for the evening."

"Huh?" Then Brandy shook her head. "Never mind that. *Mama's* coming. Do you hear me, Shelley? *Mama.* It's not enough I gave up my Friday night line-dancing lessons for this, but *Mama?* God, Shel, there isn't enough indigestion medicine in the world to get me through this. What am I going to do? Besides killing her, I mean."

"I don't— Wait a minute!" She grabbed Brandy's hand and led her back to the main dining room. "Al . . . oh, Al," she called out, so that her uncle, who had been admiring his reflection in the silver on his flask, turned, cocking one eyebrow at her.

"You summoned me, my dear?" he asked, then bent over Brandy's hand. "Ah, my favorite beverage, that is, *person*. How wonderfully agitated you're looking this evening."

"Thanks, *Unc*," Brandy said, winking when he stepped back, nonplussed. "Oh, relax, I'm not telling anybody."

"Uncle Alfred, I've got a mission for you," Shelby told him as she turned him around and sought out the corner table reserved for Brandy and Gary. Gary waved to her, rather like a shipwrecked sailor hoping for rescue, and Shelby's gaze shifted to the woman sitting beside him.

Mrs. Mack sat on her chair, dressed all in black, her posture hinting that she had never in her life encountered a single comfortable seat and hadn't been expecting to find one tonight. She was thin as Brandy was pudgy, tall as Brandy was short, and if she'd smiled in the past twenty years no one could tell that by the frown on her face now, a frown that looked as if it had been chiseled in the rouged stone of her face. If she had been born a man, she probably would have become a general in somebody's army. Hopefully not ours, Shelby thought, shuddering.

"Uncle Alfred, do you see that lady sitting beside Brandy's friend Gary?"

Uncle Alfred, tonight affecting a monocle he'd found stuffed in his tuxedo pocket, raised the glass to one eye and looked in the direction Shelby had indicated. "Oh, dear."

It hadn't taken Brandy more than a second to understand what Shelby planned. "Yeah, Al, baby, *oh, dear*. And this mission Shel mentioned, if you should choose to accept it, is to keep that old bat so dotty with your attentions that she forgets to tell me how fond she always was of Gary's old girlfriend. Along with all the other stuff the old bat goes on about," she ended in a near grumble.

The monocle dropped from his eye to hang nearly to his waist on a thin black ribbon. "There will, of course, be recompense?"

"Name it," Shelby said as Mrs. Mack lifted the beautiful swan-shaped napkin and peered at it as if it might not be housebroken. "Price is no object."

"Very well, my dears. We'll discuss my payment later. As for now—into the valley of death rode . . . Well, however that goes. I never was much for committing great works to memory, the exception being Slappy Jack's racing form, of course."

"Thanks, Shel," Brandy said as they watched Uncle Alfred lift Mrs. Mack's hand and bow over it. "Oh, lordy, would you *look* at her? He's sitting down—and she's positively *melting!*"

Joseph, or perhaps Francis, saw Uncle Alfred and Mrs. Mack, and quite naturally broke into song, quite unnaturally singing "The Impossible Dream" from *Man of La Mancha*. Then again, maybe it did fit the situation. . . .

A few more parties drifted in, and then the rush began in earnest, Quinn standing next to Shelby as she welcomed each new group, directed them to their reserved tables.

"Fred and Hilda," he whispered. "Ruth and Jean. The Hunsbergers, all six of them." Then: "I'm going to spend the rest of my life sticking close to you, telling you who everyone is, aren't I?"

"Are you?" Shelby asked him, her heart skipping more than a single beat, rather like Joseph searching for yet another chord.

"If you'll let me, yes," Quinn said, looking at her

intently, wondering when his timing had gotten so bad. Or maybe it hadn't. She couldn't ask questions right now; she didn't have the time. She had time only for answers. At the moment, that worked for him. "Well? Will you marry me?"

Chapter Thirty-three

"Mayor Brobst, how lovely to see you this evening!" Shelby all but bellowed, mindful of the old woman's unreliable hearing aid. "Please allow me to escort you and Mrs. Fink to your table."

She spared a moment to look at Quinn before picking up two of the special menus and leading the ladies away. "I do remember *some* names," she told him, then made good her escape without answering his question.

How could she answer his question? She didn't even know if he was serious. How could he be serious? Not when there was still so much, so very, very much to talk about . . . not in those hopeful fifty years but now, tonight.

After seating the ladies, she motioned to George to follow her into the hallway that led to the rest rooms. He did so happily, looking eager to escape to any place where he wouldn't see the small lectern and attached microphone where he would give his speech at the end of this first seating, then twice more, if he didn't drop dead first.

"What's up?" he asked hopefully. "The microphone broke?"

"No such luck, George," Shelby told him kindly. "Besides, your wife told me that you're going to be terrific. You aren't nervous, are you?"

He reached into his pocket and pulled out the file cards on which Quinn had written his speech. "There's a couple of jawbreaker words in here. . . ." He took a deep breath, then let it out slowly. "You know, all we wanted to do was get old lady Brobst to spring for the wall—that's all. How did we end up doing all of this?"

"It's my fault, George. I'm sorry," Shelby said, patting his arm that strained the seams of his ten-year-old brown suit. "And now I'm going to make it all worse. George, I don't want to ask this, please believe me, I *really* don't want to ask this, but—would you really have killed the mayor?"

"Killed? Killed the *mayor*? Old lady Brobst?" George's face went white, then beet red. He threw back his head and laughed, looked at Shelby, and laughed some more. He pulled a large blue and white handkerchief from his pocket and wiped his streaming eyes. "Wow. That's some head stuff, isn't it? Like, you know, a shock treatment, to take my mind off the speech? Thanks, ma'am. I feel lots better now. Kill the mayor," he repeated, shaking his head as he walked away. "Man, if that don't beat the Dutch."

Shelby smiled after him wanly, then took a moment to visit the ladies' room, repair her makeup, and gather herself. Okay, she thought, staring at her reflection in the mirror. It wasn't George or the regulars. If he laughed that hard at her suggestion that he might have been plotting murder, she really didn't have to ask the second question, whether the regulars had been behind the letter, the kidnap attempt.

Which, no matter how many times she thought about it or, as Tony would say, no matter how she sliced it, ended up with Quinn Delaney being the only other person who could possibly gain anything by frightening her into leaving East Wapaneken, going home, and allowing him to get back to what had to be much more interesting projects.

Because it couldn't have been Somerton. He loved her too much to scare her that way, no matter how desperately he might want her to come home.

And it couldn't be Parker, because he obviously didn't care enough to scare her into coming home.

About damn time.

Oh, yes, those men knew Quinn, recognized him. Recognized him because he had hired them, set them on her so that he could do his Sir Galahad impersonation. Get into her life. Get into her bed. Get her out of town.

"No," Shelby told her reflection, her voice small and uncertain. "No," she said again, straightening her spine, putting more conviction into her voice. "No, no, *no*. I don't believe it. I simply don't believe it."

She pressed her hands against the front edge of the sink and leaned forward to look deeply into her own eyes. "You've never had to think for yourself in your entire life, Shelby Taite. Never had to trust your own instincts, make your own way, sleep in a bed you'd made for yourself— and that's both literally and figuratively, by the way."

She raised her hands to her collar, smoothed her neckline, turned left, then right, examining her appearance. "You sure *look* grown-up. Isn't it about time you *acted* it? Isn't it about time you stopped looking for ulterior motives and just accepted the fact that maybe you made a few mistakes, that he made a few mistakes, but that you love each other? You really, *really* love each other? Or are you going to spend the rest of your life being a jerk? That's what Brandy thinks you are, you know. A jerk. Looking too deep, thinking too much, and not listening to your heart. You know your heart, Shelby—that part of you that probably didn't really exist until you hopped a bus to reality.''

Smoothing back her hair, she took a deep breath and allowed it to ooze out of her slowly, taking with it the last of her worries. "And you know what, lady?" she ended, grinning at herself. "He didn't do it. He did ... not ... do ... it. No ifs, no ands, no buts. Not anymore. And I don't care who did do it. It's just not important. Not anymore. *So there!*"

She saluted her reflection, smiled as her heart and her mind finally ended their battle—it wasn't everyone who came to a great epiphany in a ladies' rest room in East Wapaneken—and pushed open the door to the hallway, feeling certain about her feelings for the first time in ages. Maybe for the first time in her life.

Bettyann Fink stood just outside the door, watching Shelby as she walked out, but not entering the rest room herself. "Wasn't there someone else in there with you, dearie?" she asked quizzically. "I heard voices."

Shelby blushed, feeling the heat rush into her cheeks. "I was talking to myself, Mrs. Fink," she admitted, shamefaced.

"That's all right then," Bettyann Fink said, nodding her head. "Do that myself all the time. Especially when I'm talking to Amelia, which is pretty much the same thing. Lovely evening, dearie. We're certainly enjoying the music."

"That's nice, Mrs. Fink," Shelby said, then quickly made her getaway, just in time to cover her ears as George tapped the microphone and an earsplitting screech of feedback filled the room.

She stood at the entrance to the hallway, not wanting to cross the restaurant while George was speaking, and watched Quinn as he stood next to the cash register, looking at her, his dark eyes clouded with worry.

She smiled and threw him a kiss. Felt her heart wing across the room with that kiss.

I love you, Quinn mouthed to her as Francis volunteered to fix the microphone. *Marry me.*

Shelby nodded, blinking back tears, and George began to speak.

The poor man was drenched in sweat, his hands shaking so badly the index cards fluttered, his voice rather high and tight as he offered nervously, "Testing, testing," then cleared his throat and wiped his perspiration-dotted brow.

There was a slight shuffling of chairs, a murmur of voices, a giggle or two, most probably at poor George's expense. And then his voice got stronger, and he started again, and the room went silent except for the sound of this one man's voice. The voice of a generation, saying what had to be said.

George read the names of those who'd served, of those who'd died. Quinn had inserted most of the regulars' original notes into the speech just as they had written them; simple, stark, so emotionally devastating in that simplicity.

All around the room, men and women resorted to hand-kerchiefs, wiping away tears without thought, without shame. Yes, this was a party of sorts, but it was also a celebration of heroism, a dedication to remembering, a promise to remember always.

"So that's it," George said, concluding his speech. "That's why we're all here tonight. Older, maybe wiser, and with a debt still to pay to those who didn't get the chance to get older, wiser. To remember those who didn't get the chance to marry, to hold a woman in their arms, to see their kids grow up, to watch the ball games, drink a few cold ones in the park during Community Days . . . or be able to say good-bye to those they loved when the time came for good-byes.

"Theirs was the ultimate sacrifice, one we, the lucky

ones, may still not comprehend. They deserve our respect, our honor. They deserve to have their names displayed here, in their hometown, for generations to come, generations who, God willing, will never have to know such a terrible war. So thank you, boys, all of you who are here tonight. And thank you, Billy . . . Chad . . . Tommy . . . Johnny . . . Dougie . . . A. J. We didn't forget. We'll *never* forget.''

There was silence, complete and utter, for several seconds. Then Quinn stepped forward from the cash register and began to clap. Slowly everyone in the restaurant stood up and added their hands to the tribute, until everyone was standing, everyone was clapping.

Tony stood outside the kitchen with his cooks, his long arms draped over Julio, over Stan.

Francis and Joseph hugged each other.

George rejoined the rest of the regulars, and they all stood, red-faced and embarrassed to be the center of attention, yet standing tall, proud, medals pinned to their suits because their uniforms had been long outgrown.

And everyone cried.

It was beautiful, Shelby thought. Just the most beautiful thing she'd ever witnessed.

She used her knuckles to wipe at the tears on her cheeks, until Uncle Alfred handed her his handkerchief. ''I don't remember when I have ever been so moved,'' he said, then reached into his pocket. ''Here, Shelby. My poker winnings from last night. See that they get to the proper party, all right? And Shelby? You were right to do this. I'm proud of you, my darling. Very, very proud.''

Shelby nodded, biting her lip to keep it from trembling. ''Quinn wrote the speech,'' she told her uncle, standing on tiptoe to try to spot him over the crowd. ''He did a fine job, didn't he? Can you see him? Where is he? I need to talk to him.''

Uncle Alfred kissed her cheek. "Only talk to him, my dear? I think, as a Taite, you're capable of much more than that. Now go on; I'll handle things here. I'll just go mingle with the clientele, see if I can prod anything else out of their pockets now that George has softened them up."

"Thank you, Uncle Alfred. Thank you so much," Shelby said, hugging him.

He returned her hug. "Now, isn't this nice? What are you thanking me for?"

Shelby pulled back, but kept her arms around him. "For so many things," she said, blinking back new tears. "For having helped create me, as you've called it. For telling me about your adventures. For all but daring me to go out, try my wings, not just *settle*. Without you, none of this would have happened. Quinn wouldn't have happened. *I* wouldn't have happened. I would have just been Shelby Taite, empty shell. Now . . ." She hesitated, smiled. "Now I feel like a whole person, my own person. Oh, Uncle Alfred, I do love you so."

She hugged him again, then turned and made her way through the crowded tables, still on the hunt for Quinn. She was stopped several times, to be thanked, to be hugged, to be kissed by Mayor Brobst, who then bellowed in her ear for a good two minutes.

He saw her coming, watched her slow, happy progress just as he had watched her talking with Al, hugging Al. How had he ever thought her to be a cold fish, just another of the Rich and Repulsive he'd lumped into one big group, never taking the time to realize that each person deserved to be judged on his own merits and not just categorized by the number of zeros in his bank balance.

"Quinn!" she said at last, holding out her hand to him

so that he could draw her through the last of the crowd, pull her into the entryway. "We have to talk."

He had once dreaded hearing those words, had dreaded saying them. Now he wanted nothing more than to talk to her, to listen to what she had to say. He pushed open the door and led her outside, around to the side of the building. "Can we kiss first?" he asked, backing her up against the stuccoed wall, leaning a hand on either side of her head, taking the world and reducing it to just the two of them. Just here. Just now.

"No, we can't," Shelby said, but she smiled as she said it. Smiled with her mouth, smiled with those big brown eyes that were full of love, tinged with mischief. "First, I love you, Quinn Delaney. I love you with all my heart and will love you forever."

Quinn grinned and leaned closer, damn near leering at her. "And I love you with all my heart. Forever. *Now* can we kiss?"

She pushed him away. *"Second,* I want to tell you that I didn't know. Not at first, not for a long time. I'm so bad with names, and I don't think I ever *really* looked at your face."

"I know. I'm a rat. You've already told me that one. But you weren't supposed to see me. I was only here to watch you, that's all, make sure Somerton's baby sister didn't get herself in trouble. But I walked into Tony's, and there you were. You looked right at me, didn't recognize me. I have to tell you, Shelby, that had me mad. Damn mad. I thought I was more memorable than that."

She lifted a hand to his cheek. "And you are; you are. I can imagine how angry you were when I didn't remember you."

"No, you can't." If she wasn't going to let him kiss her, he had time to tell her the whole of it. "I don't like the rich, Shelby. Never have. I took one incident in my life and allowed it to prejudice me against an entire class of people—except Grady, my partner, but nobody can help liking him. I even set out to romance you, to give the little rich girl the adventure she seemed to want.''

He sighed and shook his head. ''But I couldn't. I just couldn't do it. I was too busy falling in love with you.''

Shelby blinked back tears. ''Oh, Quinn, that's the nicest thing anyone has ever said to me.''

''Nice? You sure do have your own way of looking at things, don't you, sweetheart? But wait, there's more.''

''Yes, there is. My one regret, I suppose. I wanted to do something on my own, be responsible for myself for the first time in my life. But I was never out on my own, was I, Quinn? You were there almost from the beginning. Somerton's safety net. That's why he didn't just come and get me, because you were watching me. Baby-sitting me.''

Quinn had thought as much. He bent his head, kissed her forehead. ''Shelby, you got here on your own. You got yourself a job. More, you *kept* that job, made a real success of it. My God, look what you've done for this town. Did you ever see so many people hugging each other, feeling good about themselves, doing good for their community? You went with your strengths, and those were your ability to organize people, put on a grand party—and to see nothing but the best in people. You know, there aren't a lot of Main Line heiresses who'd even *look* at the regulars, let alone do what you did.''

Now Shelby really did cry, her chin trembling, her tears hot on her cheeks. ''I never thought of it that way. . . .''

''Well, you should. You're just about the kindest, most loving, accepting, *extraordinary* woman I've ever met. No, scratch that. You *are* the kindest, most loving, accepting, extraordinary person I have ever met.'' He smiled, tried to lighten the mood. ''Even if you can't remember anyone's name.''

Shelby laughed weakly; then a thought entered her brain and stuck there. Something Quinn had said earlier. "You don't like rich people? How rich would that be, Quinn?"

"I told you, I'm over that. I've kicked myself about my stupidity for about a week now." Then he grinned. "How rich are you, anyway?"

She avoided his eyes. "Pretty rich," she admitted. "And it does still bother you, doesn't it? I mean, I used to think about men wanting to marry me for my money, but I never thought about a man *not* wanting to marry me because I have money. Until I marry, or when I'm a bit older, I just receive an allowance from the income, but then I get the whole amount to use as I wish. Is this really going to be a problem for you? If it is, I suppose I could refuse to accept the inheritance."

Quinn sobered fast. "You'd do that, Shelby? You'd refuse the money to make me happy? You'd live on my earnings— which aren't all that shabby, by the way."

She nodded, firmly. Definitely.

"Wow," he said, feeling humbled, more than humbled. "Um . . . how much money are we talking about here anyway?"

Shelby averted her eyes. "Thirty million dollars."

Quinn stepped back and rubbed at his mouth with one hand, realizing that mouth had gone very dry. "Thirty million," he repeated. He gave a short, self-deprecating laugh. "You'd turn down thirty million dollars. For me. My God . . ."

She stepped away from the wall, bent, and picked a lone dandelion on the grass, twirled it between her fingers. "So, do you want me to turn it down?"

Quinn began to laugh. He laughed so hard he had to sit on the grass, pulling her down beside him. "Darling, I may not be the smartest man in the world, but do I have *idiot* tattooed on my forehead?"

"Oh, Quinn," Shelby said, falling into his arms. "I love you so much."

He lifted her chin, thinking this would be as good a time as any to stop talking and start kissing this woman he loved. But she broke away from him and stood up once more.

"I have a confession to make."

He stood up as well and looked at her closely, still trying to collect his thoughts. "What? You eat crackers in bed? You're not a morning person? You can't cook?"

She narrowed her eyelids, glaring at him. "You know darn full well that I can't cook," she said. "But that's not it. It's that . . . it's that . . . well, I got this *letter* in the mail. A threatening letter, telling me to leave town. And then there was that kidnap attempt or whatever it was, remember?"

Quinn's jaw tightened. "I remember."

"I thought it was you," Shelby said as quickly as possible. "I thought, once I'd figured out who you were, that you were tired of baby-sitting me and sent the letter, tried to scare me, just so I'd go home and you could quit the job, get back to more interesting work."

He stopped her nervous pacing by simply grabbing her by the shoulders, forcing her to look up at him. "Shelby, I quit the job, as you call it, the morning after we went bowling. That's when I knew that this was a whole hell of a lot more than just business, that *you* meant a whole hell of a lot more to me than just business."

"Oh," she said quietly. "That's . . . that's very *nice*. But aren't you angry with me for thinking you were the one who sent the letter?"

"Letters, Shelby, in the plural. While we're in confession mode, let me tell you that I broke into Brandy's apartment, rifled through your purse, and found the first letter. Then I copped a second one from your mail the morning of the kidnap attempt. I may not have been officially *on* the job anymore, but I still *did* my job. And, no, I'm not upset that you thought it could be me, although I wish I would have thought of that, because then I would definitely have had this talk with you and not let you lure me into bed instead.''

"*Lure* you into bed! Why, you—''

"Gotcha," he said, then frowned. "But I did investigate, tried to figure out who'd sent the letters, who'd hired the goons. And I think . . . well, I'm sorry, but I'm pretty sure it was Westbrook.''

"Parker?" Shelby remembered thinking about Parker as a suspect, remembered dismissing that thought. "But I don't understand. Why would he do something like that?''

"Well, I thought about that," Quinn told her, reaching out and taking her hands in his, running his thumbs over her skin. "I mean, he knew where you were—everyone knew where you were, sweetheart; you don't cover your tracks too well. He could have just driven up here, told you he loved you, begged you to come home.''

"I don't think so," Shelby said quietly. "Because he probably couldn't take the chance that I didn't love him. Which I didn't, which I don't. So he tried to *scare* me into coming home? I never planned to be away all that long. Why couldn't he have just waited?''

Quinn lifted her right hand to his lips and kissed her. "For one, sweetheart, I think he guessed that I was making my own pitch, and worried that I might be succeeding. But there's another reason, one I really don't want to tell you.''

She squeezed his hands. "Tell me.''

"All right, but this is tricky, because I didn't exactly break the law to find this out, but I did bend it a little. Westbrook is broke, sweetheart, worse than broke. He's been skimming money from his investors, embezzling funds, and if he doesn't get an infusion of money soon—

that would be your *small* inheritance, sweetheart—he's probably headed for prison.''

Shelby bit her bottom lip as she gave this information some thought. "I don't care," she said at last.

"That's good, because there's more. He has a mistress."

Shelby actually grinned. "Now I really, *really* don't care."

Quinn's grin was wider than hers. "That's good, because he actually has two of them."

Shelby laughed out loud, relief flooding through her. "I thought there was something wrong with me," she told Quinn when she could catch her breath. "I thought I was unlovable, cold. But it wasn't me; it was never me. It was *him.* Oh, Quinn, I feel so *good!*"

"Good enough to finally let me kiss you?"

She tipped her head and smiled up at him. "That depends. How much do you want to kiss me?"

He drew her closer into his arms, knowing just what to say. "I think I'll die, right here and now, if I can't kiss you right here and now. Is that what you wanted to hear?"

Shelby's arms slid up around his shoulders, one hand pressed to the back of his neck as she pulled his head down to hers. "As Brandy says, that works for me. . . ."

Chapter Thirty-four

"Somerton? It's me, Shelby."

She counted to three while Somerton collected himself, then smiled as he said, "Shelby? Shelby, is that really you? Are you all right? Where are you?"

"You know darn full well where I am, Somerton Taite," she told him, "and you've known all along. That's why you sent Quinn to watch over me. For which you have my undying thanks. Don't you want to know why I called? I wanted you to be the first to know that we're getting married."

She could hear Jeremy in the background, rhapsodizing over the fact that she was on the other end of the phone, then listened as Somerton, his hand over the receiver, said something that sounded like, "Married. Yes. That is what she said. What? Yes, yes, I'll do that. I'm sure she'll value your input on both her gown *and* the flowers. Now calm down before you strain something."

Shelby laid back against Quinn's chest and put a hand

over her own receiver. They'd spent a lovely night in his bed, and a lovely morning, until she decided that she really should call Somerton. "Jeremy is rhapsodizing, I believe. Isn't that sweet? You like him, don't you? I mean, you aren't upset about him or anything?"

"Not on your life, sweetheart. And remind me to tell you about something Somerton did last time I was there. You'll love it."

"Pardon me?" Shelby said, taking her hand away from the phone as she sat up once more. "Say that again, Somerton, all right? I want Quinn to hear this."

She held the receiver so that they both could listen, looking at each other as Somerton repeated himself. "I *said,* there's a warrant out for Parker's arrest. He's—"

Quinn grabbed the phone, no trace of humor in his voice as he barked, "Somerton, it's me, Delaney. Who told you there's a warrant out for Westbrook?"

"Who told me? Let me think. Oh, and by the way, you still haven't asked me for Shelby's hand in marriage. We'll see to that later, all right? Now . . . was it Dex Sandler, yesterday afternoon at the club? Or maybe it was Mimi Brock, at last night's Celebrate June for Our Dolphin Friends dinner? Well, no matter. Everybody was talking about it."

"About Westbrook being under arrest," Quinn prodded, trying not to lose his patience. "He is under arrest, isn't he? Locked up? Or is he out on bail?"

"No, you must have misunderstood me, Quinn," Somerton said. "I meant that everyone has been *talking* about Parker, which is what led to the warrant, I believe. I don't know quite all the particulars, but someone started asking some rather pointed questions about Parker, about his business, and everyone began saying out loud what they had only been thinking, and then someone, I don't know who, visited the district attorney's office."

"Grady," Quinn said to himself, then only grinned at Shelby as she looked at him quizzically. "Okay," he said, raising his voice to interrupt Somerton, who was now saying something to Jeremy—something about garden weddings definitely being "in" this season. "So somebody stumbled onto Westbrook's con—I meant to say, problems—and someone from the district attorney's office paid him a visit—and then what? Sounds to me like this investigation went a little fast."

Somerton sighed into the phone. "You do want all the sordid details, don't you? Very well. Someone went to see Parker, and someone in Parker's office became quite agitated and, that same day, paid a visit to that somebody's office downtown. Asking for immunity from prosecution, I believe the term goes. That same day, Thursday, I believe, the warrant was put out for Parker's arrest. And, before you ask me, no, nobody has seen him since. What? Oh, yes, Jeremy, quite right. Jeremy says Parker's done a flit."

"Damn," Quinn said, picking up Shelby's hand and squeezing it. "Westbrook is on the lam," he told her, already mentally packing her bags to get her out of East Wapaneken. "All right, Somerton. We were calling you to say that we were planning to remain here for another week or so—your uncle wants to collect a paycheck before he comes home. But now we'll be leaving today, even if Al stays."

"Al? Who is Al? Are you saying Uncle Alfred is there? That he's *working*? I don't believe it."

"We'll tell you all about it later. Right now I just want to get us packed and out of here."

He put down the phone, then picked it up again immediately and punched in some numbers.

"Quinn? What's wrong? You said he'd be arrested; you told me that last night. I don't see why you're so upset now, if you already—"

"Shh," he said, kissing her cheek, then said, "Grady, it's me. Yeah. Nine o'clock. On a Saturday morning. No, I'm not drunk. Don't hang up. Westbrook, remember him? There's a warrant out for him. Do you know anything about that?" He listened for a moment, then grinned in spite of himself. "Yeah, as the driven snow, right. Okay, listen to this. He's skipped, taken off; they can't find him. Now, what would you do if you were broke, being chased by the cops, and needed to get out of the country? Needed to, before you left the country, make sure you'd have enough money to keep yourself in the style to which you damn well want to stay accustomed?"

There was another pause at Grady's end, during which time Shelby almost forcibly ripped the receiver away from Quinn's ear so that she could listen, too.

"If I almost got away with it when I wasn't even trying to get away with it . . ." Grady said, thinking out loud.

"Right. That's what I thought, too."

"So you woke me up to ask me what you already know? G'bye, Quinn, I'm going back to sleep. Take care of her."

Shelby took the receiver from Quinn's hand and replaced it on the hook. "You and your partner believe Parker might actually try to kidnap me? For *real?*"

Quinn stroked her cheek and tried to push her back down on the mattress, divert her mind for a while. "Now, sweetheart . . ."

The next thing he knew he was sprawled on the floor and Shelby was pulling on his white dress shirt from the night before, the shirt that made up part of the trail of clothing from the living room to the bedroom of his small apartment.

"Don't you 'now, sweetheart' me, Quinn Delaney!" she exploded, searching through more clothes that lay on the floor. "You're full of it, both you and your rude partner. We said we're staying here another few days, and we're staying here another few days. Besides, I'm meeting with the Memorial Committee at Tony's in fifteen minutes to add up our profits. Where are my *damn shoes?*"

She was angry, more than angry. She was frightened straight down to her bare toes. To think that she had been engaged to marry a criminal—one with two mistresses, no less—was one thing. To believe that he was now going to kidnap her, hold her for ransom? *Oh, no. No, no, no.* That was just too much!

"Shelby, listen to me," Quinn said, rummaging among the evidence of last night's passion in order to find his own shoes. "It's just a hunch, but it's sure a hell of a lot less than a thirty million-to-one shot, and you know it. The guy obviously doesn't think like the rest of us."

Shelby stopped in the act of pulling on the fairly wrinkled slacks to her Armani suit. "He thinks like you, at least," she said, her fingers clumsy as she zippered the slacks and closed the single button. "And I don't appreciate being frightened, Quinn. You're scaring me."

"That couldn't be avoided, sweetheart," Quinn said, following after her as she headed into the bathroom, picked up his toothbrush, and squirted paste on it. "I just wish you were scared enough to let me take you home. I mean, hey, I'd love to hear that Westbrook turned himself in, or that someone caught him trying to hop a plane to Brazil. But he's been banking on you for too long, sweetheart, banking on your being his salvation. And, one way or another, I think he still sees you that way." He hesitated a moment, then added, "As the golden goose."

A shiver ran down Shelby's spine, and she put down the toothbrush and walked into Quinn's arms. She pressed her head against his shoulder. "All right, now I'm really scared. Not angry, scared. And I'm not stupid. I've lived with the threat of kidnapping all of my life, and I know the consequences of acting as if security isn't always necessary. But I really want to say good-bye to everyone, Quinn. Can't we at least do that?''

"Yeah, babe," he said, stroking her hair. "We can do that. Now let me throw on some clothes, walk you *home* to shower and pack, and then we'll head to Tony's in time for the meeting. All right?''

"Thank you, Quinn!" she said, standing on tiptoe and kissing him. "But your Porsche will never hold all my luggage. I'll just pack a few things and we can come back for the rest, all right?''

Quinn agreed, knowing Shelby needed to feel she would be back in East Wapaneken again. He'd agree to dyeing his hair purple, if it would get Shelby moving. Not that he didn't think he could handle Parker Westbrook III and his two hired goons if the occasion arose. He just didn't want Shelby in the way if that happened.

Twenty minutes later, with a worried Brandy bonded to Shelby's side as if she'd been smeared with glue and stuck there, the three of them headed off down the street, on the way to Tony's.

"I'm going to miss this place so much," Shelby said, squeezing Brandy's hand. "I'm going to miss everybody, especially you and Gary. It's difficult to imagine life without you now."

"You can come visit anytime, sweetcakes," Brandy said, tossing a concerned look in Quinn's direction. "And, hey, if you want to send Jim Helfrich and the limo to bring me to you, well, I wouldn't say no. Oh, damn," she said, stopping on the pavement just before the alleyway. "I forgot the envelopes Tony gave me to hold. Donations, you know. You two go on ahead, and I'll be right behind you."

They walked the second block slowly, with Quinn holding Shelby's hand, with his gaze sweeping the roadway as he watched the coming and going of several cars. Looking ahead, he could see several more cars in Tony's lot, which wasn't unusual. As a matter of fact, nothing seemed the least bit unusual or out of the ordinary.

That made Quinn nervous, more on his guard. Not that he wasn't always on his guard. But he was never nervous, never unsure of himself. It had taken falling in love to do that to him.

They'd just stepped onto the blacktop of Tony's parking lot when it happened.

The freestanding sign that listed the day's specials, a low sign on wheels placed at the edge of the parking lot, had blocked Quinn's view just enough that he didn't see the man crouching behind it.

Without a sound, the man stood up and made a run at Quinn.

Shelby screamed.

Quinn recognized the guy as the one who had tried to pull Shelby into a car, and cursed himself for being right the one time in his life he didn't want to be right.

He shot out an arm, deflecting the man's fairly well telegraphed punch, then stepped forward, planning to chop the side of his hand against the guy's neck.

The son of a bitch countered the blow. Great, Quinn thought. Damn all the interest in martial arts these days. Just what he needed. A guy who thought he knew how to fight.

But then, he probably didn't know how to fight dirty.

Quinn did. He turned his body to one side, balanced his weight on the balls of his feet, dropped his arms to his sides, and all but begged the guy to come at him again.

Shelby ran into Tony's yelling for help, completely bypassing the police chief, who was nearly invisible in his normal stance at the poker machines. "Someone's after Quinn! Hurry!"

Then she turned and ran outside.

Tony grabbed a cleaver, breaking into a pretty damn good imitation of a run. Joseph and Francis knocked over two tables on their way out the door. The regulars pushed and shoved their combined bulk out of their booth, bringing up the rear.

By the time Shelby was outside once more, Quinn was standing over his attacker, his chest heaving, his fists still clenched as the man writhed in the street, both hands clutching his most tender parts.

"Quinn, you're all right!" Shelby yelled, running toward him across the width of blacktop.

"No!" he called to her, still trying to catch his breath. "Go inside. For God's sake, get back inside!"

But it was too late. A dark sedan pulled into the parking lot, brakes screeching, and a man jumped out of the passenger door, grabbing Shelby's arm.

"Parker?" Shelby couldn't believe it, even with the man standing in front of her, looking more frightened than she did, if that were possible. His fear gave her courage. His rumpled, custom-made tennis whites, probably the only clothes he had on him when he ran from the police, made her laugh. "Parker, you *ass.*"

Unfortunately, Westbrook's fear did not give her physical strength, at least not enough to pull free of his grip. He twisted her arm behind her back and began shoving her toward the open car door as the driver yelled, "Come on, come on, *move it!*"

That was when Mayor Brobst and her '67 Caddy, arriving a tad late because of her usual Saturday-morning appointment at Maude's Curl, Cut, and Color, pulled into the parking lot.

Quinn could see Amelia Brobst glaring at the scene as she peered through the steering wheel from the opposite end of the parking lot, as Bettyann Fink shouted in her ear. Amelia laid on the brake and the horn, and gunned the engine in warning.

Quinn looked at the man on the ground and decided he wasn't going anywhere anytime soon. He looked at Shelby, who was wincing as Westbrook tried to make her walk toward the car. She wasn't making his job easy, bless her, not that she couldn't do with a little help.

Which she got.

In spades.

Francis, bigger than Joseph by a few pounds—which was like saying that maybe having two tons of bricks fall on your head would be less painful than having two tons plus five pounds of bricks fall on your head—grabbed Westbrook from behind, catching him in a bear hug and lifting him straight off the ground.

He then deposited him back on the ground, from rather a great height, and Joseph took over.

Joseph kicked him, right in the Third's hopes for a Fourth.

Meanwhile, Mayor Brobst gunned her engine again, put the Caddy into gear, and aimed that tank of a car straight at the sedan that was suddenly moving toward her—and escape—in what looked like a serious game of chicken.

Quinn held on to Shelby and watched, knowing deep inside that Amelia Brobst was a real gamer. She wasn't going to back down. Not a bit. Not Amelia and her hearing aid and her straw hat with the flowers on it . . . and her Caddy, which had all the stopping power of a Mack truck.

The sedan kept going.

The Caddy kept coming.

Shelby closed her eyes.

The sedan swerved at the last moment, heading straight into one of the late Mayor Brobst's shade trees, finally putting at least one of those pavement-tilting bits of bad planning to good use.

The regulars, feeling a bit left out, as Tony and his two helpers were all holding cleavers over the goon still lying in the street, went over to the sedan, ripped the driver's-side door clean off the car, and yanked the driver out onto the ground.

"Shouldn't somebody rescue them, darling?" Shelby asked, having at last opened her eyes. "Parker and his friends, that is."

"All taken care of, my dear," Uncle Alfred said as he joined them on the blacktop. "I phoned the police as soon as you came into the restaurant." He looked at Parker, who was in the process of being bounced back and forth between the decidedly playful Francis and Joseph, and winced. "There but for the grace of, etc.," he said, flinching once more.

A siren wailed in the distance, definitely heading closer, as East Wapaneken's part-time officer responded to Uncle Alfred's call.

Uncle Alfred looked at Quinn and winked. "All's well that ends satisfyingly, or whatever. Delaney, my boy, do you think I ought to alert the chief, or should we just let him continue with his game? Oh, why not . . ."

Epilogue

The Taite mansion gardens were every bit as beautiful as nature could make them, and then had been further enhanced with Jeremy Rifkin's considerable decorating talents.

As it was mid-September, he had ordered pots of chrysanthemums, hundreds of them, to line every walkway, to fill in beds where the summer flowers had begun to fade. Blooms of white, yellow, and pink nicely balanced the flowing sky blue draperies that seemed to hang in midair along the center path that led to a flower-bedecked arbor where the minister stood, waiting.

Rows of wooden folding chairs neatly disguised beneath white covers tied up with sky blue bows lined either side of the grass bordering the brick walkway, and nearly all of them were already filled.

The regulars and their wives and children took up four rows on the bride's side, so that Francis and Joseph had been asked to sit on the groom's side to even things out a bit. That didn't seem possible, if the person being told had never laid eyes on Francis or Joseph, but it worked beautifully.

The remainder of the seats were occupied by Mayor Brobst and Mrs. Fink, all the waitresses and kitchen staff from Tony's, Tony himself, and many of his regular customers. Tabby sat up front on the bride's side, her arm tucked through Uncle Alfred's, her six children—all under the age of twelve—sitting all stiff and starched on either side of them. Uncle Alfred was looking quite spiffy, and hunting for a handy exit. . . .

Only Mrs. Miller was missing, swearing that Shelby's alien friends would kidnap her, brainwash her, and—Tabby said, "She should be so lucky, the old bat"—"have their wicked way with her."

There were two large tents on the grounds, two soaring white constructions complete with temporary canvas walls that held clear plastic inserts that resembled windows in a church. In one were more decorated chairs, several dozen round tables with swan napkins on them, and a large table holding a five-tiered wedding cake.

The second tent had been set up for an elaborate buffet. Jeremy had, of course, overseen the menu. Well, most of it. There was lobster, filet mignon—listed on the menu with one *L*—rack of lamb, and fresh salmon. There were six different vegetable side dishes and four varied salads. There was champagne, the best, and several varieties of wines.

And a large keg rested in an ice-filled tub in one corner, right next to the cases of Snapple. Jeremy had learned to live with this, even when Quinn declared a definitive "No" when the man asked if he could decorate around the tub with some bunting and flowers.

As the sun moved across the sky, at just about three o'clock, Quinn found himself standing to one side of the

altar, dressed in his rented tuxedo. The white one with
the sky blue bow tie and cummerbund.

He had his hands loosely clasped in front of him as the
organist changed from quiet background music to a more
familiar tune.

Two of the caterer's staff walked up the aisle, picked up
the ends of the folded aisle cloth, and carefully retraced
their steps, leaving behind a forty-foot-long path of bright
white linen.

And then she was there, standing just at the edge of the
aisle cloth.

Beautiful. She was the most beautiful woman in the
world, and she was smiling at him. Coming toward him,
her full sky blue taffeta skirts swaying with the movement
of her hoop petticoat, her bare shoulders rising above the
rows and rows of sky blue lace, protected from the sun by
a huge sky blue picture hat complete with white satin
streamers.

Quinn stepped onto the runner, advanced toward
Shelby and held out his arm to her as she reached the
fifth row of chairs, just as they'd done in rehearsal. "I
don't know how anyone could look gorgeous in that dress,
wife, but you've done it."

"Shh," she warned him, her brown eyes twinkling. "It's
what Brandy has always dreamed of, ever since she was a
child. I couldn't say no. Besides, I think we both look
rather sweet."

Quinn put a hand on hers, squeezed it, then walked her
down the remainder of the aisle, the same aisle he and
Shelby had walked down two weeks previously, with many
of the same guests in attendance. Only Grady was missing,
having taken what he called a "cushy" assignment that
would keep him away from the office for at least a month,
"which is just what you deserve after leaving me stranded
here, Quinn, old son."

Quinn and Shelby parted at the altar, each stepping to one side as the organ swelled with the traditional fanfare that marked the beginning of the *Wedding March.* Gary, standing next to Quinn, swayed a little and, as his best man, Quinn quickly propped him up again.

"You have the rings?" Gary asked frantically, looking as if he'd been stuffed into his white tux, then all but strangled with the white bow tie. "You said you had the rings. Do you have the rings?"

"I've got the rings, Gar," Quinn told him calmly. "Now buck up. Even Mama is smiling."

"She should be," Gary said, taking out a large white linen handkerchief and mopping at his brow. "I can't believe you two are sending her to Europe."

Quinn, whose suggestion to Shelby that they send Mama Mack to the moon had been shot down by his new bride, only smiled, then nudged Gary with his elbow as Brandy, on Somerton's arm, stepped onto the runner.

"Oh, God," Gary said in awe, gulping as Brandy made her way down the aisle, a vision in Chantilly lace. "Would you look at her, Quinn? Would you just *look* at her. . . ."

Quinn looked across the aisle at his wife. Watched as her chin began to tremble even as she smiled, as her brown eyes lit with tears and laughter and love.

"I'm looking, Gar. I'm looking. . . ."

ABOUT THE AUTHOR

Kasey Michaels is a *New York Times* bestselling author of more than sixty books. In addition to writing for Zebra, she also writes historical romances for Warner Books and short contemporaries for Silhouette and Harlequin. Kasey lives with her family in Pennsylvania and is currently working on her next Zebra contemporary romance. Kasey loves to hear from readers, and you may write to her c/o Zebra Books. Please include a self-addressed stamped envelope if you wish a response.